The Android and the Thief

by

Wendy Rathbone

The Android and the Thief Copyright © May 2020 by Wendy Rathbone and Eye Scry Publications. Second edition. (First edition, now out of print, was previously published by Dreamspinner Press.)

A publication by:
Eye Scry Publications
http://www.eyescrypublications.com

TITLE: The Android and the Thief
ISBN: 978-1-942415-34-3
Author: Wendy Rathbone
Cover by: Wendy Rathbone

For Della, the love of my life.

Android: *in the sixty-seventh century, a popular but often derogatory (and incorrect) term used to label designer vat-grown humans who are born adult.*

Chapter One

Trev

Trev let the cascading liquid from the pink waterfall flow over his full bodysuit. The neon waterfall was the main decorative feature of the museum's interior and his only means for navigating from floor to floor to avoid the laser traps and heat sensors.

The material of his suit was lined with sensors that absorbed the dampness and made him invisible as he climbed up fake, jutting rocks to the museum's third floor. So far he'd avoided all security detection.

It was the middle of the night in Fire Town. The museum sat in the center of the floating city's main cloud. Getting in unseen had been a peach. Back at his flier, parked at the end of the street, he'd drenched himself from head to toe. But the time it took getting to the side entrance and breaking in allowed his suit to dry out too much to avoid detection for long. The waterfall solved that problem. Now, climbing the waterfall forced him to rely on all his talents. He could perform flips and wide leaps, scamper across narrow ledges at great heights, fit into tiny ducts, and run soundlessly down streets or dark corridors without getting winded. Climbing this wall should have been easy, but the rocks were slick with a green, alien algae he had not accounted for. He'd assumed this palace of knowledge that catered to the rich was better maintained. He'd been wrong.

The comm on his wrist chimed underneath the seals of his suit. He ignored it. Set on low, it wouldn't trip any sensors, but it was annoying him. "Breq, leave me alone," he muttered softly to himself. He should have left the comm in the flier.

"Fuck." His left foot slipped. He'd left his grav-boosters behind; they would've fucked up the security system big-time. For this job he relied on experience and physical strength alone.

He grabbed frantically at an emerald-tinged rock just above his head, fingers sliding along its surface, heart rate increasing a fraction as he tried not to flail. His right foot still had a pretty good purchase, and his right hand was half-pressed into a crack between two rocks. He took a slow breath, accidentally let a little neon water into his mouth, and sputtered. It tasted of metal and scum, lichen, and—unexpectedly—honey. That would not do.

He focused, clinging to the wet wall as a continual cascade the color of party champagne poured onto his shoulders and head, clumping his dark bangs into his eyes where they had escaped his tight hood.

Take it slow, he prompted himself. His fingers discovered a bump in the rock and closed over it. He lifted his left foot and felt along the wall for another crack, found it, and rebalanced. He had about fifteen feet to go.

Slowly Trev crawled up the soaked rocks and through the pouring falls until he landed on the third floor, dripping thin puddles the sensors would ignore. He'd found the building's vulnerability to water when he'd studied the security system and its layouts, discovering that two years ago the building had flooded due to a maintenance oversight and the alarms had not gone off. The following morning, workers had opened the doors to a mess. A report had been filed and repairs made, but the system had not been updated to tag the encroachment of water as a threat, and the cascade of the waterfall left the sensors unaffected. Obviously the program ignored the motion of water. An oversight, to be sure, and one Trev enjoyed exploiting tonight.

He had calculated the air temperature and humidity, knowing he had just under three minutes before his suit and its embedded sensors began to dry and his invisibility to the museum's security system failed. He had plenty of time.

He knew exactly where he was heading. Aisle 3, Case 2.

He moved with practiced stealth past arching alcoves containing innumerable treasures. The museum's lighting made everything clearly visible. He navigated with ease.

Case 2's lock did not have an alarm, but there was one hidden inside, underneath the velvet. The object inside was worth a lot, but for some reason extra alarms had not been installed. It took him about ten seconds to pick the lock, and another ten to slip a sensor neutralizer under the artifact so he could lift it out.

The item was too fragile to be handled or exposed to air. Encased in seamless crystal, it was something to look at but never touch, for fear it would crumble to instant dust.

Through the transparent casing, Trev could see it clearly. He smiled, blinking at its beauty. It was an imperfect white page, slightly yellowed, the fading artwork of a mushroom behind an ascending rocket. And four beautiful words. *The Machineries of Joy.* The real-book he'd been looking for to complete his collection.

"I'll be the antihero of the Bradbury cults," he whispered to himself on the dry air.

When the museum found this one missing, they'd search the black markets for a while but never find it. One of hundreds of items he'd stolen—most for the Damicos, his adopted family, who sold them at great profit—but this one he was taking for himself, and he would never part with it.

He glanced around. This particular alcove was filled with Bradburys, but this was the one he wanted. With not even a twinge of conscience, he put the real-book in a protective pouch at his waist, turned, and headed back for his climb down the waterfall.

Trev could not help the satisfied feeling he got at the weight in the pouch rubbing the edge of his hip. It made his climb down, although more precarious than going up, easier and quicker.

He slipped only once as the pink waters lashed him, dropped the last three feet to the pool, and waded out of the shallows and into the foyer of the lobby.

Just then the air turned red. An alarm crowed, shocking him. He froze. Somewhere, somehow, he'd miscalculated.

The orange glow at the front doors, only thirty feet away, was a sign that the lasers were coming back online.

Trained to perfection, his body shed the shock and flew into a sprint. As he ran, he reached into another pouch and pulled out a candle tube, illegal on nine hundred worlds. He aimed it at the glass doors, fingers flashing over the code buttons to unlock it, and pressed the diamond-shaped trigger. The doors shattered and he ran through them, his feet crunching broken glass, and never looked back.

The streets of the floating city were wet, the clouds low and humming, backlit in gold from late-night air traffic. Some of that traffic would already be heading his way.

The walkway, striped in rainbow neon from the advertising screens mounted on just about every building, was clear. The demisters in the gutters kept the fog at bay. Trev was fast and light on his feet, but out here he stood out like a beacon. He used his candle to shoot at the demisters, fog rolling up behind him as he ran. Cameras would be recording. His programming talents were vast, but he couldn't immobilize them all, so he pulled his hood down over his face and kept going, a thief on the run, a ghost in the mist.

*

Trev had left his flier parked at the city's edge, near the wall and its force field that kept people from walking off the island platform and falling to the planet below. As soon as he got inside, the doors closed down around him and the comm on the dash went off with a soft clang.

"Breq. Fuck." He didn't answer but instead concentrated on building power for a straight-up takeoff.

Screaming alarms blared behind him; lights glittered from incoming police vehicles. He ignored them.

Thirty seconds to full power. It was an eternity. But finally the flier responded. He shot up through the fog and was out of the clouds and into clear skies. Traffic glittered above him. He edged into its glowing stream, glancing through the floor windows to see if anyone followed. Nothing.

The flier spoke. "Three hundred miles to destination."

"Thank you. Lock on for 250 mph."

"Cleared." The system recited an altitude setting.

The car shot up again and forward, bypassing all local traffic.

It would take a little over an hour to reach home. Trev sighed, pulling off his hood and combing his fingers through his wet bangs.

The comm message still blinked on the dash. He switched it on.

Breq's face appeared on a screen, steel-gray eyes darting. "Trev, you're late. You're going to miss early breakfast if you don't get here within an hour."

"I don't usually eat breakfast. Besides, it's the middle of the night. I have a life, you know."

His oldest brother's face twisted a little. At thirty-two, with his trim, tall physique and thick hair, Breq could have been good-looking, but his features were too hard. "You? With a lover?"

"One of many. I have a harem."

Breq rolled his eyes. "Sure, Trev. A harem of books. And not a one of them offering even a bit of decent porn."

"You went through my stuff?"

Breq laughed. "The breakfast and the meeting's been set for four. Just before dawn. Be there, or Dad will have your hide."

"So that's why you called? To remind me of the meeting?"

"That, and to bother you in the middle of the night."

"Yeah. You're annoying as hell. There, you win."

"What else are big brothers for?" At that, Breq leaned forward and ended the transmission.

Trev leaned back and closed his eyes. Breq, their father, even the book in his pouch—none of it mattered, really. It was all a game, just biding his time, because in two days he'd be gone anyway.

His hand trembled against the pouch and his prize, still fastened securely to his hip. He tried to draw some comfort from the object, as if it were a good-luck totem telling him all would be well. But ahead of him, all he could see was darkness for a long way. His throat threatened to close up. His fingers curled into fists.

The flier leaped closer to the stars.

*

Trev flipped the autopilot off and took the flier's controls. He loved this part of the approach and wanted to relish it one last time, for after tomorrow he would no longer live there.

The Damico floating mansion came into view, first no more than a star's-breadth of light, then growing pearlescent and tender

9

upon the dark as Trev approached. Its massive triangular structure gave off an opal-blue glimmering against the early morning darkness, set against a backdrop of mist, puffy clouds, and two quarter-moons.

The architecture itself belonged in a museum. Designed by artisans from Lyric Prime, one point of the upside-down triangle sat upon fifty acres of floating earth. It was surrounded by a thickly columned porch painted white, the sides overflowing with blue and green vines sparked with white flowers. The surrounding landscape consisted of lush gardens, dense, grassy fields of high-flowing willows, and redwoods nearly as tall as the mansion itself.

From this distance, Trev could see the edges of the land like cliffs dropping off to nothing but air and cumulus. Beneath that, massive machines kept the island afloat in the sky. He maneuvered around back, slow and precise, to view the inner-lit, sculptured waterfalls surrounded by flowering creepers—honey-yellow, sensitive red. The water rushed and splashed in white froth over the uneven edge of the land and into the air, only to vanish one hundred feet out. Invisible force fields caught it up and recycled it to the top of the falls again like overwrought fairy magic. The falling water was the color of mercury.

It was 4:00 a.m., but as usual for the Damicos, the houselights were all on, as white as snow, making the scenery all the more glamorous and wavery.

Trev flew into the massive underground garage and parked beside twenty other fliers, most of them designer models bigger than his own. He entered the mansion through the underground portal, a round door made entirely of dichroic glass that drew up as embedded electronics sensed his approach and scanned him to confirm his identity.

An androgynous voice intoned, "Welcome home, Master Trevor."

To his right was an elevator, to his left the winding steps. He had exerted himself enough tonight, so he took the elevator to the topmost, widest level of the mansion where his father's meeting rooms and the main dining hall lay.

In the elevator, Trev combed his fingers through his feathery dark hair. He'd changed in the flier en route, and now wore a blue silk suit, white shirt, and gold tie. He'd locked the Bradbury in the safe of his flier, planning to retrieve it later and hide it in his room.

The doors opened onto a foyer that led to the dining room. Everything dripped luxury and wealth. The foyer itself was designed like a king's antechamber, with paintings on the ceilings and marble and crystal sculptures in every nook and cranny. All the doorways were framed in gold, carved with intricate floral designs. But enough was never enough for the Damico family, who owned interests in ten planets and had investments, mostly shady and uninteresting to Trev, in a hundred more.

Dante Damico lorded over it all and held every trust, corporation, and investment close to the vest. He doled out salaries and occasional gifts to his sons and daughters. He had no wife and no lover. With his extreme ability to control all around him, Dante was like a god.

Trevor was the youngest son, adopted at the age of two but treated by Dante the same as all his children—with a strict hand and a cold heart. Trev had received the best education money could buy, fine food, clothes, and toys. But as payment for all of that, he'd been indoctrinated into the criminal side of the family. Because of his willowy frame and acrobatic abilities, they put his aptitudes for overriding computer security programs and performing physical theft to good use. He could hack complex security systems, could squeeze into tight spaces, could run like a gazelle.

As he stepped into the dining hall, he saw his family just finishing up their early breakfast. They were night owls, so technically it was dinner. Before noon they would all sleep until the night woke them again for darker deeds.

Three sisters and three brothers all sat facing each other. Dante was at the head of the table. A half-dozen scurrying servants—real people, not robots—entered and exited, bringing plates, taking plates away, refilling wine goblets.

Dante did not look up as Trev entered. He merely picked up his wineglass and raised it in his direction. "Nice of you to finally join us, Trevor," he said.

Breq, in the seat closest to their father, smothered a laugh with the back of his hand. No one else seemed to even hear or care that Trev had just come in.

Trev hurried over to his seat beside his next-up brother, Blair, the second-best fighter in the family. The only person to ever beat Blair in hand-to-hand was their sister Sonye. Those two were their father's bodyguards, and rarely did Dante go anywhere without them.

"You're in time for the cake," Dante said. He turned to the servant doling it out. "Make sure the biggest piece goes to him, the corner piece with the roses."

Trev clenched his fists in his lap. The thrill of his personal caper was fading. The Bradbury was an astonishing possession, but little made up for the cloying control Dante held over the entire household, including all his adult children. Dante knew he hated cake, and frosting most of all.

"So, Trevor, where were you tonight?" Dante asked.

Trev had no life to speak of, save thieving and working for his father, which also entailed thieving. "Just out," he murmured.

Breq piped up with a smirk. "He has a lover."

His oldest sister, Rory, said, "Trev does? Really?"

Sonye squirmed in her chair, her deadly hands looking so gentle and slim folded over the table beside her plate of cake. "I don't believe it. He's turned down every one of *my* friends, even the ungendered ones."

His middle brother, Vance, said, "His lovers are books. He was probably at an all-night storyteller bar."

"Genetics wasted good features on him," said his middle sister, Arla.

Only Blair remained silent, the one sibling who never taunted him. Maybe it was because Blair was not good-looking and didn't want to bring unwanted attention to that. In fact, none of Trev's family were beautiful. Handsome, yes, dark-haired and olive complected, with manners and proper health care, quick minds, bright eyes, solid bodies, but they were all too hard, too spoiled, to be called beautiful. Trev was the beautiful one, people said, the duckling who'd grown into a swan.

"Well, Trevor?" Dante prompted.

Trev, who'd been staring at his gigantic piece of cake and clenching his stomach muscles, lifted his chin. "Three, actually."

"Three what?" his father asked.

"I have three lovers."

Breq let out a loud guffaw, drawing a glare from Dante.

His other siblings all snickered.

Trev continued, not allowing himself to show any irritation. "It's quite a feat to juggle them all, since all of them are single-partner oriented. And if one chimes while I'm with one of the other two, well, it's a challenge."

Breq said, grinning, "You're the worst liar ever. And to tell a lie about lying is, well—"

"Overkill," Sonye finished. But unlike Breq, she wasn't laughing.

Dante spoke. "Of course I allow all of you to have your own private lives, as long as they don't interfere with our arrangements. But this meal is a prelude to our monthly family meeting. And I expected you all to be here for it."

"I'm here in time for the meeting," Trev replied, returning his gaze. Less than two days, and then he wouldn't care anymore.

"The family early breakfast is part of that meeting."

Trev wanted badly to argue. But arguing led to punishment. And punishment involved whippings. At twenty-three, he still received them. So did his siblings. Instead he said, "I apologize, Father. Did I miss anything?"

Dante raised his gilt-edged napkin to his lips. "No. But need I remind you all that if any dalliances outside the family fetch you trouble with the legal system, I will not have your back?" Everyone stared silently at their plates. "Now, eat your desserts."

Trev took a long breath, picked up his gold fork, and speared the cake.

Chapter Two

Khim

Secret missions.

Warehouse-sized sleeping chambers with triple bunks, where the air grew stale even with the compressors on high.

Flower-shaped black starships built for one purpose: to unfold layers of petals revealing thousands of death lasers. Crewed entirely by android soldiers trained for combat at all levels, the ships were referred to by the rank and file as the Planet Killers.

It was not a real life.

But it was Khim's life. All he'd ever known.

Android was the term for his kind—vat-grown humans—even though they were all made of flesh and bone and blood, not metal; they were not machines like the early versions of augmented men from centuries ago. They had creative minds and nervous systems that felt pleasure or pain. But none of that mattered. These androids were manufactured, human-shaped toys, sex dolls, soldiers, slaves. Androids programmed to obey, programmed to serve.

Khim, born with the body of a twenty-year-old and the dubious, chipped-in memories to go with it, had been a soldier for ten years. He crewed on the ship *Doom in Shadow*. Six foot four, trim and well muscled, he could handle any weapon, knife, laser gun, sunburst cannon, photon rifle. He could even wield a sword. If no weapons were on hand, it didn't matter. His body was a weapon. And his mind. He could make a weapon out of anything at hand if need be, be it toothpicks or toilet paper, a comm chip or a comb.

He fought battles without any clue as to why they were happening. He simply followed orders. It was not his place to question politics or learn the reasons behind what he did. When he was younger, he had kept track of his kills. But after the first year, he'd stopped. How many died at his hand did not matter, for he was just a tool. Morality, the evilness of deeds, conscience or lack of conscience, the violence, the battles, the deaths—they were all attributed to those who gave the orders.

Khim never had any choice.

It was on the sixtieth morning of his tenth year when everything changed.

Khim had awakened, as usual, in the dim bay of *Doom in Shadow* where the sleeping berths lined the decks three-high. Two hundred fellow soldiers slept over, under, or beside him, all gendered male, all of a similar mold, with variations only in hair, eye, and skin color. Blue, green, yellow, or purple were common hair shades, with the occasional blonds and brunets. Khim had won the genetic lottery for blond, with eyes the color of late blue dusk and skin his digital file "paperwork" called henna.

Something had startled him, and not the sounds of the two androids below him having sex. That was not unusual. Something else had brought his senses to full alert. He sat up, his sheet falling away, and sniffed the air.

He smelled the air compressors, with their slight metallic sweetness, along with the breaths of two hundred men, sour and humid, making the open area seem closed in and the atmosphere heavy. He smelled the cloying, brackish scent of sex wafting upward to his third-level bunk, but that was it.

Nothing else stirred him... so then why was his heart pounding?

All the alarms of the ship sounded at once, loud and clanging. Red strobes bounced off floors, ceilings, walls. It took only seconds for every android in the sleeping bay to don their leather boots and one-piece gray uniforms with the sunburst insignias on their cuffs.

Orders pounded through a chip in Khim's head: he was to go to the docking lines. Whether they were boarding another ship or completing a planetfall, he didn't know. But as he passed the weapons room amid scurrying men and shouted commands, he was handed a gun belt, a shoulder holster, and a backpack of extra ammo. His heart rate increased, but not dangerously. It was only his body reacting to the projected excitement he would face.

Khim ran with his gear and glanced briefly out the rectangular portholes of the corridors, wondering what they might be facing, but he saw only familiar darkness pricked with stars.

As he turned away to face the lines of other androids, he lost his sense of balance when a nearly incomprehensible thing occurred. The deck beneath his feet curved up, as if the ship were buckling, and sent him sprawling. He slid fast and dizzily into a bulkhead, watching as cracks began to form in the corridor. A panel exploded to his right in a hot green-and-orange cloud, the pieces of metal slicing through the air, hitting the men in the backs, buttocks, and thighs as they tried to crawl or run away.

Khim looked down and saw that his right hand was gone. His wrist ended in a red spurt, though he felt no pain yet. Another explosion sounded overhead, and he knew then this was not a survivable event.

At that thought, miraculously, the bulkheads that weren't compromised began to form round, black openings. One opened beside him and sucked him in. It was a life pod, and if it still functioned, he might have a chance. But before he could even assess his possible turn of luck, another explosion blotted out all sight, sound, and feeling.

*

Something tasted green. There was a hot sound. An edge of raving—raving? that didn't seem right—against his skin felt bright, smelled of tumbling light as white as nerves. He could see only wrongness in the gray fog that surrounded him.

Khim's instinct to fight jerked through his body. Jerked again.

A voice from far away said, "He's convulsing. Grab him. Hold him down!"

He did not understand. Was someone in danger? He should get up, see if he could be of assistance. But as he tried, his body jerked tight again as if a hundred ropes embedded in his flesh held him in place.

He heard the hot sound again. But how could sound be hot? It was as if he inhabited his own blood-rush coursing through his veins and was drowning in it. He bounced along in red shoutings, corridors of red, oceans of red never-ending, without time or construct. Everything around him seemed to yell like a great wailing wind, and he fell forever through it, limbs flailing for purchase, arms looking for something to wrap around.

One time he thought he saw a dimmer light, heard voices.

"Make it work," one voice said.

"He's worth a fortune," said another. "If you lose him, I'll have you fired."

More uneasy time passed. He was buffeted amid great strands of shining strings that clanged in his ears.

The voices returned.

"But the hand was grown from his own cells."

"It won't mesh, I tell you. Too much radiation damage at a cellular level. It won't kill him, but it won't allow the fresh hand to reattach."

A crackle. A sputter. His own voice coming from a place so deep inside him he could barely imagine it. "Thirsty."

Something touched his lips.

Everything went black.

When he woke again, his eyes opened this time and a room slowly built itself around him. Layers of soft lights at first, and crisscrossing shadows. Then he saw the walls of dimmed white, but mostly he watched the ceiling staring at him with the texture of thin gravel, gray beyond the strange, boxy machines that hovered over him. His mind tumbled upon itself trying to make sense of it. Sluggish. Communicating recognition failure three times before it whispered a clue.

Hospital.

From that one word, he was able to gather more fragments.

Buckling decks. Warships. Androids. Explosions.

He remembered a hole in the wall. The escape pod.

He did not remember anything else, but it was now apparent to him that he was no longer aboard *Doom in Shadow*.

He tried to move, but bands held him down at wrists and ankles. At one time he might have had the strength to break them. But not now. His strength was no more than that of a drop of water suspended in zero-g.

He slept and woke and slept again. After a while he was allowed to sit up with the help of a robot nurse.

Eventually he saw his new hand, dark silver now, a perfect hand in every way except that it could not feel. It could flex at a thought, could grasp loosely at things like spoons or rails or the edge of a sheet. But it could do little more. It certainly would not be able to wield a weapon.

The technology of the hand did not seem to mesh one hundred percent with the working of his brain.

One of his human commanders, a general he'd never met, came to his room after he was mostly healed and said, "You'll get by, but never again as a combat soldier on the front line."

"I understand," Khim said, though he really didn't. Because what else could he say?

As if reading his mind, the general said, "You'll be auctioned for the best price. The military needs its investment back. But never fear. You'll simply find placement elsewhere. No more war for you. Which, for many, would be considered a gift."

"But I have no other skills."

The general frowned, looking at him intently with crisp green eyes. An assessment without affection. A look of almost longing, but with no personal investment in it. He patted Khim's good hand just above his wrist. "We'll see. Think of it as an adventure."

Khim might have been naive to the ways of real humans, but he was not stupid. He knew the word *adventure* could never mean anything good for his kind.

Chapter Three

Trev

On the second-story landing, Trev paused, looking down the hall. No one was about.

After the family meeting, everyone had headed for bed, their minds no doubt filled with visions of their dark plans for the evening to come.

Trev had the Bradbury stuffed in the waistband of his trousers. He hoped to make it to his bedroom at the far end of the corridor without running into one of his siblings. Two of them, Breq and Blair, shared this floor with him. There were additional guest suites and one other door kept locked.

The punishment room.

They'd all visited it many times. A pole stood in the center with chains and cuffs coming off at angles up high and at ankle height. The Damico children might be left locked and cuffed alone to think about what they had done to displease their father, until Dante finally came to finish the punishment. He whipped them enough to hurt but not enough to bleed. The pain always left tears and an immediate will to obey.

That had been happening since they'd each reached the age of reason.

Trev remembered his first time in the punishment room. He'd been about six. He also remembered his last time. Six months ago. The worst part of being sent there was the waiting. And being left alone chained up, naked to the waist and naked to the cold air, for that room had never been warm.

They all had lived so long under the sadistic manipulations of Dante that they never questioned it. Each sibling took their punishment with wordless obedience because the rewards were great. Dante meted out power and money and material goods, effectively spoiling his children so they would do anything for him and put up with anything from him. There wasn't a better life to be had, Dante often reminded them. And no way out, for the Damico influence reached deep into the civilized galaxy. They all knew if they ran, they could never go far enough, for their father would always find them. Anyway, running out on the Damico family would also warrant a punishment worse than death.

The money, prestige, and name didn't matter to Trev and hadn't for years. The first time he saw his father kill another man—a guard who had supposedly sold information to the competition in some top-secret business deal—he'd decided he would find a way to escape. He'd been seventeen at the time and had run for the bathroom to be sick. Later his father told him, in a kind and loving voice, "You do what you have to do. You get used to it." And Dante had petted his son's head, cupped his face gently, and kissed him on the forehead. All with the same hand that had slit a man's throat fifteen minutes earlier.

Now Trev had a plan. And if it worked, he'd be free forever from the reach of his father.

He walked past the punishment room, and a trickle of icy air skittered down his spine.

When he got to his own room, he stood in the center of the ornate suite, always tidy as he liked it, and surveyed his private domain. From the sweep of maroon curtains to the inlaid marble shelves that held his crystal-encased collection of ancient paper books, to the beautiful bed draped in fog- and rain-colored satins and silks. He would miss it all. Most of his real-books were rare but modern editions. The Bradbury he now took from his pack was worth more than all of them a hundred times over. It was 2632 years old and could never be taken from its case. It would instantly crumble.

Trev sat on the edge of his bed and stared at it. The gleaming case surrounding it gave it a glow as if it were alive and had been ever since the twentieth century when this author had lived and typed on old mechanical machines in dusty libraries, composing the elixirs of his dreams.

Trev had dreams, but they weren't magical. Not like these stories. He lived in a future beyond these stories' small futures, but he longed for those pasts, those boyhood days in plain green towns, those impossible Martian landscapes where gold-eyed beings lived in chess cities, those nights when real carnivals of dust and autumn arrived on trains. He'd never known anything like that.

The pounding air-waterfalls of the gardens where he'd grown up, here on this floating mansion estate, might be magical to some, but he'd found the life dull. He'd become the best acrobat thief, the smartest security systems programmer. Books could have been written about his antics, his capers. But he simply did not like the cavalier idea that money was more important than happiness. Or a human life.

Oh, for the life of a shoe salesman. When he'd once made that comment aloud, his brothers and sisters all laughed. The joke became a family motto of sorts, quoted after a big job or a particularly hard day.

It wasn't that Trev really wanted to sell shoes. He did love the challenge of getting himself in and out of tight spaces, as he had done tonight at the museum, but he never felt free. Not for one moment. The perpetual enslavement to his father, no matter how gilded the cage, brought resentments so deep, at times he thought his mind would break.

Trev lay on his bed, clutching the Bradbury at his side. He leaned back into the softness of too many pillows.

Tomorrow, he thought. *Tomorrow, everything will change.*

Chapter Four

Khim

Strangers bathed his body in lilac-scented water. They brushed him down, naked, with gold body powder. They rimmed his eyes with blue shadow and caressed his lips with a soft pink sheen.

Khim might have fought them off if, beforehand, they hadn't made him breathe the curling zotic smoke from the pleasure wands the grooms waved all about his face and head. The smoke aroused him against his will, made him pliant, dizzy. Paralyzed his vocal cords—an invisible gag—and took away all aggression. Aggression under command orders for expert frontline fighting was his own past means of survival. Bereft of that, he had no sense of what to do as his body betrayed him by following every command of the grooms, every lead.

The grooms, three human boys who looked no more than nineteen, seemed pleased at his response. But mostly they seemed bored, applying all the makeup and powder as if they'd done it a hundred times before. Their touches were professional, gentle, not cruel. But except for that gentleness, they seemed uncaring about what he might be going through.

Created to obey, Khim had no words within him for a protest.

Brought onto a small lighted stage on a thin laser-leash by a fourth handsome groom, Khim could see nothing beyond the glow that contained him but shadows and darker man-shapes upon those shadows.

Knowing nothing of this new, nonmilitary world, he felt vulnerable and exposed, and fear fluttered through his stomach and into his chest. He knew what this was about—sex and its darker underpinnings. It couldn't be otherwise, for he was naked, painted like a doll. He'd witnessed androids fucking without inhibition, but he'd never wanted it for himself. Never felt aroused by his own kind. Never had the sex drive some of the others seemed born with. If something was wrong with him, he never thought about it or cared. He got his pleasure from battle, from storming alien worlds and using his weapons to subvert, kill, destroy. It was enough for him.

But that was no longer his life.

This new thing was something so completely "other" to what he was trained for. He didn't want it.

But his mind and body were like separate entities now. In this moment, upon this stage, as he tried again to find words to deny, to protest, to negate the proceedings, nothing happened but a few twitches in the sleek, round muscles beneath his henna skin. His voice was cramped down low in his throat, unwilling or unable to come out, and he was turned upon the dais as if he were a doll for all those out there in the shadows to ogle and critique and assess.

If there were conversations about his viability, his virility, his *beauty*, they were silent, through private systems and digital conveyances. He was privy to none of it, and Khim abhorred that even more.

The groom who'd led him into this dark area leaned away, put a hand up to his ear as if listening. Right after that, the groom made a motion and touched Khim on the wrist. He forced him to lift his right hand up and turn it, showing off the silver gleam of the metal that had replaced the flesh-and-bone hand he had lost in the explosion on *Doom in Shadow*.

It all took just under a minute. Then the grooms led Khim off by the glowing leash into a dark corridor beyond the little stage, where he was able to overhear just the barest of harsh whisperings.

"You can never outbid them. They have money to burn."

"Damn Damicos. They'll just sell him over and over and over again."

Khim was led away before he could hear more, having no idea what any of that meant.

Later, he was allowed to dress, though the makeup stayed. Then he was bustled alone into a flier the size of a small shuttlecraft and shipped off to his new owners.

*

Khim was led by several different people, all human and all fairly well dressed, through at least four different systems of doorways, which branched off toward varying corridors, steps, and elevators. These were not well-lit, public places, but more like taking a roundabout journey backstage, behind main floors and through hidden passageways.

Khim wore plain black cotton slacks and a pullover blue shirt. His shoes were more like slippers, also black. No one told him anything about where he was or what might be expected of him. But his eyes still worked perfectly, and his perceptions still fed his mind in alarmingly straightforward analyses, all from leftover battle programming that he'd been able to maintain for ten years even in the most panic-stricken of situations. Though for the time being he could not talk due to whatever drugs they'd given him, he could readily observe. And absorb.

The flier had brought him to a large city, a floating city that overlooked a world like a blue jewel. Khim had never seen anything like it and knew none of the names for where he was—city, planet, or even system. He only saw that the city was huge. Set down in the middle of it, he was told to hurry from the door of the flier to a side door of a tall silver building topped with three dark spires that pointed to the stars.

Once inside, he had expected to go up. Instead the people who ordered him to follow them took him downward into the underbelly of the city where, through hard, rocky walls, he could hear the chugging and churning of unseen alien machinery, probably part of the vast engine that kept the huge city afloat in the clouds.

His journey ended in a dark room with no windows and only one door, the walls lined with pipes and grills. A single fan chattered from the ceiling. Along the far wall he could see, through the dimness, a row of five cages with vertical gold bars. Two were occupied. Three were not.

His handlers led him to one cage. Inside he saw a single cot, a toilet, and a sink. They opened the cage door and pushed him inside.

Immediately he turned, though his body was sluggish, and without thinking tried to push his way out, but the barred door slammed against his side. One of the men yelled at him. "Step back!"

His body obeyed as his left foot slid along the smooth flooring of his prison so that the door could close all the way. His mind reeled.

"You'll have food brought to you three times a day," one of the handlers said.

Nothing else was said. They turned and left.

Khim stood looking toward the shadowed entrance imploringly, as if that action alone might bring them back. He felt as if he hadn't taken a breath since he'd been drawn off the stage, bought and sold, and placed into the flier.

Now he filled his lungs. The place smelled of old dampness, gritty and sharp and sad.

He blinked quickly against a sudden warmth. Swallowed hard. He never cried. Not even when the blood of battles sprayed through the air and ran thick into his eyes.

But now. This.

His breathing began to catch in his throat. To distract himself, he glanced around. The walls of the cage to his left and right were solid cement. He could not see the other five cells. But he had seen two occupied cages. Two people were in there with him. Two others locked up as he was. He had only seen their forms long enough to determine by their physical imperfections that they were human and alive. He listened to see if he could hear them, but all was silent.

He opened his mouth to make a sound. Nothing but a choking reflex came out. The zotic drug still ruled his veins.

A second later a voice whispered from one of the cages to his left. "The drug takes three or four hours to pass. But it doesn't matter. They'll just dose you again before they take you back out. Every night it's the same. Every night."

He wanted to ask *For what?* But he knew already. He hadn't been sold naked to a roomful of dark customers for anything but what his body might be able to provide.

He had other questions, but the voice seemed to predict them. "My name's Valo. There's one other person in here, Tabor. He never talks, on or off the zotic. You're in the basement of the Rainspeer Hotel. The private and secret underfloor. They call it the House of Xavier. It's an elite all-male club. There are more of us in a second room next door. Seven at last count. You make eight. I guess business is booming. But don't worry, you won't remember much of what happens there. They give us all the drugs we want. The worst part is the boredom. The waiting. Like right now. And, of course, never being free."

Khim went to the bars and put both his hands—the flesh and the metal—on them, gripping. The voice kept talking.

"We get medical attention every morning. We get three squares."

A strange thumping sound began in another one of the cells.

"That's Tabor. Sometimes he likes to hit the wall. They repair his knuckles with synthiskin, and he's good to go."

Khim closed his eyes and tried to think, but his mind was fogged.

The voice again. "It's not like they are completely thoughtless. Go to the wall of your cell on the right. See the recessed square? Touch it. It's holovision. The list of plays is endless. A hundred lifetimes aren't enough to see it all. I'll give you a list of my favorites. We can watch together. Tabor's not been much company. It's good to see someone new."

Khim did not want to watch plays. He wanted to think, but couldn't. But when he could think, he knew what he'd be doing. He'd be making weapons out of anything he could. He'd be planning and scheming. He was an android with nowhere to go, no papers, programmed to obey, but also programmed to fight. His whole life was about fighting. But always on orders. This would be different. He'd have to get around to the idea that his actions would need to be under his own orders. It was a new way of thinking, but he would embrace it. He had no choice.

But right now he was so tired. The drug, no doubt. He went to the cot and lay down. The voice that called itself Valo continued to drone. He turned to face the wall, put the pillow over his head, and the voice faded.

Sometime later he woke, and for a moment he was back in his sleeping berth on *Doom in Shadow*. He could hear the gentle breathing of his crewmates, two hundred of them, and smell the dry, faint sweetness of the processors. Hear the faint mutterings of machinery in the bulkheads.

26

All that was instantly replaced with another reality, less known but all too real. Sounds of rhythmic thumping. Low voices conferring. And air danker than he was used to. He sat up and saw the cot he had slept on, saw the cell and the shadowy room beyond it. The bars. The locked door.

He cleared his throat, and it was a tangle. He coughed twice. His throat finally made a sound.

The voice from the other cell began again. "You can talk now. It's been long enough. Did you have a nap? How do you feel? What's your name?"

The interrogation annoyed him, but he answered with one word. "Khim."

"Well, Khim. You slept about three hours. It's late afternoon now. Do you remember coming here? Do you remember me telling you my name?"

His mind was vat grown to be superior. He might have been trained mainly for the handling of weapons, but he was not simple. "Valo. And Tabor's the one wrecking his knuckles."

"Good! You're not as bad off as you seemed to be when you first arrived."

How had he seemed? Khim couldn't know. He hadn't seen himself. And he'd been drugged.

Wordlessly he went to the toilet and relieved himself. Then he examined the sink, seeing what might be stored there. He found nothing but a cardboard toothbrush with tiny white bristles, a red bar of soap shaped like a heart, and a thin linen towel. A roll of toilet paper sat on a recessed ledge.

He turned to view the cot. On it sat one pillow, fairly large; a single mattress, surprisingly soft; and one black blanket. There was no change of clothes, no other furniture, not even a dust ball in the corner. He went to the square on the wall Valo had mentioned before he'd gone to sleep. He pressed it, and a tri-D screen flickered to life. It was built deep into the cement. Only the screen showed, but he could control it by touching it. Images flickered of laughing people, chattering characters. And a thousand channels to choose from.

He felt the screen, assessing that it seemed to be made of diamond alloy; not even his metal hand, with all his force behind it, would be able to break it.

He turned to survey the room. Turned again. The feeling of being trapped closed around his heart like a thorn-gloved fist. He went to the edge of his cot and sat, elbows on his thighs, and rested his head in his hands.

Valo was still talking, but Khim heard none of it. Finally he found his own voice. It came out strange and airy at first, then rumbled to full-fledged volume. "Valo, have you ever tried to get out of here?"

He heard the other man sigh. "It's funny. Everyone asks that as their first question. But it's impossible, you see."

Khim pressed the heels of his hands—the metal one like cold fire—to his eyes. Nothing was impossible, his mind told him, and yet in his life every choice had been taken from him, for he'd done nothing for ten long years but what he was told to do. Nothing had really changed. He simply had new commanders now. New bosses.

He said, "Valo, when do they come?"

"They bring dinner in about an hour. After that the grooms prepare us. Sometimes the parties last all night."

Khim took a deep breath, his mind sinking back in on itself at those words. He could fight, but not while drugged.

Valo said, "If you're thinking you could fight them off after dinner, the food's drugged, my friend. If they see you haven't eaten, it doesn't matter. They douse you with it in the mist of the showers, in the oils they use on us, in the scents. And a final dose with the wands. You can't avoid it. Here in our cells, during the day, it's allowed to wear off so we don't get too sick, so we can recover for the next night. It sounds terrible, I know. But there's no escape."

For a long time, he sat, letting the holovision play softly but not looking at it. Valo kept trying to engage him again, but Khim ignored him.

His mind recoiled, came up sputtering as if it had been drowning, looked at this new reality, and recoiled again. He tried to make sense of it. He knew what was happening, or about to happen, to him, but that was not the question. This was more about what it felt like, because he was having new feelings he'd never experienced

28

before. Strange fears. Flights of wings in his chest. Dread like bile in the back of his throat. It made him feel too vulnerable, like the kid he'd never been, though he did have a few programmed memories of blurred childhood scenes. He had rarely accessed any deep feelings about killing because that was all he knew. It didn't require him to feel. Perhaps this new life wouldn't either. Why, then, was he experiencing so many new sensations? A discomfort at the audacity of men? Why had he never considered it before?

Another hour passed, and Khim had not moved more than to breathe or flex the muscles in his arms and legs, which ached slightly as if weakened by the zotic. Finally a door at the far end of the basement clanged open. Two men, dressed in all black with holstered lasers at their hips, entered. Trays floated in front of them.

The men were of average height and weight, both with short dark hair and not overly muscular. Khim decided it wouldn't require much effort to take them down given half a chance. The thought gave him a small hope, better than nothing.

They delivered the food to the other two cells first. Khim's dinner came last. It smelled differently from the prepackaged, preheated meals he'd grown used to as a soldier. There were crisp greens on one side of the tray and what looked like a fresh steak shining in its own juices. His stomach rumbled at the sight. He could not remember the last time he'd eaten.

One of the men slid the tray under the bars on the floor and into Khim's cell. The man looked at him, one eyebrow raised, and said, "Now I see why they paid so much."

Khim felt his body heat at the statement.

The second man came over to stare. "Androids always make people gawk, but their personalities are for shit. Some of them are viper-mean, I've heard. I hope the military obedience chip in his brain still works."

"They pretty much guaranteed it."

Khim knew what they were talking about. The chip was for weapons handling, though, and for battle. Part of that was training he'd never consciously fought. But with an understanding of how the chip controlled emotions like fear, dread, and loneliness, he knew it didn't actually control *him*. He still had freedom of action and thought. But if they didn't know that, maybe that could be an advantage.

He took the tray from the floor and brought it over to his cot, ignoring them.

The men stared at him for another few seconds. "He's big. Remind the grooms to double the zotic dose for him."

"Definitely."

They turned and left the room, not lingering.

Khim looked at the good fresh food, inhaling the aromas of meat, buttered broccoli, and a baked potato dripping with all the trimmings. He was hungry, but a tremor of sickness rose up inside him at their words.

He heard sounds from the other cells of the other two men already eating.

Khim lifted a plastic fork and stabbed at the meat, bringing it to his mouth. Taking a bite from the edge, it melted onto his tongue, making him salivate. This place was obviously a wealthy establishment if their kitchens could produce something this fine for their slaves. A carton of wine accompanied the food, as well as small paper packets of salt and pepper and a paper container of fresh water.

Despite the tightness in his chest and stomach, Khim continued to eat. But halfway through the meal, a fog rolled up in his mind and he remembered what Valo had told him.

They drug the food.

Chapter Five

Trev

Trev woke a little after noon. It was still the same day as the early-morning meeting. He'd spent his last evening with his family controlling computers at a remote location, setting up an illegal power takeover for Dante and assisting Blair with a building map for some meet and greet he had to secure beforehand. Trev paid little attention to the details for meetings and setups and takeovers. He only supplied information or broke into highly secured complexes when hands-on as well as computer skills were needed.

Trev's brothers, Breq and Vance, had gone off to oversee an important but secret party for the very rich and the very decadent. Trev knew Dante owned underground brothels, and not to be outdone, Dante's abodes of the night were posh and extreme. There was nothing he would not organize if enough money was involved. Trev stayed out of that end of the business, telling his father he wanted nothing to do with any of it. He had never set foot in one of those places and never would, didn't even want to know their names or where they existed. He refused any work concerning them, which had almost garnered him a whipping. But then Dante had taken him aside and said, "Your drives are different from your brothers. I respect that. These matters that feed the appetites are different for everyone. If you want to read books instead of fuck with the rich boys all night long, that's your right."

It had seemed an almost underhanded acquiescence on Dante's part, dismissive and yet nonjudgmental.

Trev was not a virgin by choice, merely by circumstance. He simply hated people. The fact that he was physically beautiful made his brothers and sisters joke about his love life, but if Dante overheard them, he frowned on that. Dante never required Trev to work the underground, human-trafficking end of the business, and after that day he'd never mentioned Trev's love life again.

The morning finally came.

Dante approached Trev just outside the dining room and patted him on the back. "Good work tonight, son." He cupped his hand around the back of Trev's neck, warm and gentle, pulling him into a brief embrace. "I don't think I thank you enough for what you do for this family."

Trev knew his father was under stress. He'd heard him yelling on his comm for hours that night to various parties. Trev did not hear actual words or details, just the raised voice, and he kept doing his own list of jobs as quickly and efficiently as he could.

That efficiency had not gone unnoticed.

Dante said, "There will be a substantial bonus for you this month."

"Thank you, sir." Trev's cheeks heated a bit at the praise. He tried not to think of what Dante would do once he noticed, after today, that Trev was gone.

Though Trev would have been justified in hating his father, he did not. It was the family business he hated. Dante himself was actually very conscientious, even caring, loving. He might be a bad man, but not completely evil. In Trev's mind there was a difference. Or so he told himself. This man had legally adopted him as a favor to a friend of a friend. That was all Trev knew or cared to know. Dante had given Trev everything, and Trev was not ungrateful. He was just done with this life and needed to make himself a new one. That was all.

This time at early breakfast, Trev had more to eat than cake, though he was nervous and not hungry. He looked around at his family, all present, back from their nightly meetings and depravities, and felt not one ripple of remorse or grief that he'd not be seeing them again.

Except for Dante. A part of him would miss his father.

Everything was in order. His Bradbury was tucked in his secret safe. After he was gone, Trev knew Dante would never let him go in his mind. His room would not be touched or changed. The staff and his siblings would be ordered to stay away from it. Maybe someday Trev could reclaim his things, but that was the least of what was on his mind now.

He barely heard the dinner conversation, which focused for a while on how something had gone wrong at one of the brothels. Someone had been injured. Or killed.

It was a big deal, a probable lawsuit. And a loss for the company that held that business in trust. Dante was pissed, and Trev figured it was what he'd been shouting about during the night. He did not want to know anything about it, and closed his mind off to any details his brothers were complaining about. It wasn't good dinner conversation anyway, and quite soon Dante put a stop to discussing the subject during the meal's first course.

Dante was pissed about the money, of course, and his shelter company's reputation. He didn't care that there were injuries or possible deaths.

But Trev heard Breq say, in a sly tone, "It could've been the best draw ever. If Torrel hadn't had such a big mouth, we could've covered all the evidence, all trace, and whacked that zotic supplier for inferior grade. No one would have had to know. The police—"

Dante slammed his hand on the table. "Enough. No more! It's done. We lost this one. And I hold you accountable, Breq."

"Not Torrel?"

"He'll be taken care of, as will the supplier. But on my order and when I say. Not you!"

Trev took a deep breath. *Taken care of.* Those were not words you wanted to hear come out of Dante's mouth.

"Well, it's too late. We lost him for good now, and our investment with it."

"I said no more!" Dante's voice came slow and even. That was the tone he used when he meant it. If Breq said one more word about it, he'd go to the punishment room for sure.

Trev would be so glad after today to never return. He took a deep breath and faked being hungry after a long night of family business.

*

By nine in the morning, everyone was in bed. It was as if the Damico family were allergic to the gentle spread of cream-frosted sunlight down the halls and corridors of the floating mansion. They were shadow dwellers, dealers in the dangers and thrills that occupied the landscapes of darker hours.

Trev remained wide-awake. When he left his room for the last time, he took nothing with him but the clothes on his back and the fake chip ID his private client had provided.

All the backstory work, which he'd helped create, had been done now. By the time he left the Damico mansion, he would no longer be Trevor Damico, but Trevor Varain from the Omicron system. His palm print, retina scan, and brain pattern would all now match that name.

He walked through the family great room, seeing little of it except that it was ornate and grand, decorated with so much original art and sculpture that it crowded the vast checkerboard floor space and hovered over fancy couches and pillow-backed chairs. A fountain with two eight-foot embracing angels splashed noisily in the foyer. Aside from a couple of circular, humming robot cleaners, there was no other sound.

Trev took the elevator to the underground garage. The security system recognized him, and all the doors opened soundlessly. He got into his flier and started it up. Later it would be found abandoned in Fire Town. He'd already made plans for that.

As he drove away from the mansion, Trev circled it once for a last view of the trees, the waterfall cascading over the land's edge, and the house itself, a triangle-shaped work of art that glowed in the early light. As he was about to turn the flier, he looked toward the upper story and thought he saw a curtain move and then a ghostly face framed in black hair. That window opened to his father's rooms.

A chill washed over his skin.

The sight of his father's face watching him pull away was one final dig at his confidence. As if his father were somehow saying Trev would never have the last word. But that was paranoia talking, and guilt, for he and his brothers and sisters had freedom to come and go at will for hours, even for a day. Trev, at twenty-three, was not required to account for every trip he made in the very flier Dante had given him when Trev turned sixteen.

Trev put all thought of his father behind him, took the tracking system off-line, and hand-piloted his flier up into the sky.

He drove to the city of Mooncast, twenty miles from the mansion. The floating metropolis was bigger and more beautiful than Fire Town, except for the underside with its jagged edges of land dripping vines and pipes all around its forty square miles of buildings and roads.

He pulled into a garage, leaving the flier unlocked and the password open so that the vehicle could be taken away by the person he'd hired to abandon it.

When Trev arrived at the address he'd been given, two men in black suits were waiting for him. One said to him, "Do you have your new ID?"

"Yes."

"Mr. Archimedes is ready for you."

"Thank you."

Trev stepped into a large sunlit office with a back wall made entirely of glass showing a panoramic view of the Mooncast skyline. With its ball-tipped spires and white swirls of sweeping rooflines, it could have been a city made of the foam of ocean waves.

A small man stepped forward, slimmer even than Trev, with a shock of white hair on top of his head, the sides cleanly shaved. "Mr. Damico, I am Archer Archimedes."

Archimedes was flanked by a taller man in a gray suit much like Trev's father would wear.

The man held out his hand, and Trev took it. "I remember you." Trev had met this man once long ago at a private party of Dante's. Trev had been twelve. The man had talked to him about computers; he had been kind.

Mr. Archimedes nodded. "You were not followed, were you?"

"No."

"Good. This is my attorney, Mr. Shinn."

Trev nodded. The attorney did not hold out his hand, so Trev kept his hands at his sides.

"The two men outside are police who work for me," Archimedes explained. "There is already a judge in place on the next floor. After you sign the documents, witnessed by the judge, they will take you to North Star. The confession has already been written out. All the details and why the money you stole cannot be accounted for. You cannot be sued for it since you own nothing. The judge will sentence you to one year. North Star is for nonviolent offenders, practically a resort. The year will go quickly. And in payment, you will have your brand-new identity and a bought-and-paid-for island in the air all your own in the Omicron system one hundred light-years from here. Your father will never find you. You will be wealthy and free to live your life as you wish. Is our agreement still standing?"

"Yes."

Mr. Shinn came to Trev with a thin, shining digital paper document. "Please put your thumb print here, and here." Trev did as instructed. "This contract with Mr. Archimedes is now binding. You may now proceed."

Archimedes had pale blue eyes and thin lips, but he lifted the edges of his mouth a little sadly—or maybe that was barely controlled glee. He said, "Thank you. My company's reputation will remain clean, its assets untouched, and both of us will be wealthier for what you are doing."

In truth, Trev knew Archimedes had embezzled, over time, nearly one billion credits from his own firm, leaving investors poorer. He'd finally been caught and needed a quick scapegoat. Trev had learned of the situation online and recognized the name. He carefully queried Archimedes about his predicament, bypassing all security and making sure his message reached the businessman's personal comm.

Having recognized him, Archimedes was ready to listen to a deal.

This man, perhaps one of the only men equal in wealth to Trev's own father, had the money and connections to help Trev disappear. They came to an agreed-upon plan. Archimedes's problem was solved. The older man would not go to prison. He would get to keep his company, which provided jobs for hundreds of thousands of workers.

And Trev, as Trevor Varain, would admit to the crime through his computer-sleuthing expertise and do the time for him. The story was in place, the funds untraceable, the judge paid off.

All that remained was a year to serve time in a veritable resort, and then he'd be free. "The deal is set," Trev said quietly.

"May you live a healthy and long life," Archimedes said.

It seemed peculiar to Trev how the biggest criminals in his life—his father, and now this man—could show such politely innocent and charming demeanors. How they lived with themselves and slept through the night, Trev didn't know. Nor was it his concern.

Now all he cared about was that he was finally going to be free.

*

The prison flier had seats for twelve. Half were empty.

Trev, hands cuffed in his lap, wearing a gray jumpsuit given to him in the judge's quarters, sat in a window seat and stared at the passing clouds.

All the passengers were male. A uniformed guard piloted. Another, armed with a laser in a thigh holster, sat on a bench seat facing the prisoners.

Trev was not afraid. He'd researched the North Star facility. It had gardens and gymnasiums. Private cells and job opportunities. He actually could have brought some of his belongings with him and been allowed to keep them. Like books. But they were safer left in the Damico household.

The other prisoners in the flier looked harmless. One man was heavyset and red-cheeked, blinking rapidly. Another looked like he'd barely reached the age of adulthood. Yet another picked at a hangnail, seeming downright bored. These were not dangerous men. Trev's own brothers and sisters were chillier than this lot. He would do just fine.

As Trev watched the sky traveling by his window, he saw a black dot on the horizon. Another flier. They were in the middle of nowhere, but it wasn't unusual to see other air cars in remote patches of sky.

The driver of the prison flier spoke softly and rapidly into a wrist comm. The car slowed and took a turn toward the approaching dot which, as it got bigger, looked like another air bus, gray with a red stripe. Prison grade.

Both fliers slowed until they were side by side, hovering in midair.

"Hey, why are we stopping?" asked the man with the hangnail.

No one answered him. The fliers connected in midair, and the door opened.

A uniformed guard boarded. He glanced over the prisoners, then came down the aisle to stand beside Trev's seat. "You're to come with us."

Trev looked up. "Me?"

"Yes. There's been a change of plan. Your prison assignment has changed."

"I'm sure you've made a mistake," Trev began. But already his heart was speeding up, his throat thickening in fear. Had something gone wrong?

"No mistake. You're Trevor Varain, yes?"

"Yes."

"New charges have been added to your sentence. New evidence came to light. You'll have a trial if you want one, but in the meantime, you're to be remanded to North Star's sister facility, Steering Star."

"That's maximum security," Trev said, standing. "That prison's in space."

"I see you know your prisons. Good for you. Then there will be no surprises. Come with me." The guard grabbed Trev's upper arm and pulled him up.

Trev had to concentrate to keep his legs from shaking. In the worst of situations, he'd trained his body not to react in alarm, not to panic. Slithering in and out of buildings, leaping past the grandest of security systems, the ability to keep his cool had saved his life on more than one occasion.

He took a deep, leveling breath, but it sounded too loud in the small space of the flier. He followed the guard up front and crossed the threshold into the small tunnel that connected the two hovering fliers.

"What new charges have been filed against me?" he asked.

"I don't have that information. You'll find out soon enough."

Trev entered the second flier, which, to his relief, was empty. They'd commandeered it specially for him, then. And that could mean only one thing.

Dante had found out about his plan.

Chapter Six

Khim

In Khim's mind was a blue place behind a transparent wall, a place like an ocean cave where treasure might be found, where he stored what he called his forbidden "I am" thoughts. Such as *Is this all my life will ever be?* and *Will I feel my death in my head or my heart?*

Sometimes his questions and answers came to him there, in the glassy blueness, like little poems he should never have had one thought to composing.

His mind might question, *Why are we created to be sad?* Answer: *Because you are lonely.*

Or *How does one set a trap for a dream?* Answer: *Bait it with candles and red aster incense.*

In that place lay madness. For what did he know of real life, or candles, or red aster incense? When he wasn't fighting in wars, he played games of war. In his off-hours he watched action-hyped movies or read books about weapons, histories of other wars, encyclopedias of random facts about war. Not fairy tales or poetry. Not fantasy or romance.

He had those weird questions he stored away, and the weird answers, and he thought he might have liked to taste, just once, the words of a fairy tale on his lips. But he had been trained away from that, convinced it wasn't for him, that he would not find worth in it and it would waste his time. He believed in everything he'd been taught so he could be the best warrior. He had had no reason to think otherwise.

Now he found himself grappling for more imagination because the fog, and the drugs, and just the thought of hands on his body were not what he'd trained for, not welcomed, so alien and distasteful that he no longer wished to immerse himself in "real life."

He needed escape. He needed to bait a dream.

When Khim had arrived at the basement of the brothel, he had some clues as to what awaited him. Sex service.

Of course he knew what sex was. He knew that service would mean submitting his body to another's demand for pleasure in that way. He'd never liked others of his kind in the barracks, so did not understand the need for a partner in order to achieve a brief release, and he had never shared that with another.

He would hate it in the brothel. He expected unpleasant things.

After he ate his dinner and the zotic rushed through his system, he could only blink in dumb wonder as handlers opened his cage and led him through the basement shadows to a tiled room with faucets and hoses and drains in the floor.

He saw the man who'd spoken to him when he'd first arrived. *Valo.* And a third captive, the silent one, Tabor, who thumped the walls with his fists. Khim noted groggily that they, like him, were fairly startling in appearance. Valo was tall and darkly muscled, with wide dark eyes and beautiful, pink-rose lips. Tabor was shorter, with golden skin that shimmered and long brown hair that brushed the edges of his hips. He had flashing green eyes and reminded Khim of a sculpture he'd once seen on an alien world that supposedly depicted an incubus demon from the underworld. Tabor had slanted brows and a strange, alluring glare.

They were all three stripped down to bare skin in the space of two breaths and shoved forward together under sprays of warm water coming from all angles of the tiled room. The water smelled faintly of lemons.

The zotic had them pliant, lethargic. Tabor swayed as if he could barely stand on his own. His long hair clung in wet ropes to his chest and back, making him look even wilder.

Valo kept glancing in Khim's direction, no longer talkative under the control of the zotic; his pupils were dark, his looks lazy, and he might or might not have even known Khim was there.

Khim wrestled against the drug with his mind. Trying to stay aware, observe, assert himself. But every time his thoughts crested to form anything more coherent than obeying his handlers' commands, he would have a sensation, both mental and physical, of falling in endless loops. It made him dizzy to keep trying to think, as if the drug were punishing him for the effort.

Tabor must have been trying to think too, because he fell in the bath several times as the handlers scrubbed their bodies with brushes and cloths heavy with foaming soap.

Valo just kept making groaning sounds, almost as if he were laughing, and his large member was very erect.

Khim felt nothing like that from the zotic, but when he looked down at himself as he was washed, he saw that he, too, was erect from the effects of the drug without even realizing it. As was Tabor, who squirmed now on his hands and knees, all soaped. Khim watched as one handler held that feral-looking guy down with a hand on his back, and a second handler inserted a soft tube into his backside.

Khim felt his breath catch and a kind of fury, where for a brief moment he wanted to kill that handler—not because Khim cared about Tabor, but because some instinct inside him wanted this dream to end, and that slave's nightmare, as well as his own, was just beginning.

For ten years he had killed without conscience. Murdered. But war was war. It had its own rules, ethics, and reasons. Right or wrong, he'd been indoctrinated not to question his orders. Programmed. For the mind, whether vat-grown android or natural human, was easy to influence.

Sometimes he felt rage when he killed, but not toward himself, mostly toward the conditions that required so much violence. But never such fury as he felt right now. Which was strange to him, because wasn't killing just about the worst thing one person could subject upon another?

Maybe not. Maybe enslavement was actually worse. Maybe causing continuous suffering to another for a dark act of pleasure was an evil of a richer grade.

Of course it was all evil, and as soon as Khim's fury tried to surface, his system bombarded him with wave after wave of disorientation and he couldn't find the energy to lift even a finger against those who manipulated and controlled him.

Now he was pushed forward into the water stream, and down, until he fell to his knees on the tile. The sting of his weight hitting the floor was muffled by the drug. Something soft entered him from behind, sluicing him inside with warm water. Horrified, he wanted to be sick but had no will to follow through with that urge.

Though the touch was clinical, it didn't matter to him. He did not want it. He'd been given no chance to refuse.

While one handler worked on him from behind, another soaped up his hair and rinsed it.

The ministrations to Khim ended first. The other men went through a depilatory step and more rinsing. Khim had been bred to have no body hair except for his scalp, eyebrows, and eyelashes—another reason he'd been prized for the sex market when he could no longer serve as a soldier.

Khim was taken to a dryer where his hair was arranged and various lotions and scents were put on his skin. One handler dabbed gold dust around his eyes. The second oiled his behind—yet another violation he wanted to move away from, followed by another urge to lash out, to fight, immediately quelled by the zotic.

His eyes stung in a strange response to his horrible helplessness. If he shut them, the dizziness from the drug got worse, so he opened them and watched the handlers. His own two were male and wore tight shorts and tank tops, not seeming to care that their job got them soaked. They acted indifferent. Perhaps they were drugged as well, yet under better control of their faculties than the slaves they handled. They did not seem aroused by what they were doing, but once in a while they spoke to each other with furtive smiles.

"He's a big one." "Such beautiful eyes." "This one will be the star tonight, for sure."

They also gave short, clipped orders. "Turn." "Left." "Follow." "This way." "Bend." "Legs spread."

They did not console with their words, but they weren't rough. Neither were they gentle, nor at all sympathetic.

When all three slaves were lined up, naked and glistening with lotions and powders, one handler came up alongside them and doused them with sweet smoke that smelled like strawberries slightly singed.

All the colors of the drying room, a jumble of pink-framed mirrors against red walls, ran together in Khim's vision like a distorted, melted painting. His mind numbed out. He actually lost a little bit of time, maybe minutes, for it seemed he had only blinked when suddenly he found himself in a large room full of people mingling, drinking, and smoking. He did not remember walking there.

Khim and about a dozen other naked slaves stood on a sort of stage overlooking a party where more colors assaulted him, mixing and merging as if the whole event were being held underwater.

The room's lighting was turned low, a dim bronze effect that made strange shadows on the wineglasses and on the wide white walls. There were low tables and lots of puffy-looking couches, love seats, and settees. Some were backless or had a pillowed rise at only one end, and they looked old-fashioned. There were also recessed alcoves framed by velvet curtains with gold cords, all standing open, showing plush beds within.

Khim's mind took an inordinately long time to process it all, moving at a sluggish pace as if he were half-asleep. His body tingled. His skin felt flushed, as if all the longings of his frustrated ten years of life were brimming to overflow in this very moment, his body poised to a tense and focused need. He'd rarely felt this way—such focused lust. Such a fever. He'd been bred for fighting, not for any purposeful sex drive.

The drugs in his system changed all that. Now he waited with the others to be chosen. Hot. Itching. Aroused. As if the very blood in his veins were boiling.

And he hated it.

Already the moans of the slaves beside him echoed as the extra drugs they'd all been given took over, ruling their bodies with pure desire. The zotic caused a sort of selective muteness—none of them could speak—but humming, moaning, and groaning all came from a different part of the brain.

Khim refused to give in to his own moans collecting in his throat. He made a vow that he would differentiate himself from all the others in any way he could. If that meant not moaning, then he would remain silent.

Out the corner of his eye, he saw Valo and Tabor. They stood out from the flock, both more beautiful than anyone in the room. Already Tabor was getting attention as tuxedoed customers, all men with the look of the very rich, moved closer to where the demon-eyed man stood so they could appraise and inspect him. Tabor bared his teeth even as he moaned in pleasure at the attention.

There must have been a dress code, because everyone wore formal attire: tuxedos or tailcoats with glittering satin vests and black ties, or brushed silk kimonos. There were men of varying ages and sizes, all well-groomed, behaving as if this lavish party were the most normal event of their week.

Khim had expected women to be in attendance as well, but they were not. Then he remembered what Valo told him. House of Xavier was a men's-only club, very private, very exclusive.

Just as Khim thought Tabor would be the first of them to be chosen, with men surrounding him as if he were some rare and magical sylph, looking up at him with hunger and licking their lips, a voice below Khim said, "What can you do with that metal hand of yours?"

Khim's gaze fell on a man with bright red hair, shaved on one side, and a complexion that looked almost sunburned. He had no voice to reply. And even if he had, he would have no answer to that question.

When he did not react, the man laughed louder, bringing the attention of other men to his side.

An image of every weapon he'd ever used flashed across Khim's mind. But he could only stand there, vision blurred. And listen to that laugh.

The next thing Khim was aware of was that out of all the men standing naked on the stage, it ended up being him who was chosen first and instructed to move down the steps so that he could join the party in whatever fashion the guests saw fit to have him.

His heart rate increased, then subsided once more to that sleepy, drugged rhythm. His throat felt tight, his lungs almost too tense to take in air.

"Is that a real android?" someone to his left asked.

"That's what they promised in the invitation," said another.

"Bring him to the couch."

"Oh, of course we'll all share."

Khim barely felt the hands on his lower arms, leading him forward, or the hands at his back, pushing. One palm cupped the curve of his hip briefly, then was gone.

He wanted to flinch. To run. But his body moved as directed, as if he had no will of his own. And of course he did not. The drugs in his system saw to that.

The couch was red velvet. The men surrounding him were mostly wearing black tailcoats with white shirts and black ties. Most had hollow gazes of empty hunger that appeared ugly to Khim, who again had thoughts of weapons and what he might easily do with them in this room, at this function, where the wealthy and depraved congregated.

Khim blinked. Blinked again. The room and the men surrounding him wavered.

A push from behind made his knees catch the side of the sofa, and already dizzy, he lost his balance and went forward. He caught himself on his metal hand, not feeling the red velvet underneath it but aware of how his weight indented the cushion. His sudden stumble resulted in more hands reaching toward him, not to balance but to take advantage. Hands went to his face, shoulders, back, thighs. Hands caressed his buttocks. Fingers brushed his lips, parting them. One unwelcome finger entered his mouth just as he felt a hand between his buttocks, another finger probing there.

His eyes shut on white blankness. His teeth clamped lightly at the finger in his mouth, and a voice in his ear said, "Now, now. No biting."

Another voice exclaimed, "He bit you?"

"No, it was just a muscle response to Chin, there, putting his finger up his ass. I don't think he was quite ready for that."

"It's his first night," said another.

"Ah, that explains it."

"Well, he better not bite. I intend to thoroughly use that beautiful mouth."

Laughter.

Though Khim heard all this, his thoughts protesting every word and tone, he remained helpless. Of course he wanted to bite that finger! It had been his intent. But his muscles did not obey more than to keep breathing. And that attempt at a clamp down was nothing but his mouth relaxing around the intruder, strangely accepting. It was infuriating.

He tried to blank it all out of his mind—what they were doing, how they were arranging his body. Fingers in his hair, at his waist, and inside him from behind. Someone forcing his legs apart. Someone reaching under him and grabbing his erection. He did flinch at that, at least inside, where he felt flutters of both anger and pleasure begin in his stomach and tangle up into his chest. The touches felt crazily erotic but horribly offensive. They were holding him down, invading him, forcing him. He was not programmed for this. His training was to fight until he could no longer fight. At that point, all he had ever hoped for was a quick death.

This was worse—this was not a fair fight. He could have taken a beating easier than this. This strange, dark, hungering hell, this vulnerability of being so exposed and uncontrolled among strangers. This horror that his body responded to it as if it liked it, when really it was the aphrodisiacs working on him combined with the stunting of his own personal power.

He smelled pipe smoke and old leather. The velvet of the couch pressed against his cheek, and someone raised his back end and pushed more than a finger into him now where he was soft and yielding and quivering. Khim didn't care if it was smooth and effortless and he was hard in the hand that stroked him. It was still rape, still an attack, and he very badly wanted to look up and over his shoulder at whoever had taken the lead so he could memorize every detail of his face and someday, when things had changed, he could hunt the man down and slice him open and watch him drown in his own blood.

The first rape came with much peer encouragement, laughter, and even applause.

Still mortified, a bitterness rose in Khim's throat. The drug did not take that away. He would have to live, for now, with that acrid taste permeating him. His nostrils widened as he fought to breathe.

Hands were on his mouth again. Was that another mouth on the hardness between his legs? He couldn't see. Sounds became muffled. Time distorted. Erections pressed into his face, his mouth. Someone slapped his jaw twice, hard. Liquid coursed down the sides of his face. Semen or tears? Both.

The bitterness in his mouth filled him until he gagged, and he was struck again as someone said, "He's certainly not trained in the art of that!"

All that was left for his mind, which seemed to fracture over and over like multiple breaks in fine ice, was to wait. And wait. For it to be over. For the night to end.

He didn't want to think anymore. He didn't want to exist.

He did not want to understand what was happening, and yet he couldn't help it. After loyal service to a high-end military organization, this was his life?

He was a sex toy now. Nothing more. And despite the physical pleasure that the drugs made him feel, his body responding sensually and even craving more, his mind knew it for what it was. Rape. And he did not want it.

It was so hard to think, so hard to understand that what was happening to him was nothing he could control or ever change. How he hated his body now, a body that betrayed him through drug-spiked blood. And all of it happening to him as if he were submerged in liquid, floating, moving in a weird, ecstatic dance that felt good, too good, even as it enraged him.

After a while, what they were doing to him began to hurt. Badly.

The transparent glass holding back the blue place in his mind where his true self lived cracked again and again, an internal, echoing, breaking crash. Gunshots in his mind. Flashing darks. Exploding novas. Body wet. Face wet. Throat knotted with screams or sobs or dark, deep yells he could not give voice to. His hands, metal and flesh, formed fists in the cushions hard enough to tear them. Hard enough to make muscles contract, stand out against his skin underneath endless caresses, his jaw clenching, back seizing, eyelids fluttering.

With a pent-up, raging, alien roar he came up so fast that naked bodies went sprawling. The couch overturned, red cushions flying.

Khim did not have time to think. His body simply reacted. He turned, his arms reached out, and he grabbed the man who had been behind him—not the first and not even the fifth, maybe a repeat. He clamped his hands on either side of the man's head and gave a swift, strong jerk.

48

The room had gone instantly silent. The sound of the neck breaking was like a single clap. The man fell limp at Khim's feet as he let go of the body and automatically crouched in defensive warrior posture. Then his warehouse programming took over, and he lowered his hands and folded them submissively in front of him, bent his head, hunched his shoulders. At that moment, and not one second before, he realized with horror that the zotic had lost its hold upon him, leaving only a lingering cloud of mist where once had stood an open door to the dancing pleasures of hell.

He'd been a very, very bad boy.

Sudden shouts went up around him. Men in uniform with lasers drawn. The House of Xavier was exclusive and wealthy. Of course it would have round-the-clock specialty guards.

Khim immediately put his hands up in surrender; his knees gave way as he crumpled to the floor. His mouth opened. What came out was a strange, strangled sound.

The men surrounded him. Some began to kick and lash at him with their boots. Others yelled for them to stop. In an automatic submissive response, Khim crouched low over his lap, put his hands behind his head to protect it, and let them have at him.

He felt very little and heard less as boots and fists impacted his sides and back. But someone finally yanked him forward and upright, cuffing his wrists. When he lifted his head, a fist slammed into his face. He felt the warm blood coat his upper lip.

He looked around, dazed and bloody. People were running for the exits. The room had cleared pretty quickly. Now two expensively suited men stood in front of him as a third, a customer who was still quickly getting dressed, yelled, "I'll sue for this! Everything you have! He was my friend. He was my friend, and your *thing* killed him."

Khim glanced through his still-red, enraged vision at the naked body that lay untouched on the floor. All the other slaves, he realized, had been rapidly escorted away. The only ones left in the room now were himself, a half-dozen security men, the dead man, the dead man's friend, Khim's two handlers from the baths, and two dark-haired men in black suits who looked like they wanted to murder him.

One of the men in suits said, "Why isn't he on zotic?"

"He is, Mr. Damico. Triple dose, as ordered," replied one handler.

The second dark-haired man said, "This can't happen. Our father will be very unhappy."

The friend of the dead man said, "Well, you better figure something out because I've already chimed the police."

"Torrel, you're an idiot," one of the black-suited men said. "Every witness here would have been paid nicely."

The man said, "I *have* money. I don't want to be paid. I want justice for Chin."

They all glanced uneasily at the broken man sprawled at their feet.

Khim was shaking now, flanked by security on all sides. They seemed not to care that he was still naked and covered in blood and semen. His side ached. He might have a broken rib. Inside his rectum, he was burning, liquid dripping down the insides of his thighs.

One of the security men asked, "Orders, Mr. Damico?"

Both suited men looked at Khim. Now he could see their resemblance. They were obviously brothers.

The taller one said, "Hand him over to the police, then. We own him, but if we turn him in for murder, at least we won't be held accountable."

Khim trembled harder. The police? He would most certainly be executed.

"Breq, don't you think we could—"

"Shut up, Vance," the taller man interrupted. "It's over. Dad's gonna be pissed at losing his investment, but it's the only way."

So, Khim thought through his glittering daze, their father owned the House of Xavier.

The one called Breq looked Khim up and down as if appraising him for a fight, or a modeling job… or perhaps another rape.

The man who had just finished dressing said, "Fuck you all. This club has a reputation for being safe and clean."

"It is safe and clean," Breq snarled. "This has never happened before. Obviously the drugs wore off. We'll need to investigate why."

He turned to Vance. "Take some men and go find Lig. Find out what the fuck he actually sold us!"

The man named Vance hurried off.

Now Breq turned his attention back to Khim. His dark eyes, pinched with a cold light, met Khim's, and Khim stared back—still horrified, still in shock. And yet the drugs had waned and an unbidden image came: he saw himself taking the man by the throat and pressing in with flesh and metal hands, watching that cool glow in the deep-set gaze slowly dim until nothing was left of the human.

The killing instinct in him should not have surprised him. It was what he'd done for ten years. But war was different from murder. The dead man at his feet had been raping him, and he'd reacted. But this man had done nothing but hold his stare.

Khim's breath puffed in a jolt of disgust. At the man, and at himself.

Holding Khim's gaze as if it were a test of wills, Breq said, "Take him away. Clean him up and turn him over to the cops."

"Yes, sir."

Khim was forced to look away first as two strong guards led him out, followed by his handlers. But now he would remember that face forever.

He was allowed a brief shower under close supervision. Gone was all privacy. He had no hope he'd ever get that back. But then, had he ever really had it in the first place?

As his thoughts cleared even more under the hot water, the last vestiges of the zotic a distant shiver in his veins, he felt a strange gladness under all his pain and horror.

His life would end. That was good. He had never wanted to be sold to a place such as this and knew he'd never become used to it. Death was better. Or prison, if he were spared. Still locked away, but at least there he would be drug free, able to walk about on his own and fight whenever he felt like it. That happened in prisons, didn't it? Fighting, and an existence apart from humanity?

That would be fine, actually. Better. He hated the human civilizations anyway. It was best to be apart from that. There would be rules in the prison, but he was used to that. And with his strength and size, he could keep the other human prisoners at bay with little effort.

Yes, this was all better. If he survived, if he were not sent to immediate execution, he would be better off.

His fate was turning now. He could feel it.

*

At the police station jail, Khim was given a drab gray jumpsuit to wear and soft-soled black shoes.

The police had come quickly to the House of Xavier. Seeing he was injured, they had taken him to a clinic before booking him.

Khim's fractured rib had been knitted well, his broken nose set and healed, his internal injuries medicated. But his muscles still ached.

There had been no time to sleep. In the early morning hours, he arrived for his arraignment. He had no rights. His lawyer entered his plea for him. Strangely, the judge spared his life. That should not have been the outcome, but the judge had seemed to side with Khim during some of the proceedings, questioning the drugs, the rape, and the fact that Khim had been trained as a soldier, not a prostitute.

The Damicos did not show for the arraignment or his guilty plea. There were angry lawyers in that small courtroom, as well as his own attorney—a lawyer from the Damicos?—who managed to convey a great amount of disgust at the conditions her client found himself in and begged beautifully for leniency from the judge.

And the judge responded.

It was the only kindness Khim had ever been shown in his entire life.

That lawyer and the judge both saved Khim's life that day.

Now he found himself aboard a silver flier with a red stripe painted on its side, bound for Steering Star Correctional Prison, which orbited the planet. His stay there would be for life plus twenty years. Translation: seventy years. Since he had a lifespan of 190 and was only ten years old, he would actually know freedom from the prison in some distant future he could barely envision.

If it still existed, would he be forced to go back to the brothel? He had not even thought to ask.

He glanced out the window of the flier, where clouds like melted gold floated by. He'd been to the distant stars and back and had tramped around colonized worlds in every setting, from green jungle to sapphire ocean and burning beaches. He'd camped in iron-scented desert sands and trooped up jagged peaks to alien vistas overlooking pink acid lakes or ammonia snowdrifts. Sometimes he wore helmets or other breathing apparatuses. Other times the planets were physiologically friendly to human lungs and brains. He'd seen brute armies die, alien cities implode, whole moons and planets broken into jeweled pieces of emerald and ruby floating in space. But he'd never been captured, never seen the inside of a prison.

Part of him was looking forward to it.

Another part of him, the part behind glass in a blue cave where he might've had a semblance of a heart if life had given him half a chance, turned away. Didn't want to look or know. Begged to be shut down.

Life was bound by things no one could control. Humans, animals, and androids alike.

But the voice of his heart said, *It's unfair. It's as if we're all dead before we ever get to live.*

Khim barely noticed the single tear hot against his cheek.

Chapter Seven

Trev

From the outside, as the flier had begun its approach, Steering Star appeared spectacular. It looked like a big mechanical octopus, the center hub black and lit up with huge, white-gold squares of windows, while eight appendages stretched out at various angles, comprising eight abutting sections. Several wings housed docking bays.

Two more fliers were approaching from the left side. Below lay the glimmering opal jewel of the planet Gideon, which looked so close but was now so very far out of reach.

Trev had grown up in the clouds and knew most of their cities, but he had also been to the planet below many times. Now, in his new home high above the world, he would be able to view it rotating beneath him at all times as if to taunt him. Reminding him, and all the prisoners of Steering Star, that they could look but never touch. The setup was ingenious. Insidious.

As the flier attached to a dock of connective doors on one of the eight appendages, the other two fliers did the same, all three floating side by side against the backdrop of an endless black and starry night.

The two guards in Trev's flier stood, beckoning for him to get up from his seat.

His skin rippled with a wave of fear. He'd been feeling that fear all along, but now it fully woke inside him. His blood felt chilled in his veins. "Maximum security" meant this place housed the most violent of criminals. Trev was anything but violent. He knew how to fight—his older siblings, Blair and Sonye, on the orders of Dante, had trained him since he was very little—but he had never actually been *in* a fight. He was so much better at avoidance, at running away.

A thin film of cold moisture coated his eyes. He blinked it away and stood, even as his throat tightened in dread.

A soft voice at the back of his mind began.

One step at a time. You can do this. Do not look forward. Do not look back. Just walk.

He moved toward the waiting guards, his hands locked in cuffs in front of him. He had so many questions he wanted to ask. Why the last-minute transfer? When could he see an attorney about the new charges? What were the new charges?

Instinct told him to remain silent.

One guard led him through the portal. The other stayed at his back as if he were a dangerous man. As if he might try something in the middle of space, with no weapons and no idea what awaited him on the other side.

Trying not to stumble, keeping his head high, Trev followed two armed guards from the door of the flier through a sealed airlock and into a long gray hall, well lit but with a distinctly oppressive atmosphere to it. Two more round portals opened, emitting more guards and about half a dozen other prisoners of varying ages and sizes, very unimpressive—except for one who stood out.

He was over six feet tall with glistening golden hair pulled roughly into a tail and fastened with a strip of cloth. His features appeared so in proportion, so perfect, that Trev realized he was looking at a rare being, one of the slow-growing numbers of vat-grown humans that so many in the galaxy erroneously referred to as androids.

Curiosity rose in him. Why would an android be in the prison system? They were indoctrinated against crime, made-to-order, very controlled. If any androids did run amok, they were almost always immediately put down. The checks-and-balances system for androids was strict. At least that was what the companies that made them advertised to the public.

If this android was a criminal sent to maximum lockdown, then obviously he was dangerous. Maybe his infraction was minor, but he was an escape risk? Or maybe his owner had a soft heart and paid to have him spared but serve time as any human who committed a crime would?

Whatever the reason, his presence was quite disconcerting.

There were seven new arrivals in all, and the guards lined them up and made them march down the corridor until they passed through a doorway and into what looked like a staging area.

The guards uncuffed each prisoner, one by one, and ordered them all to strip.

Trev hesitated, and a guard yelled, "Hey. Are you deaf? Strip!"

His hands shook as he undid the fastenings on his jumpsuit and let the cloth fall away from his slender body. He looked up as he pushed off his underwear to see that he was the last one to finish. Standing at the end of the lineup, he could see them all, their naked backs bent, glistening with nervous sweat, some of them heavily tattooed. He'd never understood the draw of tattoos and had none. As he looked ahead, he saw the android had none either, his impressive torso unblemished, unmarked, save for what looked like newly healed faint bruising on the left just under his shoulder blade and more red marks on his side just below the ribs. The other unusual thing about the android was that his right hand looked to be made of metal, not skin.

Trev shivered, though the prison station air was not cold. He did not like feeling so vulnerable. He did not like being around so many people, all strangers. Sure, he lived with three brothers and three sisters, but he did not hang out with them very often. He did not attend parties, only occasionally went to functions his father hosted, and only if ordered. And then he never stayed long.

Now the guards motioned for the line to move. Trev had no choice but to follow, silent and obedient. They were led past a lit-up arch that doubled as a sensor that scanned their bodies. He found out right away what happened if that sensor detected anything unusual.

An alarm went off, a low squawk. The second prisoner in the lineup, a young man with very pale skin and no scalp hair, was taken out of the line and given a full-body cavity search right there in front of them all. A guard with a displeased look on his face stuck a tongue depressor with a light on the end into his mouth, far enough to make the man gag, then made him bend and spread. The guard donned a white glove, put his fingers between the man's buttocks, and shoved, obviously feeling around not too gently as the prisoner gasped.

"Nothing," the guard reported to the door guard, whose arms were crossed over his chest, looking bored.

At that moment, Trev thought he might very well panic. If nothing was found, why had the alarm sounded? Would it go off for him?

56

The android was the third prisoner in line and passed without incident despite his metal hand. Trev could see beyond the doorway to a room where the sound of recycled water hissed in the bulkheads. He could already smell the coarse soap.

As he approached the doorway, he saw the other men who'd been ahead of him inside the shining white room already under various water streams. Again, no privacy. Most of them seemed not to care, all turned to the walls, but Trev wasn't used to this. Exposing himself in front of strangers? Not his style. But he had no choice. Even in the less secure facility of North Star, where he had first been headed, he would have had to go through this type of process. There he'd been told he would have his own cell, though, and that the prison held no violent offenders. For the sake of the payoff, his mind had accepted the situation. But now everything had changed, and he faced an unknown future among the types of men that, even in the Damico family business, Trev avoided.

Trev passed through the arch. The alarm did not go off. His muscles went slack with relief. He hadn't realized how tightly he'd been holding himself.

He entered the steamy room and stood under a spray of warm water, staring only at the white wall, trying not to notice or be noticed by anyone. A soap dispenser tube stuck out of the wall. When he put his hand to it, his palm filled with a slightly earth-scented foam.

There were guards close by, so of course he was not in any danger at the moment. But Trev had a slender, small build, and with the pretty looks that his siblings had often teased him about, he was the type men took advantage of in prison. Just because he could fight didn't mean he *wanted* a fight. He decided he'd do best if he worked at bringing as little attention to himself as possible.

He soaped his skin and hair with a minimum of effort and was done in a minute.

When the water shut off, the dripping men lined up for towels. Trev was first in line this time, being closest to the door. He had no idea who was behind him and did not look. A guard handed him a white towel, and he wrapped it about his body and moved back into the long room to where a new man stood. He wore blue coveralls and had a medical wand in his hand.

The guard nearest Trev said, "Move forward."

Trev moved to the man with the scanner, who said, "I'm Dr. March. Stand still. This will only take a few seconds."

Trev stood as the man lowered the scanner in front of and over Trev's head and face, slowly moving the scanner down. It glowed green and blue and made a faint purring sound. Dr. March did not touch Trev but angled the scanner over every part of his body. He didn't seem to care about the towel and did not ask Trev to remove it.

Trev could hear the breathing of the men behind him, silently waiting their turns.

Finally the doctor said, "Health condition green. Pass."

Trev frowned.

A guard said, "Move forward."

Trev moved along until the doctor was behind him. At the end of the room was a low table he hadn't seen when he first walked in. On it were piles of neatly folded gray drawstring pants and pullover shirts. A guard said, "Find your size. Dress."

Trev found the piles that held smaller sizes, grabbed a pair of pants, and pulled them on. As he did so, he turned and saw the android getting the scan and the doctor scowling. "Remove your towel."

As Trev watched, the android held his towel to one side. The scanner ran over the bruising on his back. "Two broken ribs, newly healed." The doctor continued to run the scanner lower past the curve of a hip, over the back, and slowly over his buttocks, which were like carved amber, taut and muscular. "Internal abrasions. This one needs to be on antibiotics for at least two days. See that it's noted."

A guard nodded, holding a hand screen and entering information into it.

Then the doctor said something to the android, low and soft. To Trev it seemed a weirdly out-of-place, kind gesture, though he could not hear the words. The android shook his head, eyes suddenly going downcast.

Trev felt his body tense again. What had happened to that guy? It didn't matter to Trev that he was vat grown and owned, the man had obviously been abused. *Internal abrasions?* That meant careless intercourse. Or rape. The idea made him cringe. The android was gorgeous enough to be a sex toy, but when vat-grown beings were sold into that line, they were trained and bred for it to minimize injury. Why would this one be so injured? Why was he even here?

He watched as the android brought his towel back around his body, and Trev noticed again the silver right hand, an add-on accoutrement that lent even more mystery to the guy. For a flash of an instant, he thought he saw the big body shiver, just once, betraying vulnerability and shot nerves.

The android was motioned to the table, and Trev looked away as he walked up. The big man went to the other end where the largest sizes were sorted and picked up a pair of pants. Out of his peripheral vision, Trev saw him drop the towel and climb into the pants, tightening them at his trim waist once they were in place. The man was quite a specimen, to be sure—no blemishes and, strangely, no body hair except for a thick golden mane and beautiful arching brows. He had perfect proportions. Trev decided that, yes, he had to have been in the sex industry. He wondered if that made him less or more dangerous.

Trev shrugged into a white T-shirt and a pullover gray shirt, straightening it. He found soft black shoes and black socks and sat at a nearby bench to put them on, all under the watchful eyes of the guards. The android came to the bench to do the same, sitting about a foot away and completely ignoring Trev. He smelled of lemon and something else that made Trev's skin prickle. Like fresh-baked bread. It triggered a memory from childhood of sitting at a table and a servant placing a plate in front of him, hot french toast streaming with pale yellow butter and thick bronze syrup. The memory brought a weird contentment, and he blinked rapidly, reorienting himself to the harsh room, the other men dressing, and the prison where he'd now be living.

The soap they'd used in the shower didn't smell like any of that; the android must have exuded some mesmerizing odor on his own. If he was made to please others sexually, it would probably be a prerequisite, though Trev was ignorant of all such matters.

A guard stood against a wall where another circular door had formed as if by magic. Trev saw a long metal corridor. The guard announced, "When you're done dressing, take a plastic pack from the table, one each, and line up outside this door."

Trev and the android were the first to finish. They stood at the same time. Trev let the android go first. Each took a clear plastic case that contained toiletries—soap, soft comb, depilatory shaving packs, washcloth, tissues, towel, and a thin, short toothbrush.

When all seven men lined up, having apparently passed the physical, the guards led them down the long corridor that fed into the main hub of the prison. No matter who they were or whatever horrible things they had done, all the men looked nervous, pissed off, depressed. No one talked.

The wall on their right was transparent. The star fields beyond it stretched into forever.

Trev saw the android in front him turn to gaze at the view. Trev looked too. The opalescent edge of Gideon shone at the foot of the wall, mostly hidden by the deck upon which they walked, but the colors were still startling, vibrant. And all of it seeming so close.

When they reached the end of the corridor, another guard stood at the entryway. He had a device in his hand that looked like a gun. "Hold out your hand," he ordered the android.

The big man obeyed, and the guard pressed the muzzle of the gun to his wrist. Trev heard a click. "Identchip in place for Khim 18367."

So that was the android's name.

Trev stepped up.

"Hold out your hand."

He obeyed.

"Identchip in place for Trevor Dante Damico."

Trev's face instantly heated. So his new identity had already been compromised. He smelled his father's hand in all of this. Fuming, he said, "There must be some mistake. My last name is Varain." He began to spell it out.

The guard frowned and checked a digital readout on the gun. "Damico," he said. "That's what it says. And that's who you are. The system's confirmed it."

As the guard spoke, Khim turned quite suddenly, and his face had contorted to a strange, almost horrified expression.

Trev backed up a step as the android let out a hiss. Meeting his eyes, he leaned into Trev's space. It was as if the gaze tried to spear him, the man's irises paling to the color of blue ice—sharp, accusing, hate-filled.

"Face forward!" the guard ordered, glaring at Khim. Then, "Next."

Trev tried to take a deep breath. What had just happened? Had he almost been attacked? Did this android named Khim think he knew him? Trev would have remembered if he'd ever met him before. Or even seen him. Khim's attributes were not forgettable.

He stared worriedly at Khim's back as they shuffled through yet another door. The man held himself with a power and grace that gave away nothing. That shiver Trev had seen before? No sign of it. Maybe it had all been in his imagination. Khim walked easily, not as if he'd been recently injured or felt any pain. Khim's long hair left trails of wetness on the back of his gray shirt, the pale ends curling a bit in the dry, recycled air. Whatever fastening he'd had for the ponytail had disappeared.

Trev himself was actually trembling. His own still-damp hair made the skin on his neck crawl.

As soon as he was settled, he needed to find out how to make an appointment with an attorney. And somehow, some way—though it was the last thing he wanted—he needed to contact his father.

As the new inmates entered the main hub of the actual prisoners' living quarters, Trev saw a large central plaza surrounded by five levels of cells. Metal walkways connected each line of cells on each level and grid stairs led upward. Every cell was free of bars, but that was not because the cells held no locks. What kept them enclosed were invisible force fields. From holos he'd watched, Trev knew that if you tried to pass through one, it would give off an electrical shock and toss you into the air. Force fields were highly efficient. Sound could pass through them, and air, but not people.

Already Trev could hear the sounds the prisoners made— shouts and yells, the low hum of conversation. In the plaza area, some prisoners roamed. Two men were running cleaning machines over the already pristine, shining deck. At the end of each stairway stood a robot sentry, human-shaped but with backward-bending, insectoid legs and made entirely of metal. Their faces were smooth silver with glowing red eyes.

Trev had seen robots like that before. He was familiar with how they worked because he'd actually built one as a child. They were fairly simple mechanisms, dependent upon their programming. He'd never thought to be afraid of a robot, but in this environment, the sentries looked sinister.

"This is A Block," one of the guards explained, loud enough for all to hear. "This is where you're all assigned. For now." Then he gave them a quick overview. "Visitor hours are on Fridays. If you have cases pending, your attorneys are allowed to visit you at any time. Mandatory lockdown is from 9:00 p.m. to 6:00 a.m. Random lockdowns occur during the day, and you must report to your cell when you hear the alarms. There are two media rooms on this block, and two exercise rooms. You are to keep your clothing and personal hygiene tidy at all times. Meals are at seven, noon, and six. If you miss a meal, you cannot make it up. All rules are posted in each media room, exercise room, and the cafeteria. Read them. Memorize them. Deviation from any rule results in checks. Get three checks, and you earn solitary confinement for a minimum of two days. You do not want that. Believe me."

It went so fast. Trev locked it all into his mind as quickly as he could. He intended to get through this, for whatever time he would be required to be there, as smoothly as possible.

Keep a low profile. Do not bring attention to yourself.

He was a Damico. He'd been raised to be strong.

At that thought, he had the sudden realization that his actual name, Damico, might help him. The Damico family was known and feared. He wondered at the irony. The very thing he was running from might be the very armor that would protect him now. Name as reputation. With it came a fear of reprisal from a crime family that left no loose ends. Ever. Trev was one of those loose ends now, but the other prisoners in the facility didn't know that.

The guard who assigned the cells led them down the center of the open plaza. Inmates stared at them filing by. Some made low comments under their breaths. Trev noticed most of them had their eyes on Khim.

But one man with short brown hair and a rumpled jumpsuit, the sleeves rolled up to show muscular forearms, met Trev's eyes and said

62

to some hard-looking companions beside him, "Pretty boys always get a special welcome."

Trev's face instantly heated, but he'd learned from his brothers and sisters to never avert his gaze in a confrontation. He gritted his teeth and glared back.

The man's eyebrows rose, and his lips curved into a surly smile.

Trev thought he might be quick enough to take on the bigger, more muscular man because of his acrobatic ability and fighting skills. But he would not be able to win if the man and his companions ambushed him as a pack. With robot sentries at every turn, the chances of that happening were hopefully slim.

Most of the men roaming the area had nothing better to do than watch the new prisoners. None actually approached.

One inmate, who stood closer than the rest, with bangs long enough to cover his eyes, said, "I thought androids who broke the law were put down, not locked up."

The guard said, "Step back, Connor. Mind your business."

"Yeah, yeah," Connor said, moving a pace backward. "It's a threat to the rest of us, though."

"You're all threats or you wouldn't be here," the guard replied, toneless.

The truth was that vat-grown humans were physically stronger than natural humans. Perhaps even mentally superior. But in Trev's mind it wasn't an issue. There had always been power differences between humans. Life was not fair or just. It was naive to think otherwise.

The group approached a stair. The guard in front stopped. He turned to face them, motioning with his hand for Khim and Trev to move forward. "You two! Follow me."

Another guard came up from behind and took over with the other five men.

Trev and Khim followed the guard up one flight of stairs. At the top of the second level, the guard led them past a half-dozen cells, some empty, some with inmates quietly reading or napping.

The deck they were walking on was a tarnished silver grid-walk that clanged faintly with their footfalls. The cells were fitted along a tight line, the walls separating them comprised of solid metal about six inches thick. The lighting for the level ran in a single seamless tube along the outside tops of the cells, a soft greenish phosphorescence easy on the eyes but bright enough to keep shadows from collecting. Inside the cells the lighting seemed to emit from above; the entire ceiling of each cell was a luminous square, white with a faint tinge of chrome.

The three stopped at an empty cell. "Number 482 is your new home, fellas," the guard said.

The android's hands formed into sudden fists, and he stepped back, frowning.

Khim said, "I refuse to share a cell with this person." He did not look at Trev as he said that.

Trev waited, watching expectantly. He had no idea why Khim had immediately despised him, but he'd seen the reaction when his name was revealed.

The guard said, "You don't have a choice. Live with it."

"And if I refuse?" Khim stated, voice sharp but level.

"You'll bunk in solitary until the warden's schedule clears to meet with you and hear your complaint."

"Solitary is a private cell, yes?" Khim asked.

"Indeed," the guard replied. "But it is very uncomfortable. I don't recommend it. Some inmates leave quite disturbed. You can find out for yourself, or you can stay here and ask your advocate to voice your complaint. The food here is warm, the beds have sheets, you get a shower once a day, and you have clothing on your body. The same cannot be said for solitary."

Khim said, "It would be quite easy for you to switch me out with another inmate."

"Easy?" the guard echoed. "For who? I'd have paperwork, and then, well, there's the sheer annoyance of you, which has already begun. I don't like to be annoyed. Nor do the other guards. If you annoy us enough, we can make your stay here even more unpleasant."

Trev held his plastic kit tight to his chest and remained silent. Now the guard turned to look at him. "Besides, how is this little shit gonna give you any trouble? Look at him. He's nothing."

64

Trev noticed that the guard had tattoos for eyebrows and very thick lips, his face chiseled as if he'd had a lot of sculpting done. He looked less real than Khim, who had been custom-made. His voice had a tenor tone that cut.

The guard asked Trev, "What the fuck did you do to piss him off?"

"Nothing," Trev said.

Khim made an almost-strangled sign of anger, turned his back on both of them, and stomped into the cell.

Trev felt the guard nudge him on the arm. As he entered the cell, the force field came up.

Both turned to look at the guard, who said, "You're new. You get locked in the first day. That's that rule."

Trev swallowed hard, stepping away from the entry and the faint hum of the shield. He'd been close enough to feel it prickling the air with its static. If he'd been any closer, it could've shocked him with a punch that might have propelled him across the room.

He looked around. There was a single metal toilet in the corner, no privacy. Beside it was a small metal sink and an inlaid nonglass mirror above it. A rack for towels, like a seamless extension of the wall, protruded alongside the mirror. Below that was a single shelf. They were intended to share all the space for their toiletries, which wasn't much. Good thing they didn't have a lot.

Trev looked at the premade beds with a heavy sigh. Bunk beds. Each had a single pillow and a dark green blanket folded back with a white sheet underneath. The mattress was also sheeted white. Khim had already placed his kit on the lower bed. He did not acknowledge Trev at all.

Trev turned away and went toward the towel rack. He unpacked his kit, careful to take only half the space, placing his towel and cloth on the rack and the rest of his stuff on the shelf. When he was done, he folded the plastic tote and placed it too on the shelf.

Khim was standing by the beds, arms crossed, very still. He might've been staring at the back wall. His kit lay on his bunk, unpacked.

Trev said, "My name is Trev."

Nothing.

Boldly, "Do you think you know me? Because I—"

"No. I don't think I know you," Khim interrupted, unmoving.

"Then why did you tell the guard what you did?"

"I don't like humans. Natural ones, that is."

Trev tilted his head, thinking carefully about his response. "I don't like them much myself."

That got Khim to turn his head slightly. The vivid blue eyes assessed him. "I don't care what you like or don't like. You will stay away from me. You will not touch me. Ever."

The words came to Trev edged with hate. He said, "I'm not even supposed to be here. Hopefully I'll get out soon anyway."

Khim looked away.

Trev came over to the bunk, noticing that Khim's body tensed as he got closer. "I call dibs on the top," he said, trying to sound nonchalant and keep things light.

But it was already too late.

Khim snarled, "Dibs. Are you twelve?"

Trev decided to play along. "Twenty-three." He went to the end of the beds and looked at the structure. It was nothing to him. He could climb sheer walls if need be. He put his hand on the upper frame and pushed, drew his body into a curve, and flexed as he jumped, landing on the top bunk in a neatly seated position.

Khim ignored him, picking up his kit and moving to the sink to unpack it.

Trev watched him, taking in every detail of the android—no, the man. They really were not androids in any sense of that term. Their bodies were clones, mixes of whatever DNA their clients might want. He wondered where this one came from.

Quietly he asked, "Are you really vat grown? From a warehouse somewhere?"

"Definitely. One of the lie-down models. Can't you tell?" Sarcasm twitched his lips.

"No," Trev said, ignoring the sarcasm. "You're not pliant enough, nor have the temperament for it."

"You don't know me. Don't act ignorant. They make models for all needs. You should know."

66

"I don't know. Why should I know? I've never owned an android."

Khim didn't answer. He finished putting his things on the shelf and approached the bed. Trev watched him sit on the edge of the lower bunk.

Trev leaned back against the cold wall. "I don't understand what I did to make you hate me. Other than being human, that is."

"I was made to be a soldier. I hate everyone equally. Don't flatter yourself."

"So I was right. You aren't a lie-down model. Were you in the star wars? The military?"

"I know how to efficiently kill in 152 ways, with or without a weapon. So you best be careful around me."

Trev's eyes widened, but he almost laughed. If the android really were dangerous to others, he would not be here, would he? He would've been put down immediately. Wouldn't he? Trev's skin prickled. "I'll remember that."

He took a deep breath and thought about the doctor running the scanner, talking about intimate internal injuries. Pictured the incongruous metal hand. The hand might've been the result of military combat, but the other? "Is that how you got injured?"

"You can shut up now."

Changing the subject, Trev said, "I shouldn't be here. I stole something. It was completely nonviolent. I was to go to the sister facility, North Star. They call it 'the resort.' But instead I got sent here. I don't know what happened. A mix-up."

"I don't care."

Trev saw Khim pull his legs up from the floor. He figured he was either sitting back now or lying down. Trev said, "I need to find out what happened. Then you'll be rid of me when they realize their mistake."

"Yes. You said that. Now shut up."

"We're stuck in this tiny cell together. We should at least try to get along."

"I don't require that or want it. Nor do I wish to speak further with you."

Trev was mystified. His charm and unthreatening demeanor always pulled people in when he wanted it to. "I'm not really a bad guy, okay?"

"Shut up."

"I am *not* your enemy."

"Yes, you are. You just don't know it yet."

"What does that mean?" Trev asked lightly.

Suddenly he felt movement, saw Khim come up like a dark shadow over the top bunk as if he'd teleported there, his bent knees holding him balanced on the edge, his fist coming forward.

Trev reacted instinctively and caught the fist—the flesh one, not the metal—which impacted with a smack against his lifted palm only inches from his face.

"I said shut up. I'll knock you out if I have to."

"I can fight," Trev said, still leaning against the wall, legs crossed, knees up. He knew the moves, of course, and he was fast, but right now his body was trembling. He hoped Khim couldn't feel it. In any hand-to-hand, Trev was good, but not against the superiority of a soldier-programmed android.

Khim poised on the edge of Trev's bunk, so close to him now, almost fevered with fury. His skin had a glowing sheen and was so smooth and perfect it looked like gold satin.

Trev leaned back. Their hands were still connected. One push from Trev and he might be able to unbalance the bigger man. After a few long seconds, they dropped their arms at the same time. Their eyes held each other in another kind of combat. Trev did not want to be the first to look away, but the day had been long. The worst day of his life. He'd always been alone, but now he felt that more than ever. And this unfriendly and dangerous android, an anomaly in any prison, was his cellmate. His eyes stung. He glanced down, lashes shadowing sudden unshed tears.

Khim's full, beautiful mouth twisted, became ugly. He bounced back and jumped to the floor. Trev heard the impact like a shot.

Khim disappeared into his bunk again.

Trev moved until he lay supine, head on his pillow. He looked steadily at the glowing ceiling, waiting for his heart rate to slow, the shaking to stop.

This time, he shut up.

Chapter Eight

Khim

Khim's heightened sense of smell detected the acrid edge of fear and the scent of cold salt as the eyes trained on him went into an overproduction of moisture. His other senses detected a faint muscle tremble. Yet the man named Trev sat calm on the top bunk, holding his gaze with irises the color of the dark plains of Umbria. Umbria had been Khim's last planetfall before *Doom in Shadow* exploded, before arriving at Gideon's cloud cities that harbored deep, secret dungeons.

He'd liked Umbria. A quiet planet with red skies and a landscape of endless brown prairie with tufts of tall pale grasses and beautiful singing winds that caressed the skin and crooned in the ears. It would've been an even nicer world had it not been strewn from continent to continent with bloodied corpses and ruined cities, some there because of him and his battalion and some because of another enemy they'd fought on that turf—an enemy from a distant world they'd been ordered to exterminate for reasons the soldiers in his squad were never told.

But he was here now. And he didn't care that his cellmate had interesting eyes or that he'd reacted with surprising quickness to Khim's closed fist moving toward his face, or that he'd talked to Khim as if they could be friends.

This man was a Damico. Of course he'd denied it, saying his name was Varain. Khim did not know why that would be, but the guards had the truth. Computers didn't lie. His cellmate was a Damico, and that name, on Gideon and in the cities that floated above it, meant one thing to Khim: they were the ones who'd witnessed him murder a man named Chin. The ones who owned the House of Xavier. They were the ones who owned him. That meant, technically, his cellmate owned him. And whether Trev claimed ignorance of that fact or not, Khim would never be prepared to be his friend.

He heard Trev move on the bed above, most likely to lie down. After that, Trev did not make another sound for a long time.

Khim was tired. He had not slept since yesterday, since his nap in the dungeon cage. He'd been drugged, raped, beaten, and arrested, had cursory medical aid, and then he'd come here. He was exhausted.

He glanced at the bed, then up at the ceiling. He would've preferred a way to dim that ceiling glow-light, but there was nothing to be done about that. He looked back at his pillow and the neatly turned-down bed, then pulled his legs onto the mattress and lay back, hands crossed over his stomach.

Above him, the underside of the bunk was a solid dark metal, almost black. The pillowcase smelled faintly of bleach. He could hear the echoes of men's voices from all around the plaza area and conferring in separate cells. Once in a while, a shout shot out over the vast space. Khim was used to noise like that from living on a starship in close confines with others of his kind; it didn't bother him. He would soon learn to tune this place out as well.

But right then the sounds, the new scents, and the fact that a Damico was situated right above him greatly annoyed him.

His body ached in a kind of fierce way he'd never felt before, not even when he'd been injured on duty. Not even this last time, when he'd lost his hand permanently—and that still stabbed where it connected to his wrist—or when he'd been told he would be sold.

This ache came from deep within like a violation of spirit. Some might've laughed to learn he had that thought. But of course he had a spirit. All humans did.

He had new skin grafts that felt all right, but his ribs hurt. And when he had jumped angrily onto Trev's bunk, a sharp pain had twisted in his gut. Pain from the rapes still radiating, making his teeth clench. His lungs heavy. His throat thick.

He'd never been raped before. And he had never raped anybody himself. He was programmed against that sort of behavior, as well as against uncommanded violence against humans. His threat to knock Trev out, not to mention the murder he had committed less than twelve hours ago, were highly disturbing. Something in his mind had changed abruptly, and he did not know how to deal with that.

Of course it had to do with the rape. He wasn't made for that sort of treatment. Not mentally, not physically.

He had a dim memory of fumbling, first-time sex as a teenage boy with some nameless, faceless person whose gender he could not recall. The memory was faded and uncertain. It wasn't even his. None of his scant memories before age twenty were his. Knowing that, he rarely allowed them to intervene or affect him.

Any androids in the training labs, right after being "born," who rejected memory programming or all programming, were usually taken away. Destroyed—or so the rumors told. Or maybe they were somehow altered, fixed. That would make more sense. It took a lot of energy and time to grow a fully adult human. His kind were an expensive lot.

He had suffered a bit of that amnesia, but the scant memories his brain did supply had been enough to get him past all the training tests. He kept quiet about that "blank past" aspect of himself. He did not want to be "taken away."

Khim stretched his legs out, flexing his thigh and calf muscles, the material of the drawstring trousers abrasive against his skin. An echo of his internal pain still radiated through him. He closed his eyes and saw again the dead man on the floor, the one they'd called Chin, with his head at a strange angle, his naked torso sprawled. Khim had seen dead bodies far too many times. He'd even killed a lot of them. But that was war. This was different, more personal, a feeling of wrongness about not being ordered to do it; it was more like revenge. Something he'd been conditioned against.

But at the time he'd broken the man's neck, a strange release had come over him, as if a huge weight had lifted. Then reality flooded back and he was appalled. That killing was on no one's order. He should not have been able or even willing to do it, no matter the reason. His indoctrination process had been firm and clear. He was never to operate as a soldier or an assassin on his own, not even in self-defense. He was supposed to sacrifice himself first, prepare to die, before harm came to another. Unless command orders were given, he was not really a killer. Just because he knew how did not mean he wanted to act on that knowledge.

In this moment, on this day, a sympathetic attorney and a soft judge were the only reasons he had lived. Apparently, being gang-raped, even if you were an android with no rights, still sickened some humans.

But now it was as if some dam inside him had cracked. He had killed once. On his own. Proof that he could. And he'd already threatened his cellmate. Was he finally breaking? Would he get worse?

If so, he could not count on always having sympathetic judges and lawyers.

If he was going to survive, he would have to control his impulses. That meant not getting to know people, not letting them in, not caring if they insulted him or even hurt him.

But just knowing a Damico family member shared his cell made his brain feel as if his careful barriers were breaking down all over again. He had wanted to hurt Trev. And if Khim could believe him, Trev didn't even know why.

He needed to make an appointment with his advocate in the prison as soon as possible. He needed a different cellmate, both for Trev's protection and preserving his own fragile sanity.

Absently he rubbed at the area of skin where his metal hand met flesh. His eyelids fluttered. His body felt strangely cold, probably due to lack of sleep and food.

Slowly he moved around until he was under the blanket. He turned onto his side, facing the wall, and huddled into himself, one hand between his thighs, the other—the metal one—tucked under his chin. Just before sleep he determined to himself that he would keep control, not allow himself to lash out again.

But along with that thought came the unbidden image of Chin, sprawled and broken in the House of Xavier. Khim had stood beside that corpse, damaged and trembling, his body released from torture for a moment of almost pure pleasure—to be able to just breathe, to not be touched anymore so that it hurt, to not be manhandled in intimate, degrading ways where strangers had no business.

A deep part of him was glad the man was dead.

Lying in his bunk, trying to block out the strange sounds and smells, he heard that other self in the blue space whisper in the back of his mind.

Never again. No matter what you have to do.

It was an instinct that blocked out all else.

Survive.

But the word was a contradiction. To survive he must *not* be violent. For violent androids were dead androids.

Right then, he feared for the men in this prison if they ever laid a hand on him. He feared he would lose his mind once and for all.

The judge and attorney had been idiots. He should have been put down.

Breath trembling in his throat, body tightly clenched, Khim finally fell into the escape of darkness. And sleep.

Khim's sleep was iridescent. Liquid. He heard distant voices echoing as if through a long chamber, and his mind rocked in a warm zone, relaxed and safe.

He dreamed of the day he was born, new and fresh, with stirrings of brief memories that felt real, stretched like blue sky across his mind… like summers he had never experienced, like nights dripping with rain and stars where people thrived and laughed and cried and lived.

He remembered thrashing in a coffin of warm fluid, a taste of sourness, feeling that swirl of sloshing warmth all over his skin as rough hands pulled him up and he took his first gasping breath.

Khim knew many things about himself in that single moment. He was twenty years old. He knew four distinct languages and the words for twelve others. He had clear memories of schooling— reading, math, and science, and later as a teenager, major weapons training. He had a memory of a military boot camp at the age of nineteen. And yet he could not have really been there, because right now he was looking down at his body for the first time, sitting in a pool of fizzy blue liquid, the first shush of oxygen being pushed into his lungs through his mouth and throat—the act of breathing.

A man in a shiny blue jumpsuit that looked waterproof said, "Who are you?"

His mind supplied the answer. "Khim 18367." His voice came out scratchy. He coughed twice.

The man looked at a digital paperboard. "Schooling?"

"Watersign High School. One year at Colcar College with a half degree in xenomechanics. Karfax boot camp training, four months."

Water sloshed as he found his hands and brought them up to his face, looking at them.

"Good. That checks. Parents?"

"Mary and John. Died when I was five. Raised by my Uncle Joe."

Then Khim felt the new skin of his brow furrow. He tried to remember their faces and couldn't. "Uncle Joe" was a name only. But the man with the paperboard didn't ask him to describe the people he named.

Khim struggled to remember them. Nothing.

"Good," the man said.

"Who are you?" Khim asked, trying to shake off the discomfort of his incomplete memory. He had an urge to stand, but as he moved his legs under the water, they quivered, and he did not feel confident in his strength yet.

The man's mouth curved up. "Aric. But that doesn't matter. You'll be leaving here shortly. You are a soldier now, enlisted to fight on the battle cruiser *Doom in Shadow*."

"I know what a soldier is and that I am trained to do that job," Khim replied. "Thank you for telling me."

Aric looked at him strangely when Khim said "thank you." He glanced at the digital reader. "Guess you were raised to be polite."

"I don't know. I guess I was." He remembered only snapshots of any personal upbringing. His mind tried to summon more.

A boy running down a beach yelling at birds called seagulls. Lying in a field of sweet-scented grass, staring up at the stars with a strange longing in the pit of his stomach. A voice from a shadowed room saying, "It's an honor to enlist, to fight the good fight. You will be a hero."

The word *hero* made his heart fill and tremble. The memory was trying to convince him he chose to be a soldier. It was an obvious lie.

"You will be feeling your strength come up to normal levels in about a minute. Then we'll get you out of that tub," Aric said.

"My body seems to be shivering," Khim said. "Is that normal?"

"Perfectly normal as your muscles and nerves settle in. You aren't cold, are you?"

"No."

He tried to figure out why he was shivering. He knew that something was strange; his memories were distant, of another time and place, another boy. They were grounding moments, but they only made him feel divided. Was this normal? When he had been asked, "Who are you?" he had immediately answered a name and number. But who was he aside from a label? Not the boy on the beach—that did not resonate. Why he knew this so quickly, he wasn't sure, but he understood intuitively he had no family, no friends, nothing but a job. His skin was so shiny and new, his body stretching out for the very first time.

His mind answered his question before he could ask it.

Who are you?

He was someone who had not lived before this very moment.

At that thought, the shivers overtook his breathing, his vision blurred, and the warm liquid surged against him as he tried to curl inward.

He closed his eyes tightly, saw a dark spiral in his mind. It spun, drawing him down and into it.

Aric's voice seemed to echo. "Khim, can you hear me? Can you hear me?"

He did not answer. He thought he might be choking, because his throat seized as he sputtered and coughed.

He heard Aric speaking in a low tone. "Need assistance, sector five, vat 18367."

Khim heard footsteps in sets of three pounding on a metal floor.

Aric's voice. "Get him out of there now."

Hands came under his arms and pulled. More hands wrapped around his wrists and tugged. Fingers grasped at his ankles. He was lifted through the warmth, and the air hit his entire body. He heard the liquid lap the sides of the tub, sluicing from his skin. Smelled rain. The hands that held him set him gently onto a soft platform.

He was coughing, his limbs stretching out, grasping, flailing. A sound came up from his throat, a strange, welling cry. A salty taste ran over his lips.

Aric. "Can you save him?"

Something poked at his mouth. Fingers lifted the lids of his eyes, and the soft greenish light of the room entered. A cold hardness touched his chest.

Another voice. "Heart rate and pulse normal. He's breathing on his own. There's no event."

But Khim continued to choke.

Aric said, "But he's struggling to breathe."

"He's crying."

"I've never had one do that before."

"It happens. They want their mommies sometimes."

Laughter.

"Hey. He can still hear you. Besides, this one's parents died when he was five."

"It'll pass. There's a shock to the system. Some are born laughing. Are you new here?"

Aric's voice. "Been here a week."

"You'll experience it all. Get him dried and standing and get the protein drink into him. Then get him on the running wheel. Nothing like physical exertion to remind the mind what it's here for. Survival. And this one here is a soldier, so for him it will be all about the fighting."

Footsteps receded.

Eyes still shut tight, Khim heard every word. He understood it all in a flash.

I'm not the boy who lay back in a field gazing at tangles of stars. I'm a soldier made to assess the situation and survive. I have not lived until today. I am a designer-model "android"—Khim 18367— and I do what I am told.

No one had called him that word—*android,* the derogatory but popular term for his kind—but his mind supplied it from somewhere in his downloaded education.

The realization left him listless. Alone. A feeling like hollowness that started in the stomach and fed to all the regions of his body, settling finally in his brain.

His sobbing began to recede as he felt something soft moving all over his body. A towel, drying him. Slowly it moved to his face, blotting his damp-streaked cheeks, running over his hair.

Khim took a breath, opened his eyes. Aric stood over him, blue eyes looking down at him from a pale round face. "I'm sorry they laughed. I don't believe in being mean, even to an android."

Khim's stomach muscles contracted as he sat up with ease. He was getting stronger by the second. He looked around at the room where he saw the vat he'd come out of, a black tub like a tube attached to various pipes and machines with screens that flashed white numbers and lines. The green-gold light came from high up.

He lifted his gaze. Tubes of light made crosshatched patterns on a dark ceiling. The area he was in was huge, filled with vats much like his own, all closed for the moment. A corridor stretched in front of him as far as he could see, and as he looked about, he saw the place was comprised of hundreds and hundreds of those vats. The air came into him now, softer, dry. He swallowed tears, blinked.

"Will I train more here?" Khim asked when he could finally speak.

"You'll have some indoctrination classes."

"With others like me?"

"Yes. Other android soldiers. You understand quickly. It's all there in your brain, but most take an hour or more to assimilate what they are and why they're here."

Aric brushed the cloth over his shoulders. He was gentle. Khim heard a soft tone to his voice. He liked it.

Aric said, "You're more sensitive than the others I've birthed."

"Am I?"

"I wouldn't have pegged you a soldier."

"What, then?"

"The pretty ones, they—" Aric stopped. "Never mind."

"Sensitive. That's a bad thing."

"You'll have classes about how to build the walls in your mind to toughen you, harden you."

"Why?"

"Less emotion, less suffering."

"That's a good thing?"

"Yes."

Khim processed that. He understood all too quickly, all too well. He was nothing more than a tool, to survive as best he could without undue torment. Aric was right to tell him not to feel. He'd do best to clamp down on emotion, be tight and efficient with his thinking, and use his mind to survive only. Nothing more. It should begin now. Why wait? The weeping was painful and uncomfortable. He did not want to repeat that scene.

"I'm hungry," Khim said.

"Good." Aric ran the towel down his waist, soft and gentle.

Khim had liked it at first, but now he knew what he was, and that tenderness would prolong his discomfort. So he said, tonelessly, "You may stop now. I'll finish drying myself. Will I be given clothing?"

Aric stood back, head tilting. "Are you all right? Honestly, if you need more time or anything. Like I said, most of you take an hour or more to get it together."

"Clothing?" Khim repeated, taking the towel from Aric's stilled hand.

"Of course."

Khim finished drying his body, assessing it to be perfect in every way—the skin shining with a bronze tint, the muscles well-rounded and hard.

Aric brought him a thin white cotton jumpsuit and a tube of protein that, when Khim put it to his lips, had the awful consistency of sludge. He drank it all, tasting a mild sweetness. Then he dressed.

Aric put a hand on Khim's upper arm. "You look much better. Are you ready to get out of here?"

Khim looked down at where the hand touched him. He did not want it. No more softness. No coddling. "Yes." He stepped away.

Aric dropped his hand and moved back.

Maybe he should thank Aric a second time for being there for him, so attentive and maybe even a little worried. But the man was only doing a job and felt nothing real for him. Khim owed him no thanks.

Khim adjusted his body on the bunk, waking briefly to see a bare beige wall before his eyes and a black metal ceiling. He reaffirmed where he was by the sounds and scents of the prison. One hand was fisted, clenched against his chest. The other, the metal hand he could not feel, had moved down and gripped a handful of sheet by his thigh, responding to a command in the mind to hold tight.

Khim was shaking. Just a little.

He closed his eyes, still so tired from all he'd been through. The auction. The dungeon at the Rainspeer Hotel. The high-powered party at the House of Xavier. The men all over him, on him, in him for their own decadent pleasures. And now he'd dreamed his birth. That had not helped him at all in regaining his peace of mind.

His heart beat more rapidly than he was used to. It felt as if his chest had been sliced open and the blood-filled, pulsing organ that was his life force were exposed to the degradation of air, of life, of reality. His soldier personality and all his armor had been peeled away.

Who was he? Khim 18367. A soldier. A fighter. But he wasn't even that anymore. He was left with nothing but himself, an ex-soldier now, a being made of anger and resentment and pain with a few leftover memories of a boy in the grass, a boy on the beach, and an uncle in the shadows who'd told him it was noble to enlist to fight a war. Khim was educated, but he couldn't even remember anymore how that had come to pass.

As his muscles stretched, he felt the persistent ache from the rape deep inside, felt the men on him again, the velvet of the couch, and he struggled to squelch the memory. But it was too recent. He realized he must still be in some shock.

Not acceptable.

He had twin pains: his birth, and now what was left of his life.

He shut his eyes tighter, turned his face into the pillow. There were exercises he had learned for control back in the vat warehouses, the indoctrination rooms. Systems for entering alpha states to calm the nerves, keep off-duty aggression at bay. Meditations for building barriers—like the glass wall Khim had constructed—against the core self. An out-of-control android was a dangerous android. Androids were always threatened with being "put down."

All androids, first and foremost, were taught to be submissive, their brains trained to back down, back off, give way. Even the soldier androids, trained in combat, were submissive to all superiors, and they learned to bow heads, turn away, take a step back, even kneel and bend their torsos tight over their laps if the situation warranted it. They were stronger than natural-born humans and needed to remember that their strengths did not define their stature. They were the lower class, the inferior-though-perfect models of humanity. They were never to be the light in life, only mirrored light. Only an echo of the spirit that drove men to greatness.

From the warehouse classes, Khim remembered the wires, the lit-up sparkling helmets hooked to machines that rewarded calmness and encouraged the mind in the art of riding the alpha waves in a serenity of tolerance and acceptance. Tiny shocks stabbed at the brain to punish any hint of rage, impertinence, jealousy, even competition. Sexual response was allowed but given no erotic or romantic encouragement. It was a function of the body, like eating, sleeping, pissing, breathing.

Somehow he had lost the sense of all of that now, forgotten the programming completely, because what he felt was anger. Rage. He had killed a man. He had jumped onto Trev's bunk and threatened to punch him. Something inside him was broken, and he was having a lot of trouble calling on those alpha waves now.

When he was aboard *Doom in Shadow*, he had been able to put his mind in that state at will. His off-duty hours were calm. He slept without nightmares. He did not take lovers, as some androids did with each other, because he did not like to be touched. But that was his only flaw, created from a moment during his birth experience when he'd made a promise to himself not to be coddled for his own sake. To prevent pain, to never suffer.

He lay very still in his bunk, heard the murmurs of men outside the cell through the quiet hum of the force field and Trev in the bunk above him breathing in deep, even rhythms. Trev still slept.

For both of them, sleeping was the only escape from a brand-new setting they had not yet become accustomed to.

Khim wanted only to sleep again, and he attempted to push his thoughts in that direction.

It took a long time before his mind finally responded to his efforts at achieving an alpha state. After that, he sank into a more restful slumber, his beaten and abused body welcoming the chance to rest more, to heal.

Chapter Nine

Trev

Trev woke from a dream of rain. On the acreage of his childhood home, floating among the clouds, it often rained, and flowers with sugared scents bloomed in the earth suspended upon giant antigrav devices underneath the estate.

A loud clanging, like an alarm, had startled him from sleep. Sitting up, he thought for a moment he was back home in his bedroom surrounded by his books, his computers, all his childhood belongings.

Then he glanced around and saw the beige walls, the glowing ceiling, the metal deck outside the force field of the prison cell. With a jolt, he reoriented.

Khim was up already, a bit disheveled. His dark blond hair glistened in the harsh light and lay in disarray about his shoulders and head, strands pushed messily against his forehead. He couldn't have been awake for long. They had both slept away the afternoon, exhausted, wrung out.

Outside their cell, men lined up in the plaza. It must have been the dinner hour. But neither Trev nor Khim could go anywhere until their force field was unlocked.

Trev pushed his own thick hair from his forehead. It was shorter than Khim's, but heavier, and sometimes stuck up from his forehead in annoying spikes.

Trev lifted his legs over the edge of the bunk. He hopped effortlessly to the floor, landing as gentle as a cat. He had to pee but was nervous about that. The cell was so small. Khim was so close. He'd never lived this close to anyone in his life. He stood leaning with his back against the frame of the bunk beds.

Trev felt nervous about everything to do with this place. He wasn't sure how he would bear it, but a voice in the back of his head coached him.

One step at a time. Forward.

It was the same calm voice that he'd learned to listen to when he broke into buildings, evaded complex security systems. The voice kept panic down, created a coolness in his mind. It had saved his life on more than one occasion.

For what seemed like an eternity, Trev waited by the edge of the bunk. Khim stood forward and to his right, staring at the side wall, hands limp at his hips. Unobserved, Trev was free to look at him—at the straight line of his back; the way tendrils of his hair were caught under the collar of his gray shirt; how the metal of his right hand mirrored the white light, the beige walls, and the hard, dark floor in a glancing abstract of quivering curves and spinning portals. The other hand looked so ordinary in comparison, so bare.

Trev wondered again what had happened to this man. Certainly a hard life, being an android, which to Trev was very unfair. He had already surmised, from their very nonprivate medical scans, that Khim had been sexually assaulted, a secret Trev would not reveal and which, he hoped, the other new inmates had not picked up on during their orientation. But how had Khim lost the hand? Why had a new one not been grown for him?

The voices from outside their cell, on the decks and in the plaza, had changed from an uneven humming and occasional shouts to a low rumble. Promise of food gave hungry men focus.

Trev's bladder stabbed. Finally, he moved forward and past Khim, looking over his shoulder. "I have to use the—"

Khim turned away to face the entrance, his bulk casting a shadow over the sink as if he did not hear him.

Trev stepped up to the toilet and undid the fly of his drawstring pants.

When he finished, he washed his hands. He turned. Khim stood looking out from their second-floor vantage. Trev moved up alongside him. Khim gave no indication he even knew he was there.

Men in gray passed by on the deck outside, shoes clanging, moving down the stairways. It was easy to see where the cafeteria was from here by following the two long lines of inmates in the plaza.

A louder clatter drew Trev's attention. A silver robot sentry came up the stairs. It moved with a strange alien grace on backward-bent legs like an insect. It came straight for them, stopping at their cell. Its red eyes scanned them from an oblong, almost featureless head. Its right wiry arm snaked out, and its metal fingers danced over a control panel on the frame of their cell.

The shushing hum of the force field ceased as the invisible electric barrier came down. Through a small hole in the center of its dark metal face, the robot said, "You are to join the end of the dinner line to the right of the plaza. Make no trouble."

Trev and Khim stepped forward at the same time.

Trev was closest to the stairwell. He expected Khim to move around him, ignore him, and stride off. Instead, Khim just stood there. Afraid to say anything, Trev turned and moved forward. He could feel the man at his back, following him, his footfall surprisingly soft on the metal for all his height and muscular bulk.

Trev took the stairs quickly and walked across the clean plaza floor to the end of the long line. The men in front of him ignored them. But more men came up behind them, talking and chuckling. One came up alongside Khim. Trev turned to look.

The man, who had several days' growth of beard but no hair on his head, said, "Hey, new guy. It's tradition when you're new that you eat last."

Khim did not look at him.

Trev raised an eyebrow.

"Hey, did you hear me? End of the line."

Still no reaction from Khim.

The man must have been a head shorter than Khim, but he stood tall and dominant. "So anyway, Hercules, we're cutting in front of you guys unless you wanna do something about it."

The man and his entourage of four scruffy-looking guys of varying heights moved past Khim and Trev and squeezed in front of them.

Trev didn't care. The voice in the back of his head was calmly repeating, *Stay invisible. Bring no attention to yourself.* But he wasn't sure what Khim might do. He waited.

Khim never moved. Nor did he meet the man's eyes. It was as if the man did not exist. This seemed to annoy the loudmouth, even though he'd gotten ahead of them, gotten his way, and neither Trev nor

Khim had protested. He shouted back over his shoulder, "Hey, Herc, you should thank me for filling you in on the rules."

Khim's gaze stayed fixed, unmoving. He did not respond.

The man turned to his friends. "It's an android, you know. It has to do what you tell it."

Another man said, "That could be fun."

Horrified, Trev had no idea what to do and hoped they would move on, but they kept talking.

"They're programmed not to hurt humans. They won't fight back," the first one said.

"Yeah, Deb," said another, "but why is he here?"

It was exactly the question Trev had been asking himself this whole time. And the comment about not fighting back made his skin cold. For Khim had struck out at *him* in their cell, and it was only his own quick response that had prevented a fist from impacting his face.

Deb said, "So, why are you here, Herc?"

Khim ignored him.

"Guess he's not talking."

Trev wanted to move to the very end of the line as more men came up behind them. But he didn't know how to make his exit look natural. So he kept standing directly in front of Khim, body tense, skin prickling.

Suddenly another man with dark hair, who'd come up behind Khim, moved forward and looked at Trev. "I know you." Trev could only blink in confusion. "We haven't met, exactly," the man said. "You were just a little kid. But I've seen your face in holos." Trev shook his head. "You're a Damico, right?"

Trev gulped. "My father—"

"—is Dante Damico. Yeah. I know him."

Then something very strange happened. The man came up to Trev and embraced him loosely, then said, "I'm Kant. These men giving you trouble?"

Trev said, "No. It's fine."

"And your friend here?"

Khim's eyes slowly slid from their fixed position to look directly at Trev. Trev did not have to say one word as Deb, from the

86

front, said, "Hey, we don't have any trouble with the Damicos. We were just razzing the 'droid, Herc, there."

"Yeah, he's with me," Trev said softly.

Kant looked at Deb. "You heard him. Herc's with him. So cut it out."

Deb said, "How were we to know a Damico was standing right next to us? You old-Earth Italian guys all look alike."

Kant said, "Now you know." He turned his gaze back to Trev. "You're welcome."

Trev nodded, trying not to flush. He'd forgotten the notion that his very name might be the one thing that could protect him, despite the fact that he had no doubt it was Dante's doing that had brought him here instead of to "the resort."

Trev glanced quickly at Khim, whose eyes were almost slits, the blue of the irises glinting from between dark gold lashes. He saw Khim's upper lip quirk in an almost snarl.

He turned away. The line moved slowly. Khim did not leave, but he still said nothing. It was very strange to be followed by a guy who seemed to hate him.

It took about ten minutes before they got to the head of the line where the food was being served. Many were already done eating and were stacking their trays on metal counters marked DISHES.

Trays laden with food came on a slow conveyer that automatically slid by at table height, coming out of the wall and going back into a space a few feet along. Each man took one tray in order of their lineup as the trays passed by. There were no choices here.

Trev took a tray and, turning, looked over the room for an empty table. He saw one toward the back and headed in that direction. He did not have to turn around to know that Khim followed. Even here.

Trev sat at the table's end, nervous still, and almost flipped his tray while setting it down. His sealed drink tipped over. Khim moved around the table and sat as far away from him as possible at the other end—but it was still the same table. That was interesting, despite the amount of space between them.

Trev looked at his food. A round roll. Something that looked like meat with a thick brown gravy over it. Green beans. An apple. A thin yellow slice of something that looked like pudding formed into the shape of pie.

He was used to only the finest of foods, but he didn't care. He was starving. He picked up a plastic fork. As he did, Kant called to him from behind. "Hey, Damico. You can sit with us."

At the sound of the word *Damico*, several men at nearby tables came to attention.

Trev looked over his shoulder.

Dark-haired Kant, who looked about thirty-five but might have been much older, waved him over. "C'mon," he said. "I'll introduce ya."

It was the last thing Trev wanted—attention, notoriety, befriending *anyone* who was friends with his father. But if he denied the invitation, he'd look like a snob. If he accepted it, he effectively abandoned Khim. Although Khim had done nothing to ingratiate himself to Trev. They were only cellmates by misfortune, and by accident. He owed Khim nothing.

With a heaviness in his chest, Trev got up, taking his tray to the table behind him. The men made room for him. He noticed the inmates who'd been bothering Khim were now eating three tables over. They hunched at their trays, but their gazes wandered. They glanced now and again at Khim, and they certainly noticed that Trev had left him alone.

Kant said, "I was surprised to see you here in the food line. You're one of the Damico boys, I know, but I've forgotten your name."

"Trev," he said.

"Ah, the youngest. I've known your father for almost twenty years."

Trev had never heard of Kant. He certainly had not seen him at any of his father's parties or places of legitimate business. Trev stayed quiet and listened, wondering what Kant was in prison for, wondering why this man, who was definitely serving time, appeared to be so loyal to a Damico. Fear? Debt? Love?

Certainly not the third.

Instead of elaborating, Kant introduced Trev to his three companions—Thrash, Macon, Zamora. They were all dark like Kant, like Trev. They did indeed share a distant Earth culture, all descended from the Italian line with thick, dark brown hair and brown or blue eyes. One was dark-eyed but pale like the walls of the cafeteria. The others were caramel or brown, like Trev himself, whose skin had the tint of coffee with cream.

Trev began to eat. He barely tasted the food, which was unremarkable but at least filling. He asked between bites, "How do you know my father?"

"I worked for him for nearly nineteen years before I got thrown in here. I'm serving three, out in two with good behavior. One year to go. Thanks to Dante, who put in a good word. I was facing more time, actually."

Trev did not risk rudeness to ask what he'd been charged with. He figured it was something Dante was into. But Dante was always protected, always covered. His men should have been too, but sometimes things slipped through the cracks. Trev knew, though, that Dante took care of the loyal ones. If you weren't loyal, well, you ended up entombed in space. Trev did not think about that much. It was just a fact of life, something he'd known since he'd seen his father slit a man's throat.

Kant did not ask Trev what he was in for either. An unspoken etiquette between inmates. But he did say, "Guess you won't be in here for long yourself. Your father's reach is long."

"Yes. It is." Anger stirred, making Trev suddenly feel sick. He put down his fork.

He felt depleted, overly tired. Still… again. The whole day encroaching, like being spaced. The revenge of dark fathers who never wanted to lose control.

He wanted to leave, go back to his cell. Instead he sat very still, forcing himself to take even, small breaths.

The men around him did not seem to notice Trev's sudden bout of nerves and kept chatting.

Trev did not hear them. He glanced toward Khim, whose golden hair draped against his cheeks, hiding his face as he ate. Alone. What had the android done? It made him almost crazy to wonder about it.

He watched as the men who'd cut in front of them in the food line got up, taking their trays to the far counter. They walked as a group, with purpose. Other prisoners flinched when they passed by. They headed for the exit but detoured toward Khim. Trev heard Deb speak in a low tone. Khim kept staring at his tray, placing slow, deliberate forkfuls of food into his mouth.

Deb laughed, said something else.

Trev strained to hear but could make out none of the words.

"What's with the Hercules guy?" Kant asked Trev. "He your friend?"

"No. Cellmate. And that's not his name."

"It's his name now. It'll stick. Prison is like that. He's lucky the nickname is flattering and not disgusting or X-rated."

"Khim. His name's Khim. And we just met."

"Well, whatever. He's going to see trouble in this joint. So it's good he's got you on his side."

"Yeah." But Trev knew Khim didn't want him on his side. Khim hated him. Trev just didn't know why. But hatred or not, he couldn't forget the moment during their orientation when the doctor had announced Khim's internal injuries, then leaned in and spoke to him softly. He couldn't forget that the man, who was really not any more an android than anyone else in this room, despite his metal hand, had obviously been abandoned to the prison system.

Who would ever do such a thing to another human being, no matter their status?

He watched as Deb and his group kept hovering near Khim.

Finally, Trev stood. "I'm done. Nice to meet you all." He did not even look at Kant or the others. He went to the counter, placed his tray upon it, then sauntered over to Khim.

Deb and his men saw him approach. Deb gave him a leering grin, a waggling eyebrow. "Damico. Just having a friendly chat."

The men left quicker than he could blink.

Trev said to Khim, "They're total assholes."

Khim did not look up. He took a slow sip of water. "I don't need your help."

Trev felt as if that fist from earlier had finally impacted in a delayed reaction. "I didn't say you did."

He should have felt grateful that Khim was going to ask for a transfer, should have been filled with hatred for this strange man before him. Instead the heavy feeling inside him kept growing, and he wasn't mad, or enraged at Khim, just sad. It was his father he wanted to rail against. But he had not made up his mind whether he dared to contact him.

Tomorrow he would make an appointment with his lawyer, find out what the extra charges were, see if he could get out of here on his own.

He turned and headed out of the cafeteria.

*

On Steering Star, the doorways to the eight sections that jutted out from the hub were round. The metal opened like flower petals, pulling back when the portals opened or closed. His first morning at Steering Star, Trev had been instructed to go to Door 8 to be taken to a private room to see his lawyer.

A robot sentry met him there, its red eyes unnerving, its disconcertingly long arms folded at its chest plate. It stood, waiting for him as he walked up. One spindled arm lowered toward him. "Your wrist," the robot said.

Trev held it up and the robot scanned his identchip.

"Trevor Damico, you have a visitor."

"I know," Trev rolled his eyes. He hated robots.

"This way, then."

Trev followed the robot through the portal and into a long corridor, much like the one he'd come through into the prison. A long floor-to-ceiling window opened onto the stars at one side. He could see a lineup of fliers docked at various bays just below the window. This was obviously the route the guards and visitors came in by every day. From the major cloud cities, the fly time would be anywhere from twenty minutes to three hours.

The stars flashed at him. Majestic. Distant. Devoid of atmosphere and planetlight, they drenched the black, thick as rain up here. The tile under his feet was hard and gleaming white, the walls streamlined with no soft colorings or art to adorn them. The warmest thing was those cold stars, caught and held within a darkness that never ended.

They came to a wider section of the corridor that curved, and the window ended. A hall led to many doors, left and right. The robot stopped at the third door.

"Here you are," it intoned.

The door slid open with a hiss. Trev stepped over the threshold, his shoes hitting soft, plush carpet, his lungs reacting to slightly thicker air and the scent of high-designer cologne.

There was a flat square table made of fake wood. An off-white couch that looked brand-new stood against one wall. Three chairs of black faux leather surrounded the table. In the chair farthest away, with its back to the wall, sat a man in a high-end silk suit of deep blue, a flashy tie of pale lavender, and a scarf of white silk that trailed almost to the floor. His neat dark hair reflected every glance of light. His eyes were carved of the darkness of the void itself.

"Hello, son."

Trev felt his body jerk in an uncontrolled start. "My lawyer—" But he couldn't speak further, his voice sticking in his throat.

"I already talked to your lawyer on your behalf. Come. Sit down." Dante's voice was always as smooth as a slow, dark sea. It soaked into the pores. It made you feel at peace even as your skin chilled in the man's presence. Trev envied and even loved his father's charisma, but he'd always been intimidated by it as well.

He swallowed, but his throat ached and his mouth seemed incapable of making any moisture to soothe it.

"What?" asked Dante. "Don't I even get a hello? Or a 'good to see you, Dad'?"

"Dad, I—" Trev tried to speak. Lost his voice again.

"Well, I'm glad to see you're all right." Dante put his hands on the tabletop, folding them neatly. "I've missed you."

Trev stared at him. He'd been gone for a little over a day. And all this time his father had known where he was. What a fool he'd been to think he could ever trick Dante. Escape him.

92

"This facility is quite the architectural feat. Like a giant spider floating on an invisible thread. How do you like it, Trev? Is it as interesting on the inside as well?"

Trev thought he might crack. Forced himself to take a breath. "It's... a prison," he answered hesitantly.

"Well, of course it's a prison. You broke the law. Now I'm doing everything I can to help you, son, but it's looking very bad."

"I was already sentenced. For a year. It's done. But it wasn't to this facility. They say I have other charges—"

Dante held up his hand. "Oh, that first sentence. I already cleared that for you. The charges have been dismissed. You've been cleared of any malfeasance. Mr. Archimedes confessed to the whole deal, admitted to coercing you. I'm sorry if he took advantage of you, Trev. Men like that cannot be trusted. I thought I taught you that."

None of that was true. But this was the story that Dante would now tell the world. To save face.

Trev blinked. His chest quivered. "Then why am I here?"

"There was a small matter that came to the attention of the authorities. Well, it seemed small to me, but they didn't think so. I did do what I could to help, of course."

"What matter?" Trev's eyebrows furrowed. He wished in that moment for a different father. A different life.

"Why, the matter of the Bradbury, of course."

Trev gasped.

"It was just one book, after all. I couldn't see why they made such a big deal. But, my dear boy, you do realize it's a priceless artifact. They found it in your car, abandoned in Mooncast."

"I didn't leave it in my car," Trev sputtered.

"No, my dear boy. You left it in my house. Of course I could not have an item like that in my residence. You put all of us at risk."

Trev looked at his lap. His hands wove together there, damp, shaking. Softly he said, "I want my lawyer."

Dante leaned forward a bit. "Your lawyer's here, with a deal I helped procure. I want you to remember what I've done for you. The prosecutor wanted to give you ten years. I had it reduced to five. Unless you're a bad boy while you're doing your time here, in which case they will add to your sentence. I just wanted to see you first. The warden allowed it. Of course, he and I go way back."

For a moment Trev thought he might be sick. Five years, and the warden here a friend of his father's. If there had been a deeper hell he could have climbed into, he didn't know of it.

"You'd best sign the papers your lawyer—my lawyer—has drawn up for you. If you don't, your deal will be forfeit. You'll get ten or more. I did what I could for you."

Trev looked up. Through his anger and a lifetime of pent-up resentment, Dante's face blurred. "No one ever would have known. You put the Bradbury in my flier to frame me."

"But you stole it. You have to pay for that."

Trev suppressed a sob. He shook his head. "No. I'm paying for leaving *you*!"

Dante's smile was flashy. "You never left me, Trev. You're my favorite. I had your back the whole way as that man Archimedes took advantage of my best boy."

The words were sinister—worse than anything his father had ever done to him, including punishments at the whipping pole. He'd been such a fool to think he would get away. Ever.

Trev took a shaky breath.

Dante had the audacity to look sympathetic. "Five years is not so long," he said in the pampering tone of voice he'd used when Trev was a child and had gotten a scrape or a cut. "And your home, your room will be waiting for you when you get out. I will take you back into the fold." He sat up, chin high. "And you'll be grateful."

Trev's voice had vanished again beneath a welling of emotions, too many to name or count.

"Your brothers and sisters send their love," Dante added.

With a hissing breath, one word burst from Trev's mouth. "Fuck!"

"Now, now. I raised you better than that." Dante stood and walked around the table. "Normally prisoners are not allowed to touch visitors. But I acquired this room specially. No monitors. For us." He came up to the side of Trev's chair, patting him on the shoulder. "Now, can I have a hug?"

Trev stayed seated, looking straight ahead.

Dante sighed loudly. "Well, know that I love you, son." He sighed again. "My favorite, most beautiful boy, please stay safe."

Trev's eyes stung, but he would not give in. Not now. Not after all that his father had just said to him, including "I love you," which was about as ridiculous as anything the last twenty-four hours had contained. Dante didn't know anything about love. Possession, yes. But love? For years, Trev had tried to believe it—that Dante could love, did love him. He made excuses for his father, convinced himself everything Dante did for his children was out of love. But people were toys to Dante. All people, including his children. His chessboard was all pawns, even if he favored some over others.

Trev had never felt such outright hate for his father as he did in that moment. It filled him with a dark cold that dragged through his body like splinters of ice.

He heard the footsteps recede across the carpet. The cologne scent dissipated as the door hissed open, then closed.

Only after he was alone did Trev finally let go of his voice. It echoed through the room, a low scream tangled with a burst of shouted rage. Then he put his hands to his forehead and rubbed. Hard. He stomped his feet up and down on the plush carpet. Let out another moan.

Then he sat back, listless now, and waited for his father's lawyer.

Chapter Ten

Khim

The showers, smelling faintly of bleach and raw, bland soap, were noisy and echoed with men's voices. Khim hated it. He'd taken communal showers daily with his own kind, but never with real humans. He felt awkward and clumsy and out of place. And afraid. Not for himself, but for the others. If anyone made a move on him, especially there, he could not guarantee the outcome. He was no longer the controlled android he'd been born to be.

He entered a stall in a more shaded corner, not looking at anyone or anything, not paying attention to where Trev had gone.

A few minutes earlier, they had walked to the showers together, wordless, not friends, only cellmates on the same schedule. He hoped that would end. Today. When he asked his advocate for a change of cellmates.

Khim only followed Trev out of habit. It was because of his residual programming, the leftovers of brainwashing. He was never to step in front of humans but always to walk behind them. He fought side by side with other androids as equals, but humans were the superiors. Always.

It was a lie. But his body followed that lie as if it were true.

Khim took towel, soap, and the clean trousers, shirt, and underclothes delivered that morning by a laundry robot, and he placed them on a bench. He quickly undressed, stood under the tepid spray, and cleaned himself. It took about thirty seconds, then another thirty to wash his hair. When he was done, he re-dressed in under two minutes.

Naked and half-naked men came in and out of stalls. Khim did not look at them. Or look for Trev.

He did not feel any need to wait for Trev. He owed him nothing. He wanted to leave the musty, steaming air of the showers as quickly as possible. So far no one had noticed him or cared to notice him, but he did not want to take any chance of running into Deb and his gang.

He threw the wet towel over his shoulder, placed his soap and shampoo back into its plastic container, and strode into the corridor. Water trickled from his hair down the back edge of his jaw. His collar soaked up some of the drips. In the space prison's crisp air, it would all dry quickly.

Back at the cell, he combed his still-wet hair and used the toilet, checked to make sure his bed was made. It was. Neat and square as if no one had ever slept there. Trev's bunk up top was also made, but more haphazardly. Wrinkled.

Khim did not touch it. This was not the military. He didn't think the guards would care about military corners on blanket covers.

Khim left the cell and approached the robot sentry at the bottom of the second-level stairs. He held out his left hand, the flesh hand, toward the robot, wrist up. "I need to make an appointment with an advocate for this morning."

The robot's hand waved over his wrist, scanning. "Khim 18367, your advocate is Mr. Weatherford. I will ping him for you for eleven this morning, Door 7. The sentry there will escort you. If that changes, I will notify you."

"I understand." No need to thank a robot.

The breakfast lines were forming in the plaza, two trails of men going into two entrances of the cafeteria. Khim hesitated. After last night's debacle, he thought he might wait until he could be certain to be at the end of the line. It didn't bother him to eat last; he preferred less of a crowd. He thought about going back to his cell to wait, but instead he took the stairs to the second level and stayed on the open deck, leaning his abdomen against the rail and scanning the facility. Trev came up the stairway farther down the deck and headed for their cell, his thick dark hair wet against his forehead. Khim noted Trev's agility as he hopped the steps two at a time.

It still hurt Khim to climb stairs, but he told no one that fact. A robot had delivered antibiotics to him the night before, and another dose would come tonight. He had one more day of the medicine and he'd be done. He wasn't going to think about any of it after that.

Khim could watch Trev freely from his vantage, unobserved.

Trev was a very slender man, with lean muscles like a cat. Young too, and he held himself with the demeanor of privilege—chin high, shoulders back. Wiry, energetic, Khim could almost see a blue static fizz around him as he moved. Pure fantasy, of course. His mind provided the image, no doubt because Trev was so self-contained yet seemed completely unaware of that fact. The man was quick and bright. Khim had learned to read humans a long time ago so he could best judge how to behave with them to make the least amount of trouble. But reading Trev, he realized, was a waste of his time. He'd be rid of him soon, though. Trev was a Damico. Khim didn't want to cross him, but he didn't want to please him either.

Trev did not appear to know that his family owned androids, but it didn't matter to Khim. Trev was the brother of the men who'd sent him here, the son of the man who'd owned him and had thrown him into that brothel. To avoid dissension that could lead to unwanted violence, he needed a different cellmate.

He thought about last night's dinner, how Trev's presence had protected him. That made him pause. He'd considered for half a second that Trev did not seem like a bad man. But of course he had to be.

Trev was in prison. Maximum security. And he was a Damico.

Khim watched Trev enter their cell. Scanned the plaza again, saw Deb and his cohorts moving along one of the lines. His muscles hardened. He had the strength to take those men down in about ten seconds, twenty if they were armed. But he could not use his strength. It would be his death sentence for sure.

The best course was to avoid.

About two minutes later, Trev exited their cell and turned in Khim's direction, moving toward him.

Khim suppressed a sigh.

As Trev passed him, he said casually, as if he were actually respecting Khim's boundaries, "Aren't you hungry?"

Khim didn't answer.

Trev shrugged and moved like a panther down the stairs. At the bottom, Khim watched a robot sentry halt him, scanning his wrist. "You have a visitor," it announced. "Door 8."

"Thank you," Trev said.

Khim let out a huff of air. One did not thank a robot.

Trev moved off across the plaza. He was going to miss breakfast.

When the lines shortened, Khim descended the stairs and stood at the end of the nearest one. He was one of the last to take a tray and a seat. Deb and his gang were across the room, but they saw him. He pretended to ignore them, but of course all his senses were tuned directly onto them.

When they finished, they came by his table, which was empty but for him.

"Hey, Herc," Deb said. Khim kept eating, eyes fixed on nothing. "If I were to tell you to bend over, you'd have to obey, wouldn't you?"

Khim chewed on a piece of buttered toast, focusing on the flavor, how the butter was actually better than the kind they'd gotten on *Doom in Shadow*.

"Are you one of those rape models? Inquiring minds want to know."

Khim swallowed.

"You're certainly pretty enough. But rumor says you're military."

Khim did wonder where rumors got started. Not from Trev, he decided. Trev didn't seem the type to talk about others, unless he'd told Kant while they had dinner yesterday. But Khim had watched that scenario, and throughout the dinner, Trev had spoken little and eaten little.

"Well, Herc, which is it?" Deb grinned. His bald head reflected almost white in the cafeteria lighting.

Khim took a sip of water, slow and casual.

Deb said, "The sentries aren't everywhere all at once. Be wary, Herc, or you might find yourself in a place where we can test our theory."

Khim put his water down, looked up, and met Deb's hard eyes. "You want to fuck me?"

Inside, he'd gone very cold. Like when he let all his senses focus on his guns, on slaughtering the enemy one after another after another, the spray of blood, red and brilliant under alien suns, rising up in perfect ruby geysers.

Deb laughed. "Fuck you? I will break you."

Khim nodded. "In a place where no one will see. I know. And they won't see, but you will know the wonders I can do. With my body." He held up his right hand, the metal sparkling. "And with this hand. In secret places that are soft and yielding."

Deb danced back, then forward again. "You think you can get the better of me, *fucking asshole*? Think again."

"I am thinking about it," Khim said. "Vividly."

He'd never talked to humans this way before. It both terrified and exhilarated him.

"It would mean your death sentence."

"Well," Khim agreed, "if anyone saw. If we were caught, then yes, you are correct."

Deb actually flushed. "You wait. You just wait. And don't stop looking over your shoulder. Just because you have a Damico in your cell doesn't mean he'll always be around."

Khim simply nodded. But what Deb said was true. Trev would not be around. Not if Khim had his way and changed cellmates. A quiver passed over him. What was he getting himself into?

    *

Khim waited at Door 7.

Trev had been gone the whole morning. Probably in meetings with high-powered lawyers, the best that rich men like him could afford. Maybe Trev would get out of here soon. But Khim couldn't count on that. He needed—wanted—to change cells.

The robot sentry scanned his chip. The round door twisted open. A sentry on the other side waited to escort him to his advocate.

The corridor offered a familiar view of space. Khim had seen that view a thousand times and catalogued a thousand different shades of dark, depending on the proximity of suns, shiplight, planetlight, nearby auroras…. The stars had a unique ability to reach inside of him and make a fist. Then twist. He had actually liked being on a starship, despite the atrocities of war.

The sentry took Khim down the corridor and to a hall that led to offices. The first office door was open. The name on the door read "Mr. Julian Weatherford."

The sentry announced, "Khim 18367."

A man behind a desk looked up. He had long black hair tied into a braid. The desk was covered with little statues of animals carved from wood: wolves, bears, deer.

Khim's footfall went from hard floor to padded carpet. On the walls of the office were paintings of woods in moonlight, of ruined cities like broken chess pieces covered in vines. The room seemed closed in but serene.

Weatherford had a bunch of digital papers lined up in front of him, as if he needed multiple readouts for his job. Maybe he did. He said, "I see you only just arrived yesterday. How was your orientation?"

Khim said, "Normal, I think. I've never been in a place like this before."

Weatherford smiled. "You're here for murder. You know that this is completely anomalous for one of your status."

"A death sentence was narrowly avoided," Khim stated.

"It was. Because of that, and what—who—you are, we will be monitoring you carefully. Any step out of line involving violence and it's the end of the line for you. You're on your last strike with the law. I'm sorry to say it, but it is the truth."

"I know the truth."

But he hadn't known. This was a prison. Did they expect him not to fight, not to defend himself?

"Do you think you are a danger to others?"

"Isn't everyone here a danger to others? Isn't that why they're here?"

Weatherford looked at him thoughtfully, as if assessing him. "I can see that you're polite and well trained. The question, and the problem, seems to be how you respond when provoked."

This was not what Khim had come here to discuss, but he was interested. He could only nod.

"I could order you placed in solitary for your own safety. But seventy years of solitary? No man would survive it. At least, not mentally."

Khim's eyes widened.

"Here's the layout as I see it," Weatherford said. "If you are provoked, if someone attacks you, you must endure it. It's the only way. It's wrong, I know, but you cannot be involved in altercations. I will see that the sentries keep an extra eye on you, but that's about all I can do."

No one Khim had yet seen among the inmate population could best him, but his status meant the opposite. He could potentially be bested by them all—if not in reality, in theory. He took a deep breath. "I understand."

"How are your injuries?"

"Adequately healing."

"I do see that the severity of them was what perhaps caused leniency in your sentence. And yet abuse of androids is within the law." He sighed, looking down at his readouts. "We have had androids here before, but very, very rarely. But I can say the prison population may respond to you oddly."

Khim nodded a second time.

"You should know you may come to me at any time with any problems."

"To have those problems solved, or to talk?"

Weatherford smiled. "I'll do what I can."

Silence. Khim wanted to ask to be moved to another cell, but he'd started to have second thoughts. The problems he'd already faced, which Weatherford had confirmed might worsen within the prison system, could all be curbed by the presence of Trev. He hated Trev and his family. He didn't want anything to do with Trev, but could he use the Damico name to get by? To avoid confrontations, as his mind told him to do? To stave off provocation?

He did not want to die. Living was a struggle, but something inside him kept waking up each day, willing and ready to face that struggle.

102

Weatherford leaned back. His chair bounced a little, springy. "So, what did you come to see me about?"

Khim started to speak. Stopped.

Weatherford wove his hands behind his head and stretched his elbows out. "I have read all of your file. You were a decorated soldier. No insubordination, no record of trouble at all. Your battle injuries sidelined you. In all fairness, being sidelined was not a life you had ever been prepped for. To deal with that may not be in your skill set. I can get you into group counseling. You are not the only one in this prison who is a victim." He paused, then added, "Of rape."

Khim's nostrils flared slightly. "The man I murdered was the victim. Not I."

"Point taken. But experiences like these cause problems. Shock, post-traumatic stress, aggression, depression. What happened to you was legal, the murder you committed a crime. And you had no previous record in ten years of any wrong behavior. You are a victim of your situation, and it is the only reason you're still alive."

"You may insist upon that label of 'victim,' but I have never known any other way of life. I don't need the counseling." Then he remembered this guy was not a robot and added, "Thank you."

Weatherford brought his arms down, leaning on his desk. "You are a trained killer. All legal. Then you killed in self-defense. For anyone else, still legal. But not for you. I don't think that's fair, and I don't want to see you put down."

Fair? This man was talking about fairness. How naive and sweetly innocent in a place such as this. Khim wanted to laugh.

"So I want you to come to me before you take problems into your own hands. Do we have an understanding?"

Khim could have broken him in half just to show him how fair life really was. How could he talk to this man honestly, openly, if he was such an idiot? Weatherford was not a problem solver. He shuffled prisoners into cubbyholes and hoped they stayed there and made no trouble.

He managed to grate out one word. "Yes."

"Good. Is there anything else you wanted to ask me?"

"About my cellmate, Trevor Damico."

"I don't discuss inmates with other inmates."

"I just want to know if I should have anything to worry about from him." Khim frowned slightly, watching the other man's response.

Weatherford's eyes darted about the room. "He's not violent, if that's what you're asking. That's why he's in with you. It was not a random pairing."

Khim nodded. His time here had been wasted, except for that one fact. Trevor Damico, he now knew, was a man he could most certainly use.

*

When Khim returned to his cell, Trev was there, curled on the top bunk facing the wall. Asleep. His gray pant legs rucked up about his dark slip-on shoes, showing his black socks. The trousers were loose on his small frame, bunched about his narrow hips.

Five minutes until lunch.

Maybe things had not gone well for Trev with his high-powered lawyers. Khim couldn't make himself care.

Weatherford had promised Trev was nonviolent. Weatherford insisted they'd been deliberately placed together. Why? So Khim would not be provoked?

Khim was here for seventy years. When Trev left, who would they put in Khim's cell then?

After five minutes, Trev still had not awakened. Khim left the cell and went to his customary position on the second floor deck, watching the inmates line up.

Sometime later, he joined the end of one line. He ate his lunch in peace. Deb and his group had apparently already eaten and left.

Khim thought about how Trev's status had so effortlessly protected him from harassment while Khim had to withstand the taunts of bullies. If he was going to survive, he needed to be smart.

He put an apple in his left pocket, a roll in the right. At the exit, a sentry stopped him. "You cannot take food with you outside the cafeteria."

"I did not know."

"The rules are posted in the exercise rooms and media rooms, and there is a posting right here in the cafeteria."

Khim produced the roll and tossed it in a nearby trash receptacle. "I'm new. I'll go read the rules now."

The sentry's red eyes pierced his gaze, and then the head swiveled away.

Khim walked out.

When he returned to the cell, Trev looked as if he had not moved. Khim set the apple on the sheet beside his pillow, then bent to get onto his own bunk, folding his long legs underneath him, and reclined against the wall.

He waited.

Chapter Eleven

Trev

Trev awakened slowly, eyes swollen, stuck shut. His father's face kept flashing across his mind. He clenched his fists hard, wanting to kick and beat at the wall.

It would do no good. Chest tight, he focused, took slow breaths, and rubbed his hand across his eyes, clearing them. He slowly turned over on the mattress. A round yellow-green object came into view.

Trev pulled his legs up, then balanced on the edge of his bunk and leaned slowly down with the grace of a dancer. He had heard Khim breathing, so he knew he was there.

The man in the lower bunk was sitting very still, legs unfolded flat in front of him, looking back at him with vivid, dark blue eyes. All upside down.

"What's this?" Trev threw his arm over his head and waved the apple with its fluorescent green skin through the air. He was surprised he had a voice, all his emotions still sizzling too close to the surface.

"You missed lunch."

"I have a headache."

"I don't know how to procure aspirin except through the infirmary."

"Why are you suddenly talking to me?" Trev asked. It could not be that this person who'd tried to punch him yesterday had such a sudden change of heart.

"You spoke first. I answered."

"You made it very clear you don't like to talk."

Khim said, "Yes. I did."

"So what's the apple payment for? What do you want?"

"Why do you think I want something?"

Trev was getting tired of hanging upside down. He pulled himself up and sat contemplating the apple. Every muscle in his body ached from emotional exhaustion, but his head was the worst pain of all.

There was an old myth about the apple of sin. Well, so be it. He opened his mouth and bit into it, reveling as the sweet juices dripped down his throat. Chewing, he replied, "Everyone seems to want to take something from me today, not give me things." He didn't want to think about the morning. His father. He clamped down the quiver of depression in his chest—he'd cried enough—and took another bite. His stomach woke, telling him he was very hungry.

"Because of your name, people here seem hesitant to provoke you."

Trev heard a tone in the words that was like a wavering chord of gold. Khim was designer made right down to the voice. Liquid. Sibilant.

"Damico." Trev's breathing was easing up now that he had something else to concentrate on. "I hate that name. But it is true that it generates respect."

Khim said from below, "I would like to purchase your— protection."

Trev nearly choked, swallowed a piece of the fruit whole. He leaned over the edge of the bunk, perfectly balanced, to look at the android upside down again. "What?"

Khim blinked up at him. "You do look ill. Did your meeting not go well?"

Trev winced. "How intuitive. Did I hear you say you want to buy my protection?"

"Correct."

"I don't even—but—but why?"

"I believe I've lost the ability for aggression control. And the rules for me, even here, are not the same as the rules for all."

It was more information than he'd heard Khim say altogether in twenty-four hours.

Khim continued. "If I slip up and hurt another human, I will be put down because of what I am. I would very much like to survive, at least for a little while. I don't like to be touched, and what control I have seems to dissipate when that happens. If you are there, in an intervening sense and as a Damico, events of provocation would be fewer, and I might get through at least the next few months alive."

"Events of provocation," Trev repeated. "You mean that asshole Deb."

"Among others."

Trev righted himself again, stretching his legs out and hanging them over the side of the bunk. It had never occurred to him that Khim would be under such a great threat. Of course he'd had his own problems on his mind, but this man he shared a cell with was in actual, immediate danger.

This was serious. If what Khim said was true, the man was not even allowed to defend himself. That would end quite badly for him, with his looks, in a prison for violent offenders.

"Uh, what currency do you have?"

"Currency?"

"To pay me," Trev said. This was intriguing. And it was taking his mind off his own problems. When he thought about it, he realized he actually could help this guy.

"Well, I gave you the apple."

"Oh yeah." Trev felt himself smile a bit. "Thanks. It's buying you this consult." He flinched. He heard his father's voice in his words and hated it, hated himself for taking that stance with a man in peril.

"What would you want that—that I could give?" Khim asked.

Trev heard a strange waver in that beautiful android voice. He had already made up his mind. "Simple." He leapt down off the bed, turned, and faced the man in the lower bunk. "A friend."

The look on Khim's face turned to horror.

Trev frowned. Then his cheeks flushed. "Oh no. No! Not *that* kind of friend." He raised his eyebrows in a sort of truce. "No. Okay?"

Khim shook his head, face in a half scowl. "I don't know what you mean, then. I don't have friends. Or know about that sort of thing."

Trev knew androids were given false childhoods. "Surely you have some memory of 'that sort of thing.'"

"My memories are faulty. At best. It's a problem, but one I've kept to myself."

Trev couldn't imagine not having memories. He looked at the way Khim sat, muscles taut, aloof, alone, and so beautiful. It was like looking at a work of art, a sculpture, but one that had been defiled, hollowed out, used, and ruined. If you touched it, it might crumble under your very fingertips, like one of his fine old books encased in crystal.

His heart trembled when he imagined what the man must have been through. But you could not encase a man in crystal to save him.

"Okay then, so you'll learn," Trev said. "If you agree to work on the friendship thing, we have a deal."

"Yes. You will tell me what to do, and I'll do it."

It was Trev's turn to scowl. "No. It's not like that. I don't own you."

Khim's face darkened.

Trev could not quite read the emotion there, but it wasn't good, so he added quickly, "It's two-way, friendship is. You hang out. Talk a bit. Back each other up. Remain loyal. Oh, and bring them apples when they have a headache."

Khim's chest rose as he took a deep breath. The muscles around his eyebrows relaxed. But his eyes still glittered with mistrust. "All right."

"All right," Trev echoed. He stood there, watching the other man glower in the shadows of his bunk. The day had been a very bad one, but at least his cellmate didn't want to beat him up anymore. That was a tiny, tiny win.

Trev went to the sink and washed his face. He knew he must have looked terrible throughout the entire conversation. He pushed his bangs back with wet hands, neatening himself.

He turned back. Khim was still seated on his bunk, arms crossed.

"I need to go for a walk. Move around a little," Trev announced.

Khim simply nodded. "I'll come too."

*

The remainder of the day went smoothly. They explored the prison, finding the exercise rooms and media rooms were much bigger and more luxurious than they'd expected. But they could not explore for long—the dinner hour came quickly.

That night Khim was allowed to join Trev at Kant's table. No one said anything against it, but no one spoke to Khim, either. Trev felt awkward. He was quite hungry; he forced himself to eat quickly so he would have an excuse to leave.

Kant asked, "How'd your visit with your lawyer go today?"

Trev took in a sharp breath, shrugged, and kept eating.

"That good, huh?" Kant slapped him lightly on the shoulder. "I thought your father would have you out of here before the rest of us could blink."

Trev made a sound halfway between a chuckle and a moan. "Yeah, right. My father. It's a little complicated, even for him."

As Trev spoke he was conscious that Khim's posture stiffened beside him. He remembered when Khim had said, "I refuse to share a cell with this person." But it was because he was a Damico that Khim had made the friendship deal with him.

The dark hole inside him expanded. He lost his appetite.

He stood, tray in hand. Oddly, Khim mirrored him, though there was still food on his plate.

Trev muttered, "It's been a long day."

Kant said, "It takes a while to settle in here. But you're a Damico. You'll do fine." He glanced up at the tall android. "Not sure about him, though."

Trev heard the tone not as a threat but more a warning. His skin prickled. Khim, as usual, had no response.

Wordlessly Trev dumped his tray and headed out, Khim following behind him.

He moved across the plaza to the stairs and went up two steps at a time. When he was on Level 2, he turned to look, and Khim was right behind him.

110

"It's two hours before lights-out, but I'm tired. I'm going back to our cell. You don't have to follow me."

"I have nowhere else to be. And I do not trust any of these men."

Trev sighed. He wished he could be alone. His depression from the day was getting the better of him. But he had no energy to argue.

Once in their cell, Trev shucked off his shoes, pants, and shirt. Underneath he wore the white T-shirt and gray shorts like all the other prisoners. He folded his clothes and placed them on his shelf, then brushed his teeth. He was aware of Khim the whole time, sitting in his bunk with his knees up, hands against his shins, facing the side wall.

Trev peed, then leaped onto the top bunk, settling gracefully and saying a soft "Night" as he went.

Khim did not answer.

Trev shifted under his blanket and turned toward the wall. He lay very still, listening to the tense pulsing of his heart.

It was ridiculous. The whole day had been. But it wouldn't do to let others know too much. How his sentence had been increased and he had no chance of getting out of here for five years. How his father had betrayed him.

He remembered being very small, maybe four years old, and there was a big party at the mansion. Dante had shooed away Trev's nanny and surprised his tiny son by dressing him himself. There had been a silver box with a big red bow. Inside was a tuxedo, twin to his father's but made to fit Trev. Dante took his time with him, making sure every ruffle was in place and the tiny bow around his neck was properly tied. Trev even had new, shiny black shoes. Dante combed Trev's hair until it shone and put a bit of spray on it to hold it back from his face. Then he picked up his son, and they looked at each other in the big mirror of Trev's closet. Trev was a miniature copy of his father.

"Look at us," Dante had said. "Aren't we amazing?"

Little Trev said, "I love you, Daddy. Thank you. This suit is pretty."

Dante laughed. He kissed Trev on his plump, flushed cheek. "This is your first party, little boy, and I'm going to show you off to everybody."

The promise was kept. Dante barely let go of Trev all night, introducing him to just about every guest. He doted on Trev, kept his hand on him even when Trev was not in his arms. His older brothers and sisters smiled at him, but they were also jealous. "Pet," fourteen-year-old Breq had called him at one point when their father wasn't looking. "Like a trained dog."

"Am not!" Trev retorted hotly, then grinned as Dante lifted him up again. He put his short arms about his daddy's neck and smirked back at Breq, who rolled his eyes and turned away as more guests greeted them, saying, "Mr. Damico, is this beautiful boy your new adopted son?"

"He's been with us two years," Dante replied. "He's very special."

Trev had basked. He also liked that he was adopted. It set him apart from his siblings.

Trev had tried to convince himself for so long, even through the worst parts of his life with Dante Damico, that he was well and truly loved. But that conviction became harder and harder the older he grew.

On his side, with his pillow bunched under his head, Trev's eyes filled and he clamped down hard on his emotions. He bit the insides of his cheeks. Shut his eyes. Sniffed.

He heard Khim get up, use the toilet, brush his teeth. He heard the soft shush of cloth against skin as he disrobed. There was a tiny vibration in the frame of the bunk as Khim climbed in below.

Trev thought it was stupid that Khim was going to bed as early as he was. But that was the deal. Khim wanted to stick with Trev to minimize "provocation."

After a while, through his misery, Trev heard Khim's rich voice rise up, saying, "It is but one day in a universe that is sixteen billion years old. That's how I got through every day of the war."

For a moment Trev thought he was dreaming. Khim did not seem the type to offer up pleasantries. Or comfort.

"Yeah," he replied with a shaky breath. "But it's a fucked-up universe."

Silence from below. Trev took it as agreement.

*

It was strange at first. Trev had a pet android following him around. Well, not an android. Not really. The man was fully human. The unfortunate circumstance of his birth was what wrongly defined him.

But the strangeness of it all wasn't just what Khim was. Trev's perceptions played tricks. When he moved and Khim moved with him, he felt a sort of electrical field behind him, a pulsing as if Trev hauled a gold-drenched light wherever he went. And there was that odd scent of fresh-baked bread. Cloying. Hunger inducing.

They woke to the clanging prison alarm at six sharp. Breakfast would come at seven. That gave them an hour to procure fresh clothing from the robots at the laundry, shower, dress, and neaten their bunks and their cell. During this time they were allowed to make future appointments with advocates or lawyers if need be, through the sentries assigned to their cell level.

On day three, Trev jumped down from his bunk. He'd slept almost twelve hours after going to bed so early and depressed the night before. The air felt cold against his legs; his nose burned from the dryness. He hurriedly put on yesterday's clothes, his back to the toilet where Khim was. He hated their lack of privacy. He'd never get used to it.

At 6:05 a.m. the force fields on each cell hummed off, and the ceiling of their cell glowed white. Sentries passed by to make sure all the men were rising, all accounted for.

Khim and Trev left and passed by the laundry room, gathering clean clothes for the day.

In the shower room assigned to their block section, Khim followed Trev. They chose stalls side by side. Other men were already there, the steam from the stalls rising in the air. Luckily none of them were Deb and his gang. No one called Khim "Herc" or even seemed to notice him. So far. Inmates barely glanced their way, too busy hurrying to get in and out so they could be first in line for breakfast.

Khim was quick and efficient at disrobing, then re-dressing, but Trev caught just a glimpse of his tall, muscular body. The bruises on his ribs already looked healed. He also noted, with not a small amount of self-conscious nervousness, how perfectly streamlined that body was. How beautiful.

Trev was not used to taking note of people in that way. And now it would not do to notice, since Khim was only his fake friend and still didn't even seem to like him.

Khim ignored everyone, including Trev, not looking once in his direction while they were dressing in fresh clothes.

They left the shower, tossing their day-old clothing in a bin where a robot stood watching with red eyes.

At breakfast, Deb and his gang showed up as usual. One of the men, not Deb, passed very close by Khim, accidentally bumping him.

Trev said, "Watch where you're going."

"Damico scum," the man said under his breath so that only Trev and Khim could hear.

Trev was not sure what to do. Should he stand and confront the guy? Or pretend he hadn't heard? But the man was already two tables away before he could even think about reacting.

Kant and his men showed up a minute later. Breakfast ended peacefully.

As they walked across the plaza, Trev turned to Khim. "Let's check out the starboard exercise room."

Khim looked supremely bored. "Intriguing," he replied tonelessly.

Both exercise rooms were quite large and fully equipped. Trev and Khim ended up spending most of the morning using the equipment and walking the indoor track.

As they were spotting each other on weights, Trev watched Khim wince once. He asked quietly, "Do you still have pain?"

Khim's eyes narrowed. His mouth straightened. Finally, he replied curtly, "The exercise helps." Then he got up and walked to the far side of the room and mounted a cycle gingerly.

Trev was cut off from asking any more personal questions. He understood that Khim was still raw, both physically and mentally. Maybe his wounds would never completely heal. Trev didn't know the psychology of androids, but when it came to pain of any kind, he thought they were probably the same as humans underneath.

114

Both had removed their gray shirts and wore only their T-shirts above the waist. The way Khim's muscles rippled in the white light of the room got the attention of a lot of men. Eyes furtively glanced at him, then at Trev, then away. Other men in that room were bulked up as well. Some of them looked as if working out was all they ever did. In a way, Khim fit in nicely. If he hadn't been an android, probably there would never be much trouble for him. Especially since he could fight.

Trev slowly made his way to the cycles. He climbed onto a cycle two down from Khim. They rode for half an hour, then drank from water fountains that extended from the wall.

To cool off, they sat on a bench near the far wall, which was clear and showed the star field beyond.

Neither man spoke.

The lunch alarm sounded.

*

After lunch they decided to check out the larger of the libraries.

The room curved outward at the edge of the prison hub, the tall white ceiling trailing in a half arc to a broad window that took up the far wall and showed off the stars. Sometimes fliers floated by, their engines leaving a strange red plume against the black. There were couches along the solid walls and lined up end-to-end in the middle of the room. Robot sentries stood at either side of the entrance and at the far corners of the room, their scarlet eyes observing all the open space. It was interesting that the prison afforded this luxury.

This particular room supplied digital books that could "chip" right into the brain through an earbud. You closed your eyes and you could read. A blink turned the page. Trev preferred his collection of real-books back home, but he tried not to think of that.

They used the plush couches in the main room to sit and read. The rules posted on the wall stated they were allowed to take one book each per night to their cell.

Trev chose a Bradbury, of course, with the fitting title *A Medicine for Melancholy*. He glanced over at Khim. "Which one did you choose?"

"*The Art of War.*"

Trev said, "Sun Tzu. I haven't read it. Aren't you tired of war by now?"

"The supreme art of war is to subdue the enemy without fighting," Khim quoted.

"Okay, then, that applies directly to the situation at hand. Maybe that's something we both should read." Trev relented, leaning back.

They were quiet for two hours.

An alarm rang out, echoing, interrupting their reading. A voice filtered in behind the alarm. "Random lockdown. You are to report immediately to your cells for the count. Any inmate not in his cell by the count of five minutes will receive two checks."

Three checks meant automatic solitary for two days, Trev recalled. Khim and Trev rose, checked out their books with the sentry, and hurried across the plaza.

They reached their cell with a minute to spare before the force field automatically reset.

A sentry came by, reciting their names and telling them to hold their wrists up facing the entrance. The robot scanned their identchips through the field, acknowledged they were present, and moved on.

"Well," Trev said, "at least we got books." He bounded up onto his bunk, using one hand to increase upward momentum, and landed on his feet, knees bent. "Damn. Forgot to take off my shoes."

Khim stared at him.

"What?" Trev asked.

"Most men would climb up using the end of the frame."

"Well, I'm not most men."

"I can see that."

Trev suppressed a grin. Khim was making small talk. It was a first. However, it didn't continue.

They spent the two hours of lockdown in silent reading.

Chapter Twelve

Khim

A new day came.

The shower seemed busier this morning. Damp and steamy. They had to wait longer than usual for stalls, and getting two side-by-side today was not going to be possible.

When they were at the front of the line, one stall became vacant and Trev motioned for Khim to go in first.

Khim went, knowing Trev was right behind him, and if not next to him, then at least in the vicinity. He smelled the clear but rough edge of the soaps they all used, and the plain shampoos. The overchlorinated water came on with a sharp smell. He undressed quickly, placing his dirty clothes on the bench next to his clean clothes and towel.

The spray was hot. At least there was that. He could soak his muscles for a moment, and the water felt good on his lower back where he still ached.

Sounds of splashing and echoes of splashes filled the room. Men's voices reverberated off the tiled walls. Laughter as someone told a dirty joke. It was ironic to Khim that even in prison humans could find humor.

Khim soaped up fast. Shampoo foamed in his hair. He was almost done, ready to rinse.

Someone cried out. Pleasure or pain?

His heart began a panicked rhythm. He heard a slap of flesh on flesh. Heard grunts and a moan. When the men in his unit had sex with each other, it could sound like that. He'd grown used to it.

So two men were having sex in the showers. So what?

He closed off his mind to the sound. But he heard whisperings and chuckles. Even closing his eyes and sticking his head under the water to clear off the shampoo didn't drown out the muttered command from several stalls down.

"Shut up and take it."

The mood in the showers changed eerily. Khim could feel it. The echoes of men joking, or laughing, dimmed. Men went silent. The air, already humid, became swamped with fear.

Where was the sentry?

He heard men rapidly filing out. He heard spigots go off, the splashing of water diminishing. And more groans. And cries. Three voices, maybe four.

He breathed in, and his chest began to shake. He turned off the water and grabbed his towel.

He could still hear the muffled cries, some more chuckling, more groans.

Trev appeared suddenly at the entrance to Khim's stall, half-dressed, his clothing soaked, his dark hair in his eyes. "Let's go," he said.

Still wet, Khim dragged on his pants and grabbed the rest of his stuff. He came out to stand by Trev. The problem was they would have to pass that stall to exit.

The sentry at the door looked nonfunctional, and the laundry robot was outside, in the hall where it did the least amount of good.

Trev followed Khim's gaze to the frozen sentry. "What the fuck?"

Khim said, "I have no clue."

"We can't be here."

They moved quickly, but not before a man with a white towel around his waist hopped out of a stall and glared. One of Deb's men. "Look, it's Herc," he cried out with a loud laugh. He looked half-crazed, maybe high, his reddish brown hair sticking up. "Deb says you have to do what humans tell you to do. Is it true?"

Khim barely heard him. He only had eyes for the man in the stall bent over, held down by two others. All were naked. A sort of dizziness swept him, and he saw again the red in front of him, velvet and soft where they had pressed his face down to the couch as someone entered him from behind.

He blinked. The shower was on in that stall, steamy wet air covering them. The two men standing were aroused. The third, bent over and bleeding, was not.

Khim calculated that in under ten seconds he could probably take them all with his bare hands and maybe a little help from the bench if he could lift it high enough and crack it over their heads. "Stop," he heard himself say. His voice was low. As if stuck in his throat. "Stop." His body went into a posture of attack; he didn't even think about it.

He felt a hand on his bare arm. "Don't."

It was Trev.

Khim looked down to where Trev touched him, going livid. He yanked his arm away.

Trev said it again. Calm, but commanding. "Don't."

Khim backed away a step. A wave of submission surged over him at Trev's tone. Would it be enough to stop him from attacking these men?

"Damico." One of the guys in the stall was another of Deb's men. Deb was not there.

Trev said, "Yes."

The men in the stall let the other man go. "Just having fun," they said, coming out and grabbing their towels. They were rough-looking, both with small eyes and unappealing bodies. Nothing, Khim thought, like the posh men of the House of Xavier. It didn't matter that this was a prison and that other place a silk-wrapped boudoir—they were all rapists.

And he wanted to kill them.

But the attackers were quickly gone, and Khim stood in his bare feet in the puddles of warm water while Trev went to the shaking man, still bent over in the stall, and said, "Are you badly hurt?"

"No" came the low response.

"What's your name? I'll call a guard."

The man stood, hunched into himself. "They call me Pig. But I'm Jay. And please don't call any sentries or guards. It'll just get me into more trouble with that gang."

Through narrowed eyes, Khim watched Trev help the man up. "He's bleeding," he stated without inflection. It was all over the tile, pink now as it mixed with the water going down the drain.

"I'll be fine," Jay said, grabbing a towel.

The tightness in Khim's chest was not receding. He turned his head away, had the urge to go to his knees, bend over himself, let this place beat him to death. He raised both his hands to the sides of his head. He could feel his hair against the palm of his left hand. The right hand felt nothing.

Trev said, "You need a doctor."

The man had his pants on now and was rapidly tying them. "No."

Khim moved to the door. The room was starting to spin. He lowered his hands.

Trev was beside him, and Khim didn't remember hearing him walk up.

"Khim. Are you okay? We need to get you out of here. You can't be a part of any altercations."

Khim nodded tightly, watching as Trev walked up to the frozen sentry. Steam smudged the silver surface of its face, chest plate, and arms.

"Don't touch it," Khim said.

"I built one of these when I was a kid."

"If you fix it, they might assume you broke it."

Jay came up behind them. He was smaller than Trev, young, blue-eyed, pale. He said, "They do something to its time mechanism. It'll pop back to life in a minute."

"Let's go," Trev said.

Khim followed him. Jay followed behind Khim.

Khim walked as if nothing were wrong. As if the weight of the prison did not press in on his ten-year-old skin. As if seeing the naked victim on his knees with his blood going down the drain did not leave splinters in his eyes.

Just over four days ago, there had been blood on a floor by a red velvet couch.

He did not remember any time in his life, even in the worst of battles with his bunkmates dying around him, when he'd felt so stripped of the psychic armor he'd pulled around himself the day he'd been born.

The plaza was too bright. Men lined up for breakfast, showered and clean and orderly.

Khim did not feel the least bit hungry, but he followed Trev, trying to keep only that one focus. Concentrate on the slender gray form in front of him, with the swatch of dark hair on its head. Pretend nothing was out of the ordinary.

The three of them got in the end of the breakfast line. Khim did not look for the culprits, but he would never forget their faces. He memorized faces well these days. It was becoming a habit.

When they got their trays of food, Trev headed for an open table in the back. Kant and his men had already gone. No potential friends waved them to a table.

Trev sat and scooted along the bench to make room for Khim.

Khim moved too quickly and brushed against Trev as he seated himself. Shock zinged through his body and he huffed a swift breath, putting his hands on either side of his tray. Both of them were fists, one light, one dark.

Trev turned to him as if nothing were wrong and whispered, "It's okay. You don't have to react to anything now. It's just breakfast."

But it wasn't okay. Right then there was so much hate in him. His glass wall, which surrounded his core self, was growing ever thinner. Khim did not know how he would survive it. Everywhere he turned there was an enemy.

Jay sat across from them, pale hair hanging in his eyes, still damp. His look was turned inward, thin, unhealthy. But he kept forcing weird smiles.

Khim could not look at him without seething. Maybe if the man had been stronger, none of this would have happened.

A lightning bolt of pain centered in his chest at that thought.

Khim began to eat, stabbing at eggs automatically, chewing, swallowing, not tasting.

Trev looked a little put out, but took charge anyway, his eyes dull and disturbed. He said, "Jay, do you read?" Jay nodded. "What do you like?"

Khim blotted them from his mind. He knew Trev was making small talk to calm the situation. He didn't have to listen to it.

Breakfast ended not a moment too soon.

Standing in the plaza, Trev said, "Weight room?"

Khim nodded. Physical exertion was one solution for burning off excess negative energy. He couldn't wait to run on the track, speed on the cycle, pound the punching bag. He'd loved the exercise rooms on *Doom in Shadow* and had spent a lot of time in them.

Jay tagged along without a word. Khim did his best to pretend he wasn't there.

After fifteen minutes at the weights, Khim stripped his shirt off and let the sweat sheen his skin. Already he was starting to feel better. The knot in his chest was untying. His stomach muscles relaxed.

He did not talk to anyone, but he was aware of Trev's presence close by at all times. And he was aware that Jay only fiddled with the machines and weights and other apparatus, and did little else. Lazy. Or listless.

Sometime later, while he was on the cycle, someone said to him, "Hey, Herc."

He pretended not to hear and they went away.

He kept expecting some repercussion from the shower scene. Maybe the attackers would come looking for them. Maybe there would be a random lockdown.

Nothing happened.

It took about three hours for Khim to feel almost fully relaxed. Oxygen reached the bottoms of his lungs again; he no longer wanted to kill everyone in sight.

Before lunch, Trev and Khim went back to their cell to relax.

Khim immediately lay down on his bottom bunk.

Trev stood by the head of the bed for a few seconds as if undecided. Finally he said, "You all right?" They were the first words spoken between them in hours.

Khim said, "Surviving," then gave him the warrior thumbs-up.

Trev smiled at that before he leaped onto the top bunk.

Chapter Thirteen

Trev

A week later, Trev lay on the top bunk reading, while outside their cell the lights strobed. Another random lockdown. It might last half an hour or two hours. They never knew.

Khim was reading on the bottom bunk.

The lockdown had happened while they were in the media room. Trev checked out the book he'd been browsing, a novel about Earth kings in a medieval setting, not realizing how close to the final page he had been.

He opened his eyes. "I'm finished. Now what will I do?"

From below, Khim said, "What are you reading?"

"*A Consortium of Kings*, from an author of twenty-second-century Earth."

Khim's left hand reached up over the rim of his bed with an earbud clasped between two fingers.

Trev took the bud and handed Khim his own. "I think you'll like mine. It has horses."

"I've never seen a horse. I don't know if you'll like mine."

Trev inserted the bud and closed his eyes. The first sentence was about Marines storming a star base. The next sentence involved laser guns mounted on saucer ships.

Khim chose volumes about war, battle, combat, or even sports fighting.

Trev chose books of Earth literature, fantasy, poetry, memoirs, and twentieth-century science fiction.

It did not surprise Trev that Khim was smart. When they had traded books a couple times before, Khim had seemed to enjoy Trev's choices. He did not seem to mind pretty words on pages at all. But Khim still chose action and spy novels. Sometimes he chose poetry too, such as that of ancient samurai or Chinese poets from the time of Genghis Khan.

The last time they'd traded books, Trev had been a little shocked to see lines on the page like:

The Forbidden City, the nine-tiered palace, loomed in the dust
From thousands of horses and chariots headed southwest.
or
And the wind, that has come a thousand miles,
Beats at the Jade Pass battlements....

Trev said, opening his eyes to rid himself of alien marines, "No poetry this time?"

"Sorry," he heard Khim mutter.

"Well, I would think maybe a soldier with other things on his mind would be bored with poetry."

"In some old-Earth cultures it was required that a warrior learn to write poetry. The best warriors wrote the best poetry, needing to stay in touch with that which might ground them. Or perhaps otherwise go insane."

The response moved Trev greatly. "Maybe we should both read more of that stuff, then." He grinned. It was nice to hear Khim talk, relaxed and content. A rare moment.

He wanted to ask, badly, how Khim's own experience related to that. Instead he bit his lower lip and kept quiet. Khim was too sensitive still, and they did not know each other well enough yet.

When the lockdown ended, it was dinnertime and Jay was already waiting for them by their cell door. He must've run there as soon as the force fields came down.

Trev noticed Khim withdraw again as the three of them walked together to the dinner line.

Chapter Fourteen

Khim

Khim had not realized he could spend as much time reading as working out and enjoy both equally. When he read, he could escape the prison, both the physical one and the cage of his own thoughts.

The moments he enjoyed the most were when he and Trev were alone together. Jay hung around far too often for his tastes.

The random lockdowns happened at least every other day.

Today another lockdown came early, just after lunch, and they'd been shut in their cell all afternoon.

Restless, Khim had done some push-ups on the floor. He had been reading, but he'd gotten bored.

Trev was napping but woke when he heard Khim moving around.

Trev sat up, his dark hair falling over his forehead. His face was a little flushed despite his naturally tanned skin color; his eyes looked thickly glazed. "Still on lockdown?" he mumbled sleepily.

"Yes."

They both glanced at the softly humming force field.

Khim wondered if Trev knew how closely he sometimes watched him. Their deal was to stick together. Khim followed Trev's lead without really thinking about it. Always a step or two behind. He had memorized the man's gait, his stance, the way his body moved effortlessly across the floor as if his feet weren't really touching the surface. It hadn't been more than a few weeks now, and he knew which hairs at the nape of Trev's neck curled and which ones were always straight. He knew exactly where the pullover prison-gray shirt wrinkled against Trev's waist, the exact point where it clutched his hip, how sometimes it caught at the fabric of the cotton trousers and rode up against the curve of his backside.

Now Trev pushed himself forward on the bunk, crossing his legs and leaning out a bit. "Hey."

Khim was already looking at him, so he wondered why Trev seemed to think he needed to call out to get his attention. He frowned.

Trev said, "I got these as a gift from Jay. You know, for helping him out."

Khim took a deep breath, not wanting to see anything Jay had given Trev. One perk about lockdown—Jay was not there for a while.

But Trev waved a deck of playing cards in his face. They were shaped like triangles, but they were regular, with four suits and the usual number of kings and queens. "You know how to play?"

"Of course." Khim stared at Trev's deft hands as he shuffled them. "Gin. Rummy. Poker."

"Let's go, then."

"We don't have a table."

"Jump up. Sit on the end of my bunk," Trev offered.

Khim hesitated. It seemed, perhaps, a bit too familiar, too close. But he was so bored.

He walked over to the end of the bunk's frame and climbed up. They sat facing each other, knees bent, the cards between them.

They each knew games the other did not, and they taught each other how to play them. They were both equally quick and won games fifty-fifty.

Trev looked up at one point. "We've been at this for hours, and I didn't even notice."

Khim felt his face relax into a rare smile. It had been quite a nice way to spend a day.

But as soon as the force field came down, Jay was there again.

Khim's insides grew heavy with resentment. If only he could have gone to dinner alone with Trev in peace, it might've been one of his better days.

Chapter Fifteen

Trev

Trev watched the tension in Khim come and go like flashes of lightning. One moment he'd be calm, the next all his muscles would go hard as if he were ready to explode.

The men were all like that here at Steering Star. But while they faced solitary if they lost control, Khim faced death.

Trev saw layers of emotion simmering in those dark blue eyes. He didn't think Khim knew he showed it. But Trev saw, and watched.

They were all broken here. An aggressive android, a wilting man named Jay. And Trev himself, still reeling from his father's charismatic cruelties.

The day after the rape in the shower, Jay had begun hanging out with Trev and Khim every day.

Khim continued to ignore Jay. He never responded to his greetings or his furtive looks.

Trev himself did not feel particularly strong or capable away from his old life and the things he loved, but now he found himself with two wayward young men following him around. It was because of his name, he knew. It couldn't be anything else.

He'd been alone, frightened, and confused when he'd agreed to Khim's deal of the fake friendship. With Jay, he'd made no such deal. But he felt sorry for the guy and treated him with the respect any human being deserved.

Khim obviously felt differently. Trev could sense a bitterness in him when every day Jay trailed along behind them to the exercise rooms and the entertainment rooms.

For about a week, Khim kept hold of his self-control. He exercised, he read, and he remained uninterested in idle conversation. When he saw Deb and his gang, he did not acknowledge them.

Jay, on the other hand, was a nervous talker. While Trev walked or lifted weights, Jay always engaged him. He liked to see what Trev was reading in the media rooms and would read the same thing. He would begin discussions about the books; he talked about the stories.

Because Khim did not say much, Trev welcomed pretty much any discussion.

Today, Jay was talking about a novel they'd both read. "I liked the vampire because he was cool and invincible, and he was forced to see the bigger world around him and all the lies."

"I liked that one too," Trev said.

They sat in the library alcove, sorting earbuds and gazing at the star field. It was quieter in this area than any other because the earbuds allowed inmates to watch movies individually, piped straight into their brains.

When Jay started babbling, Khim got up and walked away. Trev watched him go to the movie section and look around. The golden light of Khim filled Trev's eyes.

"What's up with him?" Jay asked. "I know he's your cellmate, but he's very rude."

Trev glanced away from Khim, realizing he'd been staring after him as if he cared. "Just like all of us," he replied. "He's been through a lot."

"I know he doesn't like me."

"I don't think it's that," Trev hedged.

"Do you two have a thing or something?"

"No." Trev felt his face heat at the suggestion. "He's just like you. He's trying to stay out of trouble."

Jay said, "By hanging with you."

"Yes."

"It's your name. People respect it. I would've thought for a Damico you'd be a lot worse. Like Deb's men. The Damicos have that reputation. But you put up with him. And you put up with me."

Trev felt slightly bereft at the statement and decided that perhaps Jay talked a bit too much. "One day at a time," he said under his breath.

He looked up and saw Khim staring at him from across the room with a strange, almost frustrated look. Khim looked down as soon as Trev met his eyes.

When they walked back to their cell with their new books, Jay went off to his own cell to await the dinner hour.

Trev hopped up to his bunk and lay back, glad for more quiet reading time. Khim stood for a moment in the center of the cell. Trev thought maybe Khim needed to use the toilet, and he turned away to face the wall. It had been an unspoken etiquette between them, giving each other as much privacy as they were able.

Trev closed his eyes and began to read, blinking to access the next page.

After a minute he heard shuffling and wondered what Khim was doing. Curious, he opened one eye, and the book page slipped away from his vision.

Khim was pacing the cell, hands making fists, head down. Back and forth he went from the edge of the bunk to the opposite side wall. It was such a small space he could only go two steps before he had to turn and go two steps back. His shoulders hunched. It looked to Trev like he was just spinning in circles. He kept taking deep breaths.

Trev sat up, both eyes open now. "Khim, what are you doing?"

Khim paced two more times before looking up. "Get rid of him," he said cryptically.

"What?"

"I can't stand looking at him. I don't want him tagging around."

"Are you talking about Jay?"

Khim stood still now, hands on his hips, head down. His hair was flaxen, with a mirror shine today. But the beautiful face was tortured.

Trev said, "He feels safe with us. You understand that, right?"

"I can't look at him. If he weren't so damnably weak, none of it would have happened. And he wouldn't be interfering with our deal."

Trev felt his jaw go tight. "He's not interfering with our deal." He could not believe Khim was saying this.

Khim put a hand to his forehead. "I can't stand his incessant chatter."

Trev had no love for Jay, but he didn't hate him. "He's not 'chattering' to you. So you don't have to worry."

Khim opened his mouth to speak. Closed it. Trev watched him, trying to read him. The man looked furious. Khim and Jay were so different, but maybe Jay's look and demeanor and the fact that he'd been raped kept Khim on edge because he related to it so deeply.

Trev said, "It's not his fault he was raped."

Khim glared at him through lowered lashes. "Isn't it?"

Trev frowned. "No."

"He invites it. The way he's weak. The way he—" He stopped abruptly, a strange pain washing over his face.

Trev said stiffly, "No one invites it. Do they?" He watched to see how Khim would take that. He'd never stopped being curious about what had happened to Khim, but short of asking him outright, there was no way to find out. No prison rumors, nothing.

"He could fight back. If he wanted to," Khim said.

"Or maybe he might never learn to fight properly, and get himself killed for it."

Khim's flesh hand clenched, unclenched. "Some do invite it."

Trev gulped. Sat up straighter, a bold feeling overcoming him. "Did you?"

Khim hunched down, head forward, staring at the floor now. The man had just been talking about fighting, but his training had him posturing like a shamed dog.

"You can't really be telling me you blame yourself for your situation, how you were born, everything about that." Trev was careful. He so wished he could know more about Khim.

"If I had proper controls, I would not be here," he replied, voice just above a whisper.

"Where would you be?"

Khim's lips twitched. "That isn't relevant."

"No?"

"No."

"If you can stand there and tell me victims are to blame for their plight—"

"It's a mind-set!"

Trev sighed. "Then you teach him how to be, how to act. If you think you're so right, why don't you help Jay?"

Khim's blue eyes were on fire. "It's not my job." He paused. "Besides, I can't even help myself."

Very gently, Trev asked what he'd been wanting to ask since he'd first met him. "What happened to you?"

Khim turned away now, moving toward the sink, head still down.

Trev felt as if he were dealing with a wild animal. "If I could understand you better, maybe I'd piss you off less."

"All you need to know is I was a soldier. I learned to fight. Now I can't do that, even when every instinct propels me to it."

"But it's more than that." Trev kept his voice steady. "You've been badly hurt because of it."

Khim's body whirled. Everything about him hard, virile, strong, and big, he trembled as if he stood on the edge of a crumbling cliff. That fierce golden light flamed in him. "You don't need to know these things! Why do you ask me as if you care? This is a simple deal between us. No more."

Instinctively, Trev drew back at the very power of him, brimming. Caught and falling. "I don't think of it like tha—" he began.

Khim turned away, breath coming out fast, and strode out of the cell.

Trev sat there for a moment, stunned. Then he said to the empty air, "What just happened?"

Chapter Sixteen

Khim

Khim moved across the plaza toward the weight rooms. In the corners of his vision were sparkling white lights, tiny fractured droplets as if, in his mind, it had started to rain.

In his chest: a raging furnace.

In his stomach: eels tied in knots.

In his brain: an electrical storm complete with howling winds.

He did not assess his heart behind its transparent barrier. He didn't believe there was any of it left.

Less than two weeks had passed, but he knew now. He was not going to survive this.

It had to end. Now.

He entered the largest weight room, the one he and Trev favored, and looked at the men. Most did not notice his presence, but some glanced up, gazes lingering, mouths scowling.

He walked the length of the room and the small jogging track that hugged the walls, ignoring the sentries, looking at the human faces. Bringing them into his mind, then disregarding them. It was less dry here; a scent bit the air, of sweat and strain. The men looked tough, vibrant, even angry. All the tough dayshine masks they wore were so transparent. Khim had heard them at night, each and every one of them crying into his pillow.

Not finding what he sought, he turned and left, making his way to the second weight room.

More stench of human. More masks to disprove grief. He sniffed about the room, scanned, searched.

And there they were. The little gang making their piss-poor, weak structure of terror at the corner of the room. Playing top dog. Laughing. Toying with a couple of strays. Enfolding them into their plans to do the grunt work, the strays too fearful to turn down the jobs.

At the very center was Deb, standing as if he wore a crown and a velvet cape instead of gray prison fatigues. Arms crossed. Telling the other idiots who followed him—who in all the universes knew why they followed a man like that?—what to do, how to coerce, take, assault, destroy.

Khim strode toward them, noting the sentries' red eyes following his progress, but he didn't care. Maybe they could read his body language. Maybe the robots were already notifying human guards, sending out a warning.

Fight in Weight Room Two. Emergency. Immediate measures necessary. Commence lockdown.

But no alarms went off. Nothing happened. Yet.

One of the gang looked up. "Hey, it's Herc."

Irony crossed Khim's mind for the second time that day. Since Hercules was known for holding up the sky, killing the hydra, capturing a boar, fighting with giants, it seemed quite an appropriate nickname for what he was feeling right now.

He walked right up to the group, stood tall with his head up, shoulders back, and met each and every man's gaze in turn. The faces of the three he sought showed themselves. Strangely, they all stood together with slimy, sloppy, dumb looks that revealed no structural thoughts of their own past what they could take for their own pleasure, for satiation, for getting high. He saw them in his mind again in the shower, naked, sexually aggressive, stupid.

Khim lifted his metal hand and pointed. "You three. Now. It's time."

Deb was sidling over to him, which Khim expected. "Excuse me, android," he drawled. "Do you have a problem with some of my men?"

"They definitely have a problem," Khim said.

"Where's your Damico bodyguard today? Did he toss you out with the rest of the trash when he was done with you, the way their kind does?"

"Do you see him with me? I come alone."

"Let's work this out, then. Like adults," Deb said slowly, body straightening, chin up.

He was the take-charge man. Khim knew the type well. In the wars he'd fought, the human leaders had this manner. They led; the sheep followed. Khim understood this structure. It was often far too artless for his tastes, but necessary.

Deb, like all of them, wanted Khim on his knees. And he would probably stop at nothing to get him there.

Khim turned his slitted gaze on him. "You want to make a deal? Like adults?"

Deb made a tsking sound with his tongue. "It's simple, really. The deal is this. You bend over for me. That's the deal."

All the men, about twelve of them, were coming in closer to surround them. Khim felt their heat and smelled their stink at his back. He had no plan, no idea what he was doing. But he was not afraid. If he was going to die, he was going to take as many of these men down with him as he could.

The storm in his head raged with satisfaction at the idea. The winds inside him snarled at each other, excited.

Khim noted casually that one of the men to his right produced a very small square of metal in his palm. At first he thought it might be a weapon, a homemade knife. But then he saw the guy wave it in a quick circle just above his head.

Something happened then. The sentries froze. He could see it through the crowd of men, the way the robots' red eyes suddenly dimmed and their limbs froze. They were cold now. Temporarily dead.

Other men using the equipment in the room began to leave.

"It's true, then," Deb said, "that you are submissive. All of your kind, beautifully submissive monsters. Aren't I right?"

Khim said, "Have you met an android before?"

"I have."

That surprised Khim somewhat but did not deter him. "Then you know."

Deb's Adam's apple rocked against his neck as he swallowed. "Bow to me, android."

Indeed it seemed Deb might have served in a war. May have even commanded android troops.

Khim felt the corner of his mouth start to curve. The winds blew inside him. He bowed. It was easy. The conditioned muscles knew what to do.

"You see that if you do not obey me, my men will tear you apart. But it's in your programming too. You can fight it, but it feels bad, wrong. Now, kneel for me."

Khim fell gracefully to his knees, controlled and effortless despite his height and musculature weighing him down, knowing the picture he presented to them all—Hercules, a golden light of a man, great, beautiful, and foreboding, offering himself like a sacrifice on an ancient altar of blood. The hard floor came up but did not smack him, did not hurt. He placed his hands behind his back, grasping them. But he kept his head raised, his eyes on Deb.

"Is this enough now?" he asked. "May I settle my score with your men?"

Deb looked down at him, smug, repugnant. "I don't think my men have done anything you need to concern yourself with."

"No?"

"Have they ever touched you? Oh, that's right, they haven't. Not with Damico always around. But even if they had, well, you're a good slave boy, now aren't you? It isn't as if you aren't used to a little rough treatment."

"Used to it? I crave it." The winds became gales.

Deb ignored that last comment. "And you can't fight back without dire consequences. Such a perfect dilemma. And here you are."

Khim knelt, body very still. "Your three men. What do I have to do for you to hand them over to me?"

"My boy, what would you even do with them? All humans are off-limits to you."

The pack of men laughed at that.

"Off-limits, yes," Khim agreed. "But only if I'm caught."

"Is that a threat?"

"I'm on my knees, and you have twelve men. Who is threatening whom?"

Deb laughed. "You even talk like an android. Like a snob. Like the filthy rich environment you no doubt come from. What did you do to land yourself in here? You're worth too much to be thrown away so easily. If you were dangerous, you would've been put down. Is your owner punishing you? For not sucking his cock right? But no, you're good at that, right?"

"All the lie-down models are," Khim replied tightly.

Laughter.

Deb said, chuckling, "The fluffer models."

"The butt-fuck models," someone said from behind Khim.

Khim held his submissive position. The winds inside him grappled for more air.

He watched as, very casually, Deb waved his hand. "He's nothing but a goddamn flavor-of-the-month doll. Wipe the floor with him."

As he gave the order, the men converged.

For a split second, dizziness threatened. Khim saw himself again, kneeling by the red couch, bent over himself, hands over his head as brothel guards punched and kicked him while a dead body with a broken neck lay beside him. His rapist. His victim.

He felt a soft shoe connect at his hip, another at his ribs. He sensed the men behind him bending down. Someone grabbed the hem of his shirt and pulled, tearing it. Khim's eyes never left Deb's defective, cruel gaze.

Something punched him in the jaw. He saw the white lights again, the raindrops. And with the rain, the inner wind came up faster. It shrieked and wept, almost doleful, but inflamed his mind in a fever as if he suffered an infection, rancid but pure, for which there was no cure. A dark weapon blooming.

His mind dimmed to a narrow focus.

The fever coiled, storm-red, iridescent wrath. The height of it crested in a dark, intrinsic justice. Dark revenge.

From one moment to the next, as short as an eye blink, men were standing. And then men were flying. Landing hard. Yelling, bodies thumping against the floor, groaning.

A knee came up to Deb's chin. The leader went down.

Khim saw bodies all around him, shifting, still alive. It didn't matter to him. The three he'd left for last shrunk together, backed up.

It was fast. Like a dance. Efficient but not without symmetry. Elegant. The splendor of hands on the sides of a pale, puffy face with a five-day growth of beard and nothing behind the eyes. The sublime turn-and-click. The pleasure of the sound of the neck cracking.

Then on to the next. His stringy black hair. His nose that had a strange angle, already having seen too many bone-knitters in its time. *Crack.*

The third, heavyset and stupid, mumbling about gods. Liquid fear running from his nose. *Crack.*

One. Two. Three.

Down. Down. Down.

"*Khim!*"

Piles of men at his feet, Khim turned. Right metal hand raised, silver-black and gleaming. Still clean, still perfect. It had all been quite bloodless.

He kept his left hand clasped hard, feeling a small metal-sharp object press against his palm. Something one of the men had, something he did not remember grabbing.

"Khim!" Trev ran forward, grabbed him by the arm, pulled him away from the moaning pile of men.

And the three dead ones.

Khim felt the touch on his arm, started to pull back, then realized Trev was afraid. Trev looked panicked.

"Run!" Trev said in a deep, desperate tone.

The voice, the depth, the *command* of it. He responded instantly, coming out of the rage and into an eerie after-storm light, following Trev's lead, leaping over writhing bodies.

They made it out the entrance where Trev, obviously not wanting to bring attention to them, slowed to a walk, pulling Khim along an outer wall, pressing him hard against it, back to front, as a line of sentries rushed by, followed by half a dozen armed human guards.

Khim felt the press of Trev's body against the very pulsings of his heart under his skin. He went very still.

An alarm began, at first far-off.

The alarm grew in pitch, its tone and color different from random lockdown. This level of emergency meant every man in the prison had to go down on the ground where he stood. Prone. Hands over the head. Legs six inches apart.

Trev dropped to his hands and knees. Khim followed, flattening himself down next to him, left hand still in a tight fist. The plaza was littered with gray-clad men spread out on their stomachs, trying to turn their heads, trying to see what was going on.

More sentries came from all directions like giant roaches skittering across the plaza floors, some taking the stairs to other levels, all weaving about the still men, checking to make sure no one moved, no one threatened.

"Stay still," Trev's whisper commanded. "Don't move. Don't say anything."

Khim realized he had begun to breathe hard. His body had an automatic response to curl up, turn away, blank out.

"Keep hold of yourself," Trev said. "Hang on."

Khim was shaking now.

Trev moved toward him, brushing against him hip to hip, arm to arm. "You don't want to bring attention. Focus. Ground yourself."

A sentry stepped up. "No talking!" it said.

Trev pushed his arm against Khim's; Khim took in the heat as a source of calm. With Trev next to him, grounding him, he closed his eyes, the other man pinpointed in his concentration. He heard Trev's breathing, the shift of his body on the tile. Khim smelled the faint soapy scent of him, the way his fear burned at the edges of that usual sweetness. He opened his eyes again, saw white tile, errant dark bangs, brown eyes holding his own as they lay facing each other; the alarms clanged, the chaos of sentries and more guards gathered in all directions.

Trev mouthed soundlessly, "Stay down."

Khim must've shown some fear in his own eyes, or aggression. Or maybe outright madness. He blinked away tears before they fell, a new sensation he had not noticed before now.

Trev nodded at him. Saying nothing. Mouth firm. Eyes holding his.

Khim felt the metal object still pressing his left hand—the hand of his identchip. If they checked it, they'd find the object. He turned away and slowly slid the metal into the waistband of his trousers.

Sentries kept moving, processing. The alarm kept sounding.

Right now the whole prison was like some strange, alien hive where insects scrambled over their collection of humans.

A sentry passed by them again, assessing. Its head swiveled. "Trevor Damico," it said in its tinny voice. "Stand."

Trev obeyed. Khim saw him straighten, pulling his shirt into place.

The sentry leaned toward Khim. Khim felt his throat quiver where his pulse raced. He clamped down on his muscles tight, tighter, to mask the shaking.

"Khim 18367. Stand," the robot said.

Khim moved to his hands and knees, slowly getting his feet underneath him until he could stand.

"Wrists up," the robot ordered.

Both Khim and Trev raised their wrists for the identchip scan.

"How did you tear your shirt?" the robot asked.

Khim said, "Uh—uh—"

Trev interrupted. "Don't you remember? Earlier in the day at the weights, it caught in a tiny snag on the metal. We laughed about it because the weights came down and we heard the tear." Trev laughed lightly.

Khim said, "Yes. We went to the laundry. They did not have extra shirts."

"He means," Trev said quickly, "that they had shirts. Just not in that size. He's not just a large, he's a triple large. But there's a lot of big guys in here so they were out of stock."

The robot said, "Quiet. Trevor Damico, the question was not directed at you."

Trev nodded, teeth worrying his lower lip.

The sentry's head moved back and forth, one to the other, watching them, processing.

The robot faced Khim again. "What are you doing in this area?"

Khim said around the tightness in his throat, "We were about to line up for dinner."

"The dinner is delayed tonight," the robot said. "Go back to your cell."

Other men around them were getting up on the orders of sentries, shuffling across the white floor.

The sentry who questioned them escorted them up to the second level. When they entered their cell, the force field hummed to life.

Trev stood in the center of the cell.

Khim stood to the side, his back to the wall by the toilet.

Trev's hair was mussed, darkly tangled against his temples, long strands falling in curves against his eyes. He had the most frantic but determined look about him, like a sprite just captured in a glass jar.

Khim thought for that one moment—and maybe it wasn't even the first time—that Trev looked quite beautiful. He forgot for a second that he had just killed three men.

An unusual burning, not quite pain, rippled up from his abdomen and into his chest.

Khim watched Trev's lips part, his chest expand with a deep breath. Then he heard Trev say, "We have to get out of here."

A chill immediately replaced the strange fluttering he felt in Trev's presence, flowing its way up Khim's spine and spreading over his entire body. "The cell?"

"No, the prison."

Khim knew that was what he meant, but he could barely acknowledge such a thought. It was so forbidden. So wrong. But not as wrong as killing three unarmed men. He shook his head as if to clear it.

"It's only a matter of time now," Trev said. "They'll figure it out."

Khim's hands were shaking again.

Trev said, "You need to sit down."

Khim ignored him, moved his hand to his waistband, pulled out the metal device. "This is how they freeze the sentries. I think it loops the cameras back onto themselves too."

Trev looked at the thing in Khim's hand. "A remote device. I know all about how they work." He took it from Khim. "Now, you need to sit before you fall."

"I don't—" Khim started to protest, but Trev's hand was on him, pulling him toward the bunks.

"Are you hurt?" Trev asked.

"No." Khim sat. "Maybe some bruising."

"They kicked you?"

"Yes."

Trev stood before him. "It was a really, really stupid thing you did!" Khim glared at him. "How can our deal protect you if you run off like that? They were out to get you, catch you off guard, and you just walked right into it? I had a hell of a time finding you."

"I sought them." Now Khim bowed his head, unable to meet Trev's eyes anymore. "The three who raped Jay, they are dead."

Khim heard Trev swallow twice. The sound was followed by a single body-shudder, then silence.

"I told you I should have been put down," Khim said, staring at his knees.

Now Trev knelt before him. "But why didn't they? That's the question. And the answer is obvious. Someone must have seen that you didn't deserve it. What did you do that you think you should be put down for? What did you do to land yourself here?"

"I killed a man." He paused. "Now I have killed again."

"Murder. I've never heard of it with an—an android. Not and have them remain, uh, living. You're not telling me everything."

"I was… assaulted. Severely injured. I had a good attorney. A lenient judge."

"Was it self-defense?" Trev asked.

"Yes."

"Is that when your programming malfunctioned? I mean, your conditioning?"

"Yes."

"Isn't it supposed to be fail-safe?"

"I think so. But I'm a soldier. We're different, trained to kill. So the conditioning is different. If you change the conditions, the conditioning changes—perhaps?" He ended his words in a question, for he truly did not know.

"I don't know," Trev said gently. "I know more about sentries than I do about the conditioning of vat-grown clones. Or brainwashing human beings."

Khim nodded. "We're human. Just like anyone else. I suppose if you break us sufficiently, all bets are off."

"They knew this and they put you in with the general population here?"

"I don't know if the lawyer and judge knew my conditioning was broken. But my advocate, Mr. Weatherford, knows."

"That's crazy. I mean for your own sake too, Khim."

Khim almost wanted to smile at those words. Trev was an enigma. "Maybe my wealthy owners are behind it. I don't know. Money buys a lot of cooperation."

"Don't I know it," Trev said. "Remember, I'm a Damico."

Khim tried not to wince. He wasn't about to reveal all of himself. He did not yet completely trust Trev. Trev was, after all, still part of the family who owned him, no matter his temporary incarceration.

Trev looked like his mind was moving at light speed. He finally said, "You really killed those three men just now?"

Khim nodded, remembering it all in a kind of blur, but still feeling the men's heads in his hands, still hearing the strange, muffled crack as their necks broke. "I think I'm going to be sick now."

Trev backed up, let him stand and move to the toilet. Khim leaned down. He'd rarely been sick a day in his life. It was so odd when the contents of his stomach splashed into the water before him. As he gagged, the bitterness in his throat increased.

When it seemed he was done, he dragged himself back to the bed.

Trev was there again. He touched his hand.

Khim pulled it away.

Trev said, "Hey, I was just checking. Your skin is clammy. You're in shock. You need to stay still, okay? Are you cold?"

142

No one had ever fussed over Khim before, not since Aric at the birthing vats, who'd pulled him from his tank.

"I've killed before."

"On orders. In wartime. Even so, I hear it drives men mad. But you were conditioned for that. Not for this."

Khim swallowed, the sourness of it all washing over him. Finally he lay back, pulling his legs up to the mattress.

He heard Trev moving about the cell, doing something at the sink. He closed his eyes. Saw men flying. Saw men writhing in pain on the gym floor.

I am a very dangerous man. I can't be allowed to continue.

With that thought in the forefront of his mind, he fell into a dissociative doze.

Chapter Seventeen

Trev

Trev watched over Khim as he finally slept.

Lockdown was still in progress. They'd probably miss dinner altogether tonight.

Three men were dead. The prison was in an uproar.

Trev tried to ignore the curdling, eerie feeling that crept over his body and bristled his veins in his legs, arms, back. It left his skin goose-bumped, prickly. As he watched Khim, it was difficult to imagine that face, now softened in repose, was that of a murderer. An uncontrolled maniac. No, not quite. Provoked. A man provoked beyond all rational thought. That was not sheer mania. In fact, it was not truly crazy. Not if there were reasons.

Khim's sleep was fitful. His arms flew up. His body writhed.

The beautiful being who fought in his sleep, who tossed from dark dreamings as Trev watched him nap, who had one of the deepest gazes of any man Trev had ever met, was being destroyed from within.

He was like a bad fairy tale come to life. An animal with a thorn wedged deeply in its brain. An artifact the best museum technicians had failed to preserve.

The man had murdered three men.

And probably thousands more in his stint as a soldier.

But none of that seemed to matter next to Trev's intense urge to save him.

This was a man who had at first refused to share a cell with Trev. Who had attacked Trev the very moment they were alone together. A man who'd said he didn't need Trev's help.

When had it started for Trev, then—this feeling, this almost automatic urge to protect?

With the apple, maybe. Or later, the sharing of books. Or maybe simply the hours they'd spent during lockdown playing cards knee-to-knee on Trev's top bunk.

Trev had lived his entire life under the control of another. Maybe that was why he could empathize. He'd never had any other choice in life but to work for Dante. He was a criminal by his father's command. He was good at what he did. The best. It was the only way he could make himself proud of who he was, what he was. If he could make his father proud and happy, then the pressure of being a Damico lessened. But happiness in that household was moment to moment. You had to make it where you could find it. Escape was impossible. Trev had thought he'd found a way out, but he'd been an idiot.

He, his brothers, and his sisters did crazy things sometimes to alleviate stress, to rebel. Everything from fighting among themselves to getting drunk and crashing fliers. Every little thing they got caught doing from childhood on culminated in severe punishment. Privileges taken, money docked, luxuries swept away for weeks at a time. And an afternoon chained to a pole in a cold room, waiting for the whipping.

The last time Trev had been whipped by Dante, he had been late too many times for the family meeting. A misdemeanor, surely.

But not to Dante.

Trev, clad only in trousers, had shivered and cursed while chained to the whipping pole, waiting. Two hours had passed that last time before Dante showed up with his suit jacket off and his white sleeves folded up his tanned forearms. Always he would say, "This hurts me as much as it hurts you."

The whippings were more humiliating than anything else. The helplessness, the lack of control—it all led to a kind of horrible inner shame of not being good enough, right enough, strong enough.

The whip made a strange crying sound as it folded the air around it. The crack of it against Trev's skin always made him jump. The sting resonated through his bones, heart, lungs, like the painful sting of a giant horror-show wasp.

Depending on Dante's mood and the nature of the disobedience, it might be five lashes. Or ten. Never more than fifteen. But past five was always enough to elicit tears. And the final sorrow was when Dante would unchain him, look him in the eye as he held his bare shoulders in his grip, and say, "You understand why I do this."

He would always have a warm, damp cloth to wipe away the tears. He would do it gently, close and personal. Then he would say, "It is because I love you."

The scene always ended in a hug and Dante unlocking the door, offering a robe or other clothing, and stating the time for their next meal, saying, "I expect you to be there."

Not all meals were mandatory. But the ones after whippings were.

The comfort Dante gave should have chilled Trev. But he always craved it, believed it. Until that last time. A whipping for being late? He was twenty-three years old. Well past childhood. He resented his lack of freedom. He resented his father. That was when he'd begun to plan how to get away.

How stupid he had been.

Trev looked over at Khim again for the hundredth time. He knew what life as an indentured being was like, knew the extremes the mind went to in order to find a way out.

Today Khim had sought out his aggressors on a suicide mission. He'd thought he would be caught.

And now Trev found himself thinking, *I have to make sure he gets away with it. I have to make sure he survives.*

He could hear men's voices from the other cells, some low murmurings, others starting to yell.

Many of the men demanded loudly, "You can't keep us from dinner! We've done nothing wrong!"

Another sound came underneath the chatter. Metal footsteps followed by booted ones.

Trev turned to look beyond the force field to the metal deck, saw a half-dozen sentries approaching from the right followed by four armed guards. They gathered at Trev and Khim's cell. The force field zinged off.

Trev's skin went cold.

"Trevor Damico. Khim 18367. You are to come with us."

Out the corner of his eye, Trev saw Khim awaken abruptly. The big man rolled out of the bunk and neatly into a standing position. He showed no emotion.

There was nothing else to do but follow the guards and sentries.

They went through Gate 6, its round aperture spinning open to let them through to a corridor with a big window showing a star field to the right.

Trev was taken to one room, Khim to another.

Trev's room was bare except for a table and some chairs. Two sentries stood in different corners.

A robot hand on his shoulder forced Trev to sit. The chair was plain, plastic, hard.

A man in a guard's uniform that was red instead of blue sat across the table in another plain chair. He had digital screens in front of him. He looked up after a minute. "Trevor Dante Damico."

"Yes." Trev had already had his identchip scanned three times on the way there.

"I just have a few questions."

"Yes, sir." Trev's heart hitched in a weird rhythm. He waited.

"Do you have knowledge of events today in Weight Room Two just before lockdown?"

"No, sir."

"Do you know of anyone who might have knowledge of events today in Weight Room Two just before lockdown?"

"No, sir."

"Can you explain what you were doing in the area just before lockdown?"

"I had come to the plaza to line up for dinner."

"The lineup procedure had not yet started."

"I was hungry. I wanted to get there early to be toward the front of the line."

The guard tapped one of the screens on the table.

"Was your cellmate, Khim 18367, in the vicinity at that time?"

"Yes. He was with me."

"You did not see him going into the weight room at any time?"

147

"No, sir. We were in Weight Room One earlier in the day, though."

"Interesting, since we have cameras in the plaza showing he did in fact enter. And we have cameras in the plaza showing that you walked across the plaza toward Weight Room Two 1.45 minutes later. You are not seen entering, but the cameras had stopped working at that time."

Trev said nothing. There had been no question.

"Another 0.51 minutes later, you and Khim are seen in the plaza area together. But for a span of 0.51 minutes, you are missing from the plaza area. None of the cameras see you go in, but they cannot detect you in the plaza either."

"I did not go in," Trev said, keeping his voice steady. "And neither did Khim."

"Khim went in before you. Then you and he are seen standing in the plaza when the alarm goes off. How do you account for that?"

"Camera malfunction?" Trev asked, eyes narrowed.

"You do know we will get to the bottom of this. Your cellmate is being questioned even now."

"I'm sure he will say the same thing I have," Trev said. "Because it is the truth." But the truth was that his pulse was raging. He could barely keep from shaking.

"Maybe some time in solitary will shock your memory back in place."

Trev's vision suddenly blurred. He blinked.

The questioner said, "Take him!"

Cold hands jerked him up by the arms and out the open door.

Once in the hall, they moved quickly. Trev didn't have time to wonder or even think. All he could do was stumble along; their hands pushed and pulled him along the corridor.

He was more afraid than he ever had been in his life. But not for himself. For Khim. Trev knew he would survive this. But Khim—Khim was in mortal danger.

They went down the hall and through several sets of doors. Farther into shadow. Into the unknown.

I might never see Khim again.

148

*

They passed a series of small doors ranged very close together. Trev stumbled several more times. He heard no sound coming from this place. Only emptiness. Only silence. A stale scent filled his nostrils.

He had a sentry on either side of him, a human guard in front, and a human guard following close behind. They stopped in front of one of the little doors.

The guard in front of him said, "Clothes."

"What?" Trev looked at the guard's no-nonsense face, chiseled, dark, firm.

"Remove all clothing."

"All of it?"

"All clothes. Now!"

Trev began to disrobe. When he got down to his shorts, he asked, "Shorts too?"

"All clothes."

Trev had let his clothes fall to the floor in a pile. The shorts soon followed.

One of the sentries bent and held a wand to the door. A series of lights flashed violet, amber, pink. The door sprung open.

"Get in," the guard who'd opened the door said.

The door was maybe five feet high. Trev had to duck low to walk through it. On the other side, an abrupt darkness came up so swiftly and fiercely around him that he lost his balance and fell. His knees hit the hard floor. Then the stars came out.

All around him, floor to ceiling, wall to wall, was blackness pricked by millions of stars. The entire room was one small transparent cube.

The door slammed behind him. He heard the buzz of the lock. On his hands and knees, naked and completely exposed, Trev could only gasp.

He became immediately disoriented and nauseated. Was there even a toilet?

149

Trying to clear his mind, he glanced about and saw a low square off in one corner. He crawled over to investigate.

The toilet was no more than a box with a darkness deep inside, but if he had to throw up, it was right there. Beside that box was an indentation in the clear floor, and sticking out, as if from black nothingness, was a spigot. When he ran his hand under it, water flowed.

That was it for the niceties. He had no bed, no towel, no toilet paper that he could find, nothing. He drew his legs up, closed his eyes, and huddled against the wall the spigot came out of.

The air felt cold, but not too cold—just enough to be uncomfortable.

Trev rested his head against his knees. *So,* he thought to himself. *Solitary is like falling through the stars.*

He wondered how many days he would be here.

He began to cry.

Chapter Eighteen

Khim

Khim saw blue salt flats. Astral-flecked skies. Starships that looked like the very stars were lashed to their hulls. Constellations cupped in the leftover bowls of ruined planets.

Fires soared and died in space. On the surfaces of alien worlds, the sounds of the pulse beams and the laser shards and the phase bullets always sounded the same in any atmosphere. Like death.

Sometimes he thought he'd never stop smelling the burned ozone of the wars.

The man in the red guard's suit was asking him a question.

Khim came out of his daydream long enough to say, "I don't know."

They had asked him many questions. Why he and Trev were in the plaza. Why they had both been gone for short intervals.

He had answered, "For the dinner lineup" and "Maybe a camera malfunction."

They were not satisfied. They asked him how his shirt got torn.

"Caught on one of the weights in Weight Room One earlier in the day."

But he had been caught in a lie. They could see the shirt was not torn when the cameras had spied him going into Weight Room Two just before lockdown. And after he showed up on the camera feeds in the plaza, standing next to Trev, his shirt appeared clearly torn.

Did he have an explanation for that? they wanted to know.

"I don't," he said.

War was an art. He knew what to do if caught by the enemy, questioned. He knew how to evade. He could withstand torture, on command, and had been conditioned to do so. He'd never questioned that conditioning. Until he was sold.

Now everything was different. Now there were new rules.

He did not notice when they stopped talking to him, but he felt the sharp sentry hands on him pulling him up, pushing him out the door. Things weren't right. He wasn't seeing right. He wasn't hearing right.

They took him farther into a maze of corridors, somewhere far along one of the arms of the prison space station, away from the hub.

They came to a hall with dozens of small doors. They stopped in front of one door. A human guard in blue ordered him to strip.

He complied, tossing his clothing toward the hard floor. A sentry unlocked the short door with a series of light flickers and shoved Khim through.

He stood, breathing hard, blind at first, seeing nothing.

Then the stars came out.

He took a deep breath, let it slowly move through his lungs. Solitary was a room nestled in the darkness between the stars. For a spaceman soldier like Khim, it was stunningly beautiful.

For the first time since his arrival at Steering Star, he felt utterly safe.

*

Khim lay flat on the clear floor, looking down, down into the depths of space. The way the stars and all that blackness spun into his brain was a comfort to him.

To the side, dangling like a jewel made of sapphire and foam, spun the blue orb of Gideon.

Perhaps he was insane to think this was not torture, not punishment at all. He didn't care. He knew he was broken. And he probably did not have very much longer to live.

He counted the days by the meals. After three were served, he knew another day had been completed. The food came in bland protein tubes, much like the sludge he'd first been fed as a newborn android in the vat rooms. Sometimes they had it in the battlefields. He was used to it.

When he slept, he did not know if he slept hours or minutes. When he got bored, he did push-ups, sit-ups, or paced his way back and forth in the tiny room across the stars.

Often he thought of Trev and wondered if he was in a room like this. Sensory deprivation of this sort did not bother Khim, but he suspected Trev might not react well to it. He allowed himself to worry about him only because it was Khim's fault they were here. Khim had made an untrained, rash, aggressive decision. It had resulted in casualties. Trev was one. The only one he felt badly about. After everything, he could no longer hate the guy just for being a Damico.

His memories returned often to battles he had fought and won, to images of old ships burning from within and atmospheres turning pink on destroyed planets.

But he continued to think a lot about Trev too, for there was little else to occupy his mind, and memories of war often ended up looking all the same.

It was interesting that he could allow himself to worry about Trev. He'd never worried about anyone before. What conditioning Khim had left after the House of Xavier ordeal responded to something in Trev. It was not just the Damico name, although that did contribute somewhat. It was something more, something he felt beyond their deal. The deal had been made to help him survive, keep the other inmates at bay.

But he hadn't expected how easy it would be to follow Trev's lead, to listen to him, to respond to his voice. And he had not considered the fact that Trev was just so likable.

Trev, it seemed, took their deal quite seriously. After Khim had run out of the cell, Trev did not have to follow.

The deal had been for Trev to keep others away, not to protect Khim from himself. But Trev took it all the way, every day, speaking softly to Khim when he didn't have to, his voice soothing, asking if he was all right or breaking through Khim's tensions by saying two simple words: "It's okay."

When that happened, Khim felt places open up inside him that he had rarely, if ever, accessed before, not even when he read stories or watched holomovies. Areas of his mind that had seemed once removed now swung wide their gates—hope at the memory of the dawning of a full alien moon, images of a real home where a fire burned and trees whispered in the night. He dreamed of one day putting himself to some task that did not involve duty, weapons, killing. Might he ever paint a picture or write a warrior poem?

It both scared and intrigued him.

When he'd had thoughts like these in the past, they'd touched him only briefly, as remote as a wisp of alien pollen on wind.

Now, whenever he looked at Trev, the oddness of hope, possibility, and comfort swept through him.

He was perhaps days away from certain death. To have these feelings probably made him the most ridiculous android in existence.

He shifted his weight on the floor to stretch his muscles, turning onto his back. Stars above, stars below.

Maybe this was a tiny introduction into what death would be. If so, he would welcome it. He would miss nothing of his life.

Except, maybe, the quickness of Trev's smile.

He lay back, allowed his lips to curve up, and fell asleep.

*

They came for Khim on what he had counted as the third day. The short door in the corner, where blackness met a dimmer blackness, opened. Piercing white light shone through, momentarily blinding him, stinging his eyes.

A voice ordered, "Come out!"

Khim stood unsteadily and made his way to the door. He felt grimy, though the room was dust free. He felt desperately threatened by the light.

As he ducked his head to get through the archway, a metal hand grasped his forearm and pulled him through.

Two human guards and two sentries stood outside the solitary cell and faced him.

One human held out a pile of clothing. "Dress," he ordered.

Eyes still stinging from the light, Khim took the clothes. He climbed into a pair of pants that were too tight and too short. The shirt also barely fit him. He said, "These are too small."

154

The guard said, "You can walk to the showers naked if you prefer."

Pleasure trickled through him at the thought of warm water. He said, "No. I'm fine."

The showers were empty as the guards and Khim entered together. Khim could not tell if it was late morning or late afternoon. Or it could have been mealtime and they'd brought him to shower while all the other inmates were eating.

The sentries went to the door. The two human guards stood to the side of the stall, looking bored as Khim stripped again, put his clothes on a bench, and showered.

Khim did not have his own soap or shampoo, but he found a dispenser in the shower and used it.

The water fell about him like a warm cape. It wakened him. He stretched muscles he hadn't felt in a long time. His mind numbed out, and he remembered a soothing moment, standing outside a waiting transport after a long, exhausting battle, caught in a hot rainstorm. By the time he'd boarded the vessel, all the blood on his armor had been washed clean. He was brand-new again, like coming from the birthing vats. All ready for his next mission.

Now he stood under the spray long after he'd rinsed off.

He heard one of the guards step forward, boot on tile. "Out! Now!"

Khim stepped away, and the spray of warmth ceased. He found a fresh towel by his clothes and used it. Then he got back into the tight garments as quickly as he could.

He followed the guards into the entryway, thinking they would take him back to the narrow hall, the short door, the star room that was solitary.

Instead they escorted him, hair still dripping, into the plaza and up the metal stairs to the second level. They stopped in front of his and Trev's cell. The force field was on. A sentry unlocked it, and a human guard motioned Khim inside.

Trev was already there, barefoot and disheveled, struggling with his mattress, which was halfway over the edge of the top bunk, nearly fallen to the floor.

Khim heard the force field hum to life behind him and the sentries' footsteps clanging on the deck.

He surveyed the cell. It was a complete mess.

His mattress lay in a corner by the toilet. All their toiletries were scattered about the floor, some under Khim's lower bunk. Their towels and washcloths lay in a pile near the sink.

Without even thinking, Khim moved beside Trev, put his metal hand under the mattress, and lifted effortlessly, pushing it up onto the bunk.

Trev turned to look at him. "Thanks."

Dark hair tangled on the high forehead. Soft, honey-brown eyes. Khim's heart skipped. He'd missed those eyes. He realized he really had believed he might never see Trev again. "When did you get back?" he asked.

"Only a few minutes ago," Trev answered. His voice came out hoarse. His face was drained of health, almost a pale gold.

"What happened?"

"They searched our cell while we were gone."

"For what?" He remembered the remote as soon as he asked the question. "Oh."

Trev turned to pick up his pillow. "They didn't find anything."

"How do you know?"

"If they did, we wouldn't both be here now."

Khim nodded, watching Trev pick up piles of sheets, untangling his from Khim's. "You hid it, then."

Trev nodded, dropped the sheets, and went to the sink, looking around. Finally he stooped and picked up a bar of soap. He threw it at Khim.

Khim caught it easily, looking it over carefully. He saw a dent in one side. The soap wasn't hard, but it wasn't soft either. He peered at the dent and saw it was a rift that went all the way through the middle of the bar. Something dark lay inside. "It's in here. That was smart."

"I didn't know where else to put it. I cut myself getting it in there."

156

Khim put the soap on the edge of the sink. He began to help Trev straighten their belongings, make the beds. Trev's hands were unsteady.

"How did you fare these past days?" Khim asked hesitantly.

Trev did not look at him. "I was sick the whole time."

Khim's spirit was raw, open. As if he continued to float among the stars. "I would not have willingly involved you," he began.

"But I am involved." Trev was frowning, his eyes glittery as he turned. He looked Khim up and down.

Khim froze, waiting for Trev to unleash some kind of fury, although Trev was not the type to hold grudges, let alone fury toward others. He watched as Trev's face contorted, twisted a little. But what came from his mouth was a laugh that grew.

Trev caught his breath and said, "They gave you the wrong size of clothes. Those barely cover… anything."

Khim looked down. His legs were bare almost to the knee. The shirt was so small it was like a crop top, revealing his tight, flat abdomen. His drawstring pants weren't even tied. There was no extra string left to pull through the holes.

"Idiots," Trev muttered, turning away again. "How could anyone forget they put a giant in solitary?"

Even in this horrible place, in the dark pit of his broken conditioning, Khim wanted to smile. No one had ever spoken to him that way. No one had ever cared to.

But his mind was drawn back to what Trev had said before that. *I was sick the whole time.* Trev looked exhausted. Khim had no idea when the sentries would let them out of their cell, so he hurried to finish sorting everything and completed making the beds.

Trev watched him, eyelids heavy. "Thanks," he said when Khim finished.

"A mattress and a warm blanket. Then food, perhaps?" Khim said. It was all he had to offer by way of medical treatment.

Trev did not leap up to his bunk as usual. He climbed slowly up the end, crawling under his covers. "I don't even know what time it is." He yawned.

"Me either. I didn't get a look at the plaza clock on the way back."

Trev turned on his side, facing the wall.

Khim said, "I won't let you miss dinner. Hopefully something other than gray sludge tonight."

Trev made a little disgusted sound and pulled the blanket tighter about his neck.

Khim sat on his own bunk and stared at the bar of soap on the sink, considering his options.

Chapter Nineteen

Trev

Trev never wanted to go back to solitary again. Sure, everyone liked stargazing, but floating among waves of suns as if being continually drawn down into the throat of night made him miserably seasick. He figured that was intentional in the design. Solitary was not supposed to be fun.

He woke in a fog to Khim's touch gentle on his shoulder. "Do you want to eat?" came the golden voice.

He rolled to the side. Khim's hand did not snatch away as he'd expected. It went with him, only drawing back a few seconds later. He could not remember Khim initiating touch of any kind before.

"Okay." He pushed his way out of the covers and jumped to the floor, looking for his shoes.

When he glanced up, he saw that Khim had normal-fitting attire again. "What happened to your summertime clothes?"

Khim said, "A sentry came by with these. Surprisingly the correct size. They also brought shoes for both of us. Also the correct size."

"They're robots. They shouldn't make mistakes. All that info is in our records."

Khim stood by as Trev sat on the edge of the lower bunk and put on his shoes.

At that moment, Jay walked by. "Hey, you guys are back!"

Trev glanced up, stomach muscles tightening. He watched Khim for a reaction.

Jay said, "Did you hear what happened?" Trev and Khim just looked at him. "You've been gone, so I'll tell ya. Those guys, you know, from the showers—uh, they're dead. They're saying they all got into some brawl in one of the weight rooms. That gang, Deb's gang, turned on some of their own."

"That's what they're saying?" Trev asked.

"Yeah. What are the odds? You know, those guys. They had it in for me." His smile wavered. His happy-go-lucky countenance was marred for a moment by a sudden spring of tears that did not fall. He looked so pale and vulnerable, wisps of his dirty-blond hair trailing along his cheeks. Trev could not guess at his age, but right now he looked no more than eighteen.

Trev watched as Khim's fists closed at his sides. He bowed his golden head. It looked as if Khim might whisk his way past Jay without even acknowledging him. Instead he took a step toward him, raised his flesh hand, and patted him once on the shoulder. "Fortune does not always favor the bold."

Jay looked up at him adoringly. "Did you just speak to me?"

Khim shook his head, looking annoyed.

Trev felt himself start to smile. Solitary did not seem to have done Khim any harm.

It had been a long time since Trev had eaten real food. He stood up. "I'm ready. Let's go eat."

*

Jay heard gossip; like a little mouse, he was everywhere at once. He sat across from Trev and Khim at dinner and bent to his food as he spoke.

"After you guys got taken away, I saw a lot of men called in for questioning. For two days they brought guys in, anyone who had been in the plaza near Weight Room Two."

"Why are you telling us this?" Trev asked.

"Because it's about you, and I eavesdrop. You know me. I heard a bunch of them talking at dinner one night. Kant, I think his name is, and others. He told them to stay resolute. Yeah, he used that word. *Resolute.* I heard him say, 'Don't mention Damico or that android he has on a leash, or there'll be hell to pay.'"

Jay shot Khim an apologetic look and shrugged. "So," he continued. "I guess they all denied seeing anything in that room where the guys got whacked. But you guys were around there, right? I mean, that's why you went to solitary."

160

Trev said nothing.

Khim said nothing.

Jay said, "So, what happened?"

"Nothing happened," Trev replied.

Jay nodded. "They didn't believe you. That's why you were sent to solitary."

Trev said very firmly, "They never told us why they sent us there."

Jay took a bit of meat and gravy, chewing around a small smile. "So really nothing happened?"

Trev nodded.

Jay looked from Trev to Khim and back again. Then he said, after he swallowed, "Thanks for the nothing, then. A whole lot."

Trev looked at Khim, who had stopped eating. His hands were in his lap, one placed over the other, the top one—flesh—gripping the metal. Trev looked back at Jay. "We won't speak of this ever again, you hear?"

Jay nodded.

Khim sat like a stone at Trev's side.

*

Trev watched from the edge of the white wall, his back to the stars so he wouldn't have to see them—the sight still too fresh from solitary—as Khim showed Jay how to work the Artflex 2000. Trev had crossed his arms over his chest, his sweat-damp hair hanging in his eyes as he leaned.

Khim instructed Jay how to straighten his arms, where to hold the straps, where to place his legs. He helped him adjust the seat. He even set the timer for him.

This scene sat right next to the one in his memory of Khim standing in a sea of writhing bodies, two dead men at his feet and a third falling from his arms, the body sagging to the floor.

Trev would never forget it.

Khim was becoming more human by the day, and more dangerous too. If he hadn't been an android, it wouldn't matter. But every step Khim took toward unpredictable emotionality placed him in a position of greater vulnerability.

Once Khim got Jay going on his own in the exercise machine, he backed away, glancing over at Trev.

Trev nodded, beckoning him over.

Khim came without hesitation. His shirt was off. His arms gleamed, copper curved muscles rippling, his strong chest stretching the cotton of his undershirt. It was like looking at a sun god. When he stopped two feet from Trev, Trev smelled the fresh-bread scent again, and a lingering sweetness. A fluttering began in his gut.

Trev said, "We need to get out of here."

"The weight room?"

They'd had this conversation right before they were taken for questioning and then placed in solitary.

"This prison. Even when I was sick in solitary, I was thinking about it all the time. About the remote you stole. It's why I hid it. It's a start." His thief instincts had come into play. He saw the challenge— had been seeing it for days now—and knew he could win it. "Tell me the thought hasn't occurred to you since I brought it up days ago."

"It has."

"I've never told you my story of how I came to be here. Now you're going to hear it. And then you'll understand how this can be done."

They sat by the stars on one of the couches, and Trev began his story.

A few times they were interrupted by Jay as he finished one set and moved on to other equipment. Khim assisted him when needed, then came back to sit with Trev.

"So you see," Trev finished. "My father cannot be trusted. Not for a moment. But maybe a few of my brothers and sisters can."

"But you can't be sure." Khim seemed to be gritting his teeth.

Trev shook his head. "But we're going to need someone on the outside. Maybe I can think of someone else."

"Are you thinking of taking the boy too?" Khim nodded toward Jay, now on the cycle, looking flushed and winded.

Trev was surprised at the statement. "I think it has to be you and me. Alone. I trust no one else."

"You trust me?" Khim asked.

"Well, we have that deal, right?" Trev let out a small laugh.

"Right. But that deal was for me."

"And me. Friendship, right?"

But they both knew it was more than that. Trev had witnessed Khim murder three men. It was Khim who was in the position of needing to trust Trev. With his very life.

"Do you trust me?" Trev sometimes thought the android still resented him, hated him as he had the first day they met.

"You saved me," Khim said, looking away. "You never again have to ask that."

*

Trev turned over his cards. "Gin."

Khim ducked his head as if annoyed, looked up through dark gold lashes. "You didn't shuffle enough."

"Are you accusing me of cheating?" Trev asked.

"Isn't that the Damico way?"

Trev did not get offended when Khim said stuff like that. Anyone else and he would've been. He gathered up the cards and handed them to Khim. "Your deal."

They sat knee to knee on Trev's top bunk. It was almost nine. Almost lights-out.

The remote sat between them, newly programmed and reassembled, hidden under a fold of blanket. They'd been working on it nonstop after dinner.

They had spent days going over the remote whenever they had the chance, during lockdowns in their cell or in the hours after dinner and before bedtime. They played cards to hide their work. Trev had taken it apart, analyzed the parts, tried to see what he could use to augment the device and give them options so they could begin their plan.

Trev had computer knowledge and had built a sentry when he was a kid. Khim had excellent knowledge of remotes used in weapons-delivery systems, so his assistance was equally valuable.

They assessed, analyzed, and tested. They checked out earbuds, one each per night, and programmed some of the information on them into the remote to transmit erroneous behavior into the sentries.

The first time they tested it on the sentry at the corner of their second-level stairwell, they had transferred a segment from a holo musical into the remote's delivery system. When they pointed it at the sentry and activated it, the sentry started to sing, in perfect pitch, a horrible song from *The Phantom of the Centauri Listening Station*. The sentry began to belt out in contralto, "The void is alive with the sound of quasars…."

Before the anomaly got the attention of other inmates, Trev hissed through barely repressed laughter, "Turn it off!"

It was days later now, and they'd fixed the thing so that it had a quick, domino-viral effect, ensuring all the sentries would be infected. They were going to introduce a contagion to the automated sentry systems of Steering Star.

Now all they had left to do was plan their way out through a series of locked spiral doors, penetrate an air lock, and commandeer a flier. Not to mention evade all the human guards who operated the complex.

"The rest of our tasks are simple now that we have the remote programmed," Trev stated, watching Khim shuffle the deck.

Khim laid the cards on the bed for Trev to cut. "Simple," he echoed sarcastically.

Trev reached out, divided the pack, then handed the cards back to him. "I've been in complexes with the highest security ratings. I remained undetected."

"But you had equipment at your disposal," Khim said.

"Yep. Bodysuits. Full-on computers hooked up to the wave. Candle tubes."

"You know those are illegal on nine hundred worlds?"

"Really? I thought it was nine hundred and one."

Khim said softly, "With the sentries down, or preoccupied, we can take their wands. But they won't work unless they are programmed to the user. I think I know a way around that, but—"

Trev watched him begin to deal. "That'll get us through the first sets of doors."

"I can handle the human guards."

"I have no doubt. Can you do it without killing?"

"Of course. I know quite well how to disarm an enemy."

Trev nodded. "They'll have weapons and more keys. Door 8 is the one where the fliers are parked. We'll need codes for after we board, too, just to break away. They still might chase us. I can disconnect the tracking system and the computer. I've done it on fliers before."

"Have you been chased before?"

"Of course. Cops on my tail." Trev grinned. "Evasive maneuvers. Loop the loops. My life before now was very exciting and grand."

"Then whyever would you wish to leave that life?" Khim asked.

Trev bowed his head, looking at his cards, organizing them in his hand by ranking. "Hmm," he said. "Another good hand."

Khim was waiting for him to discard.

Touching each card in turn, Trev said, "If you'd ever met my family, you wouldn't ask that question." He discarded the two of diamonds.

Khim's wince did not go unnoticed. Trev had seen that look at least two dozen times whenever he mentioned his father, his siblings, his name.

Khim picked up the two. "I know your father had you put here because you tried to run away. But it seems you did actually have it quite good."

Trev tensed at a slight heat in his veins. "Yeah. Putting up with a whipping now and then seems like nothing, I suppose. I had luxury. I was a real good thief. Like you in the military—the best soldier. The most efficient survivor. That's all we need in life, right? Stuff to do so we don't have to think 'what if.' People to tell us what to do and when.

No one expecting us to seriously answer the question, when we were kids or newly born, 'What do you want to be when you grow up?'"

"Young people tend to believe they have infinite choices in life. But when they start making those choices, they find themselves quickly limited. Our plight is no different."

"Or maybe that's what you kept telling yourself for the past ten years," Trev suggested. "So you could live within the limits and not feel—well, sad."

"They have medication for sadness."

"I know they do. Isn't it wonderful? The lengths we go to for control, us wily, conniving humans."

Khim looked up, frowning. Trev met his eyes. Then Trev asked the big, nagging question. "How do you know my family name?"

Khim was the first to look away. Trev watched him shrug, then saw his energy fold into itself almost neatly. He had not yet discarded from his hand.

Trev tapped the discard pile. "Waiting."

Khim seemed to grab a card at random and place it between them.

Trev took a card from the mystery pile. "You don't have to tell me. But it seems to me that you react to the name by more than its reputation alone."

Trev discarded an eight.

Khim stared at it, then looked toward the side of the bunk. He lay all his cards down, faceup. They were chaos, unorganized, a mess of a hand in any game, not just rummy. He said, "I'm tired," and jumped off the bed.

Trev had been feeling a tiny bead of heat in his stomach for a while now concerning his name and what it might mean to Khim. That heat grew a little hotter as he gathered up the cards, stuck the remote in between the cards so that it lay flat, undetectable, and banded the stack with a short piece of elastic. Then he stuck them down the side of his mattress.

Khim was at the sink, already getting ready for bed.

Trev drew his knees up, put his head on them, and waited for lights-out.

*

Over a mouthful of green beans, Khim said, "Where will we go?"

The question had been asked several times. Neither had answered or ever suggested an answer.

"I'm working on an idea about that," Trev said. But in truth he had nothing so far.

Jay came up to the table, setting down his tray. "What are we talking about?"

Khim was right with his question. Their biggest problem was, even if their plan succeeded effortlessly, with smooth efficiency, and they managed to get to a flier and managed to evade tracking, a chase, and a long-arm search, where could they go?

They had no money. No interplanetary ship. No home base.

Of course, Trev could steal all those things. But on a cloud city or the planet below, there would be more than alerts out for them and the Damico influence to avoid. Doing it all single-handedly would be a stretch, even for him.

Trev changed the dinner conversation to holovids.

Jay obligingly chimed in.

Khim had no comment, as usual. He only talked about things like that to Trev, no one else. But he did not ignore Jay anymore. He at least looked like he was listening these days, even if Trev suspected he wasn't.

As they were finishing up and the cafeteria was emptying, Jay said, low, "I know you guys are planning something. I don't need to be involved or anything. I'm out in six months, free and clear. I'll be okay. But if there's anything I can do to help, let me know. Anything. I owe you." With that, he got up and took his tray to the counter.

Khim said, "That surprised me somewhat."

"Yes," Trev said.

*

Trev said, later that night, "We have one chance. That's all. If we're caught, I get years tacked on. You may or may not be executed. Which is why we spare the lives of the guards. No killing. No matter what. Escape is one thing, but another murder—"

"And I'm down for the count. I know," Khim said.

The white ceiling light glistened in Khim's hair; his lashes made the shadows on his smooth cheeks waver. Knee to knee again, they sat on the top bunk, the playing cards between them.

"Are you okay with this?" Trev asked.

Khim's lips curved almost imperceptibly, but Trev saw.

"Are you?" Khim asked.

"Very. Maybe I can escape my father once and for all. And you, maybe you can finally live."

"The deal we made, it did not foresee this," Khim said. "Past the time of escape, you don't need to look out for me. What happens to me after is not your responsibility."

Trev looked at him hard. Took a deep breath. Frowned. "The deal was friendship."

"*Fake* friendship," Khim corrected.

"I don't remember that word when we spoke. When we agreed." Trev filled his lungs. "Khim, I know—I know you don't particularly like me. Or anyone."

"But—"

Trev held up his hand. "It doesn't mean I would abandon you. I want you to know that."

"You don't have to think that far. I can take care of myself."

A sinking feeling gathered in Trev's chest. The little bead of pain that disturbed him waking and sleeping, and communicated to him that it was more than just his name Khim despised, coiled close.

Trev said through his tight throat, "But I don't know that. Not for sure. And until I'm sure, I say we stick together. I'm not going out there into the unknown only to split ways and never know what happened to you."

"Why do you care?"

"I just—I don't know. It's been bothering me. That you'll go off and get into trouble. I know, I know you can take care of yourself.

You're beyond capable. I've seen that, but I want to see this through. All the way." As he spoke, his words became more and more difficult to say aloud.

Khim looked speechless, so Trev added, "I just think we can help each other. Stronger together, you understand?"

"In the battles I was in, men fought stronger together. But that was war."

"This is war."

Khim nodded. Very slowly, almost whispering, he said, "The deal is just different than I thought it would be."

Trev's lips pressed into a pleased smile because he heard the tone behind the words not as resigned, but open, hinting at a depth of unexpected delight. He couldn't hold the smile back. This strange man, this golden presence, the way he was like an energy that had coursed along beside Trev for all these past weeks, had had its effect on him. It was strange how it gave him something other than his own wishes and hopes to live for. How that presence made him so determined. How it warmed his heart.

Chapter Twenty

Khim

Khim watched Trev shoulder into his shirt, saw the flash of tanned skin above his undershirt, nape, spine, the curve of flesh just below the underarm—It was like seeing something precious for the first time and wanting to come forward, lay a hand there, protect. Unarmored flesh before a skirmish, a landing, an invasion. It just wasn't right.

He felt his first wave of apprehension about their plan.

He'd not had that feeling since his first battle. He'd defeated anxiety. Or thought he had.

Trev turned. Khim glanced away.

"Nervous?" Trev asked.

The audacity of him, Khim thought fondly. "No," he lied.

They had discussed timing. Strategy. Trying to foresee every circumstance, every possible hitch at all times of day. Should they attempt their crazy plan at night or during the busiest, most distracting part of the afternoon?

They went over every aspect they could think of. So much depended on technology and their shared ability to think creatively in stressful situations.

As he did every day, Khim followed Trev into the showers. The remote was back in Trev's bar of soap in their cell. There were spigots with old brown coarse stuff in each stall, but Khim hated it. It smelled of the low tide on Beta Niobe Four.

He figured Trev hated it too.

Khim soaped up, then handed Trev his personal soap bar around the edge of the stall. A hand darted out of warm spray to take it.

"Thanks."

Suddenly the sentry at the corner piped up. "What are you doing?" It skittered over to their stalls, red eyes staring in at Khim.

Over the splash of water, Khim could hear Trev breathing. He said, "I handed him a bar of soap."

He could not see Trev, but he heard him say, "Here. You want it?" Then Trev's hand moved forward, past the wall of the stall, and held the soap out to the robot.

"You have dispensers in the stalls. You do not need to share," the sentry said.

"It's brown soap in the dispenser," he heard Trev say. "I'm allergic."

"Hold up your wrist," said the sentry. Khim saw its arm use a wand to scan Trev's identchip. The sentry said, "This allergy fact is not in your record."

Trev said, "For humans, allergies come and go. I reacted to it several times as a child. I steer clear of it now."

"The rule is to keep to yourselves." The sentry moved back to its corner, the lights of its eyes like those of an animal's gaze caught in a bright light.

Khim had been holding his breath. He quickly shampooed his hair, then rinsed and moved to his bench to dress.

Trev emerged in a towel and their eyes met. Trev, soaked, hair hanging over his eyebrows, looked a little scared. And thoroughly beautiful.

Khim glanced away, putting on his shoes. He sat staring at the floor until Trev came up alongside him.

"Let's go," said Trev.

Khim got up and gathered his old clothes, towel, and shampoo, and followed him out of the steamy room.

All night Khim had tossed and turned, not apprehensive but looking forward to today. Now, as they passed the sentry, who swiveled its head to watch them go as if it suddenly had it in for them, he just wanted the day to be over.

Trev turned to him once they were out. "That fucking sentry. Fuck!"

Khim felt exactly the same.

Jay met them for breakfast. All as usual. They had brought him in on part of the plan. Khim had not wanted to do it, but Trev trusted the little man, and Khim trusted Trev.

They had not told Jay much. That way, Jay would be speaking the truth if he were questioned about them missing. They merely told him they needed a distraction at two o'clock that afternoon, as far away from Gate 8 as possible.

Jay said, as they ate, "I got something in mind. No worries."

And that was all he said. The guy had turned out not to be as squirrelly as Khim thought.

Breakfast was pleasant without Deb's crew there. Kant and his men sat with them at their table. Khim ignored the small talk and left to go to the weight room after he was finished eating. They had to make all their routines look normal.

Trev stayed at his side. Khim still kept finding himself waiting for Trev to lead, to move a step forward so Khim could come in a half-step behind. The damned conditioning would not let up on some things. Only when he concentrated could he make himself walk side by side with Trev as if he was not on an invisible leash. It didn't annoy him, but it did confound him.

Too many things were different for him now, and his life had changed so fast. He looked up and saw the high plaza ceiling, white against the surrounding backdrop of five levels of cells under green-lit lines, left to right, metal grid balconies jutting outward. The ceiling curved, the structure of eight arches meeting in the center like being under a gigantic dome.

Khim had lived in enclosed spaces his whole life. This one was the biggest—but no matter how big, a cage was still a cage.

Trev gave him a nervous look, showing white teeth.

Another wave of apprehension hit Khim, roiling through his chest and stomach.

In the gym he stripped off his shirt and worked the weights hard. He watched Trev do the same. Jay came by, but left early.

Khim had been on the cycle for half an hour. He got off and wiped his face with his shirt.

Trev came up beside him. His body glowed. He was breathless. His lashes were damp from the sweat running down his forehead. He

172

combed his perspiration-slick hair back with his fingers, then looked up at Khim, brown eyes big in his face, narrowing their focus on Khim alone.

This is the man I am following. A Damico. Stature: small. Personality: big. In fact, bigger than the biggest android I have ever served with. This is the man with whom I've made a deal and who saved me, who looks as if he has come shining right out of a dream.

Trev stood still beside him, biceps pumped, veins running down to his wrists with faint green-tinged trails. Vibrant. Like nothing Khim had ever known.

He'd never been treated with care before, never had anyone even want to be his friend. Other androids made frail friendships or fucked in the night from pent-up aggression and boredom, but Khim had had none of that. Hadn't ever desired it.

But he looked at Trev, and some part of him woke and yearned.

Beside him, Trev said, "How are you doing?"

As if he did not know how nervous Khim was. As if he cared. "Fine."

Trev nodded. "I don't know how you can be so calm. I envy that ability."

Surprised, Khim raised his eyebrows. He thought every bit of tension in him had to be broadcasting all over the room.

"I feel jumpy as hell," Trev said.

"I am desperate for this day to end," Khim said. Despite his penchant for the fight, for the thrill, he did not like this waiting game at all.

"Me too." Trev reached out and brushed Khim's forearm with the tips of his fingers, a brief, soft slide.

Khim did not like to be touched. But where those fingertips had lightly caressed, a warmth began. It suffused his skin.

He did not have words to describe the sensation.

*

After lunch, Trev dug the remote from the soap. Khim grabbed the triangle-shaped deck of cards and stuffed them in his waistband. There was nothing else in their cell worth taking.

Together they took the stairwell steps two at a time and entered the plaza. They did not see Jay.

Gate 8. That was their destination. Through that round aperture were offices and guards, but also docks and fliers and their only way out.

Without the remote working properly, they did not have a chance. But with the sentries down, and with Khim's fighting skills against human guards and Trev's knowledge of security systems, they did have a chance. A chance was all they asked for.

As they stood by the stairwell near Gate 8, Trev said, "One last time, Khim. Are you sure? Your life hangs more in the balance than mine."

Something in Khim's chest tightened at Trev's concern. "My life has always hung in the balance. Today is no different, except that I make the choice. For once, I act on my own."

Trev nodded. "Good."

Trev had the remote in his hand. He tilted it upward toward the middle of the ceiling, where they had calculated the signal would hit and bounce off in all directions. The sentries in the laundry, weight rooms, and media rooms would catch the virus in a delayed reaction, but they would all go down.

"Done," Trev said, eyes wide.

Khim watched the sentry closest to them as it jerked once, then froze. It emitted a loud pip. Then it began to sing, its alien tone blending with the sounds of all the other sentries' voices echoing together in the plaza and on the decks, a lilting chorus rising up as if the prison had become a church, the sentries the choir.

Khim was fast, grabbing the sentry's wand from its flank, fiddling with it for a few seconds, and then pointing it at Gate 8.

The angels sing
The demons croon
with songs they have learned

174

from the fifth ring of Hell

The gate opened and more sentries inside the corridor began to sing.

> *The river runs*
> *Styx to sand*
> *the ferryman bows*
> *to the evening Knight*

The musical Trev had found in the holovid section had been critically panned; it had played on two planets for all of two nights. Trev had downloaded every song of every act into the sentries' AI minds to play on an endless loop, certain words of the songs interfering constantly with their normal programming.

Trev and Khim leaped through the opening gate and encountered human guards immediately.

One said, "Hey, there's nothing on the schedule for—"

Before he could finish, Khim had him on the ground along with the second guard, passed out but still breathing. He pointed the wand at the door to close it.

The hall before them was empty. But it wouldn't be for long.

The sentries in the corridor sang. The star field to their right seemed blacker than usual.

Khim and Trev searched the guards' bodies and took everything of value. Guns. Wands. Radios.

Trev said, "We should take their clothes."

Khim was about to agree, but there was no time. Guards came running around the edge of the corridor that led to the hall of offices. Though their weapons were drawn, Khim ran straight toward them. He took down three of them with efficient neck chops—nonlethal blows—before they could get off a shot.

Alarms began to blare through the prison. First in the plaza, a dim siren. Then in the corridor where they were, a clanging that was startlingly loud.

A toneless voice announced, "Lockdown. Lockdown. All inmates remain where you are. You will be escorted to your cells. Lockdown. Lockdown."

In the hall, another voice spoke over invisible speakers. "All civilians, stay in your offices until the alarm stops. All civilians, stay in your offices until the alarm stops."

Trev was beside him, quick and quiet on his feet. "That means the workers can trip a sensor. We might too. Come on." As they rounded the corridor into the hall, they saw the line of office doors. They did not have time to be picky, ducking into the first office. Luck was with them; it was empty.

Trev went straight to the computer. "I'll hack in. See what I can do. I've done this a million times."

Khim stood at his side, amazed at how Trev's hands worked over the screen, touching as if everywhere at once, a dance of hands over lights on a display.

"Hold up your wrist," Trev said.

Khim did as instructed.

Trev pressed a few lights on the screen, then ran the wand over Khim's wrist and his own. "I've turned off the tracking devices in our chips."

After another few moments, Trev announced, "We have to get wet."

"What?"

Trev did not look up. "Is there a bathroom in here?"

Khim looked over to the corner—a door. He ran to it. "A toilet and a sink," he called over his shoulder.

"Turn on the water in the sink. Let it fill. We need to be soaked."

Khim did as he was told but said, "I don't understand."

Trev appeared at the door. "That's so weird. I was just inside a system like this two days before I was arrested. What are the odds?"

The sink was filling. Trev began to scoop out waves of cold water, dousing himself. Khim began to do the same.

The water poured, a steady stream, and Khim watched Trev bend down and put his whole head under the spray.

"Help me," Trev said.

Khim began to scoop water over the back of Trev's head, neck, and back.

When Trev looked as if he'd just stepped fully clothed from a shower, he straightened. "Your turn."

Khim bent and let himself be splashed all over. Trev scooped handful after handful of water over him until satisfied, then spoke softly. "There are lasers in the floor. They come on if they sense intruders, but they don't sense water. This will give us about three to five minutes. When we start to dry is when we'll run into problems. Oh, I almost forgot. We have to take off our shoes now and walk in our wet socks."

After removing and soaking their socks, they put them back on and headed to the office door.

"Will my hand be a problem?"

"Hmm. I forgot about that." Trev went back into the bathroom and came out with a saturated towel. "We'll wrap this around your hand. You can still have mobility."

Khim held out his metal hand.

Trev wound the towel gently around it, bringing up two opposite ends and tying it off. "I unlocked the docking-bay doors. I didn't have time to choose, so I did all of them. We can work the airlocks with the sentry wands."

"You did all that in this short amount of time?"

"I told you I'm good."

"But this is a max prison."

"It makes no difference to me what they call it. There're always breaches to any security system. You just have to make sure you find the keys. And believe me, there are many. Okay. Let's go. If you need to communicate, whisper. A voice can set off the lasers. When we get out there, we need to find the door to the stairs that lead to the docks."

"Copy."

Trev said, "Like a true soldier."

They moved, silent and dripping, into the hall, going deeper and farther toward the tip of the space prison's arm.

True to Trev's calculations, the lasers saw them as mist and did not come on as they made their way down the hall.

They heard the sentries, far off, still singing. The music was horrible, grating.

Khim wanted to laugh, yell, howl, cry. He'd never had so many emotions at any one time. He was trained for battle, but this was unlike any battle he'd ever fought. And he'd never fought on his own. He had to focus on Trev to stay in control. Use Trev's voice as a point of command.

Trev motioned him forward. The door he faced was different from the rest. It was locked, of course.

Khim waved his wand in front of it. Nothing happened.

Trev dug around his waistband for the things they'd gathered from the fallen human guards. He produced a small metal tube and stuck it into a hole in the wall. The door slid open. Before them a flight of stairs went winding down.

The stairwell was bathed in red flashing light. Khim waited for Trev's signal before barging in. He smelled ozone and didn't like the prospect of what that might mean.

Thankfully, Trev led. And yet Khim was afraid for him. He wanted to wrap him in his damp arms and hold him back. But with his conditioning, he did his best by following.

The stairs curved. They went slowly on wet, stockinged feet, chorused by the distant voices of hundreds of sentries all over the complex. Khim could make out only a few words here and there—

Herald, herald... creature of broken flesh... pain and chains... spirit flaming....

Someday, it would all be unbearably funny.

They came to a landing but still could not see the dock. Trev moved toward the railing.

It happened so fast that for a second Khim could not comprehend that Trev was just—gone.

He heard the echo of the laser bolt, then saw the black mark on the railing where it had hit.

Khim pulled one of the guard's guns and ran to the railing, spreading fire before he could even see who had shot at them. He saw the long deck of the docks, the bays like black windows before them, guards running—some forward, some back, some prone on the ground.

"Trev!" His voice came out in a strangled croak.

"Here."

He leaned over the railing and saw Trev dangling from a jutting edge of metal just beneath the banister. He hung by one hand, legs kicking the air, trying to find purchase. "If I could just get my hand up, I could pull myself up," he said, breathless.

Khim lay in another barrage of fire, then, without even thinking about it, tore the towel off his metal hand and reached over the edge, stomach catching on the rail. He clasped Trev's forearm and pulled. It took all his strength, back and shoulder and belly muscles all tensing, straining, locking. Luckily, Trev was slender, light. Khim hauled him up one-handed, lifting him over the rail and depositing him on the floor before him. He wrapped his other arm around Trev's waist and pulled him back against the far wall in case more guards decided to shoot at them.

Trev looked at him incredulously. "How'd you do that?"

Khim looked him up and down. "What? You weigh maybe thirty pounds soaking wet."

Trev muttered, "One-five-nine." Then he let out a shaky breath. "The bolt hit the rail, but the concussion wave hit me and flipped me over. Luckily I'm used to flipping myself over tall railings."

"Luckily," Khim echoed. But they had no time for more discussion. "Okay, then, I'll take the rest of them out." He could not bring himself to say "stay behind me" because it felt all wrong.

"I can help. I know how to use a laser gun on stun."

Khim sighed in relief. Khim took out two more guards from the railing, then motioned to Trev that all was clear.

Trev led the way to the final set of stairs, firing as he went. Red beams flickered all around them. The alarm siren whined. The sentries sang.

At the bottom of the stairs, they stepped carefully over two unconscious guards in blue uniforms. There were more guards standing at the far end.

Khim moved forward and laid down a barrage of laser pulses, forcing the newly arrived guards back. He kept firing to cover Trev, who advanced carefully down the dock, inspecting the bays, which all stood open due to his deft computer skills. The airlocks were closed, of course. The fliers, all in neat little rows, floated in the dark airless sea beyond.

It seemed Trev had found one he liked; he was now working on the airlock.

Khim moved from one bay to the next, using the narrow alcoves for as much cover as he could get. He could see Trev working at the door. He kept the guards back with more volleys of laser bolts and stun lines. He had two kinds of guns, both set on nonlethal, per Trev's wishes. "What's taking so long?"

Trev didn't answer. Khim saw more men in blue uniforms gathering down the dock, arriving from a doorway Khim had not known about linking another area of the prison. If Trev had seen another way in on the computer during the short time they were in the office, he'd said nothing about it.

Finally Trev called out. "There! Got it!"

Khim heard a loud hiss. He ran out from cover, shooting, and dodged into the next alcove. The airlock door was open. Trev was already inside, working on the flier door.

Khim said, "Close the door behind us."

"No time. As soon as we're through here, I will."

Khim stayed on point, hearing running footsteps echoing up the dock. At least a half-dozen men were converging on them now. "Hurry," he said under his breath. "*Hurry*."

"Got it!" Trev whirled.

Khim took a breath at the two most beautiful words ever and ran backward toward Trev. Trev was actually grinning when he got to his side.

"Get in! Get in!" Trev said.

Khim turned and entered the small two-seater flier, climbing into the far right-hand seat. Trev leaped like a gazelle into the front seat, plopping gracefully at Khim's side as the door began to hiss shut.

Two guards turned the corner and ran at them, firing.

The air exploded around them just before the door closed. Trev gave a little shriek, but his hands were moving fast over the controls.

Khim glanced over at him and saw a hole in Trev's shirt at the shoulder, the edges burned black. The skin under the hole was already blistering around a deep impression. "You're hit!"

Trev's mouth was a pale line against tanned skin. "I'm okay."

But he wasn't okay. "Damn it. They were using lethal force."

Trev did not seem to be listening. He was working the controls so fast Khim could barely see his hands. "Go," Trev muttered to himself, or maybe to the flier. "Go, go, go!"

The flier broke away from the dock, floating free for a moment as if all that had happened to them had been a dream and they were just about to wake. Then the boosters came on and they shot into the dark.

"It's not over yet," Trev said through gritted teeth.

Khim looked up through the roof window, then down through the bottom window. He saw the prison, like a giant black widow spider, hurtling away from them, growing smaller, and the other fliers, like dots of white flowering against the careening blackness, pulsing out from one of the spider's arched legs.

There was going to be a chase.

Khim worried about Trev's shoulder—he looked to be in a lot of pain. Those pulse hits were like white hot knives, and they burned deep. The pain twisted through the body like a nest of angry, stinging hornets. Khim had been hit by them several times in his past.

"I disabled the tracker, and I picked a high-end flier with suitable speed. But if we're not fast, they'll catch us."

"Can you switch places with me?" Khim asked. "I'm a certified shuttle pilot, and I've driven fliers thousands of times."

"No time," Trev answered tightly. His usually pink lips had turned a pale blue. He was still soaked through, like Khim, his gray prison attire sticking to him, his wet hair clinging to his cheeks and forehead. He was beginning to shiver.

Khim knew the symptoms of shock.

Trev said, "Too bad fliers aren't structurally equipped for foldspace." His breathing had become shallow.

"Beyond this point, our plan diminishes somewhat," Khim observed, itching to take over the controls.

"Not really. I just need to access the flier's computer. It has wave access. I need a moment only. Then I have to shut it off before they can track us." Trev's hands tapped the screens in a fluid pattern Khim could not keep up with. Trev then transferred the screen to holo, and it appeared before Khim's eyes as if floating on air.

"There. That's the destination. But don't plug it in yet. I gotta get rid of our tails."

Finally, something Khim could help with. He studied the address. Memorized it—just in case—and the coordinates as well.

Trev flew straight for the moonstone-blue planet below. Gideon was wreathed in a sapphire-white atmosphere, a swirl of green-edged fog, temperate, steady, life affirming.

They hit the atmosphere hard, and the flier shrieked an alarm. It was meant to ease in and out of space, not slam itself into barriers.

Trev made a few adjustments, hands shaking, and then they were shooting past exosphere, ionosphere, and finally into the stratosphere, where they began to encounter clouds and drops of ice hitting the windows.

The alarm went silent.

"Fuck! We left a vapor trail," Trev hissed.

He flew like the devil of mayhem himself, hurly-burly, the flier tumbling through the air. The only things holding them in their seats were the automatic armrests that had clamped over their thighs.

The sun gleamed high overhead. If it had been night, they might've had an easier evasion. But right then, Khim saw, the lights of other fliers still followed.

And then, suddenly, salvation.

They both saw it at once.

Like soft smoke lit by bronze fire from within. Like a gentle, foaming ebb and flow of some fairy-tale sea beyond the edge of a parched, white desert. Like a distant hearth calling them home.

"That," Khim said.

"I see it," Trev said.

"Fly into it."

"Naturally," Trev said, as if he'd known all along it would be there.

182

The storm looked huge, progressing rapidly, and already the winds were whipping at the front of the flier. Trev flew into angry slipstreams, fierce sleet, and the pure adrenaline rush that was their only road to safety.

The currents of wailing air buffeted them, but the flier would hold. It was made for battling storms. Just like the iron-built cloud cities and the little islands of the wealthiest families that surrounded them.

Trev took a sharp breath, blinking. Khim knew he was fighting pain, but he never once complained. Aside from tiny gasps, Trev made no sound of moaning and never took his eyes off the controls.

After a minute, when they both knew the other fliers would never find them by sight or tracking systems, they began to relax.

Khim watched Trev ease up, fingers moving slower, hands quivering.

Trev said, "We made it."

Khim felt himself smile, and it reached more than just his lips. It seemed to sink down into him deep, covering his very core. "Put it on autopilot."

Trev nodded. "Yeah. Okay."

Khim glanced at the back of the craft. There was very little room. One short couch seat. Black leather. Rather exquisite, actually. "If I help you into the back, you'll be more comfortable."

Trev started to shake his head.

"I memorized the coordinates you picked," Khim said. "I'll get us there. Wherever you've chosen to send us."

Trev's whole body began to shake now. His eyes were dim, his gaze distant as they sought Khim's face. "I just need a synth patch and a painkiller, and I'll be fine."

Khim nodded. "I know. We don't have either."

Trev let out a strange laugh. "I can't believe we did this. We really did this."

"Yes. We did."

"You'll be safe now, Khim. I'll make sure."

Khim felt a quiver in his own chest. Trev made the statement as if he'd done it all for Khim alone. As if Trev only thought of himself as an afterthought.

"We both will," Khim assured him.

Trev flipped a switch and the armrests let go of them. Khim moved up in his seat, balancing on one knee. He looked from Trev to the backseat, then back at Trev. "Can you climb over?"

Trev's eyes were glassy. "Huh?"

Khim pushed both their seats into a reclining position. Then he slid into the back and reached forward. He hooked his hands gently underneath Trev's shoulders. The gray shirt was cool to the touch, still sopping.

Trev let out a puff of air, followed by a tight sound of protest.

"I'm sorry," Khim said. "Push with your legs. You can lie down flat back here."

Trev did not push with his legs, though. He seemed not to hear Khim at all. His eyes had closed, his dark lashes making tight lines against the tops of his cheeks.

Khim kept pulling until he had Trev half on the backseat, half slumped in his lap. "Trev?"

"Huh?"

Trev's head moved a little, then fell forward against Khim's chest. Trev felt so cold in his arms. The wet clothes were not helping.

Khim looked forward, saw the darkness trying to penetrate all the windshields above and below as well as in front, saw a bedlam of rain striking the thick glass with rage.

Khim reached out and righted the front seats. He had just enough floor room to kneel so he could arrange Trev on the back couch more comfortably.

Trev kept wincing as he was moved, eyelids fluttering, but he made no sound.

Khim took off his own damp shirt, wadded it up, and put it under Trev's head.

Trev leaned into him then, whispering with tight blue lips, "Get us to that address I gave you. The guy owes me. He owes me."

Khim said, "I promise." He had no trouble following Trev's orders. He wasn't going to stop now. "Lean back."

Trev's head fell back.

Khim took that moment to examine the wound. He tore the shirt open at the shoulder, saw a clean but piercing burn. It had already cauterized itself from the heat of the bolt blast, but it was deep, a big enough hole that it would need to be sealed.

Khim tore at the bottom of his tank top until he had a strip of cloth long enough to wrap the injury. He tied it off, trying to be gentle, but Trev moaned when he finished the knot.

"Sorry," Khim said.

But Trev didn't seem to hear.

The wound looked bad, but Khim was more worried about the shock. He lifted Trev's wrist and felt the pulse. Rapid, thready. There was nothing to give him for it. Even a blanket for warmth would have been nice. But he had none.

He touched Trev's clammy forehead. "Do you feel hot or cold?"

"Cold."

"Stretch out as best you can. I'm turning up the heat."

"Okay," Trev said tiredly.

For a long time, Khim sat on his heels on the tiny back floor of the flier watching Trev slip in and out of a thin sleep. He listened to the rain pelt their tiny shell. The interior lights threw a sepia tone over everything. Khim's breath came in strained puffs as the fingers of his left hand made small circles over the back of Trev's wrist.

The air in the flier grew hot. He hoped it was enough to make Trev comfortable. At least it contributed to drying their clothes faster.

Finally, when he became confident that enough time had passed so their pursuers would be long gone, he climbed into the front driver's seat and fed the flier the coordinates for their destination.

It was strange not having Trev awake and telling him what to do. And yet it wasn't, because Trev had told him where to go, had obviously planned this every step of the way in his mind.

The flier headed on course. The voice from the console, soft and lilting, said, "Two and a half hours to destination."

Khim searched the front-seat area for anything he could find to make their trip more comfortable. A discarded sweater. A bottle of water. Anything. But the flier was clean, almost too clean, as if it had just flown right off the sales lot. He wondered whom it had belonged to.

Finally he leaned back and closed his eyes in exhaustion. The storm spilled around them, weeping in shrill, manic tones. Inside, the flier was warm and humming, a temporary haven.

Only then did Khim realize how lucky they had been.

*

Khim felt the flier slow, lean in a circular pattern, straighten, and slow some more.

Outside the windows, darkness pressed upon the little craft. Khim had slept in the front seat, sitting up. He stretched, then turned, breath catching as he checked on Trev.

The other man lay very still, but his chest rose and fell, slow and even. Khim let out a sigh of relief.

The flier was landing now, but he could not see where they were.

He squinted at the front window, through the heaving rain, and noticed a faint, tremulous glow. He could barely see through the million spears of water, but a light was there. It was real.

He pushed the front seat down and climbed into the back. "Trev. Wake up. We're here."

Trev's lashes fluttered, but he did not wake.

Khim pushed the front seat back up so he could kneel by the backseat and said, "Back door. Open." The flier door opened onto the sound of water hitting earth, puddles splashing, and the scent of mud, fresh growing things, and a raw edge of decay. The light from the flier sparked the edges of the falling raindrops with gilt, and for a moment, Khim was dazzled.

He reached out and touched Trev's chest. His shirt was dry now. Trev's hair was tangled along the edges of Khim's balled-up shirt-pillow. He needed to carry him out of there, but hated that they'd have to get wet again. He could feel how cold the air was wafting into the little flier.

But he didn't have to make up his own mind. Trev's orders were clear. Get them to this address.

He climbed out the back door, rain hitting his bare arms like ice and soaking quickly through his stockinged feet. He reached back in and pulled Trev up and into a seated position on the couch.

Trev moved a little, mumbling a protest, but did not fight him. The torn shirt bandage still held, tied against the shoulder and upper arm. Now Khim leaned in farther and put his left arm under Trev's knees, his right under his upper back. He used all his strength to turn him, then lifted him easily into his arms as he straightened under the storm's unrelenting deluge.

Trev cried out as the cold water hit him. His back arched; his muscles tensed. Khim held tight. Trev reached out blindly. One hand grabbed Khim's t-shirt at the shoulder and held on. He cried out a second time and turned his face into Khim's chest.

Even in the shocking cold, Khim's body stayed warm from an upsurge of adrenaline. He hugged Trev tight to him and walked toward the faint, misty glow as if he were made of flame.

As he moved through the watery air, a distinct shape took form before him. A house, gigantic. At least three stories, like an old-Earth Victorian expanded on, enlarged. Flagstone steps led up to tall blue double doors.

Four lanterns lighted the way up the steps, their old-fashioned, square-cut glass panes outlined in black iron. The light in them pulsed orange. The deck of the porch was polished oak, as deeply brown as Trev's eyes.

Two more lamps shone high on either side of the double doors. A digital screen by the door glowed. Khim pulled Trev close, balancing him easily, then reached forward with his metal hand and tapped the screen. From within came the faint sound of trilling bells. Khim touched the pad again, and the bells resounded.

It seemed like forever that Khim stood there with Trev tight in his arms, dripping cold water on the bright green welcome mat. Finally, one of the double doors swung open.

A man stood in flickering shadow, hair purple, glimmering, and long, tied into a braid that curved over his left shoulder. He was tall and broad, with a cool, violet-eyed gaze. He wore a frost-blue coat with tails.

An android.

Khim said, "This man says you owe him."

"Who's there?" said a low voice from beyond the greeter.

Staring at the android's eyes, Khim said, "Khim. And Trevor Damico."

The android stepped back. "You know one of them, sir."

A man stepped into view clad in black trousers and a white shirt. He wore a loose red robe about his shoulders. His hair was white, shaved on both sides.

Khim lifted his head and addressed him, repeating his statement. "This man says you owe him."

The man came forward and inspected Trev, who lay delirious, turned away in Khim's arms, still clutching the sleeve of Khim's t-shirt shirt. "Trevor Damico?" he asked.

Khim said, "He told me to bring him here."

"Of course. Of course. Come in."

It did not matter that the house was warm, that he could smell the woodsy odor of a fire burning in the next room, that the man in the robe and the android by his side were an older, strange mirror of the two of them. Khim still trusted no one.

"Sir," Khim said, "the flier outside is stolen."

"I have a man who will take care of that," the white-haired man said.

"And Trev is in need of medical attention."

"I can see that," the man said. "Renn, is the guest room made up?"

"Yes, sir," the android answered.

"This way." The man motioned Khim forward.

They went past a vast front room with a giant walk-in hearth roaring with snapping flames, and on into a more shadowy hall decorated with flaring, cobra-headed sconces.

The white-haired man opened the second door and went in, waving his hand to make light. The room flooded into being. Khim followed Renn over the threshold and saw an elaborate room, old-fashioned looking, with a giant, soft bed covered in brocade and heavy burgundy curtains closed over the window. The room had several wood chairs, a wood desk, and another door that led, Khim presumed, into a bath.

Khim did not wait to be asked. He rushed forward to deposit Trev on the bed.

"Renn, get towels," the man ordered.

A whisper of slippered footsteps, a hush of rain against curtained windowpanes.

Khim grabbed Trev's limp, cold hands in his, rubbing them. "Trev? It's okay. You'll be warm and dry in a second."

"Khim. Are you okay? Are you safe?" Trev's voice was slurred.

Overwhelmed that Trev's foremost thought was for him, Khim said, "Yes." Then, to reassure him, he said again, "Yes." And he began to gently remove Trev's torn shirt.

Trev was like a baby, allowing himself to be undressed. Khim threw the wet clothing on the floor. Trev shivered, trying to fold his body inward, curl up. His skin was clammy everywhere Khim's hands brushed it. Khim grabbed a folded blanket at the foot of the bed and wrapped Trev in it as Renn came forward with a stack of neatly folded towels.

Khim took one of the towels and mopped at Trev's hair. He took another and wiped himself down as well. Renn approached a second time with two clean robes, long, soft, and black.

"Thank you," Khim said to him.

One never said thank you to a robot, or any vat-grown slave for that matter. But this was clearly a man.

"Of course," the android replied.

The white-haired man said, "Allow me to introduce myself. I am Arch. Archer Archimedes. Trev and I have met on two occasions. And you are?"

"Khim."

"Yes. I see. Khim, if you are running from authorities and they track you here, I can hold them off for a while. If they have a warrant to search the premises, then you understand there is nothing I can do."

"Understood," Khim said.

"I have no medic here. But I have a kit. Renn is fetching it now. If, in the morning, Trev is not improved, I know someone discreet whom I can call."

"What time is it?" Khim asked.

"Nine twenty. We're on minor continent time here. You are fortunate we were still up. We retire early in this household."

"Yes," Khim said. "A lot of things have been lucky for us today."

Arch came forward, blue eyes glittering. "It is also true that Trevor Damico did me a favor. But the favor backfired. He was to take a fall for me. That didn't happen. I am under house arrest. This, all you see around you, including my—my—Renn, is to be auctioned next week to pay my firm's investors." The glittering in the eyes turned to dim withdrawal. "So I don't owe him. Not one bloody thing."

Khim stared at him, gaze unwavering. "Understood."

Just then, Renn arrived with the medical kit. Khim took it and turned his back on the two of them. He did not hear them leave but assumed they did.

He pulled the blanket away from Trev's shoulder and opened the kit, finding ample supplies. He was familiar with first aid from the battlefields, so he set about cleaning the wound and administering a syringe of pain medication.

Trev was awake but distant. He had stopped shivering, so that was good. He said, "I won't forget this, Khim. I won't."

"You're the one who saved me."

Trev's eyelashes were dark lace, setting patterns dancing across his cheeks. "Is Mr. Archimedes here?"

"He was." Khim sprayed synthiskin about the cauterized wound. It foamed.

Trev gave a little hiss, nothing more. "I'm feeling sleepy. Is that right?"

"It's quite right. You just need rest."

"Will you be here?"

"Of course."

Trev reached out. His hand closed on air. Khim saw and put his own hand there for support. Trev grasped it. "I want you to survive, Khim. I want you to live."

"I'm here."

"I know, but if you could get away. If you could find a life, I think that would make me feel like—like it was all worth it. Worlds dissolve. But sometimes we can escape them, find new paths, new worlds leading us toward a universe that is so vast. All possibility, Khim. All of it exists. Right now. Right now."

Khim said, "The shot I gave you seems to be working."

"No. I mean it. There are places, worlds, where things are different. Where you can live. Promise me you'll find them. Promise me you'll live, Khim."

Khim squeezed his hand. "You've done enough for one day."

"Promise me. Please," Trev said, tone low, commanding.

Khim, feeling neither obedient nor free of that beautiful voice, said, "I will fight to survive until the day I can no longer stand."

"That's who you are. That's who you need to remember to be."

Khim finished patching the hole in Trev's arm and secured the bandage. He patted his shoulder. "There."

"I don't feel the pain anymore. Just sleepy."

"Would you like to get under the covers?"

"Yes."

Khim helped him scoot to one side and pulled back the brocade spread, the fleece blanket, and a soft cotton sheet. "Better than the bunk beds," Khim said softly. "Better than prison."

Trev sat up with Khim's help, bent his knees, shifted. The blanket fell away. For a moment he was naked under the soft white light, eyes seeking Khim's. "I am really glad we met."

Khim felt a wave of helplessness, a kind of fervor at the vulnerable sight of him that both confused and amazed him. He helped him scoot under the covers, pulling them up, covering him. But not before he glimpsed the unchecked beauty of the man who'd saved his life, the man who had somehow hooked him into thinking he could be somebody beyond the constrained and proper laws of vat-born humans.

Chapter Twenty-One

Trev

Trev woke to the scent of fresh sheets and a clean pillowcase. A thin light leaked around a pair of heavy, dark pink curtains. He heard the faint and airy singing of birds. A man sat in a straight-backed chair by the side of the bed, chin low on his chest, eyes closed, gold falls of hair on either side of his face. He wore a torn white t-shirt and gray prison trousers.

Khim.

Trev sat up, feeling a twinge in the side of his shoulder. The heavy covers fell from his chest, and he realized he was naked. The shadows of the room rested upon each other and on the walls in pink-brown layers.

Trev saw two black robes lying across the foot of the bed along with a rumpled, discarded blanket. He wondered why Khim had not changed yet out of his soiled, hated prison clothes.

Trev pulled the robe to him and shrugged into it, favoring his shoulder, then slid from the bed. As his bare feet hit the floor with a soft sound, Khim woke.

"You're up."

"You got us here. Thank you," Trev said, looking at him. "Did you sleep in that chair all night?"

Khim shrugged. "I believe I did."

"Mr. Archimedes let you in when you gave him my name. I knew he would. He owes me."

Khim's dark blue gaze roved over his body, focusing on the shoulder.

"How do you feel?" Khim asked.

"Much better. I remember you patching the hole. I don't remember a lot, but I do remember being wet. And rain. Lots of rain. Did you carry me in here? I remember you carrying me."

Khim glanced at the curtains for a moment, then said in a careful tone, "All of about thirty pounds, soaking wet."

Trev felt his mouth curve up. Voice low, "Thank you, Khim."

"The storm lasted all night. It stopped raining about two hours ago." Khim moved to stretch, the tight muscles of his upper arms flexing, his metal hand glimmering. He stood. His clothing drooped. He looked like someone who had just been through a battle, like the soldier he'd been trained to be.

"We made it. We're out. Can you believe it?" Trev asked. Khim nodded. "What about the flier?"

"It's been taken care of. No one will track us here. At least for the moment."

Trev glanced about the room, then back at Khim. "You look like you need rest. Or at least a shower and some food."

"We can't stay here. I don't trust this man. He says he does not owe you anything. He says his house will be auctioned next week. Along with his android."

"He has an android?"

"His name is Renn, and he's been quite helpful."

"What else did he say to you?"

"Not much. He wasn't hostile. But he's in a desperate situation. Men in desperate situations are capable of, well, anything."

"He embezzled from his company and his shareholders. For years and years. Billions, maybe more. If he's losing everything now because of me, he might turn us in for a deal—"

"He won't turn you in," said a voice at the door.

Khim and Trev turned. Trev had not heard the man come in. He looked impeccable in a long blue coat and white shirt. His purple hair fell in soft waves about his shoulders.

"That's Renn," Khim said under his breath.

The android at the door said, "If he admitted to your presence here to any authority, he would further implicate himself. I came to invite you to breakfast. He'll explain things to you then. You will find clean towels and anything else you need in the bathroom. I have brought clothing I think might fit you."

Renn entered the room and set a folded pile of clothing at the foot of the bed. Trev and Khim watched him leave and close the door, then glanced at each other.

"Wow. Mr. Archimedes has an android," Trev said.

Khim raised an eyebrow.

Trev looked at him closely—the softened features, the very different way Khim held himself now that he was not on guard, in prison, or being imminently threatened with death. "What are the odds?"

"Astronomical. You can shower first."

Trev nodded and entered the bathroom; Khim liked to do things second, always following behind him.

*

The kitchen swirled with a mix of aromas. Pancakes, fried eggs, sizzling bacon. All the curtains were drawn back, and the view fell on vistas of green lawn, trees whose coin-shaped leaves sparkled in the wind, and a blue sky decorated with white clouds—all that were left of the storm.

Khim looked startlingly handsome in black trousers and a starched white button-up shirt.

Trev also wore black pants, which dragged the floor, but his shirt was dark blue.

Both remained barefoot.

The kitchen had an orange-brown polished-tile floor and a large island in the middle with stove, sink, and all the appliances a person could want if they cooked a lot of meals.

Renn was depositing eggs onto a silver tray.

Mr. Archimedes sat by the counter in a tall chair, leaning forward, reading a digital screen that lay flat before him on the dark marble counter. He looked up. "Welcome."

"Mr. Archimedes—" Trev began.

"Arch. Call me Arch."

"Arch," Trev said. "Thank you for receiving us. We had nowhere else to go."

"I see that," he said. "Even now the officials are searching for you two. It's right here in the current newsfeed. Apparently there was a fire at Steering Star, an escape, a stolen flier."

"A fire? At the prison?" Trev frowned.

Arch nodded.

"Jay," said Khim, confirming that the distraction Jay had promised had actually occurred.

"We didn't have anything to do with that," Trev said.

"They say someone made all the robot guards sing every verse of every song in that infernal musical *The Phantom of the Centauri Listening Station*. It took them hours to program them back into working mode. In the meantime, two prisoners escaped out of the maximum-security institution in a stolen flier. And no one died. You two are very good at what you do."

Khim and Trev both remained silent.

Arch waved them over. "Come here. Sit down. Do you like coffee? Orange juice? Renn, get them something to drink."

"It's all right here, sir." Renn poured fresh juice and coffee into waiting glasses and cups, sliding them in front of the two men.

Trev's stomach rumbled. The coffee smelled so good he wanted to gulp it, but he went for the orange juice first, letting the coffee cool.

As Trev watched, Khim stirred cream and sugar into his coffee and took a sip, the steam rising into his eyes. After everything they'd gone through the day before, and Khim sleeping sitting up in a hard chair, he looked immaculate, as if fresh from a vacation in paradise. His golden hair shone.

Trev lowered his eyes to the heaping plate of hot food Renn set before him. "Thank you." His stomach clawed with hunger. The last meal he'd eaten was yesterday's lunch in the prison cafeteria.

He lifted the fork he found by his plate, its handle twisted into a sculpture of a seahorse, the tail coiled into a spiral that fit perfectly against the webbing of his thumb and forefinger. He was used to fancy, but he'd never seen a fork like that one before.

Both he and Khim ate hungrily. They scooped the breakfast into their mouths until they were satisfied, sitting back and sipping coffee, eyeing each other once in a while as if neither of them knew what to say.

Renn had sat for only a few minutes to eat, and he was now clearing away pans and utensils, setting them into an automatic washer.

Arch said, after many silent minutes, "Ah, the appetites of the young. And the lawless."

Trev wondered if he detected a small amount of envy in that tone.

After breakfast they walked into the front room with the huge, glowing hearth. Trev saw a grand piano in one corner and went straight to it. As a child of privilege, he had learned to play, of course. He placed his fingers on the center keys, pressed down to hear a dulcet tone come from the depths of the instrument.

"Do you play?" Arch asked.

"Somewhat." Trev was aware that Khim was watching him. Waiting, perhaps, to follow Trev's lead.

Trev sighed, moving away from the piano and toward the hearth. The room was as ostentatious as Dante's front room, filled with art and furniture and ornate rugs, the support beams in the ceiling all intricately carved with scenes of animals and humans entwined.

Arch had already taken a seat in a plush, dark leather chair. Trev sat opposite him on a white couch, sinking into the cushions.

Khim stayed standing for a moment longer, then approached the couch and sat. Not too close to Trev, but not at the opposite end, either. His muscles were tense.

Trev could feel the mistrust in him for their new surroundings, a trait Khim clung to with the casualness of a man always on edge.

Arch's eyes followed Khim's every move. Assessing. Trev wondered what his opinion of androids might be, since he actually owned one. Did he see Khim as merely an object? Or more? He could not tell from the small interaction he'd seen between Arch and Renn if their relationship was master and slave, or something more.

He realized that Khim's proprietary attitude with Trev did not go unnoticed by Archimedes.

Trev spoke first. "Khim told me you will not be here much longer."

"The house will be on auction next Friday," Arch answered. "To help pay my debts."

"And Renn as well," Khim inserted.

Both men looked at him.

Trev raised an eyebrow, turning back to Arch. "Renn too?"

"Yes." Arch's smile looked pained. "Do not worry on my account, Trevor Damico. I am perhaps not as smart as your father, but I am much older, and I have a far reach too, and long-time loyalty bases. Your father exposed our deal, even shattered my quiet life here. My house will be taken, and my lover. But I will not go to prison, after all. You, however, he left to rot there."

Trev's face heated as he tried to process everything from those last few sentences.

Arch continued. "At first no one believed it. Dante Damico's beloved son imprisoned? You probably never saw the headlines. It's a sheer horror. For weeks he's been gaining the sympathy of the masses. More and more each day. Poor Dante. That's the surface picture, at least. None but a scant few know he engineered it all. Underneath all that, the word *beloved* takes on a different connotation, does it not, Trevor?"

Trev realized he was gripping his hands tightly together in his lap. Khim's presence beside him was anything but calm.

"You tried to escape his influence," Arch said. "A near impossible feat. And he abandoned you, all the while still keeping you on his gilded leash and gaining more power for himself both privately and professionally."

Trev leaned back on the couch now, staring at his lap. What could he say? He knew his father too well. He'd been an idiot, of course. He should get the word *idiot* emblazoned on a T-shirt. Nothing Dante did surprised him. Much of what he did amazed him. A carefully sectioned-off space inside him, protected and set apart, still held his father in a kind of awe.

He lifted his face, still hot, his insides unsteady. "I have nothing I can really say to you about my father, except you knew what you were getting into when you and I made our deal."

Khim flinched at the word *deal*.

"You knew my name. My predicament. And the risks," Trev added.

"I did." Arch leaned forward.

Trev said, "So now here we are." He held the older man's gaze for just long enough to feel uncomfortable, then said with an underlying and truly felt pain, "I'm sorry about Renn."

Arch's eyes flicked to Khim. He said nothing.

Trev said, "My father forbade me to embezzle. Said it wasn't safe enough not to leave tracks. He didn't fully understand my expertise. Give me a computer attached to the wave, and I can at least steal what you need to maybe keep Renn."

"No. They'll just take that money too. Perhaps inflate the charges. All my computers are tapped right now. There is no move I can make that is not seen. But I have no need of funds. I have extra liquid funds everywhere. Hidden for a later date, when the heat is off. It is only that which is under my name which is being taken." He held out his hand, waving it in the air. "This beautiful place. And Renn. That's the price I pay. I have gambled, I got caught. You and I made a deal. Your father has won. It's a simple game, really. One I've played my whole life."

Trev saw little emotion in the man in this strange, surreal nightmare. He seemed more jaded than defeated. "If you're being watched, then they know we're here, me and Khim."

"I am digitally observed. Computer activity, mainly. Who comes and goes from my house is of no matter. And I believe the storm obscured your arrival so that no one knows you're here. So far. But of course you can't stay long."

"We need time to find the means to survive. That's all."

"Of course. You are hidden well. Your flier is gone, with clues my man placed that will lead anyone searching for you to hunt in other directions, away from here. You were both astute. You left no tracks. And I will do my best to keep it that way. You probably have at least a couple of days, and you are welcome to stay longer. But harboring fugitives puts me and Renn on even more unstable ground. Which is why we have plans to visit a hotel owned by a friend on Gideon. We are leaving this afternoon. You two are welcome to stay as long as you like. But as I said, after two days at the outset, your danger increases.

And of course, by next Friday, this island in the clouds will no longer belong to me."

Trev said, "I don't know what to say."

Khim leaned forward. "I know what to say. We need a flier and cash. And then you will never see us again."

Trev glanced from Khim to Arch.

"To the point, I see." Arch smiled at Khim. "I can supply you with both if you can change the tracking code on the flier. When it is found missing, I will simply report it stolen. The cash will not be much, but I have some on hand, better than nothing."

Just then, Renn came in. "Sir, the hotel is expecting us at four."

"Thank you, Renn." Arch stood. "Well, I'm off to finish packing. Renn can show you around. Or you can explore on your own. The garage is one level down. I have five fliers, all spaceworthy. Take your pick, except for the blue. That one we'll be taking with us to the hotel. It will be sold too, but at a later date."

"Of course," Trev said.

Their luck might be hanging by a wisp of spider silk, but they still had it.

*

The blue flier they were not allowed to take would have been ideal. It was a Merosch, sleek and curvy and with every gadget one could imagine built in.

Trev chose the silver Lyric, opening its gull-wing doors and leaning inside. He could feel Khim's heat right behind him and immediately thought of Renn, how Arch had called him "my lover." A brief image came to his mind of the two of them together, Renn and Arch, and something inside Trev ached.

Slipping inside the vehicle, he began disabling the tracker using the holoscreen, gesturing through the air.

Khim stood beside the door, waiting. His resolute counterpart. Quite the match in many ways. At that thought, Trev's heart beat faster.

He stuck his head out. "There's a plate at the rear. We need to have any identifying exterior objects removed."

"On it," Khim said.

Trev felt both odd and happy that Khim moved so quickly at any request, immediately and without question.

When they finished readying the flier, they both stood in front of it, arms crossed.

Khim said, "I still don't trust him."

"We have to trust a little bit, Khim. What other choice do we have?"

"In our position? None, of course."

Trev took a deep breath. "We're going to do this. We're going to make this all work."

Khim turned to him as if he were about to say something, then tilted his head away, his eyes almost sad.

Trev had the urge to touch him, the way his father did whenever Trev was troubled or needed encouragement. But Khim hated touch. Trev clamped down on the sadness that began to well inside him, turned and headed for the garage elevator. Khim followed.

The elevator doors opened onto the foyer that led to the big living room with the hearth. The hearth glowed orange and brown with some kind of electric fire that looked real but never burned out. It even gave off the scent of woodsmoke.

The curtains to the right were opened to the sloping field of the front yard, verdant and forested with maples and pine. In the great room, sunlight streamed into all the corners and made auroras out of motes of dust. Everything was tidy, serene.

Trev said, "I said a man who has nothing left to lose might do anything to gain ground again. Anything. And then Renn was there. And he contradicted that statement."

"Did you believe him?" Khim asked.

"I did at the time." Trev hesitated, worrying he was overstepping, then asked, "What is your take on him?"

"I've only worked closely with other soldiers of my kind. Not servants. Not—" He swallowed. "—toys," he finished. "But he would say anything his owner told him to say, unless his conditioning is broken."

Like yours is. Trev did not say the thought aloud. He nodded. "Do you want to leave now?"

"After dark would be the ideal time."

Trev felt his stomach begin to knot. On the run again so soon, not even a day's reprieve. He knew it would be this way for a while. Perhaps forever. "Okay." His palms felt damp, his whole body nerve-racked. If anything ever happened to Khim, he didn't know what he'd do. "Nervous?" he asked.

Khim's mouth twitched. "Steady."

Trev looked at Khim's hands, the metal one so perfectly sculpted it looked like a glove, as beautiful as the flesh hand but in a different way. They so often were clenched in fists at his sides, and now was no exception. Khim looked more nervous than Trev had ever seen him. But he loved that Khim had lied about not being so nervous. It made him feel strangely protected.

*

Khim followed him everywhere.

Trev went to the piano, and Khim was there. He showed him a few chords. Minor-keyed echoes filled the room.

Khim said, "Music is like math."

"Yes, but it truly soars when you take it beyond that point."

Trev went to the kitchen for a glass of water. Khim was there too.

Trev went to the bedroom to wash up for lunch. And Khim was there. They were so used to sharing a small space, it didn't really bother either of them to wash up in the big bathroom sink together.

In the hall they heard voices—distant, emotional. Trev opened the bedroom door and peered out. Khim came to his side.

Arch stood tall against the window's white light at the end of the hall, but Renn was taller. Trev could not make out the words, but Arch's tone grew urgent. Then he took his hand and put it on Renn's shoulder. Renn leaned in and kissed him.

Just like that.

It wasn't startling to Trev, but so natural his entire body filled with warmth to see it. He looked at Khim, whose eyes were down, shadowed as if staring unhappily at the floor.

Trev leaned against the doorframe. The man at his side was anything but "steady." This was someone, Trev had realized over the past two days, he never wanted to let go. "It isn't fair that Renn has to be sold, but he refuses to run with us."

Still looking down, Khim said, "No. It isn't fair. But his conditioning is stronger than mine. He will not break the law."

Trev said, "I'm going to make sure you are never sold again."

Khim looked up, eyes big. Calm. But with an inner desolation. Again Trev had the most urgent wish to touch him. "I believe you," Khim said, "But sometimes things happen that are not under our control."

*

They ate an oddly tense but good lunch with Arch and Renn.

After lunch, Arch took Trev off into his private study and shut the door. He presented him with an envelope of ten thousand credits cash. And an ID.

"This is not the ID I had made up for you before our deal went south. Your father knows that one. This one is generic and will not hold up if anyone looks at it closely. I can do nothing for Khim. You will need to forge ownership papers if you want to keep him at your side. Otherwise, let him go."

A strange coldness at the word "ownership" wrapped Trev's heart.

Soon after, the android and the embezzler left. Forever.

Trev watched their blue flier take off into the paleness of the midafternoon sky, its sound on the air like an echoing cry.

Now they were alone again.

Trev wandered the shadows of the house, the emptiness of it reflecting his heart more than he wanted to admit. Khim sat on the couch looking at a digital screen. Playing at being steady, for the moment.

Trev remembered waking that morning, Khim sitting by the bed in a hard, straight chair. Khim had never left his side even then, and the thought increased the nervous feelings that twisted inside him. His blood kept feeling hot and cold at the same time. He needed— something. Reassurance? Or maybe a short walk?

Trev came up behind the couch, looking down at Khim, and said, "You slept all night in a chair. You should get some rest before we leave."

"You have a hole in your shoulder," Khim replied without looking up. "You should too."

"I have all this pent-up tension. I'm going for a walk. There's a garden out back, well protected from prying eyes, just off the glass porch. I'll be there."

Khim lifted his head back to the couch cushion with his throat revealed—a vulnerable position for anyone, let alone an android. But now they were alone. And something strange was happening between them.

Their eyes met, upside down. Khim's were searching, troubled.

Trev said, "Even just a half-hour nap would do you some good."

Khim said softly, "You know I will not sleep."

"I know." Something sparked between them, a fusion of light. A beam that touched the center of Trev's heart.

Neither one looked away.

Khim looked momentarily lost. He was so beautiful sitting in his white shirt on the white leather, waiting for his fate. Khim's eyes traveled over Trev's face, and the gaze went slowly from confident apprehension to adoration. Or maybe it had been adoration all along?

Trev gave a little gasp. His blood quickened. Khim's golden aura seemed suffused with a different kind of tension now—a tremble of breath, a dampness on his lips, which looked darker than normal, full. His muscles seemed held in check only by force of will.

The dusk in Khim's eyes was backlit with a rising ivory light like that of the moon on a foggy night.

"Khim." Trev's voice came in a whisper, as if he was afraid Khim would look away.

But Khim's gaze held.

"How long have you been—" Trev stopped and swallowed. *How long have you been in love with me?* he wanted to ask.

Head back, Khim did not move. He watched Trev like a careful animal just coming into the light, finally able to trust.

And Trev realized he needed to turn that question around. *How long have I been in love with him?*

Khim said, quite calm, eyes still aglow, "Make sure you're not seen."

"What?" Trev asked.

"On your walk."

"Yeah." Finally he glanced up and away. Mind reeling, he went out the back French doors and onto the elaborate glass porch. There was a sliding glass door that led down stone steps and into a jungle of greens with sweet scents and buzzing bees.

*

Trev heard the bees and saw dark yellow waves of poppies covering the undergrowth along the path. He smelled the elixirs of the flowers, fresh from the rainstorm like a spell of newness amid all the havoc and madness of the past few weeks of his life.

He stretched his shoulders, the injured one complaining but so much better now that Khim had tended it, as if it had already almost healed. He lifted his hands, ran them through his hair, tugging.

He heard himself make an oddly strangled sound. Now he forced himself to think about it, look at it from all angles—backward, forward, up, down.

I'm in love with Khim.

The thought crashed into his mind like the obvious, explosive revelation it was, hurtling through him with a million hot sparks. It was devastating. It was exhilarating.

And thoroughly impractical right now.

The earth was still damp under the grass in some places. His bare feet felt the coolness, the soft measure of calm, growing things, life clinging all around him in air and water and light.

He took a deep breath of the freshness, feeling the energy of it hit the bottoms of his lungs.

He closed his eyes as the sun's heat played on his face. He opened them again and walked faster, to the far end of the garden, fronds dipping over and around him.

Finally he came to a cul-de-sac in the pathway and followed it around until he once again faced the magnificent house, its Victorian architecture a supreme work of art.

The glass windows of the back porch gleamed in the sun, and he saw the dark silhouette of a figure there looking out. Serene and still, and as steadfast as the deepest gravity of his innermost thoughts.

Khim was watching him.

Trev's body burned.

He thought he saw a hand pressed to the glass, Khim's hand, strong and reaching out.

Trev moved toward the house faster now, holding himself back from a run. His bare feet pushed against dirt, seeds, weeds. He stopped when he reached the little stone stairs caked in dust.

Impractical. Unbelievable. Incredible.

He looked up. Khim's eyes were on him. He couldn't see their color or their expression from where he stood, only the man. Only the waiting man.

He leaped up the steps, taking the whole of them in one stride, landing lightly on his bare feet on the warm porch floor just within the borders of the sliding glass door.

Khim turned from the window in a shower of golden light.

Chapter Twenty-Two

Khim

Khim stood on the glass porch that overlooked the backyard and saw Trev's dark head as he wandered among tall green plants that waved in a breeze. Some of the long fronds were topped with blue and red flowers. Stretching to the edge of Archimedes's island in the clouds were carpets of brilliant yellow buds. They made curving, crazy paths all about the acreage.

It was the first time in his short life he had a free hour to stare out a window and think. It was why he'd come out to the porch in the first place.

That, and one even bigger reason. He had not wanted to let Trev out of his sight. Not for one fleeting second.

Every day he found himself listening, straining for Trev's voice. All the time now. The barrier inside him made of glass, or maybe of ice, was beginning to crack, beginning to melt all around him.

He closed his eyes and saw two images—a hand flattened against a glass window, a person looking out.

This was who he was deep inside. A man locked away. The one who had wept openly at his birth sat behind that glass looking out. Kept back. Held back. His breath a fog against the pane.

Khim's heart thundered. The light leaped upon the glass that kept everything out. And everyone.

He saw himself now as if he had always been made of glass—vulnerable, transparent, easily broken, and day to day never allowing the cold or heat to penetrate. And never the longing. But he was awakened now, eyes wide open; he was looking out through his glass self all the time since meeting Trev.

He opened his eyes. The back lawn stretched to the pink-edged cumulus wafting by.

He saw misty air, fresh-cut grass, and a dark-haired, dark-eyed man in a blue shirt at the center of the garden, walking slowly, hands in his pockets. He heard the assured, commanding voice of Trev in his head. It said, *Live. Survive. Heal. Do not blame yourself.*

He would trail that voice straight into the unknown if he could, realizing it was okay to be the gold cloud that followed the sun.

His life was his, but other men had unfairly claimed it. Taken him. Invaded him. Enslaved him.

Now he chose.

The sun streamed into him through the porch window. Trev was at the end of the garden path, turning. Khim put his hand to the glass. Warm. Smooth. Air came into him. The glass expanded. He was a tiny flame within the enclosure, the cage of himself, the porch room. He looked at his hands, the dark metal fist a black flower opening—not a weapon, but a man reaching out, one hand in the earth, one in the stars.

Inside he was tight, coiled, ready to break through. Shatter the glass. Ready to hear the bells of its sharp shards hitting the foundations beneath him, the broken pieces like tears falling through the mist.

A leftover tendril of fog caressed the man who now walked back toward the porch, his gait speeding, his mouth smiling. He walked to the bottom of the steps, hesitated for a moment, then leaped upward, bypassing them all and landing through the open plate-glass door, bare feet smacking the floor.

Trev moved toward Khim.

Trev. With the kindness, the acuity, the agility and beauty of angels.

"Khim, I—"

At the same moment, Khim was saying, "Trev—"

"You seem different now." Trev stepped up to him, eyes as bright as comets adrift on a night sky.

Khim's mouth opened but not for air. Heat worked itself into the backs of his eyes. He reached out, not quite ready for flesh to flesh yet, metal hand cupping the other man's firm jaw, his cheek, fingers moving into the dark brown hair.

Khim thought he could feel the texture of Trev's skin through the metal—that was how close he felt to this man—that smooth edge

208

and firmness of Trev surging up his arm. He was safe enough now to wonder at it, both feeling and not feeling, both metal and flesh.

Trev's eyebrows shifted up in a slight question, but he did not move.

Fear stirred in Khim's belly for one moment before it dissipated. Without waiting for Trev to take the lead, Khim tilted Trev's head in his hand, leaned in, and kissed him softly on the lips.

The glass of his old self shattered completely. He stood as if for the first time, fresh from the vats, liquid dripping all over him, hot and cold, hand cupping the face of a beautiful man.

Their mouths pressed, moist and warm, Trev's lips molding to his and opening slightly with such a sweet breath, like the air Khim needed so desperately.

Trev did not reach or grab or move, he just stood there and let Khim kiss him. And Khim was grateful, for he wasn't sure beyond this bright moment what he might endure or how much he could take. He just wanted to let his mind go into the kiss, both fevered and soothing, but wholly reverent.

Trev pressed in just a little, as if to let Khim know the kiss was returned, and did nothing more than that.

A breeze came through the door behind them. Wings flapped to the sky outside. Bees droned.

Seconds passed... or maybe eons. Finally they pulled back at the same time, Trev's eyes full and glowing. He was breathing hard when he whispered, "I'm glad you stopped hating me."

The light through the windows glanced off Trev's smooth cheekbones, the firm jaw, settled like sheer lace in his hair. He looked good in Arch's dark blue shirt, the stiff collar at his neck open, the hollow of his throat exposed but shadowed.

Khim's metal hand dropped away from Trev's face. They stared at each other, still breathing hard. Too many winds surged in Khim's head. But he withstood them all.

Trev said, very softly, "Now touch me with the other hand."

Anything that voice said, he would do. Khim lifted his left hand. The warmth of the face against his flesh hand, he thought, might leave a red mark on his palm. It was that intense. Slowly, he explored the contours of that beautiful face, tracing sensitive fingertips over forehead, eyelids, nose, lips. Trev's breath warmed his fingers, almost tickling. Khim's hand curved to cup Trev's chin.

Trev's eyes never left Khim's gaze.

Khim wanted—he didn't know exactly what he wanted. Or maybe he didn't want to know. Or to think. Just to feel, that was all. That was everything.

He started to lean in. Trev moved his head up to meet him.

The second kiss flared between them.

Again, Trev did not reach or grab. But it was as if they were already entangled, bodies in a tumult flying through space, careening.

Khim lost all coherence in that kiss. Everything fit, but nothing made sense.

It didn't matter. The sublime moment deserved a universe of its own. With new laws and new logic.

The black forever opening onto a new land.

When they again broke apart, lips damp, cheeks flushed, Trev brought his hands up to waist level between them, palms up.

Khim sent a question with his eyes.

"I want to put my arms around you, but… I guess I'm asking permission."

Khim thought back over the years. Ten as a soldier. Twenty years of fake memory with huge gaping blanks in it. Some amorphous, youthful sexual encounter tried to surface—not his encounter, not his memory, not even his body. He said, "No one has ever done that, that I can remember."

Trev's eyebrows scrunched together. "No one has ever hugged you before?" Khim shook his head. "Fuck."

Khim lowered his head, his gaze seeking the floor, stopping and holding on Trev's bare feet. He heard Trev say, "May I?"

Khim nodded. Forced himself not to think as Trev came into his personal space, pressed against him chest to chest, and circled him with his arms. Khim's breath caught as hands put pressure against his ribs, his shoulder blades.

Trev's head fit just right under his chin, forcing Khim's chin up, his gaze moving over Trev's shoulders to the stripes of light on the white sills, the way the glass all around made everything so brilliant, including the man who held him.

All breath froze. His throat closed. A sting in his eyes blurred his vision; the moisture in them threatened to break free. He pulled back suddenly. Trev let go, not fighting him.

He couldn't see for a moment, couldn't hear, couldn't think.

"You're okay," he heard Trev saying. "You're not going to lose control. Not with me here."

But it wasn't that—lack of control, or even a control issue at all. Or the fact that he might have been weeping. It was simply that he had never felt anything like that, or the kisses, and he wanted it. This feeling. A huge, hollow part of his life was missing this incredible force, this source of all things. The myth he had come to know and never believed in; the myth called love.

His eyes cleared, and he was again looking down at Trev's beautiful face.

Trev looked a little worried. "Too fast?"

Khim blinked. "No. Do it again."

Trev said, "Well—" and pushed his body up against Khim's again, arms going solidly around him.

This time Khim brought his own arms up over Trev's shoulders and gently squeezed.

"Ow."

Khim eased up immediately. "I forgot. The pulse burn!"

But Trev did not seem to be in much pain. He was clutching him tighter and laughing against his chest, saying between breaths, "Please, don't let go."

It was like holding a squirming, hot light. Trev's body thrummed with life. Khim could feel that energy pulse into his own body, into his blood, feeding a need, a fierce pleasure. Trev's hair smelled of the chamomile soap from Arch's guest bathroom. The dark waves brushed soft against Khim's cheek.

Every instinct in him wanted to hold tight, tighter, but he kept himself back, his embrace gentle. Trev's head moved up until they were face-to-face, arms around each other, chest to chest, stomach to stomach, thighs brushing, and their lips met again.

Their third kiss was explosive.

For how long they stood on that porch, Khim did not know. But the light outside was beginning to dim.

When they finally pulled apart, bodies hot and trembling, Khim said, not without some pain, "We should get ready to leave."

Trev looked forlorn.

*

They packed the extra clothing Renn had given them in a zippered bag. Trev wanted the black robes too, so he rolled them up and put them inside.

Khim said, "We should take the medikit too. You never know."

Trev stuck it in a side flap. Another compartment held their money and Trev's new ID. A bag in another side pocket held some snacks they'd raided from the kitchen. They'd already packed bottled water in the flier.

"We need some shoes," Trev said.

They hunted the house for anything that might fit. Everything they found was too small for Khim or too large for Trev. They decided they would have to wear plain slip-ons, which merely made them look like wealthy vacationers in designer trousers and bright pink flip-flops.

They stood side by side in front of the wide closet mirrors in Arch's master bedroom.

"I think we'll pass," Trev said.

"Except for me."

"No. It's fine. Anyone questions, we'll just say you're mine. I mean, well, of course I would never—"

"No, it's okay." Khim turned away from the mirror so he could meet Trev's eyes without any glass between them. "I'm yours."

Trev bit hard on his lower lip. Then he said, "Too bad we can't stay and get to know this place better." He reached out his hand, waiting. Khim took it.

As if everything were perfectly normal, Trev led him out of the room.

*

...with one image he would make that beauty explode into me.
— Proust

The flier shot into the pink-edged, dark sky. Already the stars had opened their eyes.

Khim did not say a word when Trev automatically went to the pilot's seat. Trev was a fantastic pilot. Khim thought he might show him, someday, that he himself was a little bit better. But now was not the time.

He could still feel the tingle on his lips, the kiss that had pretty much upstaged his entire life of alien battles, torrid rapists' brothels, inmate murders, and prison escapes. He could not remember a single moment in all his real-memory life that made him feel so wonderfully torn open, beautiful, amazed. And so filled with desire he almost could not think.

"So unless you've come up with anything better," Trev said, "we're off to Gideon. And an off-the-grid motel in the middle of nowhere."

"We will stand out more there."

"You think a bigger city would be better to hide in? They have building screens everywhere. Our pictures have probably been flashed a hundred times since yesterday. We're fresh in everybody's minds. Plus, my father—"

"Yes," Khim interrupted. "I know. He has a long reach. Spies everywhere."

Frowning, Trev jerked his head to look at him. "So, middle of nowhere, then?"

Khim nodded tightly. To his mind, nowhere was truly safe. They needed to get off-world. But none of Arch's fliers had been interplanetary spaceworthy. They needed a small ship. One that could enter foldspace—and not one of the old ones that allowed the madness of foldspace to intrude. They needed one with a shield. Then they could stay in foldspace, hide there if they had to.

But starships, big or little, were not easy to commandeer.

The flier fell into some clouds for a moment, white against encroaching darkness. And came out of the fog to the sight of two moons rising, twin silver arcs against deep violet.

Trev said, "Wow."

He took them lower, past more clouds, to the dark side of the planet below where night already rested its cloak.

Khim liked watching Trev's hands fly over the controls. The flier's traffic system always compensated for other fliers in the area, so all the pilot had to do was set the destination and relax. But Trev told Khim he liked to keep it on manual sometimes just to alleviate boredom.

But now Trev set the autopilot.

"One hour, two minutes to destination," the flier reported.

Trev drew up a computer screen. "Damn. I was hoping to make reservations using this system. But this one's tapped, like all of Arch's other computer hubs. I don't dare pull up the wave."

"Hopefully the motel takes cash."

"Well, we need a store. I can buy a handheld, and we can get some shoes. And I can put some of our cash on a credit chip in case the motel has fits about the cash." Trev leaned back, and the computer screen disappeared from the air. "There are stores in town near the motel."

"More chances of being seen," Khim commented.

"I know. But we have to get this stuff."

Khim looked down through the floor window. Far below, the cities on this side of Gideon stood out in glittered groupings of lights. In between, in the darker spaces, were mountains or rivers or seas.

"I always loved flying at night," Trev said.

Throughout the flight Trev made comments. Khim enjoyed listening to his voice, the tone washing over him.

So far they had not discussed what had happened on the glass porch, but Khim's insides were still spun by it, his mind in a fever. Trev seemed tense, but their circumstances were on the extreme end of stress-inducing.

Khim asked, "How does your shoulder feel?"

"Good. The muscle's sore. But the worst of the pain left with the meds I took last night."

Their conversations were short but comforting. The worst part of the trip was anticipating their arrival and not being able to assess their safety until they scoped everything out.

When they were minutes away, Trev took back the controls and piloted them into the little town, a collection of white and bronze twinkling lights on the edge of a sand-drifted, dry seabed.

Low buildings came into view. At the same time, they saw a sign for a small store, and Trev pulled up and parked.

Khim felt his skin prickle. This moment could be it. The end.

"I'm going in alone. I have a scarf to tie around my hair."

Khim nodded. He didn't want Trev to leave. He must've shown that on his face, because Trev touched the top of his hand gently, and Trev rarely touched him without asking first.

"Five minutes, I promise. It'll be okay."

Khim said, "If I could go with you—"

"You'll just draw more attention. I'm little and good at being invisible."

Khim could only nod, his mouth too dry to say anything more.

He watched Trev, in the blue shirt and the designer trousers that were too long for him, with the slip-on shoes and the scarf, enter the store. While he was gone, Khim could barely keep himself from jumping out of the car and rushing in after him. He pressed his hands tight on his thighs and kept his eyes open for anything unusual.

For the time of night in this time zone, the store was not busy. It looked like an outpost for tourists more than a regular daily shop-and-go. That was a plus. He and Trev looked like tourists who had every right to be there. Even a high-end flier would not be cause for discussion.

It took longer than five minutes, but Trev came out the front door laden with packages.

Khim clicked open the gull-wing back door, and Trev deposited his treasures and then hurried around the front, opened the side door, and got in.

Two minutes in the air and they were at the motel, with Trev hopping out before the engine had even purred to a stop. Other fliers were parked in the lot, but there was no one outside. Trev moved up to a lighted door, stood there a moment, and then came back to the flier. Khim stayed seated, waiting for the go-ahead.

Trev popped his head through the doorway. "Good news. The sign says there are vacancies and you can find one with a green light and slide your credit chit in. Auto check-in means we don't have to deal with people."

Khim let out a breath of relief. Trev found a room easily, near where they parked, and they hauled in their few belongings in one trip.

They stood just inside the door, looking around. It wasn't a horrible room, for the price. It had red carpet, and the decorations had a country flair, with ruffled curtains, plaid bedspreads, and lamps that looked like paddle cacti. It was small, but warm and clean and off the main highways, far from the cities.

It also had two beds, and Khim found himself unexpectedly disappointed at that.

Trev piled all their stuff on one bed, spreading it out. He'd gotten them both shoes, including two pairs in Khim's large size, black casual slip-ons and leather hiking boots. He also got the handheld and a few other odds and ends, including jackets with hoods. He swore the clerk was bored and barely looked at him as he checked out.

Beyond the motel they would make new plans, but for now they were glad to have made it through one more day on the run.

"Are you hungry?" Trev asked.

Khim realized he was and nodded. Trev was on the handheld in minutes, ordering a pizza to be delivered. When it came, Khim hid in the bathroom so it would look like only one person was in the room.

They ate, the box with the pizza spread out on one bed.

Khim said, "We're going to have to keep moving all the time. Get our food by drive-throughs and delivery. We need a starship so we can just leave."

Trev nodded. "I'm working on that. I'm a real good thief, remember?"

"Yes, you told me the story of the Bradbury."

"And if not for my damned father, I would never have gotten caught, either."

"All for a book."

"Yeah, but it's not just any book. It has elixirs and spells and stars."

A flash of white teeth as he grinned shyly.

There was something very endearing about Trev in that moment—talking about a subject he really loved, sitting in a dusty room away from prison cells and harsh environments, perched on the edge of an old bed, one knee casually pulled up.

Khim heard the desert wind come up to the door, not knocking, just brushing as if to say *I'm here*. He smelled the mustiness of age and a scent almost as if embers were embedded in the air.

Trev leaned forward, both legs over the side of the bed now, elbows on his knees. He ran his hands through his dark, shining hair, his back to Khim, shoulders slightly hunched.

Khim got up and took the trash to the recycler in the wall. He turned and in two steps was at the foot of the bed. The room was so small. But they were used to a cell, and before that Khim had shared a vast bunkroom with a couple of hundred other android soldiers, so this felt like unprecedented luxury.

Inside his chest, Khim could feel his heart clench, unclench, trip, and speed. Everything inside him had been on edge ever since he'd been sold, but nothing had prepared him for Trev. For this.

Trev turned his head and looked up. He brushed his palms over his thighs and stood. The clothing he wore was most definitely for a taller man, the cuffs of his trousers dragging the carpet, his shirttails nearly brushing the tops of his knees. The brown eyes sought his and held.

"Khim." Trev's voice came pitched low, tremulous. "Are you okay with everything? About today?"

Of course Khim wasn't okay with everything about their day— or the day before that. Prison. Escape. Pulse burn wounds. Putting his trust in the hands of strangers. Heading back out into a world of cameras, people, eyes on every corner. But he knew Trev was referring to none of that. "Yes."

Trev stood and took the two steps that brought him directly in front of Khim. "Can I—"

"Yes," he said quickly, knowing Trev was asking out of respect, not hesitancy.

Trev reached out and took his left hand. Just that one gesture, nothing more. He pulled Khim in. Khim felt as if his whole body were falling into that gravity, the thrumming, vibrating, beating life force that was Trev.

He squeezed Trev's hand. He did not remember leaning in or initiating anything, but he knew he did, because suddenly his arms were full of Trev, pulling him close, their breaths connecting, their mouths opening into one another.

Taste of salt. Fire. Extreme pizza. His hands went around Trev's waist, his arms slowly moving up. He wanted without thinking. He ached without pain.

Before he knew it, he had pulled Trev up to him. For a second he could not figure out why Trev was gasping—then he realized his grip and his own strength had naturally lifted Trev off the floor, bringing him face-to-face with Khim.

Trev pulled back in shock, still dangling. Then his eyes began to sparkle. He laughed and hugged Khim tight about the neck, lifting his legs like the acrobat he was and putting them around Khim's waist.

Khim put his hands under Trev's thighs to better support him.

This time their kiss echoed with smiles, and Trev's deep chuckles turned to groans.

They naturally moved onto the bed, lay down side by side. Trev took a breath. "You have literally swept me off my feet."

Khim's heartbeat was doing weird things. "I hope that's good?"

Another grin. "I've been waiting my whole life." Then he ordered the lights to dim and they were kissing again, bodies surging together as if maybe, if they did it just right, they could climb into each other's souls.

For a long time, they remained that way, hands roving, suggestive but slow, polite.

218

Both their shirts were unbuttoned. Trev's was half-off, his injured shoulder bare, showing its square of white bandage in the now-shadowed room. Khim's forefinger outlined the area.

Trev pushed himself up until Khim saw his face above him, looking down. "I don't do this every day," he said.

Khim allowed a small smile. "No?"

Trev shook his head. "Like, never. I'm not stupid, but maybe a few hints of what you like would help me."

Khim's cheeks got suddenly hot. "I don't know what I like."

Trev laughed under his breath. "Wonderful. The blind leading the blind."

"I know what sex is, of course. I've read the manuals."

"Manuals?" Trev chuckled.

"On my battleship, *Doom in Shadow*, my bunkmates would sometimes have sex openly with each other. And then there was the brothel—" His body tightened, mouth closing hard.

"Brothel?"

"I—that just slipped out." Khim's hands dropped to his sides. He had not wanted to tell Trev that story.

Trev noticed and backed off a bit. "During the war?"

"No."

"Where you were before the prison?"

Khim gave an almost imperceptible nod.

"Was that where you were injured?"

Khim's mouth was dry, but he could not deny Trev's questions. "I was sold, drugged, and taken there for less than a full day. That would have been my first time." Khim could not believe he was telling Trev this. He never thought he'd be able to form the words to ever speak of it.

"First time? For what?"

Khim's gaze went empty. "Sex, I guess."

Trev touched Khim lightly just above his heart.

Air caught in the back of Khim's throat.

"You know—" Trev hesitated, voice pitched to an almost whisper. "—r-rape is different from sex. It doesn't count. As the first time, I mean."

Khim had never talked about this before with anyone. He'd never spoken of his own rape to Trev. "What they did to me. I can't do that again. So if you're asking what I like, it's not that."

Trev made a little sound of frustration. Or sadness. Maybe both. "I wasn't even going to ask you to," he said gently. "You trust me, right?"

"Yes."

"Then know that I will never hurt you."

Khim wrapped his arms around him and pulled him closer, feeling their bodies conform to each other, flesh to flesh. "I do know that. Please, don't speak of it anymore."

"I just want to know you. I don't want to fuck this up. You're too special."

Khim kissed him to shut him up. Too many thoughts were beginning to clatter, too many unwanted images. All he desired was Trev, the here and the now. Any extra baggage could be left outside the door. Couldn't it?

But that was not what happened. Everything was here with them in this room, past as well as present, and a future of unknowns that terrified him in his own newness, his becoming. They did not get to compartmentalize this journey. It was a part of everything they had done and had been doing since the day they met.

The kiss was distracting, something they were good at. Something that brought tantalizing wonder back into the air between them when words got too tough. But it wasn't enough after a while. Not nearly. Not even close.

Trev's fingers kept gently pushing at Khim's waistband, wriggling under the fine material, fingertips probing at the softer areas of his body, the smooth curves at the tops of his buttocks, the tender flesh of the dent just below his hipbone.

His white shirt was long gone over the edge of the bed.

Trev's hand hovered over the fastenings now. "These are in the way, okay?"

"Okay," Khim said. And his body shivered as the clasp came undone and Trev pushed the trousers low, lower.

Khim pulled his legs out of them and turned away for a moment, getting his bearings. "Yours too," he whispered, trying not to sound as unsure as he felt.

Eyes closed now. On his back. The air on his skin like silk. Like fire. All the trembling coming from his core—it should not be right. This could not be normal, could it?

A voice in his mind spoke.

This is Trev beside you. Remember the deal. The real one, not the fake one. Trev is looking out for you. Trev saved you. Now. In the obscurity of new life. Now. Like being on the edge of an atmosphere just before the dive into space. Now. Trev wants you.

That is all.

Matter and time. Void and fire. None of it mattered on the edge of this dark town, in this room, in this hour of amnesty. Of bliss.

The mattress shuddered. He heard the sounds of cloth on cloth as Trev pushed off the rest of his own garments—pants, shirt, everything.

Khim opened his eyes.

He felt a gentle brushing against his side, the stark energy of youth, boundless and intemperate. Then flesh's touch, hip to hip, shoulder to shoulder. Hot breath upon his neck. But still Trev did not really touch him. Did not cover him, smother him, or even embrace him. He held back. He looked down.

Khim was hard, aching with want, but increasingly nervous. He turned his head to the window, where outside streetlights made the curtains into a dark gray square on the shadowed walls.

Trev hovered. Khim's body had the urge to arch up, but his muscles stayed slack. He was barely breathing. A hand touched the side of his face so gently, it was almost as if it wasn't there.

Trev said, "Khim. Look at me."

Khim kept his head turned, eyes on the gray glow of the curtains.

"Look at me" came the command again. "It's okay to let go."

The heat came into the backs of his eyes again. Was it okay? Now? In this moment? Lack of control was weakness. The leash Trev had on him had defined his boundaries, but now he was lost, searching for that leash in the dark and untamed wilds. His metal fist scrabbled for the coverlet, digging in though he could not feel it, the hand numb, alien... other.

His flesh hand, the left one, came up in the air, a fist blindly readying itself—for what? A punch? A battle? Resistance against a final, last gasp of letting go?

Trev's forehead was inches from Khim's cheek, the whisper of words muted, hushed. Loving. "I want to touch you. I want to feel you. May I? Please? Just to touch. Just to feel. Khim—"

Khim took shallow breaths. The corners of his eyes stung. He was shaking with need, exploding already within tremor after tremor. He wanted to cry out. Wanted to come up fighting, raging his passion to the stars. But he simply lay there and heard himself say, with all the pent-up desire inside him, "Yes."

Then, with more emphasis, on the undercurrents of his breath, "Yes!"

Trev moved over him, belly sliding skin to skin, body slipping along Khim's, hot, wiry, and taut with need.

He felt Trev's erection drag over his hip, his own like hot steel surging up. Khim's arms stretched. He let go of the coverlet, reaching up and grasping the man straddling him, digging fingers in his back, then sliding them lower to his buttocks.

Trev let out a small cry, a gasp. He mouthed a line along Khim's jaw. Finally Khim allowed his body what it wanted. He arched up.

Trev slid along the full length of his body in an answering thrust. Now Khim held his entire weight, Trev's legs splayed along either side of his thighs, and pearls of light detonated throughout his mind until he was made of sparks, of ash.

How long they moved together like that, he didn't know.

Once his body had crested, he came hard, pulsing between them, but that didn't stop them moving, kissing, undulating.

There was new dampness now between their sliding bodies, a slickness he loved. It heightened all they felt, the intimacy unparalleled.

Trev's mouth was all over his neck, his chest, then back to his lips. It was only a short while before Khim came again with full awareness, full force, his insides echoing with the thunder of it.

Trev cried out, and Khim felt him also pulse and twitch as he thrust in alluring, beautiful urgency against Khim's hard belly.

They lay for hours embracing, dozing.

In the middle of the night, Trev rose, pulled the blanket closer around Khim, and left the bed. But Khim was wide-awake and heard the shower come on. He pushed back the covers, found his balance against the rough, cheap carpet, and decided that he could, indeed, still walk. He made his way to the sound.

Steam floated through the tiny bathroom. The water pattered on the shower floor.

Khim, naked and unsure, stood on a towel in the middle of the floor, staring at the closed curtain.

A part of the curtain dented, folded back, and Trev's wet head appeared. "I hear you," he said. Then his eyebrows narrowed in the way of someone keeping secrets, and he looked Khim up and down, rolled his eyes, and smiled. "Fuck. Mr. Beautiful. Get in here."

Khim stepped in under the spray, the warmth an embrace, a benediction. But the second embrace was even better. Trev put his arms around him, pulled him against him.

Khim had the urge to lift him up again, but didn't—things were far too wet and slippery. He put his arms around Trev and rested his palms against the sweeping buttocks, gently caressing.

A low sound escaped Trev's throat as he leaned up for a kiss. They both grew hard again.

Merging mouth to mouth, he held Trev tight under the warm fall of water.

How do I deserve this?

Chapter Twenty-Three

Trev

Trev woke smiling. His legs were entangled with Khim's. His head rested on Khim's shoulder. Khim's breath ruffled his hair.

The room lay about them in shades of russet, woodsmoke, and thunderhead black. He could hear the purr of the desert wind.

Khim's heart beat strongly against the palm of Trev's hand where it lay against the center of his chest. Trev moved his fingers gently, feeling the satin of Khim's perfect skin, thrilling at the fact that he had no hair except for eyebrows, lashes, and scalp. Some golden strands of hair curved against Khim's neck. He could see that shimmer even in the room's faint predawn.

Fugitive, relentlessly pursued, near-broke, and planet-bound without a plan, he wondered that he could feel such contentment, such serenity.

His body was liquid, more sated than he could ever remember being. He did not want the dawn to come. A sound of protest came from his throat.

Khim woke. He moved onto his side, pulling Trev to him as he did so.

Neither spoke.

An hour passed, and the first rays of sunrise glimmered under the plain curtains.

They sat up as one.

Trev said, "We need to leave. Find a different place every night."

Khim nodded. "Just in case."

Trev placed a hand alongside Khim's face. Khim kissed his palm.

They were ready in ten minutes, all their stuff packed again and set neatly by the door. They both wore their new boots. Khim looked fine in his white shirt and black trousers. Trev had on a pair of jeans he'd bought in the camp store, which weren't dragging on the ground. And Arch's blue shirt.

Flutterings of apprehension dragged at Trev's stomach lining. He looked up at Khim. "Ready?"

"Ready," Khim said in his best soldier's voice.

Trev heard the unspoken *sir* in that answer.

They walked out into early-morning desert shadow.

Silence. A dry breeze swept bits of tumble-twig and grains of sand across the lot. At the edge of the horizon, scraps of torn cloud flagged the sunrise. Around them the green-orange sky went on forever to the curve of space. The air smelled singed, old.

They approached their flier, arms full. Trev balanced bags and entered the code to unlock it. The gull-wing doors flew up.

As Trev bent to deposit his things in the back, he heard footsteps on the asphalt lot. Before he turned, dread came like acid to the back of his throat.

He straightened, hands at his sides, and slowly pivoted.

Breq stood before him, a candle tube in his hand. Behind him stood Vance.

The black hair of Trev's two older brothers shimmered in the weird Gideon light. They were wearing dark suits, as usual. Their normally cool, detached demeanors transmitted some surprise, along with smug satisfaction.

Trev said one word. "No."

He heard Khim rustling with packages on the other side of the car. Then silence.

Breq smiled. "Hello, Trev."

Even as he shook his head in denial, Trev said, "Breq." He looked to the side. "Vance."

"Wasn't sure. Came on a hunch, a rumor." Breq paused. The candle tube in his hand did not waver. "Do you have the android with you?"

"What?"

"Father doesn't like to see his investments go missing."

"What investment?" Trev held up his empty hands.

"The one on the other side of your flier. Nice of you to break him out of prison for us. Saved a lot of time and effort."

As Breq spoke, a flash of gold-white-black flew through the air so fast the eye did not have time to follow nor the body to react.

The next thing, Khim and Breq were on the ground and the candle tube was arcing high in the air, end over end, gleaming, like an arrow that had lost its speed. It landed on the blacktop with a loud clatter.

A gasping, gagging sound came from Breq as Khim's hands encircled his neck and squeezed.

Vance ran forward and grabbed the candle from the pavement, waving it toward Khim and Breq, shouting, "Stop. Stop! That android's out of control!"

Trev stepped in front of Vance, breathing hard. "Don't shoot, you idiot. You might hit Breq!" He saw that Breq's face had already turned bright red. He was weakly clawing at Khim's chest, but his hands could get no purchase. He didn't have the strength.

"Khim," Trev called. "Khim!" He began to tremble. He couldn't just stand there and watch his brother die. He couldn't. "Khim! Stop!"

Khim kept his hands where they were, but his head slowly swiveled toward Trev. His look was incredulous.

"Stop!" Trev commanded again when their eyes met.

A look of savage betrayal hardened the perfect features.

A single sob escaped Trev's throat. "Khim! He's my brother!"

Khim gave a cry of frustration and sat back, hands coming away from Breq's throat. Then he did something that broke Trev's heart. He drew his knees beneath him, bent over his own lap, and locked his hands behind the back of his neck. He stayed that way, facedown, the dust of the asphalt settling in his beautiful hair.

Breq was trying to sit up, still gagging, hand at his throat, dry-heaving onto the ground.

Vance and Trev ran toward Khim at the same time. Vance got there first, still wielding the candle.

"Please don't shoot him!" Trev yelled.

Without looking up, Vance began to kick Khim hard in the side, saying over and over, "He's out of control!" Then he pointed the candle directly at Khim's head.

Trev slammed into Vance hard, pushing him down. "Stop it! He's not out of control. He's defending himself. And me!"

Vance fell back, ass hitting the ground, still clutching the candle. Breq was now trying to stand. Khim stayed curled over, hands behind his head, unmoving.

Trev looked around him, taking it all in. "Fuck!"

He turned to Breq, who was slowly trying to rise. "What's the matter with you guys? Damn it! What the fuck?"

Vance came up fast but stayed where he was, eyes on Khim, fearful. But he now held the candle down by his side. "That android should be put down. I don't know why Dad wants him back."

Breq said, "We came to get you, Trev. And that crazy monster Dad thinks is worth something."

At first Trev could not comprehend any of what they said. He could only see Khim, alone and still. He dropped to his knees at Khim's side. "What do you mean Dad wants him? Dad doesn't even know Khim."

Breq let out a scratchy laugh, throat still recovering. He did not smile, though.

Vance said, "You truly don't know, do you?"

"Know what?"

Breq answered. "He doesn't know the Damico Corporation owns that thing!" He looked directly at Trev. "That Dad owns Khim."

"What? I didn't know that." Tears of shock fell onto his cheeks, searing. "I didn't." Trev's hand was resting gently on Khim's shoulder.

Khim made a grumble of protest but did not move.

Trev took a couple of heaving breaths.

Breq added, "So we've come to collect him. And you. The gods only know why Dad wants *you* back." He grabbed Trev's arm, not ungently, and pulled him up and away from Khim. He locked clasps of cold metal about his wrists from behind. Then he bent and did the same to Khim. Trev could see they were strong cuffs, made for violent types.

"Breq, you don't have to do this. Tell Dad you never found us. Please!"

"Why should I?"

This, from a man whose life I just saved.

"Android, up!" Vance ordered, waving the candle tube.

Shackled and utterly still, Khim did not move.

"Android!" Vance said again. Now he lifted the tube.

"No!" Trev cried. "Don't shoot him. Please."

The candle tube was the worst. It could break walls or impart great pain to the human nervous system. It was a horrible weapon.

"We have to get to the flier now," Breq said stiffly.

Trev sniffed. The tears were still rolling uncontrollably down his face. He looked down to where Khim was still curled around himself on the blacktop. "Khim. Can you stand?" He spoke softly past the giant knot in his throat. "Khim. Please. Stand. Now."

The man at their feet moved, pushing up. In one graceful movement, he was standing tall and straight, perfectly balanced. But his head stayed down, eyes focused only on the ground.

Breq and Vance walked them to a big black flier around the corner of the building. Trev recognized it immediately—it was their father's. Sleek, top of the line.

Khim and Trev were forced into the backseat, made to lean uncomfortably against their cuffed hands. Breq strapped them in while Vance started up the flier's engine.

Trev glanced once through blurry eyes at Khim, but Khim's head remained bowed. His unblinking eyes stared at his lap as if frozen there. His inner self was astray.

Trev whispered to the lost man beside him, blinking back tears. "Khim. I'm so sorry."

But there was no response.

*

The flier took them up from the endless waves of sand surrounding the little town and the dark motel into the pinking clouds. This flier was speedier than most. The male voice in its programming announced their destination would be reached in thirty-three minutes.

Trev thought they were going back home, to Dante's upside-down triangle mansion on its island of trees, of gardens, of waterfalls crashing over the land's edge.

Instead they headed fast and straight toward the looming towers of Fire Town.

Trev wished he could get a hand free, reach out to Khim. He had tried with his voice, whispering Khim's name several times, but there was no response.

He heard his brother Vance make a call. The way Vance spoke, Trev could only assume Dante was on the receiving end. He reported that "Trev and the android are on their way."

When he finished the call, Vance said, "Hey, Trev, how come that android obeys everything you say, huh?"

Trev turned his head to the side window as blue sky and dots of cloud soared by. The horizons all around brimmed with orange light.

"Does he think you own him because you're a Damico?" Vance asked.

Trev held his breath, anger and fury warring.

"C'mon, fess up. Why does he do everything you say?" Vance turned in his seat.

"He doesn't." Trev's voice came out quiet, low.

"But you made him submit. That's pretty cool. How'd you do it?"

"Shut up, Vance." Trev swallowed against the heaviness in his throat. "Just shut the fuck up!" He was surprised that with very little air in his lungs, he'd managed to yell.

"Who'da thought you had it in you, a little guy like you," Vance said.

To Trev's surprise, Breq's fist shot out and impacted with Vance's shoulder. "What the fuck's wrong with you? He's our brother. If Dad heard you talking to him like that—"

"What? Aren't you curious? I mean, you saw it that night. Khim's out of control. Dangerous. But Trev here says one word to it—"

"Fucking shut up," Breq said.

Why was Breq defending him? Trev wondered. Did he feel guilty because Trev had called Khim off before he killed him?

Trev didn't think Breq loved him particularly much. In fact, when they'd been kids, Breq had behaved like a jealous brat. But over the years, when they had to, they'd worked well together. They did, on occasion, seem to like each other. Breq was always calling Trev on his wrist comm, but Trev thought his brother just enjoyed bothering him. Or maybe he was a little lonely.

Trev wished he knew more about what his brothers had been talking about in the parking lot. What exactly had happened that Breq and Vance had seen that had landed Khim, beaten and raped, in prison? His brothers could be sadists in business, just like Dante. But rapists? Trev didn't think so. That wasn't how they were raised, despite Dante's little side businesses in the sex trade.

But still, somehow, Khim had known them. They had known Khim. There was rage in Khim as he'd tried to kill Breq.

It explained much about the day they'd first met, how Khim had reacted so strongly to Trev's name and why he had, at first, refused to share a cell with him.

And when Khim had found himself in danger of losing control, losing his right to life over one more act of violence, it must have been terrible for him to have to come to Trev because of the power of that last name and make their deal.

Trev whispered again to the man at his side, to the air. "I'm sorry, Khim. I'm sorry."

Up front, Vance looked pissed, shaking his head.

At that moment the flier arced, turned, and descended amid the multicolored lights, tall buildings, and the huge one-hundred-foot floating screens of Fire Town.

*

They parked at a place called the Rainspeer Hotel.

230

The underground garage, lit by eerie, pale lights, was haunted with shadows.

Trev walked by Khim's side, glancing sidelong at him. Khim never lifted his head. His golden hair fell along the sides of his face, hiding any expression Trev might glimpse.

The four of them entered a stuffy, too-small elevator. To Trev's surprise, instead of going up, the car went down a long way, so deep Trev could hear the machinery of the antigrav engines that helped hold Fire Town aloft in the skies above Gideon.

When the doors opened, they entered a long hallway, thickly carpeted in off-white, the walls painted in curving white and gray stripes.

Khim froze, standing in place just outside the elevator doors.

The others turned.

"Let's go," Breq said.

Khim, hands behind his back, head bowed, did not move.

"Get moving," Vance hissed.

"Breq," Trev said, trying to get his older brother to look at him. He inadvertently tugged at his cuffs, wincing as his injured shoulder pulled. "What happened here?"

"What?"

"Can't you see?" Trev let out a hard breath. "Something really bad happened. He doesn't want to go back. Would you?"

"We're not going to the bagnio. I mean, we're going through it, but not to it."

"The what?"

"The bordello, stupid."

"Well, I haven't been here before, so I don't know!"

Breq made a face. "There's an office past the lounge. That's our first stop." He looked past Trev at Khim. "C'mon, android. Walk."

"His name is Khim," Trev said.

Breq put his hands up as if surrendering. "Okay, okay. Khim-Who-Tried-To-Kill-Me." Red marks shaped like fingerprints still blazed brightly against the sides of his neck. "Just tell him to walk, or we'll bring someone out here to knock him out and carry him."

Trev made a disgusted sound, then said softly, "Khim. Please."

Khim took a slow step forward. Then another.

Vance said, "See? He's got it wrapped around his little finger."

"Shut up," Breq said.

They all had to slow their pace as Khim took shortened, hesitant steps, seemingly ignoring them all. The way was long. It seemed like forever before they came to a door. Some small doors appeared along the left wall, but Breq and Vance passed them all.

Finally, they came to the end of the hallway and stood before two leaf-carved, wooden double doors.

"What is this place?" Trev asked.

Neither of his brothers answered.

Trev could only imagine the kind of fear and pain Khim must be feeling. He wanted to reach out to him, reassure him, but he had no business doing that. How could he reassure Khim if he had no guarantees for himself that they'd ever get out of here alive? He would do anything to help Khim, but pleading with his father, after their meeting at the prison, was the last thing he wanted to do.

Knowing he was about to see Dante, Trev's anger surfaced, a simmering combination of hurt and abhorrence gathering itself into outrage. He used that energy to strengthen his resolve and stood tall between his brothers.

The wooden doors opened inward. Khim moved just behind Trev, who could feel the trembling heat of him.

The footsteps of the four men were silent on the plush carpet. Trev smelled blooming flowers and saw vases of them, fresh cut foliage in vessels of brilliant hues—shining alabaster, alert red, and dominant purple—decorating narrow buffets along one wall.

He looked around even as Breq's hand tugged him forward.

"Ow," Trev said between gritted teeth. "My shoulder's injured, you ass!"

Breq eased up, looking at him. "I didn't know that."

"Well, fuck, Breq—the candle tube, the cuffs, manhandling me. Why are you being such an asshole to me?"

"Because Dad said you would run. And I have a job to do."

Trev wanted to spit at him, but he knew Breq was under Dante's control. They shared a father who meted out orders and gave no other options to his children.

Breq had been rebellious as a kid. It was Breq, out of all seven of them, who had inspired the most whippings. In his teen years, it seemed like Breq had been hauled off to the punishment room practically daily.

Trev turned away from him and scanned the foyer. On the wall opposite the flower buffet was a fountain spraying cascades of water into the air out of the mouths of three lions. The lions were made of black marble. They had their heads back as if they were roaring at the air. Surrounding the fountain were ferns, baby's breath, and other lacy green plants.

Just beyond the fountain was a podium, like that of a restaurant where you would approach a host who would show you to a table. A computer was built into the podium. The screen reflected only darkness.

Beyond the podium the fancy foyer led to a huge arched open wall. Over the arch, in big Renaissance lettering, were the words "House of Xavier." Further on, Trev could see an elaborate room as big as four times their entire living room at home. They stepped into this room, which was filled with tables, chairs, benches, and plush couches. A long bar. A half-dozen crystal chandeliers along the ceiling. The walls were draped in fuchsia and magenta curtains. Some of the curtains were not just decorative but tied back to show alcoves behind them, with plush beds covered in gold spreads. In the center of the room was a long stage.

"What is this place?" Trev asked.

Behind him, Khim made a choking sound and turned away. Trev jerked his head around, only to see Vance half dragging Khim through the arch. Khim was using his body to hug the wall just inside.

"Damn it," Vance said. "Move! Or do you want to be drugged again?"

Trev gasped at such harsh words from his brother, and all the strength his rage had been supplying began to leak away as he tried but could not even begin to imagine what kinds of shows were put on in this place.

"You had him in here, didn't you?" Trev's voice was loud, accusing. "He doesn't want to go any further! Why are you doing this?"

Vance kept pulling Khim, who stumbled farther into the room. For a moment Trev thought Khim, even with his hands locked behind his back, would fight. He had no doubt Khim could kill Vance with just a body blow if he so chose. But Khim's head stayed down, his hair dangling to obscure his features.

"You guys are bastards. You know that, right?" Trev said.

Breq said, "There's an office at the end of the room. That's where we're going. Now just shut up and walk. Both of you!"

They moved silently through the strangely eerie room. Trev walked, so Khim walked.

As they passed a grouping of couches with an elaborate red velvet one in the center, Vance began to chuckle. "Look familiar, android? The blood's been cleaned away—"

Trev spun out of Breq's softened grip and blindly crashed into Vance, who let go of Khim and stumbled backward. "What the fuck is wrong with you?" Trev shrieked.

Vance caught himself, brushing at his suit. "You always were a little shit."

"This situation is bad enough. Why are you making it worse?" Trev asked. Vance was his least-favorite brother, the bully of the lot of them, but this supreme coldness seemed new.

A strong voice sounded throughout the room, echoing over the four men who stood at the center. "Vance, you will make no further commentary ever again to the android. Now, my boys, come forward. All of you. I have been waiting."

Trev looked up toward the end of the room. Dante stood tall. He lorded over the entire proceedings, his silver suit reflecting the room's diffused light, making him look armored in tarnished metal.

As they approached the end of the long room, Trev saw an open door, a well-lit room with couches and desks, and flanking the door, Dante's two reliable bodyguards, Blair and Sonye.

Blair and Sonye wore suits as well, black, with white shirts and ties. Their jackets were open, their shoulder holsters visible, but Trev knew they did not need those weapons. They could fight bare-handed. Like Khim, they knew plenty of ways to kill.

Trev had learned to fight from them. He was agile, fast, but had never been as strong as they were.

As they approached the office and Dante, Vance said, "Dad, the android is still dangerous. He tried to kill Breq."

Breq said, "Trev stopped him. With a command."

At those words, Sonye and Blair tensed, eyes on Khim, following his every move.

Dante said, "Hush."

This was a nightmare. Trev had never guessed that his family were Khim's owners. He was both ashamed and horrified. They were his family. All he knew. Then he'd met Khim. But by virtue of being a Damico, he'd actually made things worse for him when he thought he was helping.

His heart began to shatter.

Dante led the way into the office, and the six of them followed—Breq and Trev first, then Khim, still never once looking up, shuffling in ahead of Vance, Blair, and Sonye.

Trev knew his father had many businesses, corporations, and holdings. He owned hotels, casinos, office buildings. Small moons. Apparently he also owned people.

Trev had suspected but never really looked at that side of things. His life had been about computers and stealth. He could steal for his father with ease, for deals Dante made with customers who would pay anything for a rare painting, information, jewels, or even something like a Bradbury. Trev was a security expert, an acrobat, and a thief. But this side of the family business? He'd never even taken a peek.

"Uncuff him." Dante motioned toward Trev, but his eyes were on Breq.

Breq obeyed.

When Trev was loose, he backed up and stood by Khim, close but not touching.

"Now Khim," Dante demanded.

Breq and Vance said almost simultaneously, "No way!"

No one moved toward Khim.

Dante's eyes were dark, like smoky quartz caught in winter light. "What do you think, Trevor?"

Trev took a half step forward, his body partially blocking Khim's. "Like anyone, any *human*, he acts in self-defense. What did you do to him here?" As he asked the question, his voice skipped over some of the words, getting lost in the depths of his throat.

"The question is what *he* did here," Vance muttered.

"Vance, did I ask you a question?" Dante said. Vance scowled. "Another outburst from you and you will leave the room." Dante turned back to Trev.

Trev said, "What did he do?"

"Only dispatched one of our highest-paying clients. But never mind that. We were uninformed as to his history as a highly efficient killer. We won't underestimate him again."

Trev spoke as if in a dream, his voice sounding distant. "Your confidence knows no bounds, does it?"

Breq gave Trev a wide-eyed look. They rarely spoke to their father as openly as Trev was doing right now.

"This isn't about Khim, it's about you, Trev. You seem to have a handle on him. Is Breq correct when he says you kept Khim from killing him?"

"I don't make Khim do anything. Khim chooses."

"Is that so? You're a Damico. He's owned by the Damicos. He's conditioned to obey his owners."

Trev felt Khim shift very slightly behind him. Trev's body heated with shame at his father's words. Shame for what his father was suggesting. Shame at being a Damico.

The room was too bright, the edges glistening in his peripheral vision. He wished for this horrible moment to fade, wished he could open new eyes and it would all be over, some nightmare from a darker place that shrank immediately upon waking.

"I don't tell Khim what to do!" He pushed the words from his mouth, hard. His chest rose and fell.

"Regardless, I want to thank you for bringing my property back to me," Dante said. "Due to unfortunate circumstances, I could not cover up the murder he committed and lock him away here myself. The crime became too public too quickly, so I allowed the authorities to take him. I thought we might not have him back here for another seventy years. But now that he's escaped Steering Star, he can never go back into the public. He will be caught and executed, and I may have power, but not enough power to prevent that. Not over a killer who has proven he cannot be held by the most maximum-security facility available. So if you want him to remain alive, this is the place for him—locked away, hidden, protected. And he can work to pay his way."

"Surely not in the brothel!"

"Certainly not. When I bought him I had no clue he was ex-military. With his skills, I have great plans for him myself. It is why you were both brought here. Do you think I have no regard for your safety? Or his? You are both fugitives now. Well, Khim is. I pulled some strings for you, Trev. I am trying to help you. Both of you."

Trev did not know what to say.

"Breq and Vance were doing their jobs. Don't blame them. I only wanted you both found and brought here unharmed before the authorities caught up." Dante smiled, teeth white. "It's the least I can do."

Trev remembered their meeting in the prison, Dante so furious, leaving Trev behind to rot with a longer sentence than the original one year, telling him to think about what he'd done. And now he was welcoming him back?

"What about me? Do I have to hide here forever too?" He asked with a firmness he hoped hid the resignation beginning to enfold his heart.

"I told you I pulled strings for you, Trev. Your charges were pending. Did I forget to mention that? The papers you signed were about your trial, which was not even on the docket yet. Of course the charges were dropped just yesterday when the Bradbury you stole was found in a distant city after a raid on a house of known street thieves. It was returned to the museum intact. But there is still the matter of the prison break, a separate crime. But judges can be influenced—"

"Stop it!" Trev shook his head angrily. "It's all lies. All of it! You wanted me punished for going behind your back, trying to escape this—this fucking madness. Now you want me to be free again. And Khim? You'll have him here as a commodity of your business to be used again and again to your own devices. To be controlled, retrained, reconditioned, even raped again if it pleases you—"

Dante's eyes hardened. "Do not speak to me in that tone! You ungrateful, privileged, whiny baby. And what exactly are you accusing us, your family, of? We do not turn our backs on each other. And this you see around you, this is business. Only that. We are in no position, any of us, to judge when it comes to that."

"Are you insane?" Trev said under his breath.

Dante ignored the interruption. "Our clients, our customers— we provide services without judgment. We keep this place secret out of respect to our clients, not because it is illegal. How dare you accuse this establishment—us, *me*—of... of rape!" The word came out a snarl. "The others we have here are designed, bought and paid for. And I just told you Khim will not serve in the brothel anymore. But it does not matter what your altruistic opinion is. The law sees androids as objects. As dolls. Made for this. Trained for whatever their owners desire of them—"

"Not Khim!"

"Yes! Even Khim! It is not my fault he was sold under false pretenses as a whore. But now Khim is mine. And he will stay here and work for me in whatever job I see fit for him. For his own safety and that of our family, he will remain undercover. It would not bode well to have it be known that we harbor a fugitive. For that, he owes us quite a lot, I would think."

As he spoke, Dante was approaching Trev where he stood next to Khim. When he finished speaking, he reached out. Trev thought he was going to touch him, but instead, Trev turned his head and saw Dante's hand rise to Khim's face, fingers gently lifting his chin.

Khim's head came up.

Dante looked him directly in the eyes. "Isn't that right, Khim?"

Trev felt bile rise. "You bought him. Now you need to place him in further debt to you?"

Without looking away from Khim, Dante said, "That is how it works with androids. What else can I do? He is not a free man and never will be. But at least I am offering him one more chance. You know best, Trev, how well I reward loyalty and obedience. That's all I ask from him for the generous offer of my protection. Khim will live, as long as he's with us. Understanding is lighting in his eyes even now. I want you both to see that if you, or he, tries to escape, you have nowhere to go. But I can always use someone with his training. Stick with me, and you have a chance. Both of you. For life. And for you, Trev, the same freedoms you once had. Neither of you will ever get a better offer."

Once prisoners of Steering Star, now they were prisoners of Dante. There was no freedom here. Only illusions upon illusions.

Trev stood his ground, but Dante was so close now, exuding a dynamic, almost savage dominance. He could smell the expensive cologne of him and the rushing flames of his power. Strong people feared Dante. All craved his love. But none more fervently than his own children.

Still, Trev fumed. He said, "If Khim stays here, hiding in this brothel, then so do I."

"No." One word. Flat. Final.

"Well, Father, you have no problem putting bought-and-sold toys on that hideous stage of yours out there. Why not try me in that capacity and see what happens? I'm not a trained fighter like Khim, but I seem to be bought and paid for too."

"That is a lie, and you know it. You are my son. Your home is with us. The Damicos."

"Your adopted son. How much did you pay?"

"I did not buy you, *child*." Now Dante's black heat was turned onto Trev.

"You've never told me where I come from. How would I know? And if you feel that way about everything you own, then why not parade me about here, let your wonderful, upstanding clients have me, fuck me any way they want?"

Dante's hand came out fast. Trev felt the sting of the slap on his face before he even registered he'd been hit. He stepped back into Khim—who did not move—and almost lost his balance.

But the pain only served to enrage him more. "Why not sell me here? To the highest bidders? Do you not think I'd bring in enough income? What's wrong with me? Am I not pleasing? I'm small, agile, pleasant. Why not sell me here? Why the fuck not?" He was yelling now.

Dante's face had darkened, and he smacked Trev a second time, hard enough that this time Trev felt Khim struggle to free his arms, as if he wanted to catch him.

Trev's body hit Khim's side, slid by him, and dropped back onto the floor. He caught himself easily so he did not hit the floor hard, but his mind was spinning, his head filled with blind fire. He stayed down, knees bent, looking at Dante, thinking about springing up and provoking a third slap.

Then he heard a voice, golden and pure. It penetrated his dizziness, angled through the waves of pain and the burning on his cheek.

"Stop. I will stay. Just don't hurt him. Don't hurt him anymore."

Trev leaned back, his hands digging into the carpet, looking up, trying to see through the haze of his anger, his hate.

Khim was speaking. Khim was addressing them all. "I'm grateful for my life. Thank you. I will do as you say. Any jobs you request. Just don't hurt him. Please don't hurt Trev."

Vance's voice shot in from the side. "I knew it! The android's sweet on him."

Trev wanted to attack Vance, beat that shit-eating smile off his face. He struggled to stand, dazed by Khim's words.

Without looking away from the two of them, Dante stated emphatically, "Vance, you had warning. You will leave this room now!"

Trev stood, still unsteady.

Dante said to Khim, "That's more like it."

"If you keep him here, then you damn well keep me here too!" Trev demanded.

Dante's eyes jerked toward him. "No. You will do as you're told—for his safety and well-being, of course—will you not?"

Trev's mouth opened, but no words came out.

Dante, looking as unruffled and cool as if he'd just come from the dressing room, said, "Breq, Blair. Take Khim away. The dungeon. For now."

Reaching out, Trev grabbed Khim's bent-back arm with both hands, as if to hold him in place. He did not ask for permission to touch him, but right then it did not seem to matter. He wasn't going to let Khim go anywhere. "No! If he goes, I go."

"No." Khim pulled back, tried to step away from Trev. "You are not going with me."

Trev clung harder as Blair and Breq pulled Khim backward toward the big room with the stage and the alcoves and couches.

Breq reached out to Trev, but his touch was gentle. "Let go, kid."

Khim pulled again, hard, knocking Trev aside. "Don't touch me!"

Hurt, bewildered, Trev stood back in shock. "But you can't do this! None of you! You can't!"

He stared through blurring eyes, watching Khim's golden head bow again as he allowed himself to be escorted away, hands still cuffed behind his back. The white shirt, Renn's shirt, hugged his back. Even in this dark place, Khim's hair fell like sunlight in soft, shining waves about his neck and shoulders. Trev remembered tangling his fingers in it. Holding all the specialness that was this man, this human man, in his arms.

He couldn't allow this.

He pushed his way past his brothers and rounded on Khim, facing him again. He heard, and ignored, Dante saying, "Trevor. Get back here now!"

He looked at Khim's bent head, saw the closed eyes, the resigned features. "I won't let them get away with this."

Finally Khim's eyes opened.

Trev looked deeply into the dark blue depths, saw a flicker, like a momentary, all-consuming pain. Khim's mouth, a straight line, quivered.

Raising up on his toes, Trev leaned into him, smelling the homemade-bread memory again, the wonder, the beauty. His cheek almost brushed Khim's as he breathed into his ear. "Khim, I won't abandon you. I promise. I promise."

Khim yanked himself back, eyes closing. Shutting him out.

The ache in Trev's chest was like a stone slowly fracturing under volcanic heat.

Dante was at Trev's side along with Sonye, and they had their hands on his arms and were dragging him toward the office again. "Get hold of yourself, son!" Dante ordered.

Trev turned away, sagging, letting them lead him back into the office. But he couldn't feel anymore. His legs just scrambled along the floor on their own. Their hands on his arms were like water. There was only a gray-edged fever, and a slight twinge in his shoulder where the skin-knitting patch flexed against the pulse burn.

They brought him to a chair and forced him to sit.

He thought he might sob right then, crumble into tiny pieces until he was nothing but dust. Instead he sat frozen, very still, hands flat under his thighs, and his slitted gaze saw Dante take a chair facing him. Sonye stood, ever watchful, ever coldly handsome, at their father's side.

"Get yourself together right now," Dante repeated, but softer this time. "You've just been through a lot. A shock. That's all."

"A shock? That's what you call—" He pulled his hands out from underneath his legs and spread them. "—all this?"

"You've had a few harrowing days, and some time in lockdown. But you hurt me, and you needed to know that. Leaving you in prison for a few weeks was the only way. It was all necessary. Now you're back, and it's all behind us. All of it."

"I hurt you? Dad, you hurt people all the time. Khim is my friend, and you hurt him!"

"He's trained for this sort of—"

"No! You admitted yourself he isn't. You bought him without knowing that and didn't bother to find out. Even so, what is all this? I knew you had brothels, but I didn't think you kept people in them against their will, *forced* them—"

"I don't. Not free humans, at any rate."

"He's human. Like us," Trev argued. "Just vat-grown. No metal parts, except for his hand, which he lost in a war."

"You know the law states otherwise. We've just been over this."

"Since when do you of all people care about the law!" His eyes were burning, his throat tight, but he refused to let his father see him weep.

"I know your escape and all the excitement made you think you formed a bond with him, but you're above that, Trevor. You are an elite part of my team. You are my son."

Trev blinked. He should not have been surprised at his father's words. Proud. Arrogant. Unflappable. Seeing himself in the upper class, above everyone else. Sitting in his cloud mansion overlooking all, lord of the underworld of both sky and sand. Dante truly was a king that no one could stop. He expected Trev to be proud to be his son. Happy. But only if Trev copied him. Only if Trev became the dutiful, good-son mirror to his father's dark soul.

Trev remembered that time when he was four, his father dressing him in an identical tuxedo for a party, then picking Trev up, holding him close as they gazed at their reflections in a floor-to-ceiling mirror. And Dante had said, "Look at us. Aren't we amazing?"

Despite being adopted, Trev looked the most like his father out of all his siblings. The last words Dante had just spoken still stirred on the air.

You are my son.

But where had he really come from?

His brothers and sisters were all from the same mother, Dante's wife, Lotty, who had died before Trev was born. There were few photographs of her, but she had supposedly been the love of Dante's life, perishing in a flier accident somewhere on the planet below.

Glancing around the strange room, the ornate office, taking in all the ornament of it, the paintings on the walls of classic, tasteful erotica of men enfolded in various pairings and groups, Trev said, "Am I really your son?"

"The circumstances of your birth are no matter. You are my son."

"But circumstances of birth do seem to matter to you. Greatly."

"We will talk no more of this. And Khim? I've done what I can for him."

"No, you haven't," Trev said. "You haven't even begun."

Dante eyed him speculatively.

There was no more talk. As if Dante had grown weary of it, with Trev only more and more insolent. Numb from the neck down, Trev could not even begin to contain the whole of what had happened to him from going to prison, meeting Khim, falling in love, and now being back in his father's clutches, his life a turmoil of pressure, change, punishment, and reward at his father's whim.

Dante left Trev sitting as he went to his desk, gathered things, arranged things, and gave soft orders to Sonye.

When Sonye finally came over to him and said, "Up," Trev asked, "Where are we going?"

Dante turned. "Home."

Trev jerked. He did not want to leave Khim. But Sonye put a firm hand on his arm.

He had nowhere else left to go.

*

Once back at the mansion, Trev stood in the middle of the garage, hands clasped in front of him, looking around. He'd thought never to see this place again, the dark garage filled with beautiful fliers—their shiny, oily scent permeating the air—or the elevator with its melodic, gentle voice welcoming them home.

When they were dropped at the first floor, the sounds of fountains filled the air along with a tender, humid scent of spring.

Dante turned as Trev stopped just inside the foyer of the great living room. "Welcome home." He reached out and drew Trev into a hug.

When Trev was younger, he'd leaned into those hugs, bestowed generously by this nefarious man when he was happy, charmed, in a good mood.

Today Trev stood stiffly, forlorn, the sense of his loss too acute for words.

He had no idea what time it was but thought that the Damico household should be asleep by now. Instead his sisters Rory and Arla entered the room. They came up to Trev and embraced him coolly.

"Your brothers will be home soon, and then things will be back to normal around here." Dante smiled.

This was insane. Complete, utter madness.

Trev tilted his head to one side and looked down, hiding his tears.

Chapter Twenty-Four

Khim

Khim paced from one edge of the cell to the other, then back. It was clean but well-worn, dark. There were no windows deep in the dungeon, only the rusted light along the edges of the ceiling that allowed all manner of shadows to gather. It made the slow fan in the ceiling at the end of one far wall, outside the cage, look like a giant, sucking hole in space.

He'd spent less than a day of his life there. Now he was back.

Five cages stood down there; the other four were unoccupied. No talkative information-dump voices, no feral sylphs pounding their fists into the cement walls.

Faster and faster, Khim paced. His muscles burned, strained. He needed to move. To not think. Not be. It was like he was a live wire, spitting and hissing; a time bomb ticking; a pressure point on a trigger. First the world you see in your sights is whole. Then it is broken. He existed in-between, where the trigger was moving, the energy building, but imminent destruction was yet to come.

Closing his eyes should have brought darkness, reprieve. But all he could see was Trev. And around his heart a strong crystal was growing, the glass structure of his birth reforming, with Khim on the inside, always looking out. And light and air and life danced upon the glass, sometimes permeating, but meaning nothing.

He tried to focus inward, heard the faint percussion of machinery in the walls. His own forced breaths. The tumble of his heart.

Trev came into his mind, lithe and bright-eyed, a hank of hair flowing against one eye. Trev walked a garden outside a glass porch. Barefoot, leaves and flowers sending accolades on a breeze. When he came back around to face the glass, he leaped all the stairs at once to land just inside the door. That smile. That shimmer of tanned skin.

Khim's chest tried to cave in on itself. He shook the memory off.

In Dante's office he had pushed Trev away. It was all he could think to do to help him. Trev's father was hitting him; Trev's father was the threat.

How could he make that stop?

The only answer was to close himself off. Obey. Do whatever it took for Trev's safety and freedom. For love, he would do that.

Khim put his hands to his face—one warm, one cold—and let out a strangled cry. Trev would have said *Fuck.* Khim could hear him in his mind as if he stood right beside him. Beautiful. Pure. Beloved.

To keep that man safe, he would do anything. He would give his body. His soul. If it would keep Trev free, he would be the best assassin, bodyguard or, if ordered, the best whore Dante had ever seen.

Khim could not properly assess time. It had been dawn when Breq and Vance had met them in the little motel parking lot. They'd flown for half an hour, traveled into the bowels of the Rainspeer. And Khim had finally met Dante. Had an hour passed since then? Two?

In the time he'd been locked down here, Khim saw no one. Heard no human voices.

He was not tired, not hungry. It couldn't have been too long.

He couldn't stop wondering where Trev was now. Would Trev stop fighting? Would he settle and accept the life he'd been given, as Khim was now doing?

It was for the best, really. This was the world they'd both been born into. One person could not change whole worlds, only the self. Things always went better if you cooperated. Khim had learned that in his years of being a soldier. He had not hated it. He had not enjoyed it. He simply lived. Did as he was told. And the rewards were food, shelter, rest, and even a bit of fulfillment for a job well done.

Trev would be well cared for if he could just learn that lesson. To Khim it was obvious. As calculating and manipulative as Dante was, amid possession and whippings, there was also love there. Such a rare thing, for Khim. It must not be squandered.

A voice came to him in the back of his mind. A birth memory.

He's crying. It happens. They want their mommies, sometimes.

Then another voice. It almost sounded like Trev.

You're a human being. And what they did to you is awful.

Khim had been sitting on the edge of the cage's neat bed. Now he got up, his fists clenching. An accident of birth. Wasn't that everyone's plight? Didn't everyone cry when they were taken from warmth, nurturing, and peacefulness at the moment of birth, or at any other moment for that matter? Didn't every child cry, shaking their baby fists against the night? Didn't everyone deserve a chance to be more than a knot of muscle, flesh, and blood pulled screaming into the vastness of a harsh and heartbreaking but glorious life?

Maybe Trev should not accept, not settle. Not fold himself into an obedient slave for the reward of less drama, more peace. Maybe Khim had been wrong. Maybe he should not have pulled away from him.

But for love, his greatest desire was to see Trev stop hurting, stop suffering. Khim would give anything to help him get what he had not been able to accomplish for himself.

Thoughts at war, Khim began to pace again.

*

Someone from the hotel, not a Damico, came into the dungeon and brought Khim food. He had on the white uniform of the kitchens. He did not speak.

It surprised Khim that after he ate and assessed his body, he detected no zotic effects. No one came to scatter the smoke of zotic over his face. No one came to drag him to the shower to wash and prepare him. No one came to brush stardust into his skin and paint his eyes.

Maybe tonight was a dark night for House of Xavier.

Well, Dante did say he had other plans for Khim.

Khim lay back on the bed and waited.

He felt the glass over his heart, newly formed, thin like digital paper. Within the structure he'd built for himself was a hollow man, his insides never fully grown, just enough to function. Enough to

248

breathe, to become an efficient killer. A nonquestioning soldier, an obedient slave. It was fine to be someone with very little concern. He didn't have to question. He didn't have to feel. There was a strange peace within, as if he were a monk who'd attained a quest and reached a higher pinnacle of being. He could float, and contentment would leak into him, serene, addictive, the right way to be.

But now behind that new thin glass, when he tried to find his way back to that, things came at him—images, feelings, a rush—a torrent of thoughts flooding in, filling the crevices, the corners, the empty long halls of his being.

Storms crested inside him, filled with activity. He saw himself turning on a red velvet couch, coming up and grabbing the man behind him, twisting the head. Killing outside of combat. He saw guards rush him. Felt the sudden pain, not only of the rape, but of the beating. In hurtling winds came prison scenes. Trev looking up at him, wondering why Khim hated him but still chasing off the bullies. Trev smiling, Trev commanding. How Khim felt when he followed him, like all the reason in the world lay in the heart of that man. All the things he ever wanted, ever needed, were in that voice since his own conditioning had broken, since all his peace and inner monk's silence had vanished.

More images swamped him. He had killed three more men and given no thought to it until Trev's voice woke him, turned him, brought him back into a kind of desperate light he'd been craving without knowing it.

Khim was broken, wounded in places he'd never before felt, but Trev's presence pieced him back together, lit the way.

When he remembered their kiss, he could not breathe. Such a short time ago—was it only yesterday? And yet it was forever etched upon him, as was their night together. Last night. Trev asking to touch him, Trev wanting to "just feel."

And Khim wanting the same.

More than anything, he wanted to feel that again. Trev in his arms, so easy-tempered and affectionate. The focused desire of his kisses. The slippery but firm body pressed to his.

Trev the thief. Trev the acrobat. Trev the youngest Damico son and the smartest, most sensitive of the clan.

Khim had fused the glass around himself in a perfect, seamless bubble. But the world outside had already infected him. He'd brought the thunder of it inside with him. The rain, the flowers, the hearths of passion. All the spilling inward, a swirl of books, fanned playing cards, singing sentries, stolen fliers, and Trev's dark eyes and sunlit smiles.

The glass no longer protected him. His conditioning was gone and could not be reconstructed. He heard Trev, standing in the pale, magnified light of Arch's back porch, say, "You seem different now."

The careful glass was cracking again. But this time it was barely there, not strong, hardly a breath between Khim and the world. A mist dissipating.

Khim folded his hands in front of him. Stopped pacing. Leaned his head down.

It was impossible for him to accept this situation now. He needed to think. *Think.*

But it was so hard now. Alone. Broken.

Trev did deals. Trev would make a plan. Swift and creative, smart and outrageous.

What to do? It was hard to think with no one to tell him.

It was hard to think over the sound of his own sobs.

*

No one came.

Khim finally slept a little. In his rest, his mind relaxed. Thoughts formed. The subconscious mind began to work. Even before he woke, he was thinking. Logistics. Contingencies. Outlines. Oh-so-fine dreams of escape in neon-blue backlit alleys surrounded by stars. In starships made of fire. Beyond the folds of space, he floated, Trev at his side.

Khim woke and waited for his food to come. It seemed like such a long time before the door at the far end of the dungeon opened and the white-clad kitchen boy entered.

When Khim heard the door, he sat quietly on the floor by the opening at the bottom where the tray slid in. He folded his legs in front of him, placed his hands together before him as if in a meditative position. The boy came forward. When he was directly in front of the bars, Khim said, "Is the food drugged?"

"No."

"Why not? Why is there no one else here?"

Slowly, shyly, the boy, who could not have been more than seventeen, said, "After the murder they were all taken somewhere else. Too many cops, I guess. The place has been closed for a while, but I hear they're going to open again. Very soon."

Khim's stomach convulsed at the thought. "I will hopefully be out of here by then."

The boy, whose hair was very curly and brown under his white uniform hat, said solemnly, "By the looks of you, I thought you were a performer. I thought you were a sex android."

"If I were, wouldn't I be on zotic and out of my mind?"

"I don't know if I should be talking to you."

"If I were truly dangerous, they wouldn't be sending you down here alone with food, would they?"

"Oh, I'm not alone. There are guards in the hall."

It was good information, and Khim filed it away for later. They probably sent the boy in for a good laugh. Or to test them both. To see what a boy of seventeen would do in a situation like that seemed rather cruel. But Khim had been surrounded by cruelties all his life and was not surprised.

The boy said, "Stand back, or I won't slide the food under the door."

Khim obediently got up and moved to the bed.

The boy quickly bent and slid the tray partway under the bars. Then he straightened and backed quickly away.

Khim's metal hand twitched. He might've been able to grab him. But then what? To mask his disappointment, he asked, "What is your name?"

"Cody."

"You don't have to be afraid of me, Cody. I promise."

Cody's face reddened very slightly before he turned and ran from the room.

Khim thought he heard laughter in the hall.

Chapter Twenty-Five

Trev

Trev did not sleep the day away as the Damico family usually did. He sat in the living room with the windows darkened, feet up on the couch—which Dante had always forbade them to do—and stared at nothing. The desolate shadows of the sculptures hovered over him. The fountain by the front door, with the embracing angels, clattered.

All the sounds and sights that he'd grown up with, grown used to, now defined a horrible, luxurious sort of despair.

The front door was locked against him, as were all the doors, programmed to deny him any exit except by permission of Dante. He had already tried to leave once, had not realized Dante had been standing in the hall, facing the room.

"Where are you going?" Dante asked.

"To the House of Xavier, of course. To see Khim."

"We just came from there."

"I don't care. I want to go back. See where he is, how you're treating him."

"You are forbidden to go there."

"I can't see him?"

"No."

"Ever?"

"No."

"That's not right, and you know it!"

"What's right is that you need to forget about him," Dante said, coming into the room. He was dressed in a sleeping gown, but he still appeared formal and foreboding.

"How can I do that? He means everything to me."

Dante frowned. He came up to the couch but did not sit. "You escaped a prison together. You formed a bond in the heat of the moment. It's not real. He's not anyone you need to concern yourself with anymore."

Trev sat up straighter, angry. "Who do you think you are to tell me what's real? You live a life of lies."

"All life is a lie. It's what you do with it that counts. Be smart, Trev. You are the smartest of all my children."

"I won't work for you. You can threaten me all you want, whip me, but I won't work for you ever again." He gazed up at his father, the darkness all around though the day continued bright and alive outside.

"You're angry right now. I understand. Still in shock. This will all pass. My son, don't you know everything I do for you is out of love?"

"It is *not* love!" Trev twisted away on the couch, feeling very much like a child instead of the man he had the right to be.

Dante chose not to argue but said instead, "You have everything here. All luxury. All that you could want or need. What is missing that you need to leave all this so badly?"

"Right now? Khim is missing."

"Khim is not—"

"He's what I want. Provide it and I'll shut up." His words surprised him. He sounded very much like his father in that moment in voice, in command.

"Is it an android you want? I can have one purchased for you if that is the price for you to stay here with us."

Imploringly, "You never hear a word I say! I don't want an android!"

"And you don't hear me. I have told you this feeling you have will pass. Maybe you shared a moment. It is nothing in the whole span of your life. I will not allow you to throw it all away for that... that thing."

"We shared more than a moment," Trev said. "And you would deny me that *thing* in the same way you deny all your children. We are things for you to control, to manipulate. Now you tell me that *thing*, as you so insultingly call him, is nothing, when he is everything to me."

"I am tired of this, Trevor. Sit and think for a day. That is what I ask. We will continue this discussion tonight."

"It won't make any difference. You never change," Trev mumbled.

But Dante was gone, and Trev was not sure whether his father had even heard him or really cared.

Now he sat in the shadows of a house that did not belong him, in a life he had never fully embraced.

After a while he got up and headed to his room on the second floor. He had to pass by the punishment room, and still, even after everything he'd been through, his skin prickled. The whippings... the gentle wiping away of the tears afterward. He remembered it all in too much horrific detail. Today it had been Vance in there, punished for speaking out of turn. A grown man, subjected to the demands of the father.

Trev had not seen Vance since his return. He figured he was in his room now, nursing the pain on his back, probably blaming Trev for everything, including Vance's own insolence. Trev tried not to care—they had never been friendly—but he could not help but believe that even Vance, whom he hated, was a victim of their father's brutal conditioning. All any of them had ever tried to do was gain Dante's approval and love in any manner they could, even if it meant sometimes being cruel to each other.

As Trev moved quietly down the dark hall toward the entrance of his own room, the door opposite his opened. Light came out of that room, elongating the shadows in the hall.

Breq stood tangled among them. "Trev," he said.

Breq was not wearing his suit anymore, but instead had on loose shorts and a T-shirt that looked two sizes too big.

Trev stopped. They stared at each other. Then Breq said, "You blew it big time, bro."

"I don't care." Anger flared again. "And you're an ass to me and always have been, so what do you care?"

"I was going to say thank you for saving my life," Breq said impatiently. "You and the android—uh, Khim—could have gotten away. He is that strong. You could have left me and Vance for dead, and no one would have caught up to you. You guys were doing good. I only caught you because I have a friend in that town who saw your fancy flier. We checked it out on a hunch."

254

Trev balked. He could see the bruises in the shapes of handprints on Breq's exposed throat. "Even if it meant escaping, do you think I would have done that? Ordered the murders of my own brothers? Made Khim, who I care about, kill for me? Who do you think I am? And Khim... he's not some tool."

Breq began to wave his hand to get Trev to stop. "I know. I know."

"Did you ever know me, Breq?"

"That's just it. We all did. We all do. That's why the rest of us are jealous. Always the smartest and brightest, Trev."

"But I—"

"You're Father's favorite," Breq interrupted. "Sure, we hate you." He smiled to soften his words. "And that moral compass of yours—what are we supposed to think? It's going to get you killed. It's already gotten you into so much trouble. The rest of us look to avoid that at all cost."

Trev felt his hands form into fists. He wanted to hit. He wanted to fight. Breq's words did nothing to comfort him. "You were there at the Rainspeer, the night Khim was. I remember you guys talking about it at dinner the day before I went to prison."

"Yes. I didn't see everything. But let's go into my room and I'll tell you."

Trev hesitated, then walked into the filtered light of Breq's room. He had been in there only a few times in his life, since his brother was so adamant about his privacy.

It was a little bit of a mess—clothing strewn over chairs, gadgets on a desk, walls lined with shelves holding leftover childhood items like starship models, electric-light spheres, old rocks and seashells he'd collected as a kid. The bed was big and all black—the sheets, pillowcases, even the coverlet. An alcove to the right led to a private bath. All the bedrooms of Dante's estate had private baths.

Trev found a leather-back chair and sat. Breq sat on the foot of his bed.

"The House of Xavier isn't a nice place," Breq began.

"I gathered." Sarcasm.

"It's completely off the map. Only for the extremes in tastes, designer drugs, designer sex workers, designer androids. There's a huge clientele for the parties it hosts."

"What about your tastes? You go there," Trev stated flatly.

"I am one of five managers. But I don't 'go' there. We don't dip into the family goods. You know that. Dad doesn't allow that."

"I know, no drugs, we don't get to keep what we steal. It's all sold, all in constant motion, constant turnover."

Breg nodded. "I was there that night. I didn't see everything that happened, but I heard the commotion. I didn't know what Khim was, that he wasn't what we bought him for. He was... so beautiful. The first chosen off the stage to come into the crowd. Everyone there wanted... well." He cleared his throat. "There was a crowd around him. I admit it was probably too much, even for someone trained in that sort of thing."

Trev winced and couldn't help the fresh tears that blurred his vision. "You let that happen."

Breq shrugged. "What was I supposed to think? When we heard the screams, me and Vance came running, but it was too late. One of our top clients was already dead on the ground at Khim's feet. A broken neck. The guards rushed in and started beating Khim. He did that thing, like when you called him off me, where he curls into the ground, you know."

Trev couldn't look at him. He nodded. "That's when he's trying to get his control back. He knows he's not allowed to harm humans, except on orders. He was in war for ten years. That's all he knew. They sold him when he wasn't of use to them anymore."

"Well, the military sucks, then, because Khim came to us as a sex model. And with his looks, who would have thought otherwise? Plus, that night the shipment of zotic that we give all the slaves, all the workers, was different. Diluted. Someone had diluted the batch on the seller's end, obviously for more profit. It wore off. If not for that, Khim would probably not have remembered that night or all the rest to come. And he wouldn't have had any strength to fight. But after all the fuckups, all Dad could do at that point was use his influence to keep Khim alive."

"Yeah. Such a great man. He didn't want to lose his fucking investment."

"Well, Dad never has been the altruistic sort."

"Well, he's an idiot. And so are you if you don't understand that androids are human beings. Just because they're owned—" He broke off.

Breq did not seem to take offense. He rubbed the sides of his neck where the fingerprint bruises were. "So, you met Khim in prison?"

Trev nodded.

"What is he to you?"

Trev hesitated. He didn't trust Breq—or anyone in his family. But he was at the bottom of the chain now; he had no one else to talk to. He finally answered. "Everything."

Breq said, "I don't know how to help you. My hands are tied."

"Did I ask for your help?" Trev did not care if his frustration with Breq showed.

Breq got up from the bed. The light from the alcove spread across the floor, making a round, glowing circle. He stepped into it with bare feet, moved across to a shelf where he picked up a handheld computer. His back was to Trev as he seemed to fiddle with it. When he turned, the light curved gently against the side of his face, and for a moment he looked soft—handsome, even—when usually Breq was so hard, so cold. It just did not seem right that this guy managed a place such as House of Xavier as if it were nothing more than a posh restaurant selling fancy wine.

Breq reached out to Trev, handing him the device.

Trev looked at the screen, a high-angle camera view of a long dark room. At the end of the room were five old-style cells with bronze bars. One was occupied. By Khim.

The bars striped the back wall of Khim's cell with parallel shadow lines. Khim sat very still on the edge of a bunk, elbows on his knees, looking at the floor. He was like a beacon to Trev's heart.

Trev looked up, blinking. "Is this live?"

Breq nodded. "If you ever tell Dad—"

Trev just rolled his eyes. "What is this place?"

"The dungeon. There are four. Where Dad keeps the ones that might run."

"The ones?"

"The whores." He gave a pained smile. "The android slaves. New ones. Or ones that are feisty. Or troublemakers. From there they get readied for the parties, washed, made up. Styled, so to speak."

Trev studied the screen, his pulse quickening. He could see Khim, but he couldn't talk to him. He couldn't go to him. He wanted to sob, but instead brought the handheld to his chest and looked up. "Can I keep this?"

Breq nodded. "For all the good it'll do you. I think you're just torturing yourself, little brother."

"Why is Khim the only one there now?" Trev asked.

"The others are in a larger dungeon. The ones that get along share rooms, live there. There are no fresh slaves coming in, which is what this block is for. House of Xavier is closed right now. The murder was, well, bad for business. It'll be opening again in another week. I think Dad might be changing the name."

That gives me one week, Trev thought.

Trev got up and went to the door. He turned back to look at Breq. "Thank you."

"Thank you for calling off your... friend."

Trev took the device back to his bedroom. He stared at the scene before him. Khim sat as if frozen in place. Trev looked at the cell, the walls, the floor, from every angle he could get the camera to move.

He studied the scene for a long, long time.

Chapter Twenty-Six

Khim

Khim had been noticing the fat, square camera for quite some time.

Off and on he watched it, up in the corner of the dank room, moving inch by inch, left to right. An old-fashioned thing. Something hurriedly rigged, which did not seem normal for this wealthy establishment.

Who was behind it? Who was watching?

After he'd worn himself out pacing, he sat unmoving for hours. Awareness of the camera never left him, but it was diluted by the tides within him. The constant breaking down of all his barriers, the glass cracking again and again, sifting down into darkness, the shards becoming their own constellations in his vast open being.

His skin kept vacillating between hot and cold, as if he were sick, in a fever.

But it wasn't sickness. It was *un*sickness, healing. Wellness. Trev's smile, Trev's eyes, Trev's body pressed to his. The sweet of him. The salt of him. The tone of voice that washed sunlit commands through the labyrinths of Khim's confused, fracturing brain.

He sat on the edge of the bunk and was remade. He sat and remade himself. He did not mourn the loss of his past self, but he mourned Trev for not being there. Mourned an emptiness where there was nothing his arms could hold on to.

He had cried a little at first. Because he was young and lost.

They want their mommies, sometimes.

Or their daddies, a little voice quipped in the back of his mind as an image of Dante coalesced at the forefront of his thoughts, then vanished.

He wondered what brand of hell Trev was in right then. Had Dante whipped him again? Was Trev being forced to play the dutiful son side by side with all his brothers and sisters?

To see Trev in such pain hurt, little claws forming around his chest cavity. Bouts of nausea. For Trev's own good, and to get Dante to stop smacking him, Khim had had to push him away.

It kept replaying in his mind. Pushing Trev back, agreeing to anything.

Of course he meant it. But only for as long as it took to find the exit.

If he pretended Trev was with him, helping to make the plan, his own thoughts grew clearer. Smarter. But the tides within him kept rolling, pushing, shoving. He was being buffeted like a shell against the sand, whittled down, formed into a polished likeness of something that used to be himself. The smooth from the rough, new from the old.

He did not intend to stay there. And he did not intend to die. He sat very still and thought about all of that as more waves of feeling slid into him.

The boy came one more time with food. Wary, alert. All in white, wrinkled and oil stained from wiping down counters, rinsing pots and pans. He smelled of dish soap, burned cream, and hot grease. Under his hat, his brown hair needed a wash.

He was a servant, Khim decided. Someone the others were using. Or would be soon. But the boy did not know that. He did as he was told and he was happy. He was young and this was an important job. He didn't know that the tables of happiness turned at a snap of a finger.

He didn't have cruelty yet in his watery green eyes. Khim thought about telling him about cruelty, mesmerizing him with the tale of a soldier sold to a brothel, but wasn't sure. Would he be able to tell it without breaking into a thousand pieces?

No. The boy, Cody, was lost anyway. Working here, delivering food to a man in a cage, trying to impress somebody, be somebody. Not caring how it came to be.

He thought again about grabbing him, if he were fast enough, when Cody bent to slide the tray.

He was dangerous when he thought like this. They had to know. Why were they leaving him undrugged? Maybe this meal had the zotic in it, then.

He breathed in air like fire. The boy bent down.

Khim moved like lightning.

The square camera tilted down.

At the sound, Khim looked up just as the tray slid under the bars. Missed his chance.

Cody stood, eyes big. "You move fast," he said shakily.

Khim watched the camera.

Not fast enough.

*

Khim did not see anyone else for long hours.

Time didn't seem to move here.

The light did not dim or brighten, and it made everything brown and ugly. Tired of the tides rolling in and out of his brain, he finally lay down.

His slumber came on, agitated. Echoing with shouts, whispers, voices calling, crying, laughing.

He woke several times having forgotten where he was. Once he thought he felt Trev on the mattress next to him. He reached for him and caught air. Heard a whimper.

Chapter Twenty-Seven

Trev

Trev had locked his door, but there was no lock in the entire house that held itself against the presence of Dante.

He sat in his bed, the covers to his waist, wearing only shorts and a tank top. The handheld lay in his lap, broadcasting the image of Khim, who was sleeping, finally, although he tossed and turned.

Affixed to the handheld were about ten different items, all manually wired in, and he used the camera feed to access all aspects of not just the dungeon the camera was placed in, but the entire system—every last intricacy of the Rainspeer Hotel.

The door to his room slid open.

Trev pulled the covers over his ugly but groundbreaking work of art.

Dante stood on the threshold. "You're up. Breakfast at nine."

That meant 9:00 p.m., not a.m. Such was the cycle of the household.

"I'm not hungry."

"I gave you an order, not a choice. I want the table full tonight. It's been too long without you there."

Perhaps Dante meant that statement as a compliment. He probably had special food prepared, and more, but Trev could only see it as a bitter attempt at taming the wild one, the prodigal son.

He got up and dressed in a nice suit. As Dante would expect.

Khim was still sleeping when he checked the screen before going to the third-floor dining room.

*

Trev sat at his usual place at the table, which was laden with platters of meat, eggs, potatoes, fruit, crystal goblets of high-end wine, and other breakfast-themed dishes.

"This is a welcome-home meal for Trevor," Dante announced. "I'd like to make a toast." He stood. Everyone else stood too, Trev finding his feet last.

"To my son." He went on to give questionable accolades, not once mentioning the prison, Khim, or the fact that Trev was locked inside the mansion.

Trev stole a look at Vance, who looked surly, as expected. As the eldest son, Breq sat closest to Dante but would not meet Trev's eyes.

His sisters were more polite. "To Trev," they each said in turn, actually smiling at him for once.

Trev ate a few bites, pretended to eat more, but was not hungry.

When the meal was over, he did not linger. He went straight back to his room to check on Khim and continue his work with the handheld.

He worked all night, writing experimental programs, testing them, bypassing system locks and codes.

On the screen, Khim slept fitfully throughout the long hours that Trev worked. Finally Trev was able to bounce a frequency off the light impulses in the dungeon and type words that resounded in that frequency. It was a crazy idea, but one he hoped worked.

Khim, he typed. *Wake up. Khim. Khim.*

Khim moved on the bed, turning over.

Trev tried again.

Khim, it's Trev. Don't ask me to explain how my voice is transmitting through the lights.

In the cage, Khim leaned up, cocking his head.

I can't hear you, so just nod if you can hear me.

Khim sat straight up, moving his legs over the edge of the bunk. He looked momentarily confused, then nodded.

Are you drugged?

Khim shook his head *no.*

Good. I'm going to get you out. When the time is ready, I'll guide you as far as the door. After that, you have to find your way back to the garage. I know you need a flier and a destination. I'm working on those things. I just want you to know I'm here. I can see you through that camera in the ceiling to your right.

Khim looked up.

My father has me on lockdown at his house. But I'm working on that too. I'm safe. And so are you for the time being. But I'm sorry your conditions are so poor.

As Trev finished, Khim stood up and walked to the front of the cage. He put one hand through the bars—the left, flesh hand—palm up as if reaching to touch Trev.

Trev smiled and typed.

I miss you, too. This isn't done. Not by a long shot.

The lights were getting hot, and he didn't want them to sputter out, so he said good-bye to Khim and worked more on his plan.

He waved Arch, but when he did not receive a response, he located Renn instead. He made promises he wasn't sure he could keep. Now, if he could only get Breq on his side.... He had no other siblings who would even consider helping him.

He waved Breq to see if he was still in and received in response a knock on his door.

He pressed the lock and it opened.

Breq entered wearing casual jeans and a dress shirt. The door slid shut behind him. Breq flopped on a couch by the bed, his dark hair slicked back, making him look hard-edged, every ounce the cool criminal. "Whatever you're gonna ask, baby bro, I'm pretty sure the answer is going to have to be no."

"I just need you to help me get out of here."

"No."

"Hear me out."

"No." He leaned back, pulling his feet up onto the couch.

"Breq—"

"I know I owe you, but Dad—"

"What if I said you wouldn't get caught?" Trev leaned forward to emphasize his point.

"Dad could be listening in even now."

"I debugged my room last night."

"You do think of everything, don't you." It was not a question. "But even if you get out, Trev, what are you going to do then? You can't bust Khim out."

"Leave that to me. The less you know, the better."

"Yeah." He scowled. "When have I heard that? Oh, yeah. Only all my life!"

"When I signal you, I need you to bring a flier around to the back end of the yard and hover beneath land's edge where you can't be seen."

"Is that all?"

"Oh, and I need you to buy an android."

Breq nearly came off the couch, feet hitting the floor with a smack. "What?"

"And then I need you to sign him over to me."

"I don't have that kind of money! None of us do. You know what our allowances add up to each month."

"I know. I'm working on that too."

Breq's eyes closed halfway in thought, the effect instantly softening all the sharp contours of his face. "Dad will catch you, little bro, before you get all this accomplished."

"I hope not."

"When are you planning all these shenanigans?"

"I'm hoping for tomorrow morning when everyone's in bed."

"Good thinking, except for one thing."

"What?"

"I would swear on all my Chibali suits that Dad never, ever sleeps."

"You may be right, but I'm just going to have to deal with that."

Breq leaned sideways, resting his hands on his thighs. "So, after all this, will I ever see you again?"

"Never in this house, if I can help it."

He sighed. "So that's a no."

Trev watched him glance briefly around the room. "You never liked me anyway."

Looking suddenly uncomfortable, Breq reached up and scratched the back of his head. "Not true."

"Nothing like finding that out at the last minute," Trev said.

They sat back in silence, not looking at each other.

Trev watched the dungeon shadows fold and unfold over Khim, turning his hair to precious amber. He remembered how that hair was like the finest of silk threads running cool and liquid over his fingers. And below that, the trusted face, the dusky eyes that held so much feeling, so much passion. He realized how soldiers, for all their courage and knowledge, aggression and violence, were made of fear by someone else's command, for if they did not act and do as they were told, they would die.

And such was life for all, although hopefully far less violent.

For Trev, life was also fear, but of another shade. All was travesty, but for Khim it was worse because he was never allowed to be real, building tense structures around his soul as if to cage a star.

At least Trev had received semblances of affection throughout his life. And he'd had company in his siblings, and his books.

Khim graced the small cell with more natural elegance and class than any of the Damico family possessed with all their silks and satins, their dark, shining hair, their colognes, their education, their hardened, toughened skins. Dante certainly seemed to feel love for his children, but it was an alien love, and something was missing. Maybe what was missing was the pure joy of a heart fired with more than just power, want, greed. Everything was planned and controlled for Dante, even his sharp-cut smiles.

Trev typed into his conglomerate of circuits, wires, screens, and devices.

Khim, I'm here. Just a little while longer.

Khim turned to the front of the cage, looked up at the camera, all his beautiful spirit yearning beyond the metal bars.

Chapter Twenty-Eight

Khim

At first, Khim thought he was hearing voices.

Trev was talking to him through the lights.

It was true, then—he had finally gone into the madlands, no turning back, no exit, no hope.

Or maybe this was some new form of zotic, and his last meal had been laced with it.

Still, the voice came. It told him to wake up. After he sat on the edge of the bed, it kept talking, telling him everything he longed to hear, everything he could never hope was true.

And finally, he believed.

Some of the better words kept reverberating in his mind, even though they were in a weird, echoing tone, not Trev's real voice.

I just want you to know I'm here. I miss you.

How he had hated pushing Trev away. But he'd had no choice. Trev needed to go with his father—or be hurt more.

He waited a long time for the voice to come back. Hours slowed in his mind as if the dungeon were approaching a black hole. Would it be forever before he heard Trev again?

He counted every bar on his cage. And then every shadow of every bar, including those of the four empty cells that threw their reflections onto the hard cement floor.

It smelled old in here, and it was creeping into him.

More hours passed, and Cody brought breakfast. So the night had come and gone, his bones aching with the reality of it all, the waiting.

Cody said, "Someone else will bring your lunch. I won't be here."

"Does it matter?" Khim did not plan to be here that long anyway, because Trev had said *soon*.

Cody looked a little sad, then shrugged. And Khim could only think of how stupid a child he was, for who in their right mind would be here of their own free will? Of course the answer was money. It was always money. Even the military who'd sold him under a history of lies had done so because of money.

He decided not to eat the breakfast. Just in case.

Something echoed off the lights, like a little mechanical shriek of adjustment. The door to his cell clicked. The sound, under the near-silent humming in the walls, was like something breaking.

When he got up to investigate, he found the door to his cage unlocked. One push and it swung wide.

Khim. It's Trev.

He almost laughed. Who else would it be?

Listen carefully, because once you leave this room I will find it hard to contact you, though I hope to follow your progress with the building's cameras.

First, I've unlocked all the doors between your location and the elevators. Can you find your way from there to the garage?

Khim nodded. He was trained military. Unless he was drugged out of his mind, he assessed landscapes, no matter the mileau, as if on automatic. Always.

Okay. I have, at this moment, your route cleared. When you get to the garage, find the purple flier with the numbers 2F893-D. It's a Collin. I've already remotely taken care of the locks. You'll have to disable the tracker yourself. You can do that, right?

Khim nodded again. He'd learned that too, in the military.

But Trev did not know that, because he said, *Glad to hear you were watching me closely when I did it at the prison.*

Khim scowled up at the camera.

What? Did I say something bad?

Khim shook his head.

Now I need you to memorize these coordinates.

Trev started listing numbers slowly. Khim memorized them instantly.

Do you need me to repeat?

Khim shook his head, wishing he could reiterate to Trev that he was not slow and never had been. Most androids came equipped with photographic memories.

Feed the coordinates into the flier. It will drop you off, but you'll still be ten miles from our destination. You'll have to walk the rest of the way. The walking coordinates are—

And another list of numbers to remember wafted down from the lights in a tinny tone.

If you can, try to park the flier somewhere inconspicuous. It belongs to the company, but who knows how long it will take someone in my father's camp to decide it has gone missing.

And again, Khim nodded.

When you reach the destination, you are to do nothing. Sit and wait. And don't forget to breathe.

Okay, are you ready?

Khim gave him a thumbs-up with his metal hand.

Then go, my friend. Now.

It felt strange to be on his own, even though he was following orders in a way. Trev's orders, which were more trusted to his mind than any man's in the universe. He'd imprinted on Trev; that was a fact. And the imprint became stronger because what he felt for the man could not be denied.

For Trev, he would do anything now. Including this risky, flimsy plan.

The door to the dungeon was ajar, true to Trev's word. He deftly skirted through, although he knew with a tinge of dread what was on the other side.

He swallowed hard, then made his way across the tiled room that led to the round shower room, the preparation area for the slaves who were sold for nights of debauchery. He saw the hoses. The scent was still there, keen from his memory, of zotic smoke mixed with lotions. Strawberries, slightly singed.

A moment of dizziness. He closed his eyes, focused against the goldenrod of the insides of his eyelids. Came back to himself quickly, to his relief.

He moved through the white room, dry for now, though the air was still humid as if the hot water pipes bled through the walls.

Beyond the next door were steps, winding and darkened, though lamps lit the way every few feet. He also saw a scratched and ancient elevator and decided not to take it. He knew only the route of the stairs and preferred to stay on familiar territory. He took them two at a time.

Light suddenly flooded the space. Someone entered a stairwell just one story above him. He saw the legs first. White pants, the uniform of the kitchens.

Khim froze. It was too late to go back down, and there was nowhere to hide.

The guy came into view—brown hair, dark eyes. Not Cody. "Hey," he said, proceeding to move by.

"Hey," Khim said, waiting.

The man turned. "You're an android. What are you—?"

Khim grabbed the guy by the collar and banged his head against the wall. Not to kill. The guy tripped backward, and Khim also lost his balance. He righted himself after his own forehead hit the banister, letting the kitchen guy drop ungracefully to the next landing.

A light spoke.

Khim, are you all right?

He didn't see a camera, but they could be hidden everywhere. He didn't worry about that because Trev seemed to have all that covered.

He nodded to the air after putting his hand up to his forehead where he'd hit himself, coming away with a smear of red on his fingertips.

You have two more levels. The cameras are on a time loop I programmed. I don't see anyone else. Go!

Khim went. Three steps in each leap this time. He came to a door that was ajar and entered a corridor with soft carpet he'd seen before. House of Xavier was to his right; the long hall to the elevator stretched to his left.

It's quicker to go out my dad's exit, said a lamp just inside the fancy foyer with the lion fountain, the podium, the sugary flowers.

Khim took a deep breath. He could do this.

He ran on the soft floor, silent and alone, toward the big arch that led to the room with the couches, the alcoves, the stage.

He tried not to see the velvet couch, so red and shining in the center of it all, but he couldn't help it. It was right there. His nostrils flared under the metallic memory of blood and death, muscles tensed at the memory of terrible intrusions and the scent of that, too, all over him. Bitter-salt.

He tripped, and for a moment was flying through the air. Then he landed hard against a black couch, half falling on top of it.

Khim! said a chandelier. *Are you okay?*

Khim jumped up quickly. "I'm not usually so clumsy," he said in irritation at himself.

He focused straight ahead and made it to the big office. The back door stood open. And another down a short hall. Trev's work.

The hall led to a garage elevator.

From there it was too easy. He took the private elevator to the garage. He found the purple Collin. He got in and quickly disabled the tracker even as he hit the charge switch. When he took off, the double doors opened for him onto a street lined with buildings and tall commercial screens. It was dark out.

He realized his time sense was really messed up. He remembered turning down breakfast only a couple of hours ago.

When he was away from the building, his pilot skills settled in naturally, and he shot up into moonlit clouds. Then, and only then, did he take a breath.

He looked down through the floor window and saw Fire Town as if it were sinking away from him, falling toward the planet below. The town appeared as a conglomeration of lights, a city of stars and of lanterns, swaying gently in the night breeze.

For a split second, he waited for them to speak orders in Trev's voice.

Then he flew on.

Chapter Twenty-Nine

Trev

Trev's plans did not come together exactly as he'd wished. He had wanted to leave earlier, while the household slept, but he was not completely satisfied that he was ready until darkness fell and the stars came out like all-seeing eyes.

With huge relief, he'd gotten Khim out of the dungeon. Just knowing his friend was safe gave him a giant boost of confidence.

He waved Breq.

"You're late," complained his eldest brother, coming into Trev's bedroom. "Dad's already up. He's going to expect you for breakfast."

"Yes, at nine. It's seven now. That's enough time."

Breq yawned. "Well, he never sleeps anyway." His hair stuck up on one side. It was obvious he'd just gotten up. "So," he said. "What do you want me to do?"

"I told you. Take your flier around to the back of the yard. Hover underneath the land where you can't be seen."

"What are you going to do?"

"I'll meet you there."

Breq looked skeptical.

"And here." Trev handed him a chip. "This is the android I want. He doesn't go on sale until Friday. There's money in that account, but it vanishes on Saturday. You can't use the chip after that or it could be traced."

"What am I going to do with an android?"

"Nothing. He won't even be there. You just tell the auction house that you have plans to obtain him later from another location. All you need are the papers in your name. Then you're going to sign them over to me. *Paper* papers, not digital. I know it's weird, but I want no online wave trail after that sale."

"What are you going to do with two androids, then?" Breq raised his eyebrows.

Trev rolled his eyes. "None of your concern."

"You know I'm doing all this at great risk."

Trev was silent. Finally he said, "If I can pay you back one day, I will. Anything I can do. I promise."

"No." Breq took a deep breath. "It's fine. I want to see you go. I want to see one of us best Dad for once in our lives."

Trev smiled thinly. "Thanks."

*

Trev wore his tight-fitting black bodysuit, soaked to the skin.

Then, like a teenager, he went out his window, which he had rigged to unlock and stay silent. As he passed through, his bodysuit made him invisible.

Stupid security systems and their ideas about water not being intrusive had become his staple in lucky breaks.

He climbed from the second floor along the outside wall, using his agility to hang from window to window along the triangle-shaped mansion. He leaped between windows so his shadow would not be seen, clung to a piece of decorative framing, and dangled.

Then he jumped, caught the edge of another window, and dropped on cat feet to the porch roof. The porch was a wraparound, technically, but it did not reach the back of the house where his room was. So maneuvering there had become part of his route.

From the edge of the porch, he dangled silently, landing on the damp, springy grass of the backyard.

Just after he landed, he heard footsteps. Someone coming onto the porch right where he'd been hanging. He scrunched into a ball along the side of the house and held his breath.

Finally, after what seemed like forever, the footsteps retreated.

The backyard waterfall splashed to his right. There was a long field of grass between it and a copse of trees. To reach those trees, Trev needed to be exposed for about three seconds.

He decided to count to five. If luck was with him and no one was looking in that exact direction, he'd be fine. But he had no way to know.

Finally he went, racing through the moonlight. His weirdly sculpted handheld invention with all its devices and wires and remotes bumped against his damp thigh. He reached the shadows of the trees and ducked down.

When he looked back at the house, the illuminated windows were yellow and square, showing no silhouettes, nothing. Good. No one had seen him.

He ran from tree to tree now, confidence growing. Little beds of flowers grew everywhere, seasoning the night. Above him, beyond scattered clouds, the stars winked with pride.

He reached the edge of the backyard after a short jog through beautiful, lush acreage. He could not see the force field, but he could hear its low hum. It ran about ten feet high and allowed small things through—birds and insects—but not humans. It was there as a security feature to keep people from accidentally falling over the edge of the island and into the air.

But now he wanted to go over the edge. He brought up his handheld contraption and fiddled with it, using a program he'd just designed to make a hole in the field.

"Hello," said a melodic voice to his left.

Trev jumped back in shock. He had not seen her sitting by the rock in the grass. The darkness turned her shape into one of the bushes that edged the land.

Sonye stood and walked over to him. "That's interesting." She eyed the device and all its dangling parts. "Why are you wet?"

Trev stood, mouth agape.

Sonye was dressed in a dark suit that emphasized her leanness. Her black hair was loose and drifted in waves to her waist. Like Breq, like all his siblings, she could have been pretty if she didn't wear her danger and fury on her face all the time. She wasn't much bigger than Trev. She'd taught him how to fight dirty because of it. *Size is not the only advantage. Not if you have a brain*, she'd told him once.

Sonye continued to speak. "It's a beautiful night. Not raining for a change. I went for a walk. Funny meeting you out here."

274

Trev would never be able to take her on. If she wanted to, she could incapacitate him. If she went running back to the house now, he had maybe five minutes before all hell broke loose.

He decided he had nothing left to do but be honest. "I'm leaving."

"I guessed."

"Are you going to stop me?"

"This has nothing to do with me."

"You're right."

"It's about Khim, right?"

Trev nodded.

"I saw the way you were with him."

Trev could not stop himself. "And?"

"And nothing. I'm just saying I saw. That's all."

"I need to make a hole in the field to get out."

"Go ahead." She had a strong voice, but it was inflectionless.

Trev began to work his program. It unnerved him to be watched, but the longer she stood there, the more he realized she wasn't going to do anything.

When the hole was complete, he could see a thin pink line around the area he could breach.

He turned to Sonye. "Thank you for not stopping me."

"Trev, this isn't about you. It's simply that I don't care. If you get caught, so be it. If you don't and Dad has a fit, I still don't care. Not about him. Not about you."

It was the strangest good-bye, and yet he had expected it. Dante had taken the heart from her somehow, more than he had the others. Possibly because she had been more sensitive than most as a child. But by age eight or nine, she'd gone cold. In some ways she reminded him of Khim.

Before Trev could respond, she turned and walked into the darkness under the grove of trees.

Trev watched her leave, then turned to face the tear in the force field. He approached it slowly. A little vertigo claimed him as he looked upon the world below, its dark clouds half obscuring the blurred glow of cities upon the ground. He could do this, he knew. But he had to put the distance to the planet out of his mind.

Slowly he lowered himself to the edge, sat with his feet dangling, then turned and positioned himself with his hands in the grass, his waist curved about the cliff. He'd studied the structure beforehand. There was a latticework that framed the land and kept back erosion below the root level. He reached down and found it, grasped it, and slowly lowered his body. The land was thick there, and he climbed down the lattice slowly, feet and hands having no trouble finding purchase. When he came to the bottom, his feet hung down and he had to rely only on handholds.

Finally he came to the last section, his whole body swaying in the air now except for where his hands gripped. He cocked his head. Below the final edge, the machinery that operated the antigrav systems vibrated minimally. He could see sections of it—square boxes of metal, grids, computer systems, fans. It was simple technology, but there was a lot of it because there were many backup systems and fail-safes. It got its power from the air.

He let go with one hand and felt around for something to grab underneath where he hung. His knees bent as he kicked his feet for balance, felt nothing. He tried three more times. Nothing.

Trev took a deep breath, steadying himself. He could do this if he kept his panic at bay. He wasn't even tired yet, but nerves were the biggest danger in this sort of situation.

He did not see or hear any fliers and wondered if Breq was even there yet, underneath the estate, and if so, could he even see Trev's legs and body?

One more time he tried to reach for something on the bottom of the island that he could grab. Nothing.

He swung his hand upward for a handhold and hung, waiting. He had a good strong grip. He could wait awhile. But not forever.

Finally he heard the flier's engine, soft on the night breeze, smelling faintly of ozone. He turned his head and saw it come up behind him, floating alongside his dangling body.

Through the open pilot's window, Breq said, "What the fuck, Trev?"

Trev said, "Get it under me and open the moon roof."

His brother cursed as he navigated the flier into position, hovering just below Trev. Trev looked down and felt one hand slip. The roof was open, but it was still too far away.

"Closer!" he yelled.

The flier moved up. It was still a long jump, and if he didn't aim perfectly, he'd hit the sides and fly off into the air. His hand slipped some more.

Now or never, he thought. And let go.

He pulled his hands to his chest, kept his knees locked, and hoped the handheld attached to his belt didn't get destroyed in this stunt.

His brother cursed again, and the edge of the roof brushed Trev's thigh, his hip, then his shoulder as he fell. His feet touched leather as he slid the rest of the way inside. Then he stretched out his legs, felt the seat encase him, and turned to Breq.

"Fuck, bro. You are clearly one crazy fuck!"

Trev grinned. "Okay. Let's go."

"You know we'll be tracked as soon as Dad finds you and this flier gone."

"All this time working for Dad and you don't know how to disable a tracker?" Trev leaned forward and had the job done in under a minute.

Next, Trev entered coordinates into the flier's console. "Drop me there, and that's it. You can take yourself and the flier home. Maybe Dad won't even notice you were gone."

"Likely chance," Breq replied sarcastically. "But I'll do what I can to keep Dad from finding you again."

Resigned friendliness from two of his brothers and sisters was like full-on sibling bonding for their family. Trev took what he could get.

"You're soaking wet," Breq pointed out.

"Yeah. It helps me evade detection with some security systems."

"I'll have to remember that."

"Not all security systems. I just got lucky."

Breq turned the flier and dived toward the planet, out of view of the house and any more prying eyes.

The flier spoke. "Twenty-nine minutes to destination."

"I hope you aren't staying at those coordinates. That's too close to home," Breq commented.

"Right under Dante's eye, but he'll never see us. Trust me," Trev said.

"Whatever you say, bro."

*

Starlight lost itself in the waves, and streaks of gray cloud smeared the black horizon. The waterfront sand looked white in the twin moons' light as the flier crested a small, weed-topped cliff.

"Here is good," Trev said.

The flier came to rest on a shiny shore in front of a wide ocean. Trev looked out the windows but could see no one. The moons reflecting the water made enough light that if anyone had been around for a quarter of a mile in either direction, they could be spotted.

"He's not here," Breq said.

"It's okay. I'll find him. Or he'll find me. This is the spot."

"Are you sure? You want me to stick around?"

"No. You need to get back. And make sure you buy that android."

"I'm not forgetting something like that."

Trev reached out and touched Breq's arm. "Thank you."

Breq reached back. A shoulder grip. "Get outta here."

The door of the flier slid open—not a gull-wing like the one he'd stolen from the prison, but Breq's flier was still a prime piece of equipment.

Trev jumped onto the sand, smelling brine and salt foam. He heard a night bird cry, its tone skittering the air. The flier door closed. Breq took off. Trev stood in the warm afterburn, a dark figure on a lonely beach.

The waves rushed, white-tipped, the current pulling back almost as soon as it came in. Wet sand gleamed. The moonlight shimmered silver on the water's tossed and torn surface.

Above the beach rose sandy cliffs that were only five feet tall in some areas, almost fifty feet farther down. The unevenness of the landscape gave the area a wild, unkempt feel.

Trev looked down at his handheld. A breeze blew over him, making him shiver, though the night wasn't cold. His bodysuit was still damp and clung to his chilled skin.

The coordinates he'd given Khim were a little way off, and he began to walk in the direction his flickering screen indicated. Trev strode along the beach between dry sand and waterlogged silt, where the terrain was wet but hard and his feet didn't sink.

Patches of beach ahead were dark, streaked with clumps of seaweed. As he came closer, something moved. He slowed his pace as a dark shape rose up from the ground and took the form of a man. Tall, hair catching gold from the glow of the moons.

Khim stood facing him.

Trev increased his pace until he could make out Khim's features—the wide forehead, the high bones of the cheeks, the strong chin. He was still dressed in that white shirt from two days ago and the dark trousers that had obviously belonged to Renn. When he was about thirty feet away, Trev stopped.

He saw Khim's mouth curve up. Khim held up his hands as if in question, but Trev knew it was an invitation. Permission.

Trev let out a soaring laugh and ran the rest of the way to him, leaping forward at the last moment as Khim swept him up into a tight hug, holding him easily off the ground. Trev wrapped his legs about Khim's waist, pressed his face to his neck, and squeezed his arms about him, breath coming fast.

For a long time they embraced like that, chests pressed, hearts drumming against each other. Trev kept saying Khim's name over and over like a prayer.

Khim whispered into his ear. "I'm sorry I pushed you away, but your father was hurting you."

"It's okay. It's all okay." Trev's body, which had been chilled, was rapidly heating up now.

Finally, Khim put him down. "You're wet."

"Had to get past my father's security. Seems all the best systems have this loophole about water."

Khim let out a soft laugh, a sound Trev rarely heard from him. "Well, now that the hard part is over, here we are. Nothing around for miles. Where to from here?"

"The part about nothing around for miles isn't true. Come on."

Side by side, they began to slog across the dry, sinking sand toward the cliffs.

After a while they came to a set of wooden stairs that climbed the cliff face, the rails weathered and warped by the sea wind and weather. They took the stairs all the way to the top and came to a path lined unevenly with rocks. A short distance away stood a V-roofed house. It looked like a gray shadow in the night, with no lights, an abandoned cottage.

As they drew closer, they could see it was neither neglected nor a cottage. An elaborate porch ran across the front, with huge glass windows on the first and second stories and no weathering to its gray-and-white frame.

"I've got the entrance code here," Trev said.

"What is this place?"

They walked up steps rippled in eddies of soft sand and approached the front door. "It's in some estate trust of Arch's from way back when he was a kid, and generations before him. He doesn't actually own it, the trust does, although he's the only name left on it. The trust is the kind that can't be touched, not even by lawsuits. Arch wasn't lying when he said he had places to go. Arch is like my father in that way. Those kinds of men always have contingencies. And more contingencies on top of those."

"Why didn't he and Renn come here when they left two days ago?"

"He didn't say. But they are coming. Next week."

"And then where will we go?" Khim asked.

"Nowhere for now. I'll be working on our new lives for some months. Until then, we stay here."

"With them?"

280

Trev could tell by Khim's stance and the way his metal hand clenched and unclenched that he was uncomfortable with the idea. "Yes. With them. I checked out the schematics. This place is pretty big."

Khim just grunted.

Trev smiled as the front door swung open after he entered a code into a box on the wall.

The inside smelled somewhat dank, and as the lights came on at their entrance, Trev saw motes of dust swirling. He moved forward without hesitation. "I think the kitchen's through here."

Khim followed, and the feeling of that was familiar and wonderful.

Trev glanced around, then went to a group of cupboards and started opening them. He heard Khim behind him, tugging on a drawer here and there.

Khim said, "There's food in cans and boxes."

"There's power to the heater and the freezer. It's all working."

"How long has no one lived here?"

Trev shrugged with a slight shiver.

"Cold?" Khim asked.

"I want something hot to drink. I've been wet for too long now." He pulled some mugs from one of the cupboards, the ceramic painted with colorful blue and green flowers.

"Tea?" Khim asked, holding up a canister.

"Perfect."

Boiling water came from a red spigot by the sink.

Khim opened the tin of tea bags. "Fancy," he said.

Trev was already shrugging out of his bodysuit. Underneath he had on a white tank top and thin cotton drawstring pants.

Khim looked him up and down. "There have to be towels around."

"Just a blanket would be nice."

It took Khim only seconds to find him one from somewhere in the parts of the house they had yet to explore. It was small, plaid, and soft. Khim draped it around Trev's shoulders.

Just that gesture was warming to Trev. Khim handed him one of the mugs already steeping. Steam rose to warm Trev's face. He put his lips to the edge of the mug, and as he took a tiny sip, the burn of the tea washed through his mouth.

They sat at a square white table with a chrome frame. The bodysuit lay in a puddle on the floor, so thin it looked like just a scrap of black cloth with legs and sleeves.

In such a short time, they had come from unbelievable, unwanted horror and excitement to this single quiet moment. An ordinary setting. Two men drinking hot tea as darkness cocooned house, land, and sea.

Trev drew the blanket closer. Sipped. Could not take his eyes off Khim.

Khim, it seemed, felt the same. His eyes wandered over Trev, intent, almost hungry.

Trev gave him a sidelong smile. "I haven't slept in thirty-six hours at least."

"We should locate the guest bedrooms."

"Bedroom. Singular. You're staying with me."

Khim raised his brown-gold eyebrows. Too polite, perhaps, to say anything.

A breeze blew about the house, rustling at the eaves.

Trev finished his tea and rose.

Khim picked up the mugs and took them to the sink, rinsing them out and putting them on an old wooden rack on the counter to dry.

They wandered through the first story, finding two bedrooms down a long, dim hallway. They were pristine, as if just made up. Both had attached bathrooms.

They took the bigger room.

Trev said, "A hot shower, then sleep."

Khim nodded, going to the closet, opening it, looking inside. It was mostly empty. Trev could see some boxes on the top shelf. Some framed holos stood stacked on the floor on the left.

Trev turned away before curiosity kept him from his much-desired shower.

Chapter Thirty

Khim

Khim took off his shirt but kept his trousers on. He pulled back the plush covers, all solid reds and pinks and blues, and got in under the crisp white sheets, leaning back against a luxurious stack of four pillows.

He did not remember when he'd ever slept in a bed like this. For him it was always bunks—military, dungeon cell, prison. Or bedrolls on alien worlds in the middle of nowhere. Their one night at the motel had had a decent bed, but nothing as plush and soft as this one.

He had found paper real-books in a drawer, old, the pages silverfish-nibbled, and stacked them on the bedside table. *Ballads from the Planets of the Twelve Realms.* A novel of adventure and time travel from the thirty-first century called *Plus Plus Light.* And ancient Earth classics, some familiar to him from his blurred, implanted memories— *Gulliver's Travels, Oliver Twist, Time Enough for Love, Harry Potter and the Half-Blood Prince.* And one more he knew Trev would like, which he now took up and opened, supporting the bottom of the book on his chest and beginning to read.

Trev came from the bathroom with a dark green towel around his shoulders and another, twin to it, wrapped around his waist. "I hung my clothes to dry. I don't suppose you found any in your room search, did you?"

"Better. I found these." He pointed to the stack of real-books.

Trev came over and got between the covers with the towel still wrapped around his waist. "Oh, wow." He put his still-wet head on the pillow and turned onto his side, facing Khim.

Khim glanced down at him, saw his eyelids flutter half-closed. "I'll turn out the light," he said quietly.

"No, wait. I love that one you're reading."

"A Bradbury. I know. That's why I picked it up first."

"What part are you on now?"

"I just started. This part, page four. 'Crossing the lawn that morning, Douglas Spaulding broke a spider web with his face....'"

"Go on. Keep reading," Trev said.

By the time Khim got to the "bee-fried air" on page six, Trev's breathing was deep and even, as if he'd come a long, long way and only now could stop and rest.

Khim set the book aside, turned out the light, and pulled the soft covers over Trev's shoulders. He scooted closer to him, then lay on his back staring at the white ceiling for a while before he fell asleep.

He woke suddenly, scared. Something was chasing itself on the air.

It was only Trev's breath against his cheek.

Where were they? Then he remembered. A house on a cliff by an ocean, by a beach.

Trev shifted sleepily. "What?"

Khim did not answer.

Trev reached out and pulled him closer under the covers. Khim's flesh hand, as if on its own, trailed down Trev's naked hip, and fire sparked up his arm to his chest.

Trev said, "Now I'm awake."

At once embarrassed, Khim moved his hand away, but Trev caught it with his own, pressing it against his skin, and said, "Kiss me."

So Khim did. And thought how lucky he was to have this man beside him a second time. It was a second chance for them both. When did anyone have such fortune as that?

Trev's mouth curved in a smile and opened to Khim's. Turmoil of heat. Blue sparks in his vision. Sweet like air in a first gulped breath.

Trev was lean and warm against him. Khim was fully hard in seconds. This man in his arms was a magician that way, made of fire commanding the brightness within them both.

The air crackled around them, between them. Their arms and legs and bodies wove together. And their minds as well, as Trev whispered, "I want you. I want you," and Khim said, "I missed you." Then Khim added, "I only want you. I'm here. Only for you."

They rolled under the covers until they finally tossed them away. Trev pushed at Khim's pants until Khim had to pause, reach down, and undo the clasp, pulling them off until there was nothing between them but skin.

Trev writhed in his arms, and Khim's desire heightened. He wanted to touch him everywhere at once. Stroke. Kiss. Lick. He found his mouth straying to Trev's neck and shoulders, chest and sternum, found a hard nipple and licked it.

Trev's body went slack, almost boneless, so Khim repeated the gesture on the other side. He whipped the last of the sheet away, and in the dimness of the room, with only moonlight seeping about the curtains, saw shadows upon shadows, the darkest of them pooling between Trev's legs where arousal fiercely rose. Khim leaned up and over him now, tracing his tongue in a line down his body. His metal hand held Trev in place at the hip, his flesh hand stroked his chest. His knees were bent at Trev's thighs, and he scooted farther down.

Trev moaned, reaching for him. Khim's palm rose from Trev's chest and clasped one of Trev's flailing hands, holding tight. His metal hand trailed from hip to cock and drew up the underside. Then he lowered his head and followed that line with his tongue.

Trev arched, then almost sat up, but Khim took his hand from his grip and pushed him down. Trev turned his head so that shadows made his face into contours of need, the whites of his eyes and his teeth flashing, his chest heaving. He brought his hand up to clutch at Khim's bicep as Khim bent and kissed him on the stomach. Khim lifted his head to move downward again and looked at him. Trev was astonishing in his beauty, more beautiful than anyone Khim had ever seen.

He wanted this. All of Trev, laid out before him in agonizing and pleasured splendor.

"Let me," he whispered against his thigh, and he took the tip of Trev's cock between his lips.

Trev's clutch on him let go. His arms and body fell back. He groaned Khim's name and burrowed his fists in the pillow at either side of his head.

Khim's tongue found the texture to be everything he craved, and he took more of Trev into his mouth, reveling in the clean taste, the smoothness, and found the supple and hard juxtapositions of arousal fascinating.

Trev's body rocked side to side. His hair pooled in deeper shadows on the white pillow. His tan skin rippled against cool white sheets. The air smelled of the ocean.

Khim had had a fleeting thought two nights ago that he would mess this up, the touching part, the sex part, for two reasons. The first was because he'd always waited, his whole life, to be told what to do. The second was because he'd never done this with another person before. Their night at the desert motel had been his first time.

Of course he knew what was what—the hows, the whys—and had witnessed others in the barracks having sex, although never looking closely, telling himself to never mind. But now he didn't need to know anything except how he felt and what Trev's responses communicated to him.

Khim hadn't known how devotion could inform someone of things they thought they were ignorant of. How love itself became a language made fluent when you allowed it purchase in the heart.

He moved his mouth down on Trev, and even his metal hand felt the tremble in Trev's hips. His lips sensed the way Trev's core became electrified, how the blood rushed to strain and swell. He moved his mouth off, then lower, tongue caressing the velvet sac, the nodes within. Back up to the damp cock, he took it fully in his mouth and his mind blazed with the exhilaration.

What had Trev done to him to make him burn so? Nothing, except be kind and generous and never use him against his will. That had never happened before. The caring. The unquestionable adoration.

It did not take long. Trev was so eager and lost inside his own body's responses. He cried out a warning, "That's it. I'm going to—" and pushed gently at Khim's shoulders.

It made Khim not want to miss a beat.

This was nothing like what had happened to him in House of Xavier. Not messy. Not dark. Not sly and painful.

This was bright, like new dawn. As fresh as something colorful growing, pushing through layers of ash and pain and blood. As if all the worlds he'd been a part of destroying, including the deep core of himself, caged behind transparent crystal, took deep breaths as their seasons and winds returned, bringing them back to life.

He took his time, reveling in the scent, the flavor, the beauty, before crawling back into Trev's arms, where Trev, breathing fast, gazed at him in disbelief. Khim lowered himself to kiss him, and Trev's arms came up and around him. He wished he could stay like that forever.

After a couple of minutes, Trev pushed him onto his side, brushed his fingers through his hair, and said, "May I?"

Always asking first, that was Trev, who would never, ever hurt him.

Khim nodded. "Whatever you like." And kissed him again.

Trev said, touching Khim's hairless chest, the hardness of the curves there, the dents of muscle farther down, "Hmm, I think I like it all."

Khim fisted his hands in Trev's hair.

Trev said, "I need to practice what you just did to me."

"Okay," Khim said. And he thought, *Practice all you want. I'm here.*

The beautiful lips took him to new worlds, his cock so heavy and full. Trev managed to get halfway down on it, and that was all. It was more than enough. Khim was nearly bursting at the first touch.

Afterward, he lay on his side, tracing the edges of Trev's face, moving his hand down to the center of his chest. He could feel the thrum of heartbeat and life force. He kissed him softly on the jaw, behind the ear, as Trev, on his back, ran his palms up and down Khim's arms, curving over the muscles, pressing his fingertips into them.

Trev said quietly, "I never thought it'd be like this."

"Sex?" Khim asked.

"Love."

Chapter Thirty-One

Trev

They did not know how long the food in the kitchen had been there.

Khim said, "I used to camp on alien worlds. I know how to make meals out of almost anything."

They found meats and cheeses in tins. Khim made bread fresh from the oven, and Trev said, "Mmm, smells like you."

They ransacked and found beer, wine, flavored waters.

The day grew hot, so they took sandwiches and beer and whatever else they could carry down to the beach.

Trev had found old clothes in another room—shorts that were too small for Khim, too big for him, but they didn't care.

Trev never tired of seeing the bronze line of Khim's body making perfect dives into the oncoming turquoise waves, then coming up spouting water, hair flipping back in sopping-wet, dark gold strands.

After their swim, they rested on towels on the warm sand, grains of it glittering on their arms and legs.

Together they dozed. To Trev it seemed as if they opened their eyes at the same time. They lay on their sides, facing each other. Khim's eyes were like the undershadows of blue in the sea, his pupils pinpoints in the bright sunlight. Khim reached out with his metal hand and ran the tip of his forefinger over Trev's ribs, trailing along the waist, stopping only at the hip where the waistband of the shorts hugged him.

"Feels cool, like the water," said Trev.

Khim bent so that his forearm above the metal touched Trev's flesh, and Trev could feel the steam rising off Khim. "Because your skin is so hot," Khim replied.

Trev half closed his eyes until he gazed at Khim through his lashes. He never looked away.

Khim never looked away.

Trev licked his lips, tasting salt. The tide sang a hushed and sighing strain. Birds cried. The sky was like melted blue wax.

Khim's eyes pulled him in until all of that—the warm sand, the damp towels, the abandoned bottles of glistening beer—ceased to exist.

Trev was not going to be able to stand this for one more minute. He pulled himself into a sit-up, got his feet under him, and stood, looking down at Khim, who lay very still, although his eyes had moved to follow him.

"Come on," Trev said, finally glancing toward the stairs.

The left side of Khim's mouth twitched to a hint of a smile. Trev felt warm sweat drip down the center of his chest. His hair was still wet at the nape.

Khim rose. There was very little covering him. The tops of his rounded buttocks peeked out from the waistband of the too-small shorts. The whole picture was driving Trev crazy.

He turned and began to jog toward the wooden stairs at the cliff.

He did not have to look behind him to know Khim followed. He could feel that golden presence, like the waves of the glinting sea at his back, only steadier, a constant furnace on the air.

They raced each other up the steps two at a time. Crashed through the front door. Scrambled down the hall, which was too long, way too long, and barely made it to the bedroom because they stopped to kiss, Khim pushing Trev against the wall and Trev breathing hard, saying, "Only a few more feet."

The white sheets received them with a cool embrace. Sand was everywhere. They didn't care.

Shorts fell over the side of the bed, legs entwined, sun-slicked bodies slid together.

Afterward, they showered and did it all over again under the warm spray, covered with soapy foam, hands and fingers going everywhere. Neither could get enough of the other.

The next day was spent much the same.

The next night, Trev found candles and brought three into the bedroom. Their light filled the room.

In bed, Trev turned to Khim. "Look what I found in the bathroom." He held out a bottle of clear oil. The bottle said it was massage lubricant, but they both knew what it was for.

Before Trev could explain what he wanted, Khim went stiff.

Trev said, "Hey, don't pull away. I didn't mean to make you uncomfortable." He rolled over Khim, pulling him forward to face him, wrapping his arms about him. "I'm sorry," he said, lips against his cheek. "That's not why I brought it to bed."

After all Khim had been through, Trev had not meant to scare him or demand anything of him he didn't want. "I know you don't—" He stopped, taking another track. "It's for me. I want to feel you inside me." He felt himself blush. "But only if you want to do that. To me, I mean. I know how it works. I just never tried it before."

"You told me you never tried any of this before," Khim said smugly, his body slowly relaxing in Trev's arms. He added, voice pitched low, "You might not like it."

Trev planted a kiss on his lips in answer.

Khim took the bottle from Trev's hand, gaze speculative. "You must be sure," he said softly. All fear had vanished from his face. What was left was pure adoration.

Trev said, "With you, I am."

"We'll go slow."

"I'd like that."

Then Khim tackled a laughing Trev and began to kiss him all over his body.

Trev luxuriated in all the attention. Every touch from Khim felt more intense than the last. When Khim's hand finally delved into the cleft of his buttocks, he started to turn over.

"No," Khim said quietly, kissing his shoulder. "Face-to-face. It might be harder, but I need to see you."

"Yes," Trev said.

Khim explored him gently. Trev let his knees bend and go wide. He tilted his hips up, and Khim reached for a pillow to put underneath him. It helped.

Slowly, Khim's oiled fingers entered him. One. Then two. He leaned down and sucked softly at Trev's cock, never enough to make him come as fingers moved in and out of him.

After a while, Trev became dazed. He felt on the cusp of shattering, completely open and ready. "Khim," he breathed. "Please."

Ever patient, Khim replied, "When I think you're ready."

Leave it to Khim to obey anything he said until now. Trev was beyond frustrated, poised on the brink of utter pleasure, hands tearing at the sheets at his sides. He heard himself call Khim's name again. Again.

Trev was hot all over. The room seemed to be swaying, as if he could see beyond the walls to the sea. Night glimmered on the edges of rapture.

Khim's weight moved over him and he reached up, blindly grasping.

"Relax," Khim said, "or it won't work."

"I am," Trev breathed, hands rubbing, then clasping over Khim's hips.

Khim pressed against him, and he was slippery and open, so it was all fine. Trev surged upward, but Khim had the control now and did not move to meet him. He felt the hardness against his opening, but no more pressure.

Trev let out a long, loud sigh.

He knew Khim was shy of this, so Trev waited.

Khim was careful as he began to push. Almost too careful, and yet Trev was glad because as he was filled, he loved that he could feel every inch and that the pressure all around him gave him time to respond fully, feel his pulse connect with the swaying of the room and recede away from all tension.

It seemed like forever before Khim finally brought them fully together. Trev opened his eyes and reached up. He loved the feeling of being joined to Khim more than he could ever articulate. "You can move if you want," he whispered.

He had felt no pain, only sensations of being stretched, wanting to push down at the feeling of being so filled up.

The look on Khim's face was bliss. He rocked very gently.

Trev saw stars as the sensitive place inside him was brushed. "Do that again," he said.

Khim obeyed.

Then they were moving together as if they knew the dance by heart.

Trev was taken up, up into ecstasy. He wanted more and curled his upper body off the sheet toward Khim. "Sit back," he ordered. "Lift me onto your lap."

Khim did as he was told in one fluid motion, and Trev wrapped his legs about the smooth, lean waist and buried his face in Khim's shoulder as they rocked to the rhythm of their hearts.

Nothing had ever prepared Trev for the intensity of this experience. He sobbed into Khim's skin, then turned his head and kissed him. Khim kissed deeply, with passion, as he pumped into Trev faster and faster.

Trev started to fall back; Khim's strong arms held him.

Trev said, "Touch me."

One of Khim's arms snaked between them and stroked him from root to tip. It was all the stimulus Trev needed, and he was crying out, coming in arcing white lace all over Khim's chest.

As a strangled sound escaped Khim's lips, Trev felt an answering warmth inside him. They fell back on the sheets, still joined, chest to chest. Trev ran his hands up and down Khim's back. Still breathless, they kissed again as Khim slid out of him, tugging, but gentle and sweet.

Trev's body was made of flame. Khim nestled against his chest.

Before Khim closed his eyes to sleep, Trev thought he saw the stars all the way through the second story of the house, as if the ceilings and roofs were invisible, as if two realities converged and nothing in that moment was solid.

*

Trev heard a crash and came rushing into the kitchen. The little glass window by the door was broken, shards glinting on the tile floor like pieces of a shattered sun.

"What happened?"

"The last of the barriers has fallen," Khim said, staring dumbfounded at the mess.

"What?"

Blinking, as if trying to focus, Khim said, blushing, "I don't know."

Khim's left hand was bleeding at the top of the palm. "Here." Trev cupped Khim's hand in his own and led him to the sink, where the water rushed. He carefully washed away the blood.

Khim said, "You don't have to do that—"

Ignoring him, not letting go, Trev said, "It's not deep. Don't need actual synthskin. Just a synth patch. Stay there. Be back in a sec."

Trev went to the bathroom and rummaged for a patch. When he came back, Khim was obediently standing by the sink, the afternoon light streaming over him in the kind of splendor that stopped clocks in midtick, stars in their paths, hearts from reaching another beat.

Epilog

Khim

A week later, Arch and Renn arrived at the house.

For all that had happened to Trev and Khim, it was a quiet arrival, casual and polite. They brought supplies. They took rooms in the upper level. There was an underground garage where they parked their flier.

At first, Khim thought the presence of others would intrude on his newly acquired happiness with Trev. He stood back, trying not to resent them, all the while knowing it was Arch who owned this place.

Khim watched purple-haired Renn approach Trev with a real-paper contract in his hand. "You own me now," he said.

"I wanted no online trail. That's why you have the papers."

Renn nodded.

Khim frowned. Trev owned Renn? His chest hitched for a moment, almost jealous, until Trev said, "You can stay with Arch as long as you wish. Maybe after that the laws will have changed and I'll be able to free you."

Renn bowed his head. "Thank you."

"Thank you for taking us in when we most needed it."

Trev turned and shot a smile at Khim, who let that look warm him all the way to his bones.

*

Later that night, Khim and Trev lay together on their snowy sheets, listening to the shushing of the tide caressing the shore.

Khim let his passion ebb and flow, softly, softly in their brand-new life.

You seem different now, Trev had said on the glass porch of Arch's estate. Khim thought no truer statement had ever been observed about him. No one had ever bothered to look at him in any depth beyond his android status. No one had ever *seen* him. Until Trev. Until now.

The days continued, leaving golden trails of the sun in their veins.

The nights spilled like magic around them, as if the whole of life were a big flower opening, engulfing them in endless burning-sweet pleasure.

For the first time in their lives, they were both free.

Contact links for Wendy Rathbone:

Join my Facebook group Wendyland. I post updates, cover reveals, snippets, sales and other fun stuff every day: https://www.facebook.com/groups/718074255203918/

Friend me on Facebook: https://www.facebook.com/wendy.rathbone.3

Follow my Amazon author page: https://www.amazon.com/Wendy-Rathbone/e/B00B0O9BMS/ref=dp_byline_cont_ebooks_1

Follow me on Bookbub: https://www.bookbub.com/authors/wendy-rathbone

Dear Reader:

Thank you for reading *The Android and the Thief.*

This story is set in a very far-flung future of my own devising, the same future as my books *Letters to an Android* and *The Moonling Prince.* Though there is no overlap of characters in any of those books, and they are all standalone reads, I use a lot of the same futuristic terminologies.

I hope you enjoyed Trev and Khim. These two are very close to my heart. I love writing about characters who have no rights escaping to a better life. It's one of my enduring themes throughout all my books. Khim's plight wrung my heart out in telling his tale, and Trev was amazing to explore while he overcame his father issues, and everything else terrible thrown in his path to freedom.

Every part of this book's process toward publishing was a joy!

Happy Reading!

Love,

Wendy Rathbone

About Wendy Rathbone

Read Wendy Rathbone… where imposters and slaves, princes and lost boys always find their happily every after.

I have written in all genres: sci-fi, fantasy, horror, paranormal, contemporary, erotica, romance. But I keep coming back to romance as the main focus. Gay romance. Male/male romance. The idea of two men falling in love is irresistible to me. It's all I write now.

All my books are available on Amazon and most are in Kindle Unlimited. So if you have the urge, go take a look. See what's on the shelf.

Male/male romance books by Wendy:

The Kingdom of Slaves Series (contemporary fantasy mm romance)

The Slave Palace
The Slave Harem
Master of Halloween (short story)

The Omega Misfits (Omegaverse mm romance)

Trust No Alpha
The Alpha's Fake Mate
Alpha's Embrace
Single Omega Dad (coming May 2020, Mathias's story!)

The Imposter Series (fantasy mm romance)

The Imposter Prince
The Imposter King

The Moonling Prince Series (fantasy, sci fi mm romance)

The Moonling Prince
The Coming of the Light

The Foundling Series (contemporary billionaire mm romance trilogy)

Rescue Me
Sacrifice Me
Remember Me

The Fantastic Immortals Series (fantasy/myth mm romance)

Ganymede: Abducted by the Gods
Zeus: Conquering his Heart

Stand Alone Novels

Sci Fi MM Romance

Solstice Gift (holiday)
Not Another Hero
Cocky Virgin Prince
Prey
Scoundrel
The Android and the Thief **(Second edition)**
Letters to an Android

Fantasy MM Romance

Lord Vampyre
Lace
Snow of the White Hills **(mm fairy tale)**
The Elves of Christmas **(holiday fantasy mm romance)**

Contemporary MM Romance

Romantically Incorrect
Snowfall and Romance (Christmas novel)
The Bodyguard's Valentine
Buying You

TRUST NO ALPHA
Wendy Rathbone

It's a world gone mad. The Alphas are out of control.

When you discover you're not who you thought you were, the nightmare begins.

KRIS

At age eighteen, life as he knows it is over for Kris. A secret to his nature he was not aware of has been revealed.

Now, kept as a prisoner in a locked room in the mansion of his wealthy father, Kris is at the mercy of Alpha laws and Alpha domination.

Things take a turn for the worse when his own litter mate threatens him, and his father starts behaving strangely around him.

Escape is his only hope. But where can he go in a world that allows him no rights?

THORNE

Marked as a dangerous Alpha, and living a secluded life alone and unloved, Thorne still grieves for the mate whose death he feels responsible for.

Years have passed, and he refuses to even try to function in normal society.

One day he discovers a young man on his property, disheveled, desperate, and scared. He acts like a runaway Omega, but he doesn't smell like one.

What is this boy? And why does Thorne feel an immediate need to protect him? To bond him? To make him his?

A non-shifter, Omegaverse love story of rescue, first time, fertility issues and an HEA. Standalone read. 65,500 words. (While Omegas are birth-fathers in this universe, there is no on-page mpreg in this book.)

THE ALPHA'S FAKE MATE
Wendy Rathbone

The Alphas think they own everything. Including people. Well, I'm here to say they don't own me, and I will never let one of those bastards touch me again.

The frenzy of their Burn cannot be trusted. I know from experience. My first time with an Alpha nearly ended in my death. And because of the laws which favor Alpha rights, and place a large number of unbonded, adult Omegas on chattel farms, my abuser can never be tried for his crimes against me.

Omegas are being hurt. Omegas are dying.

All Alphas are violent. Or so I believe. Until I meet Orion.

Ori is everything a guy could want in a mate. Six foot three. Beautiful brown wavy hair. Bright, dark eyes. Muscles like chiseled marble. He even says "please" and "thank you" at all the right times. He's got it all, except he's an Alpha.

Though he has given me a room in his home free of charge, and has signed fake paperwork saying we are bonded so I don't have to answer my attacker's claim, can I trust him?

But now I'm in danger. If I don't take a real mate, my life as I know it will be over. Can I believe in the goodness of Ori? Can I learn to love again?

A non-shifter, fake mate, Alpha/Omega love story. Rescue. First time. Omegaverse. Mpreg. Healing from sexual trauma. (All books in The Omega Misfits series are standalone reads and can be read in any order.) 61k words.

ALPHA'S EMBRACE
Wendy Rathbone

I am Misha. My name was given to me at birth by the doctor who delivered me. I have never known my parents. I live in a ten by ten space with one window, a sink and toilet, a bed and a locked door. Once a day I'm taken to an outdoor exercise area. I am allowed a limited access tablet and tutored online by computer programs. I have one friend I talk to through a tiny crack in the wall. His name is Cedric and he has trouble keeping himself quiet. When he isn't talking to me about monsters and demons, he screams all the time.

Why is my life so isolated and depressing? Because I am a Sylph. Sylphs are the byproduct of illegal Omega to Omega matings. We are all beautiful, but 99.9% are born insane. The rarest of Sylphs, like me, show no outward signs of madness or brain damage, but we live in institutions because we cannot be trusted.

All of us Sylphs who have lived long enough to pass through puberty have hypersexual disorder which makes life even more difficult for us, let alone our keepers. It is like something Alphas call the Burn, a mating urge Alphas experience once every couple of months.

But we're Sylphs, not Alphas, and this Burn thing? We experience it all the time. It's a huge problem and why we are kept isolated. Most of us don't survive through our teens because of it.

One day, a handsome Alpha comes to interview and study me. He calls himself the Chief of Staff but his real name is Geo. Like magic, I fall in love with him instantly. I do everything I can to seduce him. He will have none of it because touch between an Alpha and a Sylph is taboo. But I have plans. No matter what, I intend to bond him and make him mine. Forever.

A non-shifter Alpha/Omega-Sylph love story of forbidden love, rescue, and HEA. Standalone read. No Mpreg. 58k words.

SNOWFALL AND ROMANCE
Wendy Rathbone

A blizzard. A Christmas rescue. A man with the heart of an angel.

Hayden

Hayden knows it was stupid to think he could walk home from the office and beat the blizzard. So what if he worked out all the time until he was big and strong. So what if he hated to ever ask for help. Loners who think they can do everything themselves are just as vulnerable as anyone. His only consolation is if he dies there will be very few people who will miss him.

Matthew

The half-frozen man falling through the door to Matthew's coffee shop is more than alarming, but it's a good thing he'd forgotten to lock that front entrance or the beautiful guy covered in snow might have died in the cold.

The man is gorgeous, soft-spoken, helpful, maybe even a bit old-fashioned in his manners. Just the type Matthew always wished for but never met. Sharing a fire and a snowed-in night with him will be no hardship.

When the storm lasts more than a day, attraction blooms. But when it is over, will Hayden and Matthew's feelings fade? Or will holiday charm and a heart-warming miracle draw them together again?

Rescue, forced proximity, overwhelming attraction, blizzards, and a heart-warming Christmas miracle.

Although this book is part of A Snow Globe Christmas series, it is a complete stand alone and it isn't a requirement that you read the previous books to follow along. We wish everyone a happy holiday season.

THE SLAVE HAREM
Wendy Rathbone

The slave harem is all. If you enter, you can never leave. Contact with the outside world is forbidden.

With a secret talent for seeing auras of physical and emotional arousal, Ren, a sought-after pleasure slave, is sold to a mysterious master in a foreign land where he will become part of a collection of beautiful men.

Though the men appear welcoming, there is competition and jealousy among the ranks. And their mysterious master who is heard but never seen elicits more questions than answers.

One friendly slave, Li Po, helps Ren settle in, but it is the voiceless man, Zanti, who draws Ren's attention. With his wicked beauty and bratty scowls, Zanti is the least welcoming of them all, and Ren's training and control are put to the test.

Gay harem, slow-burn, enemies to lovers. Extraordinary and strange. Hot and cold. This book explores the many levels of sex, lust, loneliness and belonging. And maybe, just maybe, there can be love.

THE SLAVE PALACE
Wulf and Locke
WENDY RATHBONE

Conquered. Captured. Sold as a pleasure slave.

After being taken as a prisoner of war, Wulf fights his captors and is sold as a One-Night Thrall to be used and abused, then put to death. He is purchased by a high ranking master of the famous Slave Palace. Why Locke buys him, Wulf has no clue, but something about this master is intriguing. Instead of abuse, Wulf is plied with luxuries he has never known by a man who actually seems to respect him.

Jaded. Looking for a challenge.

Eminent Master Locke takes on a bet with his best friend that he can't train and tame a dangerous One-Night Thrall in ten days. But something about this slave stirs him like no other before. All bets aside, Locke has the urge to keep Wulf, as well as save his life. But Wulf is fierce, unwilling, and his consent papers have been forged. If Wulf doesn't soon submit to his role as a slave, he will be sent to death as a prisoner of war.

A sweet, slow-burn love story taking place on an alternate contemporary Earth where owning pleasure slaves is legal.

LORD VAMPYRE
Wendy Rathbone

When Lord Neverelle becomes a guest at Cliffside Keep, Vanni watches helplessly as Damion, the young man he's grown up with and secretly loves, falls for the alluring and seductive stranger. Lord Neverelle is danger incarnate, and soon takes control of the household.

Not satisfied with Damion alone, Never uses a vampire trick called "the tempt" to compel Vanni, who is swept into a love triangle that includes fiery passion and nightly threesomes.

Now Vanni must ask himself, is any of this consensual? And what about Damion—does he really want to be with Vanni, or is it all a sensual play controlled by vampire compulsion?

M/M and M/M/M romance.

The Imposter Prince
Book 1 in The Imposter Series
Wendy Rathbone

His love for an enemy prince threatens his very life.

Dare does not mind serving the spoiled and cruel Prince Darius. Growing up with him, Dare does everything for Darius including homework, bed play demands, and even doubling for him as the prince grows too paranoid to face even the smallest of crowds.

But everything changes in a single moment when Dare, while posing as Darius, is abducted by the enemy.

A captive in a new and hostile land, Dare meets another prince who seems just as indulged and rotten as Darius—until Dare gets to know him, until they fall in love. Against his will, Dare must continue to play the role of Prince Darius for real, or risk everything: his love, his land, and his very life.

His only chance for survival is to keep a secret from the one he loves, a secret that is also killing him.

A male/male, enemies to lovers novel of mad kings, troubled princes, abduction, fevers, cold dungeons, warm hearths, comfort, wine, and true love.

BUYING YOU
Wendy Rathbone

It's one thing to be a beautiful cover model on billboards, buses and magazine covers. It's quite another to be sold as one.

Prized for his looks, Dane knows it's shallow, but he is on his way to having it all. It feels good to be gorgeous, smart and have top designers from around the world requesting him.

When he returns to his hometown to participate in a small Date-For-Charity auction, it seems harmless enough—until a hooded man walks in and bids higher on him than anyone else. Dane is intrigued but nervous when he finds out the guy has vanished after the winning bid, leaving only a limo behind to whisk Dane off into the night.

Enemies to lovers, opposites attract, and hot steamy nights that challenge two guys' trust issues along with their biggest fears.

SONS OF NEVERLAND
A Deliciously Dark Male/Male Romance
Della Van Hise

Set against a backdrop of contemporary culture, *Sons of Neverland* explores the universal questions of love, sex and death - the three most crucial challenges every human being must face. Stefan London is a grieving man, suffering through the loss of his young daughter. When he goes to a science fiction convention in the hopes of meeting her friends, he encounters instead a man who is dangerously seductive. Lured into the night, Stefan soon discovers himself in a world where vampires are real, and immortality is only a kiss away.

But the price of eternal life is high, and as his handsome maker warns, "Through my blood you will learn a secret that will compel you to live forever, yet a secret so sinister it will haunt you for that same eternity."

The secret will haunt you, too.

YEAR OF THE RAM
Della Van Hise

Year of the Ram was described by one reviewer as... "A space-faring gay romance full of love, angst, and longing."

Only after Star Commander Morgan Diego becomes an exile as a result of a Galaxy Corps political blunder does he begin to realize how much he valued the companionship of his second in command - the mysterious Lucien, an Alfarian who is more elfen than human, with peculiar powers & abilities which begin to unfold as he, too, realizes what he has lost.

Separated by circumstance from his former life, Morgan is thrust into a world where he must survive by his wits. When he meets a peculiar little old man calling himself Kim Le, Morgan finds himself in a situation where he is required to master The Art - not only a form of human & extraterrestrial martial arts, but a way of living that will alter his life forever.

At the temple, he is introduced to his new teacher, another Alfarian man who begins to steal his heart - a heart which is already promised to Lucien. Torn and conflicted, Morgan struggles with the world he left behind and the world he now inhabits.

Beginning to believe he may never again return to his ship and to the friends and loved ones he left behind, he is all the more frustrated and heartbroken when a new Master arrives at the temple: a man to whom Morgan is immediately drawn both mentally and physically, a man who is strikingly familiar... yet utterly alien.

Eye Scry Publications
www.eyescrypublications.com

www.ingramcontent.com/pod-product-compliance
Lightning Source LLC
Chambersburg PA
CBHW020227260626
47156CB00002B/566